EUROSTORM

PAYNE HARRISON

VARIANCE
ARKANSAS

Variance Publishing
1610 South Pine St.
Cabot, Arkansas 72023
(P): (501) 843-BOOK; (F): (501) 843-2675

Published by Variance LLC (USA).
www.variancepublishing.com

Library of Congress Catalog Number: 2010927634

ISBN: 1-935142-14-3
ISBN-13: 978-1-935142-14-0

Cover Illustration by Larry Rostant
Jacket Design by Stanley J. Tremblay
Interior layout by Stanley J. Tremblay

Contact Payne Harrison at: payne@payneharrison.com

10 9 8 7 6 5 4 3 2 1

This book is for my daughter,

Gabrielle Mairin Harrison

An irresistible force . . . who also plays the viola!

Acknowledgements

As most authors will tell you, writing a book can be very much a spiritual journey, fraught with peril. In that vein I would like to thank the Lord for transporting me to journey's end, and to Our Lady for her instrumental intercessions along the way.

To the Main Men—you know who you are—thanks for all the backup and support.

To Bill Crus and the team at Snuffer's restaurant who always had my table waiting and kept my glass filled while I cranked on the manuscript, this one's for you.

For my agent, Mike Farris, thanks for persevering and for your salient advice.

To Rick Roseman and Steve Thrasher, thanks for sharing the foxhole with me.

For the crew at Variance Publishing, Tim Schulte, Stan Tremblay and Shane Thomson, my thanks and respects for being such a great team.

Finally, for my family, thanks for simply being the best.

Novels

by

Payne Harrison

Storming Intrepid

Thunder of Erebus

Black Cipher

Forbidden Summit

Eurostorm

EUROSTORM

PAYNE

HARRISON

PROLOGUE

A galaxy of crystalline stars peppered the desert night as a Bedouin tribesman named Abu Nadir plodded along the sandy path, taking the lead in front of a recalcitrant pair of camels. The oasis was far behind him now, and the vegetation had given way to the unforgiving sand and stone of the Rebianna Sand Sea, whose dunes—like the stars above him—seemed to stretch out beyond infinity. With a five-night journey in his wake, the tribesman still had another twenty kilometers to go before he reached the settlement of Wafti, where the dates he'd harvested at the oasis would fetch a higher price. He would've preferred to ride instead of walk, but walking freed up the second camel to carry the merchandise, and Nadir had learned from his father long ago that traveling the desert by night was easier on man and beast alike, avoiding the oppressive sun and the profligate consumption of precious water. A three-quarter moon illuminated the Saharan path for the middle-aged man, and if he was fortunate enough to avoid the brigands who still populated the desert, then perhaps this load of dates would increase his wealth to the point he could afford another camel. Then, who knew? Perhaps it was time for a wife.

Nadir halted the beasts by a large boulder, unhooked the goatskin bag from the saddle and poured a stream of oasis water into his puckered mouth. He sat down on the boulder and contemplated time and distance. Yes, he should make Wafti by sunrise, then a pitched tent and open for business. He was surveying the sky as only a tribesman can—absorbing the mystical, even divine qualities of a desert night—when he heard it. 'Twas a low drone at first, like a mosquito close to the ear, then louder and louder until the sound caused him to turn and behold a massive winged object like a dark and ominous angel emitting a deafening roar as it swept over him, close enough to touch.

And as his camels bolted, Abu Nadir emptied his lungs in terror.

Inside the cockpit of the C-7 Caribou transport, the pilot did a double take as the green-tinged image of Abu Nadir whipped underneath his aircraft. Obviously they had scared the poor bastard half to death, appearing out of nowhere in this desolate wasteland, but it was a surprise for him as well, grafted onto a long night of unremitting tension as he and his co-pilot threaded the Caribou on a ground-hugging route north across the Tropic of Cancer. From their forward staging area in the God-forsaken village of Ain-Galakka in the north central region of Chad, they had left at nightfall and flown north below the remote radar stations positioned near the southern border of Libya. The radar stations had sprung up during Libya's long-running border dispute with its southern neighbor, although the French pilot was at a loss as to why anyone would give a damn about this bit of the transcontinental pile of sand known as the Sahara.

Be that as it may, the clashes had come and gone, and with

Chad a former colony, France had come to her aid with matériel and advisors. But tonight had nothing whatever to do with
border clashes. Their mission was to fly under, then around
and behind, the radar posts before climbing to their drop-off
point north of Wau el-Kebir.

The Caribou was an old twin-engine workhorse designed to
land and take off on remote and inaccessible airstrips. This one
had been outfitted with extended tanks, plus electronics to
detect any radar beams painting its fuselage. In its cargo hold
the crew chief stared at the other two passengers, strapped into
the canvas webbing seats, both quiet, resolved, and lost in their
own thoughts. He marveled at their ability to focus despite the
stuffiness of the hold and the whipsaw action of the aircraft's
terrain-chasing turns, knowing that the only defense the Caribou had was its low-level stealth. If they were detected and the
Libyans were able to scramble even an antiquated MiG, they
were dead meat. But now they were well behind the radar
installations, for the earphones of his headset crackled with the
cryptic words from the cockpit, "Beginning ascent." And a
moment later the nose of the Caribou rose in the desert night.

Fami Wahlid groggily rose from his sweat-stained cot,
grumbling at the call of his insistent bladder. He heaved himself up to stand in the tent, his bare feet sinking into the sand
that still retained the warmth of the day's sun, but the air had
donned its nightly chill, causing him to throw a cloak around
his shoulders.

Fami looked at the black footlocker in the center of the tent,
then at his two sleeping comrades, one of whom was snoring
laconically. When they had arrived at this venue—which was
not that far afield from the dark side of the moon—the order
had been handed down from the Master that two armed

patriots should vigilantly guard the footlocker at all times. But as days crept into weeks, and weeks into months, and now months into two years, the isolation and boredom of the Libyan desert weighed on them, eroding their vigilance. To the point that Fami cursed the footlocker as he crossed the tent and exited through the flap into the desert night.

As always, the stars were dazzling as the moon headed down to embrace the horizon. Fami stumbled through the sand toward the crest of a dune downwind of the nearby tent village.

Fami was one of those poor creatures that the Gaza Strip had served up with regularity during the second half of the twentieth century: lost souls who were borne out of a steady diet of sand, little food or education, and no hope. At age twenty-three he demonstrated in the streets for autonomous rule in Gaza. For his trouble he'd received the butt of an Israeli rifle in the face, which had cost him three teeth. A brother had not been so lucky, wherein a rubber bullet that was not supposed to kill, did; and when the day was over, Fami had joined the Muslim Brotherhood, the group of true believers who knew one day they would prevail to see the destruction of Israel and her handmaiden sponsor, America.

That had been twelve long years ago, and for six of those years Fami had done little of substance, going from one tenement to another, one desert tent to another, driving a truck, running errands, holding endless parlays over coffee with cohorts who always talked about taking the fight to America but never did. There was the bombing of the American embassies in Nairobi and Dar es Salaam that garnered headlines, but little else. Fami's resolve had begun to wane. His life was slipping by him with nothing to show for it, and he was about to exit the Brotherhood when Anzar arrived.

No one knew precisely what Anzar's pedigree was, but he was definitely of a different cloth, this one. Tall, aristocratic, trilingual and obviously Western educated, he had reeked of petrodollars when Fami saw him for the first time. With those black eyes of his he could size you up in a glance, and you knew you could only be with him or against him; for with Anzar there was no middle ground, no half measures.

In the ill-defined hierarchy of the Muslim Brotherhood, Anzar had taken over the Saudi cell of a sub-group called al-Qaeda, and after a "Night of the Longknives" with the al-Qaeda leadership, galvanized it to action—all with circuitous funding from the American consumer.

The money aspect of terror worked like this: In order to embrace corruption on a gargantuan scale, the Saudi "royal" family employed a secret police to subjugate the populace with jackboot tactics that would have made the Gestapo proud. Then they threw just enough protection money at the fundamentalist clerics to get them to endorse the legitimacy of their regime as protector of Islam's holiest places. And, like a drug pusher, the regime pumped enough oil to keep America addicted to low fuel prices and leverage Pentagon protection of the Saudi oil fields from Iran. And as long as the oil kept flowing Washington looked the other way as the Saudi royals helped themselves to the biggest cookie jar in history, the American consumer under-writing their palaces, villas, yachts, gambling and orgies.

The downside was that the fundamentalist clerics were demanding more and more funds from the royal family, and truckloads of it were being channeled into Anzar's al-Qaeda accounts in Luxembourg and the Caymans.

After Anzar had seized control of the Saudi cell the Twin Towers fell, and it was only a matter of weeks before the bumbling American president launched an invasion of Afghanistan—of all places—in a pathetic attempt to lay the blame at the feet of some buffoon named bin Laden, whose only real talent was public relations in promoting himself as the founder of al-Qaeda.

Viewing the destruction on CNN in Beirut, Fami's pulse had raced as never before. Now *that* was something he could aspire to, so he went to Anzar's palatial villa on the Mediterranean coast and placed himself at his new commander's feet. To serve. To die, if necessary. But Anzar had assured him the only ones doing the dying would be Jews and Americans. "It is finished for them," he'd told Fami in the sumptuous living room that made him uncomfortable. "Their skyscrapers were only the beginning. We are going to destroy America, and Russia will provide us with the catalyst." Catalyst? Fami did not know of such words. He only knew he had elected to follow Anzar, and his master's excitement was infectious.

What had followed then was an arduous trek that seemed to go on forever—from Tripoli to Beirut, from Moscow to Geneva to Chechnya. Then, on a night such as this along the Georgian-Chechen border, Fami and a half-dozen of Anzar's men had taken possession of the black footlocker, leaving two Russian generals dead in their wake. They had traveled Georgia overland to reach the Black Sea coast where they had transferred to a most glorious boat, what Anzar called his yacht, and for days they had traveled up through the Dardanelles, into the Mediterranean, and into the Gulf of Sidra off the Libyan coast, the last two days being particularly tense as American airplanes buzzed overhead. Then the off-loading onto the beach where they had boarded a large helicopter that took them on a southerly vector, deep into the Sahara to a camp of tents and a battalion of al-Qaeda guards, where they had remained for over two years—and Fami's resolve had begun to wane.

At first Anzar had been euphoric at the possession of the footlocker, but then something happened that changed his demeanor: the footlocker couldn't be opened. Anzar had become livid, cursing a blue streak of Arabic at the Russians.

The words "access codes" were repeated over and over; and from that point Anzar was in and out of the camp with sporadic frequency. Sometimes alone, sometimes in the company of Slavic-looking men who studied the buttons on the face of the footlocker but refused to touch them.

The only task assigned to Fami and his cohorts had been to fire up a generator once a week and plug an extension cord into the footlocker's receptacle until an LED went from red to green.

But those thoughts were absent from Fami's sleepy mind now as he hiked up to the crest of the dune, opened his fly and peed into the sand, then he zipped up his pants and headed back to the tent.

"Final check!" barked the crew chief as the Caribou leveled off at 14,000 feet. The two jumpers stood up. They might have been pack animals for the way they appeared—desert fatigues laden with parachute, rucksack, weapons, ammunition and assorted encumbrances, topped off with a crash helmet and night-vision goggles that made them resemble bug-eyed aliens. Methodically, they inspected each other's gear, knowing this was a night that would not allow any margin for error.

"Stand by!" The crew chief pulled open the hatch to greet a howling wind.

Without prompting, the first man stepped forward and rested his gloved hands on the hatch frame. He heard the engines cut power as they slowed to jump speed, followed by a cuff on the shoulder and a shouted, "*Go!*"

In a moment the two were through the door with their ripcords pulled. The lead jumper, the Frenchman, felt the yank on his harness as the parasail deployed above him before he looked to his right and saw the Russian through his night-vision goggles as the Caribou began its steep descent back toward the deck.

The Frenchman checked his wrist compass, then pulled on his lanyard to bring himself on an easterly heading. The Russian quickly swung around behind him and whispered into his stem mike, "No wind."

"The pilot said the westerly flow was three hundred meters below us."

"I hope he is correct. We cannot tolerate any delays."

"Tell me something I do not know. Maintain radio silence."

And the Russian stopped talking.

On his wrist altimeter the Frenchman saw they were indeed losing altitude rapidly and if they did not hitch onto the strong westerly air current, the mission would be failed by the time they hit the ground. He checked the global positioning system readout attached to the shoulder strap of his parachute harness. They'd punched out precisely where intended and were on course, but as with Moby Dick to Ahab, without a wind they'd lose him.

As if on command, an invisible hand yanked the parasail as though it were accelerating onto an airborne on-ramp, causing the Frenchman to pull on the canopy's hawsers to get back on heading.

"*Yoooo!* There we are!"

"Eaaayah!" replied the Russian. "A real Cossack wind, this one. If it keeps up, we'll make it with time to spare."

The Frenchman examined the GPS readout again and said, "This has to be a twenty-knot tailwind. Make sure you stay inside the flow."

"Already above you, Marc. Join me."

The Frenchman pulled on his control lines and let the canopy draw in more lift, the upward force lofting him into the night. Below, he viewed the endless expanse of the Saharan dunes stretched out before him through the greenish hue of the night-vision goggles.

The two men were executing a HAHO maneuver, meaning high-altitude, high-opening jump. By deploying their canopies at high altitude they could ride the air currents for long distances and arrive silently from the sky at their destination. Indeed, some HAHO jumpers had been known to fall asleep during a long journey on the air.

The Frenchman checked his watch, compass, and GPS readouts one more time and calculated it would take about ninety minutes to reach their touchdown point fifty kilometers away. Then another ten by foot to the objective. The Frenchman would have preferred twenty for an added measure of safety, but time did not allow them that luxury. He flipped up the goggles and looked around at the incredible array of stars; there was nothing quite like the beauty and tranquility of a night parachute jump in the desert.

The death that would soon follow seemed so remote.

The *whop-whop-whop* of an approaching helicopter piqued Fami's interest as he returned to the tent from Nature's call, so he slung the submachine gun over his shoulder and climbed the dune. Peering over the crest he saw the chopper set down on the pad, kicking up a swirl of sand in the moonlight. This was not one of the dilapidated utility models that came and went periodically, but a smaller, sleeker aircraft—like a racing car. Fami recognized it at once, causing his heart to leap.

Anzar had returned.

The camp commander stepped forward as the rotor blades spooled down and in a semi-officious manner opened the passenger door. Out stepped Anzar, tall and elegant as ever, wearing desert fatigue pants, boots, and a safari jacket. A second man followed Anzar, and the camp commander seemed to go apoplectic with shock, for the second figure to de-plane the chopper stood a head shorter than Anzar, was rather slight, and wore a uniform of fatigues with some rank on the epaulets. The commander saluted three times in rapid succession as if he couldn't think of what else to do, and even Anzar seemed somewhat deferential to the newcomer.

Then something even more remarkable happened. Anzar extended his hand inside the cabin and out stepped . . . a woman! This one was fair skinned, a European surely, and wore black stretch pants and a white cotton shirt tied at the midriff. It should have offended Fami's fundamentalist sensibilities, but the effect was something of the opposite. She was not as tall as Anzar, but even so, there was something different about her. Something alien that, even at this distance, drilled through Fami's chauvinism. She had a presence that seemed to emanate from within—a presence that could match Anzar's volt for volt. A woman who was accustomed to taking care of herself.

The three arrivals turned and moved in Fami's direction and he quickly ducked down to scurry back to the tent. Despite their bonding, Fami knew Anzar would not countenance his being away from his post. He threw back the tent flap and kicked the cots of his two comrades, who came awake to a stream of excited Arabic. They both grabbed their weapons and came to attention at either side of the footlocker on the ground. Fami stepped outside, and as the trio approached Anzar came forward, arms outstretched, to embrace him.

Fami was once again transported by his leader's affection, but then Anzar stepped back and Fami beheld the stranger. It took him a moment to recognize the face in the dim light of the moon, more aged than the youthful visage that was plastered all over Tripoli, but the sight of Moammar Qaddafi snapped Fami to full attention despite his sandals and shirttail hanging out.

"Is our prize still safe?" inquired Anzar.

"Of course, Anzar," Fami stammered. "With our lives we have guarded it."

"As I knew you would, my friend." Anzar motioned and said, "Colonel . . . Anya, if you please."

Qaddafi walked past him without a word, and Fami got the close-range firepower of the woman as she glanced at him before entering the tent. Beyond the pages of an infidel's magazine Fami had never encountered anything like her, her long, raven-black hair pulled back in a ponytail.

Fami followed her into the tent, where the three of them stared down at the footlocker, oblivious to the two nervous guards. Finally, Anzar gestured to it saying, "Our prize."

Qaddafi only nodded.

Anzar said, "Anya?"

The woman stepped forward into the lantern light and kneeled down before the Cyrillic symbols engraved on the keys below the red LED keypad. From her breast pocket she extracted a sheet of paper and laid it out on top of the footlocker. She rubbed her hands on her slacks and said in French, "If the sequence is incorrect, there is a self-destruct mechanism that will render the device inoperable and kill us all."

Qaddafi wavered.

"Perhaps we should withdraw, Your Excellency, until it is opened."

Qaddafi, however, raised a hand and replied, "*Continuez.*"

Fami did not speak French, but he felt the tension in the tent as the woman carefully put her finger on the keypad. Very deliberately she punched in a sequence of numbers and was rewarded with a series of tones. She did this three times, and upon the final sequence there was a long *squeep* and a pronounced metallic *click-click-click* that caused everyone to involuntarily jerk backwards. Then silence, and the red LED displayed in Russian, OPEN SAFE.

There was a collective exhalation as the woman slowly opened the case to reveal an object about a meter in length in the shape of a potato. It was festooned with a backpack harness of sorts and the potato, too, had an LED keypad grafted onto its side.

Fami saw Anzar's eyes flare with the exultation of a zealot as he said, "At last . . . at last America will fall in ashes. . . . Well done, Anya!"

"Well done, indeed," echoed Qaddafi.

Anzar turned pensive again. "We now have access to the device. But the arming codes? Are we certain they will work?"

The woman raised the sheet of paper. "The same source for the arming codes as the access codes. The interior minister's private safe. I would say the bona fides have now been established."

"And where are the arming codes?" enquired Qaddafi.

The woman tapped her forehead. "Committed to memory. My insurance policy, if you will. Once the second twenty million are transferred to my account in Vaduz the arming codes will be yours."

Qaddafi nodded. "Money has been difficult to come by with this egregious embargo and the recent fall in oil prices, but we shall complete our part of the contract. You drive a hard bargain, Major Mikoyan, but you obtain results."

The woman smiled at Qaddafi, and then at Anzar. One of those smiles that spoke volumes as she said, "Your envoy was most persuasive. Had he not found me in the Interior Ministry security office, I might still be shivering in Moscow, waiting to get paid my back salary."

Qaddafi nodded. "I chose my envoy carefully. And he, in turn, chose you with care."

There was an awkward moment of silence until Anzar asked, "So what is it to be, Your Excellency? New York? Tel Aviv?"

Qaddafi did not answer at once. He merely stood staring at the device as a quiet rage seemed to rise and radiate from him. Fami feared to move, to breathe, causing rivulets of sweat to trickle down his armpits, when finally the colonel looked at Anzar and said, "Outside."

Dutifully, Anzar followed, and when the colonel spoke, his voice reeked with a quiet venom. "They murdered my daughter. You know that, don't you? Killed her with their warplanes as she slept in the night. America. So strong . . . so powerful. And now . . . so vulnerable. It is time they paid the price. The White House, the Capitol, their treasured Washington Monument. All will be in ashes.

"For so long they thought I was beaten, thought me afraid after Saddam fell. So I made them believe I was, as they say, 'rehabilitated.' That I had 'reformed.' That I had become a statesman." He took Anzar by the shoulders and stared into his eyes, one zealot to another, and said, "You have fulfilled all my greatest aspirations. Take this instrument and turn Washington to flame."

Anzar matched his fervor and replied, "It shall be done, Your Excellency! And the beauty of it all is that ultimately the American scientists will be able to determine the bomb was of Russian manufacture."

Qaddafi nodded. "From the radiation residue, I am told. When that happens the Americans will demand a response in kind. Then the Russians will respond. And then . . ." he gave a shrug.

"This is beyond our greatest dreams!"

Qaddafi nodded in agreement, but spoke harshly. "Security is paramount. How many know of your operations?"

"Still among the living? Fewer than a dozen."

"The Russian generals who smuggled the device into Chechnya?"

"Dead and left for buzzard meat in the Caucasus Mountains. Somewhat prematurely, I'm afraid, for my people were over-zealous and brought them to their end before gaining the access and arming codes. That is why I had to find other means to obtain the information."

"The woman, you mean?"

Anzar nodded.

"After we receive the arming codes from her?"

Anzar shrugged. "Another loose end to tie up. Regrettable, but necessary. After Washington is destroyed, the weight of the world's intelligence agencies will be squeezing every source. We bought her from the Russians, so she might sell herself again. We must protect ourselves."

Qaddafi nodded. "A pity."

"One does what one must."

"Of course. Make her final night with us a memorable one."

Anzar smiled and gave a shallow bow at the waist. "At your orders, Excellency."

And with that, Qaddafi turned and strode off toward the helicopter.

The woman had knelt back down in the sand and closed the lid on the half-kiloton nuclear weapon. She again keyed in numbers on the pad and the *click-click-click* returned. She replaced the paper in her breast pocket, then slowly looked up to Fami, who was mesmerized by the shocking blueness of her eyes, the whiteness of her skin, and the coal-like silkiness of her hair. As her eyes held his, her lips parted slightly, like a desert flower seeking the rain. The stirring she aroused within him was surreal, magical, as if he were caught in the beams of some heavenly light. Then the flap of the tent came open and Anzar reappeared, shattering the moment—and for the only time he could remember, Fami resented his master's presence.

The woman rose and dusted off her stretch pants as Anzar said, "Come along, Anya. I must tend to some camp business in the morning. We have accommodations for the night." Then he turned to the three young men and ordered, "With your lives you shall guard it. See to it, Fami." And with that dismissal, they were gone, the flap of the tent closing behind Anya as the sound of the helicopter spooling up to full power reached Fami's ears.

The ground rushed up at the Frenchman, and to compensate he yanked on the control lanyards to put his parasail into a landing flare. He executed the maneuver with great precision, even in moonlight, and absorbed the shock of touchdown with his knees for a standup landing. The canopy deflated and he quickly released his harness as the Russian came down along-side him with a tumble and an *"Ooooffh!"* But he quickly recovered and got to his feet to haul in his own canopy. Then rapidly a hole was dug, making a final resting place for the chutes, harnesses, crash helmets, and no-longer essential gear.

Marc Chartain peeled off the night-vision goggles and sur-veyed the desert night. He felt totally at home here, as well he should. A child whose family had stayed behind (somewhat precariously) in Algeria after the French pulled out, much of his boyhood had been spent in the Sahara. At a shade under two meters, with dark auburn hair, his leonine form looked as though it had been hewn from desert stone—and in a manner of speaking, it had. A glance at his broad face and green eyes made you feel as though you'd been caught in the crosshairs of an unforgiving force.

The Russian had the same hard look about him, for the Spetznaz had molded him well. Slightly shorter than the Frenchman and a bit more pumped in the muscle, Viktor Romanenko was no less capable than his companion. His blond crewcut came down to a widow's peak on a face accented by a broken nose and two black eyes that could have belonged to an undertaker.

Chartain unfolded the topographic map and spread it out on the sand, then flicked on a small map light and activated the GPS receiver. As he studied their position, Romanenko knelt beside him.

With a pen, Chartain marked the map. "We came down closer than I intended. Less than eight kilometers out."

The Russian nodded. "Less of a march, but still a long crawl. Best report in, tell them to send in Nightwind as planned."

Chartain reached into his backpack and pulled out an Iridium telephone that uplinked to a network of low-orbit satellites. It was the size of a small brick and extended an antenna that resembled a breadstick. The signal traveled a "critical path" through the satellite system until it downlinked to a ground station that patched in the receiving party's terrestrial phone system. It provided a man in the middle of the desert with a global communications system.

Chartain punched in the numbers and hit SEND, and a few seconds later a voice came on the line.

"Lightsword, here."

"Viper, here. We are on the ground and safe. Approximately eight clicks out from target. En route now. Execute Nightwind. I say again, execute Nightwind."

"Roger, Viper."

"Any word from our contact?"

"Roger, Viper. The merchandise is in the store. You are good for go."

"Roger. Viper out."

Chartain snapped off the phone, folded up the map and stood. "Lightsword says Séverine confirms the bomb is there."

Viktor reminisced. "Ah, Séverine. An extraordinary pupil. In the beginning I had my doubts, but she handled everything we threw at her. Now I am not surprised she has done what she has done. Her grandmother was Russian, after all."

"And a Cossack at that," said Chartain grimly. "Now let's be off."

And soon they were trudging through the sand.

A fire burned in the hearth of the ornate presidential office of the Elyseé Palace, but its warmth was small solace for the two men who waited for news. One of them was middle-aged with a classic Slavic face and somewhat heavyset, but a tailored suit from the Sulka haberdashery off the Place Vendome expertly camouflaged his girth as he paced back and forth in front of the fireplace. The other man was dressed in a sweater and trousers, his somewhat diminutive frame splayed over the divan as he watched the glowing embers.

Abruptly, the Russian ambassador ceased his pacing and turned to companion. "I must say, Monsieur le Président, I cannot help but marvel how calm you appear at a time like this."

A wry smile creased the weathered face. "A politician's art, Monsieur Ambassador. You are not a professional diplomat but an academic, a seeker of truth, and one who is true to his own emotions. I am as fearful as you, but I have learned to conceal it. In politics, your face is your sword, and you cannot let your sword appear weak."

The Russian began pacing again. "There is so much at stake. Not just the bomb, but Russia herself. Can we truly keep this secret?"

"So far we have, Monsieur Ambassador. The only French-man who might betray us is in a very deep dungeon in Corsica. An ignominious end to a once promising diplomatic career."

The ambassador mopped his brow. "I shudder to think what would have happened if your intelligence people had not dis-covered this devilish transaction."

"I believe the correct phrase is closer to 'stumbled upon' rather than 'discovered.' But in any case, our hands are as dirty as anyone's. It just won't do having French consuls brokering deals for Russian nuclear weapons with Arab extremists. We are honor-bound to do everything we can to recover them."

"But this plan . . . do you honestly think it will work?"

The president shrugged. "The first priority is to confirm the presence of the weapon. The second step is to recover it intact, covertly, and return it to your custody. Failing that, the weapon cannot be allowed to be removed from the Libyan camp. We will launch an immediate air strike from the carrier *Foch* cruising off North Africa, followed by an airborne assault by Legionnaires based in Corsica."

The ambassador shuddered. "And any hope of secrecy would be lost at that point."

"No doubt. Too many planes, too many troops, too many bombs. Impossible to keep a lid on."

The Russian paced again. "Our economy is falling back into a tailspin. You know that. Oil prices have fallen, but we need continued investment in our energy resources to keep us afloat. American oil companies have pledged massive investments to do that, but their Congress has threatened a "capital embargo" unless there is a full and impartial inventory of our nuclear stockpiles. The inspection team is due to arrive at the Mag-nitogorsk depot next week with their inventory lists. If this portable nuclear device is not in its proper place, its absence could derail the whole American program. And I know not what would happen to my country then."

There was a tap on the door and an aide poked his head in. "The minister of defense, Monsieur le Président."

The president rose and said, "*Entrez.*"

A short, energetic man entered wearing a double-breasted suit and carrying a portfolio under his arm.

"We have been waiting, Henri," said the president. "Any news?"

"*Oui*, Monsieur le Président. We received the signal from our operative. She has located the bomb."

There was a brief sigh from the men that at least its location was known.

"And our commandos?" asked the ambassador.

"I have confirmation they are on the ground and en route to the target."

"And the Russian aircraft?" asked the president.

"Approaching the North African coast."

It might have been the head of a cobra detached from the body of the snake and silhouetted against the moonlit sky.

Vasily Markov rubbed the crick in his neck which came from the contortion of his body lying prone on a device that resembled a chaise longue. In front of his face was a wind shield that looked out on a glorious Mediterranean night. But the trip had been long and arduous from Chelyabinsk, and nature's cosmic grandeur was lost upon him. He was muttering to himself about the lack of aspirin for his neck when his headphones crackled with, "Look out, Vasily. We are at the departure point. He is coming in to top off."

Markov's eyes scanned the starlit sky and he muttered, "*Da*," into his microphone as his hands encircled the controllers that operated the tail boom, which hung from the arse of the aircraft like an afterthought.

Vasily Markov was the tail boom operator of a Mainstay tanker aircraft in the Russian Air Force. The Mainstay was an unusual hybrid in that it was both a tanker and an airborne radar platform, providing sustenance to fuel starved planes and a long view with the sweep of its Frisbee-like radome. The lumbering aircraft had slid into the commercial air traffic lanes over Istanbul before easing southwest until it was cruising along a path parallel to the North African coast.

Markov watched, mesmerized, as the cobra's head slowly approached. He was always entranced by the image before him, for it captured the qualities of the serpent—that of silence, stealth, and death. In fact, what Markov was looking at through his windshield at 25,000 feet was a Tupolev-37 fighter bomber.

It dropped below his field of view before rising toward the tail boom like a trout approaching a baited hook. A small rectangle of lights around the fueling port flicked on and Markov deftly guided the male end of the boom into the receptacle.

"Contact," said the pilot. "I have lockdown."

"Roger," replied Markov. "Starting fuel flow now." And he flipped a toggle switch that sent the liquid gurgling down the boom and into the thirsty tanks of the cobra's hood.

During the searing latter days of the Cold War, when the operatives of the KGB had fed dispatches back to Moscow about a potent new technology that would render the vaunted air defenses of the Motherland virtually useless, even the ossified bureaucracy of the Soviet Defense Ministry became aroused. It was a technology the Americans called "*stealth*," and in a Herculean effort to match the Americans measure-for-countermeasure, the task of developing a Soviet stealth war-plane fell to the Tupolev design bureau. Twelve years later, utilizing the ever scarcer resources of the imploding Soviet empire, the result was a single operational squadron of the TU-37.

Then the Berlin Wall fell, and with it the Soviet military machine, to the point that the Russian Air Force was reduced to selling joy rides in their MiGs to young Internet millionaires in order to pay for fuel and training, while entire fighter wings sat rusting on the runways of once secret aerodromes. And of the stealth squadron that had originally deployed, only six aircraft were now serviceable, one of which was face to face with Vasily Markov as he peered through the rear windshield in the tail of the Mainstay.

While the American F-117A stealth fighter possessed a surprising boxy shape that served to deflect radar waves, the TU-37 had a much smoother look to it—rounded edges that that allowed radar waves to pass over it like a brook over a smooth stone.

Markov's intercom crackled with the Mainstay pilot's voice. "Is he topped off, Vasily?"

Markov killed the fuel flow and retracted the tail boom. "Roger, Captain."

"None too soon. Nightwind, this is Mainstay."

"Roger, Mainstay," replied the stealth pilot. "I read you."

"We have just decrypted a burst transmission from the carrier *Foch*. The field team is on the ground and you are good for go."

"Roger, Mainstay. Nightwind will comply. To confirm, field team does know that at their range I can only cruise above the target for twenty minutes?"

"They know, they know," replied the Mainstay pilot. "Now be off with you!"

"Roger, Mainstay."

Markov watched the cobra's head fall back until it was silhouetted against the setting moon, then it banked away on a southern vector toward the Libyan desert. Markov followed it with his eyes until the navigation lights winked out.

Their desert union complete, a sweaty and exhausted Anzar lay alongside the woman he called Anya, his head resting in the crook of her arm as she stroked his brow.

Her feelings for Anzar were mixed. He was elegantly handsome, charming and, on one level, she admitted their couplings were enjoyable. But the charm and Armani suits Anzar wore only masked a monster that would atomize Washington or Paris, given the chance. Deception was not in her nature, but it had become a necessity as she had easily coaxed him into a coupling here instead of waiting until they returned to Tripoli. She'd come to learn he slept more deeply afterwards.

Slowly, with weapons cradled in their forearms, Chartain and Romanenko finished a two-kilometer low crawl up to the crest of a dune where they paused to catch their breath and survey the camp below them. With his adrenalin pumping, the Russian extracted a pair of night-vision binoculars from his rucksack as the Frenchman snapped a starlight scope onto his Giat FR F2 sniper rifle. Next, Chartain unrolled his sniper pad and clipped the bipod brace onto the barrel. Then he began to search for Séverine. Meanwhile, the Russian put down the binoculars and carefully extended the collapsible whip antenna of the single sideband transceiver, then slipped on the stem microphone headset and whispered, "Nightwind, this is Viper. Do you copy? Over."

A staticky reply came back. "I read you, Viper."

Viktor keyed the mike and said, "We read you, Nightwind. What is your position?"

"Estimate seventeen minutes out. Start the beacon."

"Roger, Nightwind." And the Russian flipped a switch on the radio that transmitted a navigational tone on a different frequency.

"I only have twenty minutes over your position, Viper. If you don't lock down the target by then, I leave."

"I *know*, Nightwind. Just follow your orders."

Viktor unkeyed the mike and spat. "Pilots . . . they would not last a week in the Spetznaz. Not a day." Then he looked at Chartain lying prone beside him and observed, "But you, Marc, I must confess, might have passed muster."

There was no reply to the Russian's comment, for his companion remained rigid as a stone, traversing the scene with the starlight scope, his soul caught in a riptide between his brain and his emotions. Impatient, Chartain looked at his watch, then asked, "How long until Nightwind arrives?"

"Sixteen minutes," replied Viktor. Then he added softly, "It is time, Marc."

Chartain did not respond at once. Instead he kept sweeping the camp with the scope, until Viktor said, more firmly, "It is *time*, Marc. We may be too late already. . . . If you won't, I will."

"No," the Frenchman said, raising his hand. "No. I will do it." And from the thigh pocket on his desert fatigues he extracted a small transceiver about the size of a pack of cigarettes. He extended the antenna, powered it on, then pressed the lone button three long times.

The wait was agonizing. Part of his soul wished she would not appear, the other urged her on. Yet less than two minutes passed before Viktor pegged her with his binoculars. "There she is. Big tent near the center of the camp." The flap of the tent had parted and she emerged wearing a dark hooded cloak. She walked purposefully over the sand, like a monk toward vespers, with no hesitation in her step.

The Frenchman's pulse ratcheted up at the sight of her, at

once attracted and irritated by her resolve. But that was part of her allure, was it not? That utter confidence she bore, the way other women wore pearls or diamonds. His starlight scope followed her to the entrance of Fami's tent, and his breathing ceased as she eased the flap open and disappeared inside.

Fami rose up on his elbow, the Makarov pistol in his hand in response to the intrusion. At first he thought he was in the realm of dreams, but she stepped forward in the dull lantern light, pulling her hood back to reveal angular features and coal silk hair that tousled down to her shoulders. Fami was about to speak when she put a finger to her lips, then pointed to his sleeping comrades.

What happened next, Fami simply was not prepared for. She parted the cloak and stood naked before him except for a pair of black bikini panties that were hardly there at all. Fami stood apoplectic at the vision before him—not understanding, not comprehending, paralyzed with awe. Then she drilled him with those sea-blue eyes, and just as abruptly she brought her cloak together and whispered, "Not here," in Russian-accented Arabic, before disappearing through the flap like the wind.

Now one must understand the complete derailment to Fami's system at such an epiphany. He had been in the desert for eons without so much as the sight of a woman; and now Séverine's appearance, her nakedness, was such a wrecking ball to his Arab senses that he was blinded to any thought of danger. He might have been a parched man dropped into an oasis, and he could only follow to quench a blinding thirst.

"Viper, this is Nightwind. Over your position now. Is the target acquired?"

"Wait one, Nightwind," replied Romanenko as he wrestled with a contraption the size of an attaché case. He hoisted the metallic box in front of him and sighted its night-vision aperture towards the laundry area of the camp.

"There she is again," said Chartain.

"Does she have it?" asked Viktor.

Chartain squinted through the starlight scope. "I . . . no. No, I don't see it." He passed the back of his hand over his brow and placed his eye again at the scope. "Now what? . . . Oh, no. . . . The Arab, he . . . he's following her."

The Russian's earphone crackled. "Viper, this is Nightwind. Have you acquired the target?"

"Wait *out*," snapped Romanenko as he put his eyes back on his binoculars, saying nervously to Chartain, "What is she doing?"

"She is not following the plan. I *knew* she would do something like this. She is such a wild card that I . . . *Mon Dieu!* What now?"

Viktor gaped through the night-vision binoculars, then clamped an iron hand on the Frenchman's shoulder, saying, "Steady, Marc, steady."

Fami was twenty paces after her as she led him behind a solitary tent on the periphery of the camp. In one movement she whirled, opened her cloak and held out her arms, her tanned body painted white by the moonlight. It was all Fami could do not to break into a run, and for the last few paces, he did. She was there, like a succulent desert fruit, waiting to quench his desire. He fell into her embrace, and as he brought his mouth savagely down on hers he felt something—in his back, where his kidney was. There was pain, yes, but pain of a different stripe—a pain that paralyzed, then flowed into a sinking feeling. He tried to cry out, but his lungs didn't seem to work as he felt something warm and wet flowing down the back of his leg. He drew away and saw her looking at him, almost apologetic. He tried to scream again, dimly feeling the blade as his knee buckled and blackness swallowed him up.

Séverine withdrew the dagger a moment before he toppled over, and the finality with which he hit the sand told her the poor bastard was done for. She wiped the jagged-edged blade on her cloak, the same blade with which she'd skinned red deer on the Vercors Plateau and gutted fish taken from the Rhône. Then she shoved it back in the scabbard between the folds of her cloak, wrapped herself in it and headed for the tent.

"She had to eliminate him, Marc. He was a danger. She has brains, that one. And balls."

Chartain did not reply as he followed her through the scope back to the tent, blinded by rage and anxiety.

"Viper, this is Nightwind. You have six minutes and I have no target."

"Wait out, Nightwind," said Viktor tersely. "Target is being lased now."

Between the barracks-like rows of tents stood some tin washing tables where, when there was sufficient water, the guards could wash out their underwear. It was on the top of one such table that Viktor placed the crosshairs of the targeting laser so the metallic surface would brightly reflect the ruby photons of light.

The pilot of the Tupolev-37 stealth fighter canvassed the instruments of his weapon systems, and in particular the screen that contained data on the two laser-guided bombs in the aircraft's weapons bay. He flipped a lever that engaged the clamshell doors of the bomb bay, breaking them open, then activated their seeker nosecones. At twenty thousand feet they began sniffing the sand for the ruby photons like an electronic bloodhound. When detection was made on the laundry table four miles below, the pilot was rewarded with a flash of red letters on his screen: TARGET ACQUIRED.

Russian electronics had never been up to a precision task such as this, which was why the French had sent a technical team to the Tupolev design bureau to hurriedly graft their Dassault Jaguar targeting system onto the stealth aircraft for this particular mission.

"Viper, this is Nightwind. I have target acquisition, and you have four minutes."

"Wait out, Nightwind. She's entering the tent now."

Cautiously, Séverine eased back the flap that covered the entrance. There were three cots: the empty one belonging to the late Fami, two filled with snoring guards, and the footlocker lying between them in the sand. For all of her resolve and sense of purpose, it was here she hesitated, for when Fami had drawn the gun on her she had responded unconventionally, and in her own way, brilliantly. But in the end her seduction and execution of Fami had been an act of self-preservation. Here, faced with two helpless, sleeping men, she felt a revulsion towards what she was about to do—a revulsion that no amount of training could overcome. But she had signed on and knew with Fami's death she'd crossed her own personal Rubicon and could only go forward.

From the pocket of her desert cloak she extracted a silenced .22-caliber automatic pistol and approached one of the sleeping guards. She looked down on him and saw not an enemy, but a young man probably the same age as her brother, Philippe. Slowly she brought up the pistol until the muzzle was two inches from his left temple. She took a deep breath, thought of a mushroom cloud atomizing Paris, and squeezed the trigger.

There was a *phuunt!* as the Arab's head jerked upon impact and the small hollow slug passed through the temporal wall to bury itself inside his cranium.

At the noise, the second young man began to rouse, and the woman whirled around and leveled the automatic. Two shots sailed out the muzzle, one passing into the Arab's open mouth, clipping a tooth on the way, while the second passed through the upper left eyelid and followed the optic nerve into the brain. He fell back on his cot and there was silence—a silence that only comes with death in the desert night.

Séverine took several deep breaths to quell the palpitations of her heart, still holding the weapon over her victims to ensure no alarm was raised. Then slowly she returned it to the fold of her cloak and looked down at the footlocker resting in the sand. So benign. So horrific. She knelt down and stared at the Cyrillic keypad and the red LED display. She punched in the access codes that had been given to her personally by the deputy Russian interior minister during her preparation in Moscow and which she had committed to memory. There was the *click-click-click*, and the latches sprang free. Gently she eased the lid open and looked down at the prize.

It was time to get the hell out of there.

"Thirty seconds, Viper, then I exit."

Viktor was frustrated not knowing what to do. The plan had been to extract the bomb covertly and link up with the longrange Puma helicopter heading up from Chad to their extraction point, eight kilometers to the south. From the reconnaissance satellites the French analysts had counted nearly two hundred souls in the desert camp. A sleeping giant the commandos were loath to awaken. The Tupolev fighter impatiently circling overhead was only to be used, if needed, to cover their withdrawal. Viktor was hopeful Nightwind's services would not be required after all, but Séverine had not reappeared. Yet perhaps she would and the three of them could vanish quietly into the desert night. But timing, timing, timing was working against them and Romanenko was about to send the stealth fighter, for better or worse, on its way when he felt the Frenchman beside him tense up and say, "Mon Dieu! Tell him to execute, Viktor! Now! *Now!*"

The Russian pilot was about to disengage and bank his aircraft back toward the Mediterranean when his earphones crackled with, *"Execute! Execute! Execute!"* He double checked the weapons lock, then hit the pickle switch and felt his aircraft rise in the air as the twin 1,000-kilogram bombs fell from their racks.

Upon release, the "sniffer" nosecones on the Jaguar targeting system were drawn to the laser light below like Ulysses to the sirens' call. The on-board computer adjusted the bombs' tail fins in response to the instructions of the sniffer cone and sent the projectiles on their journey toward the laundry table four miles below.

She stepped out of the tent and despite the heft of the object on her back she made directly for the exit route. Up to now she had suppressed any thought of success, but now the exhilaration of accomplishment and escape started to overwhelm her as she crested a small dune en route to the her comrades.

"Where are you going with our treasure, Anya?"

He came out of nowhere, and how he had silently appeared behind her she couldn't begin to guess, but now she felt like a fox caught in a snare as she slowly turned to face him. As always he exuded an aristocratic elegance, even in the desert fatigues that seemed to fit him as though they'd been tailored to his form—and for all she knew, they had.

Anzar.

"They're on the way, Marc," whispered Viktor, but the Frenchman did not hear. His concentration on the crosshairs of his sniper's starlight scope was total, but the obstacle directly between him and his target was a crop of long black hair.

"Damn you, Séverine," he cursed. "Move. Fall. Get out of the way!"

"I awoke and my passion flower was not there. What was I to think? I went looking for you, and what did I find? Poor Fami. What a shameful thing to do to one so simple and given to his basic instincts."

Her hand started for the .22 in her cloak, but Anzar had anticipated her and pulled an old style German Luger from his shoulder holster. A vintage piece of hardware but still effective, probably taken from his collection. "Now then, my treasure, let us return to our tent. I must find out who sent you and what you know. I should have known you were too good to be true but, like Fami, I was blind in my own way to your charms." His voice lost its softness as he said, "Place the bomb on the ground. Slowly." And in that moment, Séverine felt an emotion that was alien to her—a feeling which filled her with remorse and self-loathing.

She was afraid.

The two laser-guided bombs had reached their terminal velocity of 120 mph, but even so, the four-mile vertical journey would take two minutes. A half mile from impact they made a mid-course correction that would bring them down at the epicenter of the camp with a detonation that would cut through the covey of tents like a scythe.

Carefully she eased the backpack to the sand as Anzar spat more than said, "Hands on your head."

She obeyed, and an evil sardonic grin came over Anzar's face as his true colors broke through the elegant veneer. "Yes, my flower, you shall tell me everything. It will take time, but you shall tell. You will beg to tell. The access codes, the arming codes, who you work for. Everything."

Fear was welling up inside her now, and she wanted to break and run. But then she heard something—barely audible on the tympanic membrane, but distinct nonetheless—a faint whistle on the night air. And in that moment her confidence returned as Anzar continued his desert soliloquy.

"I took pleasure in your body, but you must have thought me a fool. Although I might have underestimated you before, I won't make the same mistake again."

This time it was Séverine's turn to smile as she replied, "I'm afraid you just did, Anzar."

And with that she dropped to the sand a split second before a black hole the size of a one Franc coin appeared on Anzar's forehead, sending his body backward in a convulsion as the camp erupted into an inferno of sand and flame.

CHAPTER ONE

It all started with a pickpocket and a cigarette, and of all the incredible events that were to follow, it is nothing short of astonishing that the headwaters of it all flowed back to that singular confluence of the pickpocket and the cigarette on that Chicago street one April morning.

It was on Michigan Street, to be exact, near the Drake Hotel. He stepped out of the elevator, hardly distinguishable from the legions of traveling businessmen who slept in the elegant landmark on any given night. He was a shade taller than his peers and later, when the police canvassed the hotel, one young woman—a brand manager for Frito-Lay up from Dallas for the night—recalled seeing him the night before in the hotel health club as he maintained a sweaty pace on the treadmill like any trim, health-conscious executive.

Leaving the elevator he strode through the posh lobby and entered the hotel gift shop where Beatrix the cashier was filing down a broken nail between customers.

"Antihistamines?" came the question.

Beatrix looked up from her nails and into an unforgiving face that was framed by sandy-colored hair laced with gray—and a set of ghostly eyes made her shudder as though she'd felt a draft from the undertaker's wind.

"I said, do you have any antihistamines? The spring pollen seems to be playing havoc with my sinuses."

Beatrix would later recall that although his English was flawless, he possessed an accent, although from where she couldn't say. But it was the timbre of his voice that induced her to slide off her stool to inspect the health and beauty aids aisle for some packaged sinus relief. A quick scan made her turn and say, with apology, "I'm afraid we're all out, sir. But there's a pharmacy three blocks down and two over on Michigan."

With effort the customer reined in his contempt for the inefficiency and incompetence of the woman and inquired, "An *Apotheke*? Er, a pharmacy, you say?"

"Yes, sir. Out the door and to your right. Three blocks, then left two. You can't miss it."

There was a curt nod of the head and a "Thank you." Then he spun on his heel and left to recross the lobby and then out the revolving door. The doorman offered to get him a cab but he declined, thinking that a brisk walk would help defuse the excitement building within him, as one required a clear head for matters such as these. He would purchase the cold remedy, then hail a taxi, and in anticipation he reached into his suit jacket and extracted a map of Chicago and vicinity. He inspected it carefully for a moment, his chest thumping rapidly, then he took a deep breath, refolded the map and replaced it in his breast pocket.

It was a clear, crisp morning, for a late season cool front had spilled down from Canada to whip up whitecaps on Lake Michigan. In response, the Chicagoans had pulled out their overcoats and mufflers for a final wearing before the genuine onset of spring. The foreigner was no exception, but he was accustomed to colder climes, so he wore his vicuna coat open, making

his pricey tailored clothes something of a neon sign to the
Bolivians.

The Bolivians were a subculture of the pervasive gang phe-
nomenon that the Chicago ghettos had offered up, most of their
number coming illegally into the country with no money and
dim prospects, forcing many to cross to the other side of the
law to scrabble out an existence. While other ghettos pursued
drugs, prostitution, protection or numbers to carve out their
sustenance, the Bolivian gangs had curiously staked out the
arcane art of pickpocketing as the means to underwrite their
toehold in the hostile environs of Chicago's South Side.

The foreigner had halted at the intersection across from
the Walgreen's when a young Bolivian woman brushed past
him, pressing a pair of meaty, torpedo-shaped breasts into his
ribcage. The bump and momentary sexual distraction gave her
accomplice the split second he needed to reach inside his jacket
and deftly remove the alligator wallet laden with cash and
credit cards. The young woman pulled back, batted her round
black eyes at him with a "*Con permiso*" and then was lost in the
sea of foot traffic going the other way. The distraction delayed
his crossing Michigan Avenue, putting him in the caboose
position of the pedestrians surging along the crosswalk, and it
was then that the cigarette came into play.

The driver of the White Cap Delivery Service truck was
smoking in the cab, against company regulations, but since the
heater wasn't working he felt entitled. He'd taken a long drag,
extending the red flame on the tip when—as cigarettes are wont
to do—the ember fell off, dropped between his legs and caught
in a fold of the fabric to execute a spot weld on his penis.

He lurched in his seat, stomping on the accelerator when
he should have been braking, which launched his pickup into
the intersection like an unguided missile. The vehicle's right

headlight caught the foreigner gut high, compressing his internal organs up under his ribcage, and sending him through the air with twelve hundred foot-pounds of pressure. In mid-flight he rebounded off the grill of an on-coming FedEx truck, which sent his skull to the asphalt with a sickening *smack!*

CHAPTER TWO

The mammoth bells that hung in the Gothic clock tower known as Big Ben tolled their noon hour refrain, scattering the dozing pigeons from the belfry and sending their peals up and down the Thames. The sound waves wafted over Trafalgar Square, where the one-armed statue of Horatio Nelson stood like a sentinel atop its imposing column, but by the time they reached the epicenter of the city's financial district their impact had dissipated like the ripples of a pond—lost in the din of traffic as bustling office workers poured into Wellington Square in search of lunch.

He stepped out of The Exchange Building a bit tentative at first, wondering whether he should have brought his overcoat, but the sun had broken through to warm the square and send the morning chill packing, transforming a gray day into a glorious spring experience. Andrew Price trotted down the steps of The Exchange flushed with the exhilaration that comes from turning a profit of £132,000 in the course of a single morning.

Price was of medium height, a bit shy of his thirtieth birthday, and his Savile Row suit hung nicely on his slender frame. His dark hair was cut a bit moppish, but he'd done away with his thick glasses and replaced them with contact lenses, allowing his angular features to project a more rakish image.

In most every respect it could be said that Andrew Price had it made. The son of a postal worker, he'd shown early on he was something of a prodigy with numbers, and academic honors flowed to him like a stream. After Oxford he'd gone on to graduate third in his class from the London Business School, where he was courted by the elite of British industry. But Andrew Price had passed on corporate positions or employment with the larger merchant banks. Instead, he came to roost in a boutique trading firm on Threadneedle Street where he could exercise his flair for riding the market. Indeed, it would be fair to say that fewer than a dozen men, and no more than a few women in the city, had as steely a grasp of the mysterious world of derivatives, arbitrage and reverse straddles as Andrew Price, and every one in the Exchange knew it. So along with the prestige of being a youthful high flyer came the bennies—the Savile Row tailor, the spacious flat overlooking the Thames, the BMW Roadster. Yes, life was nearly as perfect as it could be for the son of a man who'd carried the Royal Mail.

Price was turning his head to follow a flash of red hair and a pair of killer legs crossing the square when a voice boomed behind him. "Andrew! . . . Andrew! Wait a moment!"

Price turned to see Arthur Topping descend the Exchange steps. Topping was managing director of Topping, Hereford & Weeks, the firm that employed Price, and in your mind's eye he fit the image of a wealthy managing director like a spandex glove—graying hair, mustache, with an aristocrat's face and a gold watch chain at the waistcoat. As he approached Price he absolutely gushed with excitement. "Andrew! I must say, you were an absolute wizard with that straddle this morning. No! Not a wizard. . . . An artist! Your trading is nothing less than sheer artistry."

Andrew might have been a modest grandson. "All in a day's

work, Arthur."

"Rubbish, and you know it. That will be a hefty check you'll collect at the end of this quarter, but until then, are you on for lunch?"

"I'm yours if you want me, Arthur."

"Aren't you the puckish one? My car's coming round. Join me at the Carlton Club."

Andrew was truly content as he replied, "Delighted, Arthur. Delighted."

The Daimler limousine pulled in front of the Vauxhall sedan parked at the curb across from the Lord Mayor's house. The uniformed chauffeur popped out and opened the passenger door as Topping and Price leisurely made their way across Wellington Square toward him. He glanced at the driverless Vauxhall with a silent *tut-tut*, knowing it would soon be towed for trespassing on a no parking zone. Then his employer and the young protégé reached him.

Andrew had just glanced at his Rolex, taking note of the time, before he stepped into the Daimler. It was the last conscious thought he had before the Vauxhall convulsed in a giant fulmination that sent a shock wave across Wellington Square like some invisible sledgehammer—flattening everything in its path and turning the gleaming office towers into a waterfall of glass that fell without mercy upon the dead and the dying.

Gideon Bloom emerged from the J Street metro station, as he had for the better part of the last half century and walked the half block to a grim granite structure that possessed all the charm of a prison in disrepair. He was a tall and slender man with a military moustache that had turned more salt than pepper—the only ornament on a countenance that imparted a flint-like disposition. He wore a navy blue trench coat with a battered fedora, and the trace of a stoop to his shoulders betrayed his sixty-seven years.

He entered the front entrance of the pillbox structure that was Chicago Police Headquarters and walked past the paunchy desk sergeant, then continued on by the display cases filled with shields of officers who had fallen in the line of duty. The desk sergeant shot him a glance that was equal parts grudging respect and contempt while Bloom regarded the sergeant as he did all rear-area bureaucratic hangers-on—with distaste.

He took the elevator to the fifth floor, where the doors opened to the undercurrent buzz of a police station awakening to a new day. Bloom walked past the Chief of Detectives suite to a cubbyhole office at the end of the hall. He unlocked the door, which had SPECIAL PROJECTS stenciled on the opaque glass, and entered. It was a small, windowless enclave with nothing more than a metal desk, file cabinet, bookcase and coat rack. He doffed the fedora from his bald head, then hung up his trench coat and sports jacket, revealing the Colt .38 Special on his belt holster that had long since become an adjunct part of his anatomy. A moment later a prim middle-aged woman stuck her head in the door, asking, "Coffee, Captain?"

Bloom didn't smile much, but he smiled at her and replied, "Black like coal, Mildred, if you please."

"Right away, Captain."

It was their standard repartee. Mildred had typed his memos, fetched his coffee, and clucked over him for the better part of a quarter century; and she was the only secretary who could actually decipher his handwriting and brew his coffee just the right shade of ink.

Bloom sat down in the creaky swivel chair that seemed contoured to his behind and glanced at the *Sun-Times*, turning the corners of his mouth down at the headline.

Mildred brought his coffee. "Something else I can do for

you?" she asked when she saw his dire expression.

"No. Thank you, Mildred. Blackhawks were knocked out of the playoffs." He tossed the paper aside to take a long deep pull of the brew.

Gideon Bloom had retired from the Chicago Police Department twelve years ago as a captain of Internal Affairs with his pension, a reputation, and scars of two bullet holes in the back, placed there by a fellow officer he would later place on a long hiatus at government expense.

Bloom had become a policeman because he felt a calling to put criminals behind bars. He seemed gifted in that regard, if not obsessed, as he rose rapidly through the ranks displaying an instinct for those quirky cases where things were never quite what they seemed. Indeed, Bloom's calling was so compelling that ultimately his idealistic wave had to crash upon the corrupted rocks of the department, and he had to choose—i.e. protect the brotherhood of policemen or uphold the law. As a young rookie he had never expected the law and the police to part company, but he came to learn that the lucrative realities of drugs and money turned that divergence into a chasm.

That the Windy City had a legacy of graft from Alphonse Capone was manifest, and when Bloom was forty-two the realities of corruption in the Chicago police weighed heavily upon him. So when he was approached by the Feds to participate in a sting operation against the drug elements within his organization, he reluctantly agreed. Twenty prosecutions later, the department was shaken to its foundation and Bloom had become a celebrity of sorts, but also a marked man. The politicians, of course, were caught in a bind: if they branded Bloom a traitor to the force by working with the Feds, then they themselves—right or wrong—would also be viewed as compromised. So they embraced him and elevated him to the post of deputy chief for Internal Affairs.

A pariah's way station.

He threw dirty cops in jail for the next thirteen years before retiring at fifty-five. Then a short time passed before he was summoned back as a "special consultant" by the Superintendent's Office because, at the end of the day, Bloom was a phenomenal detective. To convict policemen he had to be, for policemen were the slipperiest of criminals.

In the vein of detective work, Chicago was a metropolis large enough to generate that thread of distilled evil that seemed to infect big cities, an evil that manifested itself rarely, but horrifically, in crimes that churned the stomach and shuddered the soul. They usually did not splash in the papers because their victims were camouflaged in Chicago's nightly body count, and the politicians knew it was best to keep that kind of press off the grid. These were the cases that had become dragons for the aging knight to slay.

Bloom locked his door, then went to his file cabinet and spun the combination lock on the top drawer. He withdrew three files and placed them on his desk side by side. He again sipped on his coffee and opened the first, marked HOMICIDE, then methodically read the contents for the twentieth time, looking for that subtle link or heretofore unnoticed thread that could bring the macabre picture into focus. Over the last eight months, four prostitutes on the South Side had been found stabbed in various alleyways and tenements. In and of itself, this was not terribly unusual in the drug-laced battlefield of Chicago's southern venue, but what was atypical was that the stab wounds were not stab wounds, per se, like with a chef's knife or a stiletto. Forensics had established that the weapon had been a surgeon's scalpel that had entered under the sternum and deftly punctured the left ventricle. Then as a signature, the killer had sliced off certain body parts. The coroner's report stated the sternum incision had been expertly done, as had the removal operation.

Bloom read the profiler's report again and found the killer's résumé both fascinating and repugnant: he was a highly educated male, single, probably middle-aged, devoted to his profession, and felt sexually inadequate. Probably had an encounter with a prostitute in his late adolescence or early manhood and was laughed out of the bedchamber. Never forgave. Never forgot. A human inferno of rage ever since. Most likely fastidious in his personal habits and intolerant of mistakes in colleagues and subordinates.

Bloom put the file aside. He'd been through a computer sort of the Cook County Medical Society and fourteen surgeons made the initial cut. Discreet inquiries revealed three who verbally abused their staff and colleagues, and they were under surveillance. Bloom's instincts told him they would collar him soon, although another hooker would likely bite the dust before that happened. A bloodlust was never satiated.

Bloom drew the next file toward him, marked CORONER'S OFFICE. The victims here were six months in the past, but the investigation was even more chilling than the Ripper case. Within a twelve-hour period the previous fall, three gay men had been admitted to separate hospitals complaining of high fever and chills. All of them were dead within twenty-four hours. The autopsy results had been nothing less than ghoulish, for the victims had been at three separate gay bars the night before. Yet they had been infected by one of the most deadly microbes in existence—bubonic plague.

The commissioner and the mayor had put the arm on the coroner to issue a report stating the men died from "AIDS-related complications," despite their robust health, and hide the fact that in one evening some demon had visited three gay bars in Chicago and somehow had managed to put them in contact with the Black Death. There had been no victims before and—the Almighty be praised—none since, but the covert investigation had turned up nothing, so the case had landed on Bloom's desk.

The forensics techs had suggested that the victims must have come in contact with an infected flea the same way the disease killed millions during its rampage through 14th-century Europe—drinking the blood of infected rats, then biting humans. Death came within hours. The lab's best guess was that somehow the perpetrator had transported a live infected rat as the host. Fleas were introduced to bite it, then they were collected. A single flea was then segregated into a small vial the size of a capsule and the vial was left open on the bar, allowing the flea to escape and hop on a wrist of an unsuspecting patron.

As Thomas Edison once said, "Genius is ten percent inspiration and ninety percent perspiration." So it was with detective work. Since about the only place plague naturally occurred these days was in prairie dog and armadillo populations—neither of which frequented Chicago gay bars—Bloom started with the list from the Army's chemical warfare branch and the Center for Disease Control detailing where bubonic plague could be had. There were only a dozen facilities in the country where that sort of thing could be obtained, assuming it had come from a domestic facility.

Bloom had obtained a computer list of all active employees of those facilities. Then, playing a hunch, he made discreet phone calls to the chiefs of police of major cities across the country, asking whether any plague-like deaths had shown up on their radar and been hushed up. He scored. Two in Seattle and one in Miami. Then he got a computer list from the airlines of all traffic in and out of Seattle, Miami, and Chicago near the dates of the murders, compared them to the employee lists and BINGO! A man named Dentwiler who worked for a biotech firm in the San Francisco Bay Area had been at all three locations on the dates in question. He was placed under surveillance, and his home would be searched in a couple of days with a covert warrant. Again, it was only a matter of time until he was run to ground.

Bloom put the file aside and pulled open the third one, marked INTERNAL AFFAIRS. He grumbled and opened the folder to the familiar story of a dirty cop. A lieutenant in Narcotics had a picturesque family in a picturesque split-level in Wheaton. He also had paid cash for a Lakeshore high-rise condo where he'd installed a mistress with a paid-for-in-cash Lexus. Surveillance was in place, along with wire taps on his home, condo, and cell phones. If he was on the drugger's take, he'd get careless eventually and Bloom would toss another one onto the slag heap. He was reaching for the phone to call his contact at Internal Affairs when it rang. He picked it up and grunted, "Bloom."

"Gid? It's Sammy." The voice was tense. "Need you upstairs. Right away. My office."

"Be right there."

Bloom locked up the files, put on his jacket, and headed for the staircase to take him to the department's executive level, wondering why Deputy Superintendent Samuel Bracewell had summoned him.

Before Bloom had left the brotherhood of police for Internal Affairs, he'd been a lieutenant in Vice when a newly minted detective named Samuel Bracewell had landed in his division. Bracewell had it all—polish, brains, college degree, and an ambition that was always on afterburners. He could have easily joined the FBI, but he'd chosen the department. His police instincts weren't bad, but his political instincts were stellar.

He had a politically correct attorney wife and they were constantly attending political soirées for various aldermen. Bloom came to rely on Bracewell, not so much for his police work but for his paperwork. He could generate, file, copy, and track the Byzantine paper requirements of the department like no other. Bloom was appreciative and took Bracewell under his wing, letting him take credit for a couple of high-profile collars—knowing that while press ink was something that he avoided, it was something that Sammy coveted.

Just before Bloom had rotated into Internal Affairs, he'd seen Bracewell promoted to the youngest lieutenant in the department. After that, Sammy's career had continued to rise as Bloom went on to cleansing the force. Bracewell had been on the cusp of a promotion to captain of the Vice Squad, a steppingstone to greater things, when their paths crossed unexpectedly.

It was a high-priced, top-tier call girl ring. Five grand a night to well-heeled clients, a totally professional Mafia operation. Sammy had led the investigation personally and to everyone's befuddlement, it seemed to drag on and on. Then Bloom caught a call from the Feds' organized-crime strike force. Seems Bracewell's voice had turned up on a tap. It was in the bedchamber of the Mafia chieftain's personal gal pal. In a secure room in the Federal Building, Bloom listened to his one-time protégé delve into the moist depths of the Mafia hooker, all the while declaring his undying love.

Red-faced with rage, Bloom had set the headphones aside and said to the Fed, "I'll get back to you."

He caught up with Bracewell that evening as he was walking from his car to his house. Pulling up to the curb, Bloom ordered, "Get in."

Bracewell's body language was like that of a prisoner caught in the spotlight, and he meekly complied. Bloom drove to a deserted schoolyard and hauled Sammy out, proceeded to slap him as hard as he could, shouting, *"How stupid are you going to be*! What are you doing, screwing a don's piece? You're the captain of Vice!"

Bracewell fell to his knees, sobbing incoherently that he had fallen in love with the woman and couldn't control himself. Bloom, who could summon up a brimstone delivery when the occasion required it, put his face to Bracewell's and told him what to do or he'd put him in a cold, dark hole for the rest of his life. Then he turned and left.

The next day, the news cameras played the big roll-up of a prostitution and pornography ring by the Chicago PD, including a Mafia don and his consorts. Shortly thereafter, stories began leaking to the press about the "heroic" exploits of Captain Samuel Bracewell, who literally went undercover to nail the ringleaders. His wife was portrayed with equally heroic prose as she lamented that her husband's work was dirty and dangerous, and that he had bedded the don's concubine with her consent in order to bust the ring.

Sammy's career had taken off like a rocket after that, rising to assistant superintendent for Criminal Investigation, then deputy superintendent. Bloom figured he was a shoo-in for police superintendent, if he could avoid another blunder.

He walked down the hall and entered the executive suite of the PS. The secretary looked up from her word processor and smiled. "Hello, Captain. He's expecting you. You can go right in."

"Thanks," replied Bloom and he walked into the deputy super's lair.

Behind the oversized desk in the oversized office sat Sammy in a tailored suit his wife's money had paid for. He rose and said, "Hello, Gid. I think you know Max."

Bloom extended his hand. "Sure. How you doing these days, Max?"

"Not bad, Gideon. Yourself?"

"Still looking for retirement."

A chuckle. "Aren't we all." Max Cheshire was deputy special agent in charge for the FBI in Chicago. A rotund, thick-necked former defensive tackle for Fordham, he was often called the Cheshire cat for his name and ever present grin, but he wasn't smiling now. Bloom knew Cheshire was nobody's fool and accorded him the proper respect.

He turned and nodded to the second man sitting across from Bracewell and said, "Hello, Leon."

The man nodded. "Gideon."

Leon McGuiness was head of the department's crime lab, a rail-thin man with a bald head and wire-framed glasses who was constantly fidgeting as though he were uncomfortable in his own skin. Bloom didn't care much for McGuiness, but his work results were always solid.

Bloom took a seat. "So what's going down?"

Bracewell grunted. "Always to the point, aren't you, Gid? Well, let's cut to it, shall we? Seems a John Doe hit the morgue ten days ago. Got himself splattered in a crosswalk on Michigan Avenue by an out-of-control delivery truck."

"No ID?" asked Bloom.

Bracewell nodded to McGuiness, who opened a file and picked up the narrative. "Victim was a male Caucasian, very well dressed in clothes with European labels. No wallet on him."

McGuiness passed across a black-and-white photograph of the victim, naked from the shoulders up. Bloom thought he looked like a middle-aged man caught napping, except that part of his skull was caved in. He shrugged. "So?"

McGuiness continued. "Two things happened: We ran the prints through the IDFS system and came up with zip. But because the labels in his clothes were European, we filed an Interpol search request through the Feds."

Bracewell cut in. "While this was going on, we had some blue shirts canvass the nearby hotels with his photo. Seems we came up with a match. The Doe's name was Erich Stolz, assistant managing director of Bernese Laboratories, a pharmaceutical firm based in Geneva."

Cheshire cleared his throat and chimed in, "However, the print request had already been fired off to Interpol headquarters in Lyon."

There was a pause, prompting Bloom to ask, "And?"

The three men exchanged glances, then Bracewell said, "His prints came back with an ID—a perfect match, in fact. The prints say this John Doe ain't no Erich Stolz of Geneva, Switzerland. . . ."

"So, who then?"

Cheshire shifted his weight. He definitely wasn't smiling now as he said, as evenly as he could, "The prints came back as those belonging to one named Otto von Spinnemann, an *SS* Standartenführer, who was executed by hanging at Karlsrühe prison on August 7, 1947, in accordance with his death sentence handed down by the Allied War Crimes Tribunal at Nuremberg."

CHAPTER THREE

It was one of those moments when Bloom felt the earth shift under him, as though he were seeing water flowing uphill or someone else's reflection in the mirror. "Excuse me? Could you repeat that?"

Cheshire leaned forward. "The prints of this guy"—he pointed at the photograph—"are a ten for ten match for a Nazi *SS* Standartenführer, a colonel in Nazi-speak, who was hanged in 1947. It's that simple."

"It's also impossible." Bloom studied the photo. "Obviously Interpol has screwed up something. Wouldn't be the first time. I never trusted that electronic print system to begin with."

"That's what we thought," said McGuiness. "So we had the German government send the hard copy of Spinnemann's War Crimes Tribunal file." McGuiness handed over a folder. "There is a facsimile of Spinnemann's prints. They match this guy Stolz like Max said. Ten for ten."

Bloom took the file and flipped through it. He extracted a photograph of a dour-looking man in full *SS* regalia with the skull lapel pins of the Totenköpf division and a red swastika armband.

Bloom had a reaction of revulsion to the garish image, but he held up the morgue photo next to it. "Got to be some mistake. These two have different features."

"Cosmetic surgery," said McGuiness. "The guy had jaw implants."

"Jaw implants?"

"Yeah, gives a person's jaw more definition. The autopsy on the body found them. Nose, eyelash, hairline can all be altered, too."

Bloom wasn't convinced. "What was Spinnemann's date of birth?"

The others seemed to retreat at the question, then Cheshire said, "October 7th, 1901, outside of Hamburg."

Bloom raised an eyebrow. "1901? That would put him past a hundred years old." He raised the morgue photo. "This Stolz couldn't be more than fifty, fifty-five at the outside. Somebody explain to me how a man can reappear sixty years later not much worse for the wear. Never mind he was executed."

Silence, until Bracewell replied, "We can't . . . and that's where you come in, Gid."

"Me?"

Bracewell shoved across an envelope. "You leave tomorrow. SwissAir. First class, no less. Cover story is that you're the official police escort returning the remains of the late Erich Stolz to his final resting place. He had no family, so his company is taking care of the arrangements. You'll be met in Geneva by a representative of the Swiss police to make the official handoff."

"And unofficially, Sammy?"

Bracewell didn't answer at once but glanced over at a small Menorah on a shelf that held up a row of books on law enforcement—a gift from his maternal grandmother. "Unofficially? . . . Unofficially I'd like to know why a Nazi slime ball reappeared in our fair city sixty years after he was supposed to have died at the end of a rope."

The massive figure in the trench coat squatted down to examine a metallic strip embedded in the bloody smudge of a human finger. At first glance he thought the glint of the metal might be part of a triggering mechanism, but on closer inspection it became apparent it was the remnant of its unlucky owner's watchband. The face of the inspector seemed cast in a permanent scowl, like a falcon impatient for dinner; and as the figure stood up and extended to his full massive height, his hands, feet and cranium seemed oversized for even his Goliath frame.

By any measure Assistant Superintendent Grayson Salisbury was a hulk, stretching to a height of six feet six with a mane of white hair. His bushy black eyebrows framed a pair of eyes that, as legend had it, could sear a prisoner's soul with greater intensity than a glowing poker. Indeed, the word was that Grayson Salisbury could enter an interrogation room and elicit a confession from a recalcitrant prisoner with the mere presence of his towering figure.

A nickname that had followed him for much of his career was "The Bat"—not as in the winged rodent, but an abbreviation for "Battering Ram." This stemmed from his early days as a bobby patrolling the tenements of the East End. He'd stepped into a public house one night to commiserate with the clientele and recharge himself with a spot of tea. Unknowingly he had walked into a robbery in progress in which a young tough, leather jacket and all, was holding a knife to the pub girl's throat just when the massive constable came through the door. Panic ensued, with the girl being dragged by her hair into the manager's office, where the door was slammed and locked. In two strides Salisbury was across the pub and with no warnings, threats or pleas for the girl's safety he launched a massive fist through the door with such force that it was reduced to so much kindling. There was a scream, but it was the tough, not the girl, and in short order the knife was dropped, the hostage freed and the would-be mugger deposited in Brixton prison for an extended stay at Her Majesty's pleasure.

That had been thirty-two years ago, and the path from constable to assistant superintendent had been long and arduous, with the occasional triumph and the omnipresent tedium of day-to-day police work. Yet that was the reason Grayson Salisbury was here at this moment, standing in the midst of the carnage in Wellington Square. His hulking figure betrayed an electric mind that crackled with the intensity of an arc weld when he was on a case. And he possessed the mental discipline to hunker down and sift through mountains of data in searchof a single thread of information that could lead to a terrorist's door while a bomb was in the making.

Seventeen years ago Salisbury had been tapped for the Anti-terrorist Branch of the Specialist Operations Division of the Metropolitan Police, whose original mission was to protect the citizenry of London from the Provisional Irish Republican Army, but had since migrated to dealing with a new iteration of evil called al-Qaeda. Slowly, methodically, and not altogether willingly, Salisbury had climbed the ladder to the post of assistant superintendent and commander of the unit—in short, he had become *the* policeman in the whole of Britain who commanded the breadth and depth of Her Majesty's resources to prevent bombings in the heart of London, such as the one that surrounded him now.

A wave of nausea overtook him as he watched a "cleaner" perform the distasteful task of deftly picking the bloodied remnant of a woman's leg off the cement and placing it in the plastic bag. It was such an incongruous scene, for her high-heeled pump still remained affixed to her foot. As he surveyed the carnage, Salisbury cratered. For years he'd labored against the PIRA to prevent senseless bloodshed like this, throwing bomber after bomber into Long Kesh Prison, until finally an uneasy peace seemed to take root in Northern Ireland. But now there were whispers that even that was in danger of unraveling. And then came 9/11 and the London train bombings, ushering in an even darker age of more insidious evil. Was al-Qaeda responsible here? Or was it something else?

The assistant superintendent emitted more of a moan than a sigh, then walked toward the crater in the roadway where a thin, bespectacled man in civilian clothes was supervising two uniformed policemen taking scrapings. Salisbury was ill-tempered in the best of times, and his sense of frustration only inflamed the bristle in his voice.

"So what have we got, Woolridge?"

Anthony Woolridge, chief of Forensics for the Anti-terrorist Branch, had known Grayson Salisbury for seven years and had never been addressed by his superior as anything but "Woolridge."

Woolridge pushed his spectacles back up on his nose and replied, "Lab tests will confirm, but it looks like Semtex, pure and simple. Looking at the blast radius I'd put it at upwards of a thousand pounds."

Salisbury could only seethe. The ease with which terrorists acquired their implements of death was galling, as if you could pick them up in the grocery aisle. Why didn't they just have Semtex coupons in the shopping supplement of the *Times*?

He growled across the way at Arthur MacBaine, a rumpled and uncouth fellow with dishwater-blonde hair, who was Salisbury's alter-ego and chief lieutenant. "What do you have?" was all that he could say.

MacBaine flipped through his notepad and said, "Looks like we've got over eighty dead and scores more maimed and wounded. Found a license plate across the way with a piece of bumper attached. Numbers match a Vauxhall that was lifted up in Manchester a month ago. No call or codeword was phoned into Central prior to the blast. No warning. Came right at the peak of lunch hour in the square. Time and locale chosen to inflict maximum damage "

"Your grasp of the obvious is remarkable, Arthur." From painful experience in these matters Salisbury knew the PIRA usually phoned in a warning with a preset codeword, usually a half hour before it went off, giving the police barely enough time to scramble and clear the impact area. But this time no codeword, no warning, no grace period came. Only death and destruction. But it was no suicide bomber either. Like a microprocessor, Salisbury's memory culled through several file cabinets of mug shots, dossiers, interrogation transcripts, intelligence reports and informers' offerings, trying to extract the who and the why of the blood around him.

"The Troubles" in Northern Ireland stemmed back hundreds of years to when the English sovereign William of Orange had conquered the Irish at the Battle of the Boyne and awarded land grants to his English cronies, whose heirs prospered on Irish soil. But like a host trying to reject foreign tissue, the Irish had tried to expel the invaders—without success until 1918 when an Irish raconteur named Michael Collins had managed to cut a deal with a minister of the British government named Winston Churchill. They partitioned the land of Ireland into an Irish Free State in the South, and six counties in the North that would remain under British sovereignty. Although the border had taken hold, Collins was eventually killed by an assassin's bullet while Churchill eventually went on to become a wartime prime minister. And Salisbury was left to deal with the legacy of two peoples coveting the same piece of real estate. Was that happening here? Was the Ulster peace accord imploding?

He was about to put another question to MacBaine when a uniformed bobby hustled over at quick time from the rubble that had been the Lord Mayor's house. Somewhat breathless he said, "Assistant Superintendent . . . Mr. Moncrief would like a word." The bobby pointed to a man in a tailored suit standing incongruously next to the rubble. Salisbury grunted. He knew Moncrief. Head of Special Branch. Knew the man delighted in wearing a shoulder holster under his Savile Row suit so he could discreetly reveal the butt of his Walther while reaching for a drink at Mayfair parties, then smugly deferring inquiries about it with a murmured, "Official secrets." He played his Bondian image to the hilt, when in fact he was a paper-pusher. Salisbury approached him warily, and the closer he came he noticed Moncrief wasn't looking too smug. In fact, the man looked ashen. He nodded and said to Salisbury, "Grayson . . . we, we have a terrible situation."

"You have a gift for understatement," replied Salisbury. "Get to the point."

Moncrief motioned with a thumb toward the smoldering rubble of the Lord Mayor's house. "In there, a . . . a meeting was underway."

Salisbury's eyebrows arched and formed a bridge above his nose. "Meeting? What meeting?"

Moncrief seemed to grope for words. "On Ulster. A final peace accord was in the works. Now . . . inside, they . . . they're all dead."

Salisbury sensed a bad day was about to get exponentially worse. "They? They who?"

Moncrief shuddered. "Adams, Trimble, Paisley. Plus the Northern Ireland secretary. Their aides. All topped."

"*What!*"

". . . And the prime minister was to have arrived shortly."

Salisbury's head was spinning. Gerry Adams, head of the

IRA's Sinn Fein party. David Trimble, head of the Protestant majority in Ulster. Ian Paisley, the all-time Protestant Cassandra against anything or anybody remotely Irish or Catholic. Three men who despised each other in the same room. All dead. It was unthinkable. Salisbury wanted to lash out and Moncrief was the closest target.

"Why the bloody hell wasn't I told about this?"

Moncrief stammered. "All parties insisted on absolute secrecy. The old agreement was coming off the rails and they were putting together a new peace charter. Any whiff of it would have derailed everything. They wanted to meet directly with the prime minister without cameras or leaks. Insisted on non-standard protocols. The IRA was finally willing to disarm for real and for good, and Paisley was willing to soften up if he could get some language thrown in he wanted. He was an old man in a hurry, you know."

"Then who the hell was in charge of security for this?"

Moncrief stammered, "M—me."

CHAPTER FOUR

The Russian felt totally at home when he leapt from a plane in the pitch black of a night parachute jump, but ceremony brought on a feeling of profound unease. Standing at attention, his uniform pressed with buttons and boots polished to a high gloss, he could not shake his sense of awkwardness.

It was an intimate proceeding in the Salon de Tapestries of the Élysée Palace with only the president of France, his naval aide, the minister of defense, General Bertrand, the Russian ambassador and the two honorees present.

The rosewood furniture, the gold chintz and the Rodin statuary on loan from the Louvre provided an elegant counterpoint to the pair of hard men standing ramrod straight on the Tabriz rug.

The president motioned to the naval aide, who deftly lifted a slim velvet case from the antique table and held it open for the head of state. The president stepped in front of the Russian and said with great formality, "Major Viktor Ilyanovich Romanenko, for conspicuous gallantry in the face of a vastly superior enemy force, the République Française confers upon you the Croix de Guerre."

The president took the small medal and carefully pinned it

onto the flap of the Russian's breast pocket with difficulty. But once it was completed, without bloodshed, the president took Viktor by his beefy upper arms and pulled him forward to administer kisses on each cheek.

Romanenko shuddered, then muttered, "*Merci, Monsieur le Président.*"

The chief of state then stepped in front of the uniformed Frenchman and said, "Lieutenant Colonel Marc Chartain, for conspicuous gallantry in the face of a vastly superior enemy force, a grateful nation awards you the Croix de Guerre."

The medal was pinned and the kisses administered, then the president smiled and said, "I understand you were born in Algeria."

Chartain seemed detached as he replied, "Oui, Monsieur le Président. Tangiers."

"So you are no stranger to the desert?"

"No, Monsieur le Président. Not at all."

The defense minister handed the president a third case. He opened it and gazed upon the simple Croix de Guerre medal on the white velvet background.

"And your colleague?" he inquired of Chartain. "I was looking forward to honoring her as well. And I don't mind telling you I was curious to make her acquaintance. She must be quite extraordinary."

"That she is, Monsieur le Président," replied Chartain softly. "I can attest to that."

The shorter chief of state looked up at the taller soldier and asked, "So where is she? It isn't often an Élysée invitation is declined."

The stocky, gray-haired General Bertrand chimed in with, "Captain duVaal has been through quite an ordeal in pursuit of this mission, Monsieur le Président. She respectfully requested to be excused from this ceremony in order to take some therapy."

The president nodded. "Of course." Then closed the case and handed it to Chartain, saying, "You will see that she receives this on behalf of a grateful nation. If it had not been for her efforts, there is no telling what that lunatic Qaddafi might have done."

Chartain took the case and replied simply, "I'll see that she receives it, Monsieur le Président."

Outside on the portico, Chartain and Romanenko paused to say their goodbyes as General Bertrand and the Russian ambassador politely loitered at a discrete distance.

"It has been an intense six months, Marc. All I can say is that you were the best comrade I could have asked for. I did not think we had a chance in hell of succeeding." He fingered his medal. "Now look at us."

Chartain extended his hand. "Take care, Viktor. You made me understand why no invaders ever conquered Russia."

Romanenko took the hand, then their eyes locked, and to their mutual surprise they fell into a manly embrace. Then the Russian drew back and said, softly, "Don't let her go, Marc. You're a fool if you do." Then without another word he turned and stepped into the waiting limousine.

Chartain opened his mouth to speak, but couldn't muster a rebuttal to Viktor's statement, for in his heart of hearts he knew the Russian was correct.

The ambassador climbed in the other side of the limousine and, with a final wave, the Russians headed for the gate.

Chartain opened the case once more and gazed down at Séverine's Croix de Guerre as General Bertrand sidled up beside him and pulled on his white *kepi* with the two stars. "It isn't often I have to make excuses for someone under my command to the president of France, but in view of the fact she saved Paris or Washington, or who the hell knows what else, this insubordination will be forgiven."

Chartain closed the case. "And what of Qaddafi? We retrieved the weapon, but does it end there?"

General Bertrand looked back toward the palace, then said softly, "I believe the Americans have an expression for it: 'dead man walking.'"

Chartain raised an eyebrow. "Indeed?"

"Oui." The general nodded. "But how is not our concern. The deal that was struck placed responsibility for that operation in the Russians' hands. It was their weapon that he stole, after all."

"Since our mission, I'm sure he's gone to ground."

"True enough. But he'll surface eventually, and the Russians still have a knack for that sort of thing. The old KGB has put on new clothes and runs their country now."

"Too true."

"So what about you? Perhaps some leave is in order."

Chartain absently shook his head. "I'll travel up to Arrowmanches to see my sister for a few days, then stop off to pay a visit to Caisson at EPIGN headquarters before heading back to Corsica. I've been away from the regiment too long."

"Hmm. As you wish, Marc. Although I don't imagine things will be quite be the same for us in Corsica. . . . By the way, Séverine informed me she is resigning from the *gendarmerie*."

Chartain nodded. "I am aware."

"Very well, then. Give Caisson my regards, then off to the regiment with you." And with that, the General faded away.

Chartain opened the case one last time and looked down at the Croix de Guerre. For a moment he was transported to a realm beyond the here and now, where the perfumed memory of a cream-skinned neck and hypnotic sea-blue eyes made everything fall away . . . then a car horn blared on the street and his reverie was shattered. He gave the medal a last look, closed the case and whispered to the empty yard, "Therapy."

The buck was getting old, well past his prime, grazing in the Vercors meadow. He was just above timberline and below a craggy ridgeback of Alps near the Combe de la Bataille. Two young does grazed nearby, seemingly at ease; but the red deer buck was skittish, his eight-point rack bobbing up and down between bites, ears cocked, as he sniffed the air.

Séverine duVaal smiled as she peered through the eyepiece of the spotting scope and whispered, "He's clever, this one. Can't smell us or see us but knows something's up."

Her eldest brother, André, lay prone alongside her, his eye glued to the crosshairs of the Leupold scope mounted on his Weatherby rifle. "Experience," he replied. "It's what has kept him alive. Instinct for danger. Look at him. We're two hundred fifty meters downwind if we're a centimeter and the rascal is sniffing like a bellows. . . . Well, old fellow, everyone's time eventually comes."

André and Séverine were on a facing slope across a shallow ravine. It was an annual outing to replenish the family's venison supply for the coming year. They had spent the morning hiking into this venue from the family farm near the town of Léoncel, just inside the boundaries of the Vercors national park. During the afternoon they had taken a vantage point to scout for the elusive European red deer.

André ran the farm now and had always been close to his only sister—closer perhaps than to any of their three brothers—but since she returned to visit a week ago she had been remote, detached, deflecting any overture for dialogue beyond the new foal in the barn or the upcoming planting. She'd thrown herself into the daily chores around the farm with a vigor that would have amazed the Chinese, and it certainly amazed André because chores were something she'd vigorously evaded throughout her youth. Only now did she seem to loosen up a shade.

"Are you going to take him?" she inquired softly.

André carefully scoped the animal once more, then looked up and checked the position of the sun. "A little more than an hour of daylight left. Not likely to see another one today."

"All right, then. Take the shot. I estimate a four centimeter drop at this range."

"Probably. Windage is the key. Hard to say how much windbreak they're getting that close to the crags."

Séverine watched through the spotting scope as the buck raised his head once more and sniffed.

"He's put his nose into the wind. Place the crosshairs on his snout and take the shot."

"Oui, little sister," whispered André as he moved the crosshairs a shade in front of the nose. He took a deep breath, slowly exhaled half of it, then carefully squeezed the trigger on the .300 Weatherby.

The explosion reverberated over the Vercors range as the hundred-fifty-grain bullet sailed out of the muzzle at 2,800 feet per second. The missile dropped over the range as anticipated, but a lull in the wind prevented it from drifting to the right. As a result, the bullet barely grazed the buck's chest before ricocheting off a rock nearby, spooking the three deer. So when the report of the rifle shot reached them, it was like petrol on a flame, causing them to flee in terror.

André saw the small plume of dust rise off the rock behind the buck just before he bolted. "*Merde!*" he swore.

Séverine did not answer, but instinctively grabbed her Model 88 Winchester as she jumped to her feet. In one swift motion, she chambered a round with the lever action and slapped the stock to her cheek to sight through the scope. The deer were bounding up the steep incline toward a gap between pillar-like massifs that rose up like two ugly thumbs. Séverine drew a bead on the buck bringing up the rear, and in the blink of an eye she instinctively gauged distance, speed and trajectory—then squeezed off the round.

A second report echoed across the Vercors, and for a moment she lost sight of the buck from the gun's recoil. But then the animal's ascent up the steep slope halted in mid-stride. The force of 1700 foot-pounds from the bullet's arrival had shattered his shoulder before deflecting through his heart and lung and exiting through the ribcage. The animal pitched back over and tumbled down the incline before coming to rest at the base of one of the massifs.

André's hand clapped down on her shoulder. "*Bon*, little sister. Incredible shot! You always were the best marksman in the family. *Absolute!*"

Séverine lowered the rifle and leaned against her brother, as though the death of the aging buck had rid her of some demon within. She drew breath and began to feel human again as she drew strength from her family and the familiar surroundings of the Vercors. She felt pity for the deer but knew nature would have claimed him soon, and nature's death could be far crueler than a bullet's. And the venison would not be wasted.

"So, you want to tell me what has been eating you?"

André was so much like their father. Could read her like a book. But in many ways she had grown beyond the confines of her family and the tranquility of the Vercors. So she squeezed his arm and said, "Can't go into it."

"Can't? or won't?"

"Part of the job."

"But you said you quit the gendarmerie."

"Oui. But in some ways the gendarmerie did not quit me."

She slung her rifle over her shoulder and said, "Come along. We best get to our quarry while the light lasts."

And with Séverine in the lead, they strode off toward the felled animal.

CHAPTER FIVE

As the 747 lumbered over the Atlantic, Gideon Bloom settled in to the first class SwissAir seat, grateful the plump Swiss banker had passed out from his triple of Vodka Stingers.

An aging but charming stewardess approached him and said, "Care for anything, Monsieur?"

"Café, s'il vous plaît," replied Bloom. *"Noir."*

Once the china cup was in hand, Bloom sipped and thought over the case that was sending him eastward. Then he took out his briefcase and extracted the file on *SS* Standartenführer Otto von Spinnemann, a.k.a. Erich Stolz of Bernese Laboratories. He again viewed the photograph of the cold, emotionless face staring out from under a black-billed hat bearing the Totenköpf skull insignia of the *SS*. Bloom knew what the skull meant, and with a sense of revulsion began reading the file again.

Otto von Spinnemann had been the son of a university professor. At seventeen he joined the Maracker Freicorps, a band that fought against revolutionary groups in Germany, which gave him an early exposure to the concept and method of secret police action. There he met another adolescent named Reinhard Heydrich, with whom he struck up a relationship. After the humiliating armistice was signed in Versailles to end World

War I, Spinnemann joined his comrade in denouncing the Jews as the enemy that had brought down the Fatherland. Details on his postwar life were sketchy except that his family—like many of the era—had experienced great economic hardship as the German economy sank into oblivion. His father had lost his university post and the family was reduced to living hand-to-mouth in a scarring reversal of fortune. Otto eventually was able to enroll in the University of Heidelberg, where he took his degree in chemistry and became active politically. With nil career opportunities, he became a pamphleteer for the nascent National Socialist Party and by 1931 he had joined the SA—a group of thugs employed as Nazi enforcers—and it was there he renewed his acquaintance with Reinhard Heydrich, the man who would go on to formulate and implement the Final Solution.

Under the tutelage of a chicken farmer named Himmler, Heydrich built up the SD (the counter-intelligence service) and Spinnemann became his aide-de-camp working as a trouble-shooter of sorts during the war, visiting the death camps and experimenting with more efficient ways to achieve what would later become known as "ethnic cleansing." He appeared earmarked for general's rank when Heydrich was assassinated by partisans in Prague, and Spinnemann finished out the war as commandant of the Schafhausen concentration camp. Located in eastern Poland, it was built after Auschwitz and provided slave labor to some of the nearby armaments plants of the Third Reich, and served as a facility for human subjects in a range of hideous experimentation.

A curious thing about his capture: three weeks after the surrender documents were signed he was cornered by U.S. troops at night on the Swiss border trying to cut through the barbed wire seine designed to trap escaping Jews. The bizarre thing was that instead of trying to impersonate a civilian like so many of the Nazi vermin did when Berlin fell, Spinnemann was wearing his full *SS* regalia when captured. And throughout his trial he demonstrated an "in-your-face" arrogance right up to his ascent to the gallows, according to the report written by the witnessing officer. Sort of like he was asking for it.

Bloom asked for a refill on his coffee, then contemplated the rap sheet on Spinnemann—ironically "Spiderman" in German. As he did on many a case, Bloom closed his eyes and tried to project himself into the mind of his suspect. What was it like to grow up in World War I Germany under the Kaiser, the country besieged on all sides? Joining an internal security force at such a young age might suggest an underlying insecurity or sense of inadequacy. Fear. Xenophobia, perhaps, undoubtedly exacerbated by Heydrich, of all people. The architect of the Final Solution as your bunk mate. Then the economic descent of a highly educated family. Gasoline—no, nitro—on a flame. Then, later than he should, he attends university. Chemistry. Experimented with more efficient means to achieve the Final Solution. What sort of ghoulish methods did this creature come up with? The file didn't say. But something chemical, surely.

Chemistry? . . . Pharmaceuticals? A connection there? And how did the Spiderman leapfrog those sixty years?

Bloom put that one on the shelf for now. He had learned to break an investigation into pieces, solving the little ones first and building a mosaic that, hopefully, would reveal the bigger picture.

Bloom pulled another artifact out of the file. This one had been taken from the pocket of Spinnemann's overcoat when his effects were collected. It was a map of Chicago, probably purchased at O'Hare. He unfolded the map and reviewed the familiar environs, noting that it was an unremarkable map except for one thing: the suburban town of Skokie was circled in red ink. Now why was that? Try as he might to sleep, he couldn't shake the feeling he was somehow in the crosshairs.

Skokie was Bloom's home town.

Cyril Worsham carefully pried the lid off the waste receptacle marked BIOHAZARD and slowly withdrew the plastic bag liner. He held it suspended in the air and ever so delicately rotated it, inspecting the plastic for any breaks, tears or rips; then he lowered it into the larger cellulose burn bag that was suspended from an aluminum frame on wheels. He pulled in the drawstring on the burn bag, then folded over the airtight sticky seal. That done, he lifted the bag out of the frame and opened the chute marked BURN DISPOSAL. He had to pull hard against the lower pressure inside the chute, but finally he managed to pry it open and sent the bag sailing down the tube to the crematorium below.

He then returned to the waste receptacle and was relining it with a plastic bag when he heard the hiss of the airlock door open behind him. A voice bellowed, "Who left the ricin container uncovered in the lab?"

Worsham, who was contrite even on his best days, began shaking in front of the space-suited figure whose bearded face glared from behind the plastic helmet.

"I, uh-uh, r-r-r-really cou-couldn't say, Doctah Wingate. I, uh, am not allowed in the lev-level-f-f-f-five laboratory—except to clean up. Y-You might want to ch-check the s-s-security v-video."

Wingate, whose demeanor resembled Darth Vader's on a bad day, grumbled, "You're bloody well right, I will," as he began peeling off his contamination suit.

Cyril Worsham showed his security pass to the guard and walked past the sign, chiseled in concrete, that read HEATH-STONE ARSENAL. A bleak brick wall topped with razor wire shielded a bleaker compound of low-rise buildings that resembled a medical complex of some kind, but not exactly. More like an asylum, really. And in a sense, it was.

Worsham crossed the lane to a bus stop on the other side, joining the queue of low-paid office workers heading home after a long day at the arsenal. His bus arrived and he climbed up, finding the only empty seat occupied by a matron's parcel. He hovered over it expectantly but the heavyset passenger ignored him. A modest "Excuse me" would have solved his dilemma, but that would've taken a measure of self-confidence Cyril did not possess, so he stood for the ride.

Worsham was the quintessential nobody. The son of a utility clerk, he was of medium height with a pudgy body and pasty complexion that gave a perpetual rosy hue to his cheeks. His lips formed a concave oval, and a crooked upper front tooth made him look like a schoolboy in need of braces despite his twenty-seven years. His dishwater-blonde hair was poorly cut and seemed naturally unclean.

In all, Cyril Worsham was a package bordering on the pathetic. A non-starter in school, he failed the physical minimums for the Army, and his only redeeming qualities were a conscientious work ethic and the ability to obtain a security clearance. At Heathstone Arsenal he was little more than a glorified janitor, but a well-paid one due to the fact few cus-todians stayed at Heathstone after they learned what kind of grime they were cleaning up.

The bus stopped and he climbed down to a section of Brentmews Down that was home to those of modest means. He hesitated at the corner, debating whether to peel off for a pint at the pub down the lane, or to head for home. If he went to the pub, he might miss her if she came by, and his pulse quickened at the thought of it. That's the way she was, wasn't she? No phone call. No notice. Just appeared out of nowhere at the door wanting nothing more than to hump his brains out, then only to disappear like a mythical unicorn. The thought of it made his palms sweat, and by the time he reached home, Cyril was at a half trot. She'd been there twice before, waiting for him naked on the bed. How she'd gotten in he hadn't a clue, nor did he care. All that mattered was that he possessed her, her skin, her wetness, her mouth as she transported him to a nirvana he'd no idea existed.

Cyril went through the gate, then past the small garden and down the steps to his modest basement flat. He was breathing heavily as he unlatched the door and was immediately deflated to find it empty. Disappointed beyond words, he went to the fridge and popped the top on a beer. He plunked himself down on a threadbare sofa and caught his breath. Despite a plain flat, he faced a state-of-the-art video system. It was his avocation. But this time it failed to capture his imagination, for it had been over a fortnight, nineteen days to be exact, since she'd been here last. The longest stretch since they'd first come together three months ago. Was she gone forever? He refused to allow such a thought. She'd be back. She'd promised.

He guzzled his beer in an attempt to purge the thought of her but it was useless. He crushed the can with his thick fingers and threw it on the floor, then went to the bedroom where he pulled open a drawer. Beneath a stack of undershirts was a pair of black lace panties that she'd left behind after a particularly savage encounter. His pulse raced again as he picked them up and ran his fingers over the silk. The effect was narcotic and he could not refuse himself, so he went to the small safe on the floor of his bedroom closet. He spun the combination and ripped open the door to extract a video cassette tape. He took it into the living room and powered up the video system, then popped the tape into the VCR and hit the PLAY button while clutching her panties in the other hand. As the grainy low-light image of two writhing bodies—one of them Cyril's—came on the screen, his respiration quickened as tiny sweat beads appeared on his upper lip—and he moved his panty-clad hand down between his legs.

The main landing gear of the SwissAir 747 touched down with a squeal on the tarmac, and once the nose gear was on the ground the pilot engaged the thrust reversers.

Gideon Bloom felt himself pitch forward as the airliner decelerated rapidly. He gazed out the window to see the overnight flight had arrived to the dawn of an overcast day in Geneva, where a light snow was falling—the kind that melted when it hit the ground, giving the concrete a wet sheen. He stretched, then glanced at the portly Swiss banker in the neighboring chair still snoring. Such was the power of a Vodka Stinger.

Impatiently, Bloom waited through the arrival protocols, then when the seat belt sign went off he rose, grabbed his valise and filed out the door. He entered a large hallway with the rest of the passengers and was walking toward the sign marked CUSTOMS when a voice said, "Captain Bloom?"

Gideon halted and stepped out of the stream of passengers to face a pair of men standing off to one side. One of the gentlemen stepped forward and extended his hand. He was slightly above medium height, slender, and wearing a tan trench coat. His beard and hair were dark brown and he wore designer frames. "Captain Bloom, allow me to introduce myself. I am Inspector Emil Broussard of the Federal Canton Police in Geneva. I will be your liaison while you are here."

Bloom took the firm handshake. He put Broussard at around

thirty-five. And like many Continental Europeans who were educated across the Channel, he spoke English with a British accent.

"How do you do, Inspector," replied Bloom. "I appreciate your coming out to meet me."

"Glad to be of service, Captain. Your superintendent of police called our director-general personally and asked that every facility be extended. We are glad to oblige." Broussard turned to the second man. He was about the same age as Broussard but his clothes were of a finer cloth. He was also heftier than Broussard and seemed ill at ease in this venue. "This is Monsieur Alain Delmar. He is representing Herr Stolz's employer, Bernese Laboratories. He will be taking custody of the body."

Bloom shook the hand which was soft and sweaty. Delmar nodded and said, "Captain."

"We have waived Customs for you," said Broussard, "and your luggage will be transported to your hotel. After you have had the opportunity to check in and refresh yourself, we can reconvene in my office to execute the paperwork for transferral of the remains of Herr Stolz."

Bloom nodded. "Sounds like it will be a short trip for me. Speaking of the remains . . ."

"The casket will be transported to a mausoleum for temporary holding, pending the release to our custody," said Delmar a bit nervously. "Then the remains will be cremated per Herr Stolz's will."

"I see," said Bloom evenly. "Apparently Swiss efficiency is not a myth. Shall we?"

The three men started walking down the hallway, and as they passed a window Bloom looked out through a drizzle of snow to witness a forklift extracting a coffin from the belly of the 747 that bore the remains of *SS* Standartenführer

Otto von Spinnemann.

The windowless conference room was austere, appointed with a Formica-topped metal table and cushionless chairs. Bloom guessed it was used for the interrogation of obstinate prisoners and wondered if even the civilized Swiss had a rubber truncheon hidden away somewhere.

The stocky Alain Delmar opened his leather attaché case and extracted a sheaf of documents as Bloom and Broussard sat across the table. He began formally, "Now then, Captain Bloom, I think you will find everything in order." He placed the first document in front of the American. "Here is the original of the Cook County death certificate that was FedExed to us, citing Herr Stolz's cause of death as severe cerebral trauma."

Bloom inspected the document and nodded. He'd seen it before.

Delmar shoved the second document across and continued. "This is a judge's order from the civil magistrate court in Geneva appointing Bernese Laboratories as the executor of Herr Stolz's estate and granting us custody of his remains for final disposition in line with his last will and testament. With this document I am legally empowered to execute the receipt of his remains to my care."

Bloom picked up the French-language document with the court's seal and studied it for a few minutes, then said, "Forgive me, but the way I read this court order is that one Leopold Mainz, not Bernese Laboratories, is the appointed executor. And you are not mentioned at all, Monsieur Delmar."

Delmar and Broussard were more than a little surprised.

"*Parlez-vous français?*" asked Delmar.

"*Assurément,*" replied Bloom. "Now then, who is Leopold Mainz?"

Delmar cleared his throat and replied, "Technically you are quite correct, Captain Bloom. The executor is Leopold Mainz. He is managing director of Bernese Laboratories. I am his assistant and he asked that I take care of the details for him."

"I can appreciate that, Monsieur Delmar, but since I am in law enforcement, I hope you can appreciate my sensitivities to American—and Swiss—law. I'm afraid I can only release the remains of Herr Stolz to Leopold Mainz, personally."

Delmar's pigmentation shifted a shade too pink as he muttered, "I assure you, Captain, that I am acting on Herr Mainz's behalf. In his position he is very busy and his schedule did not permit him to come here in person today."

Bloom assumed his immovable object persona and replied, "Then I will be happy to go to his location and bring these proceedings to a close."

Delmar was bordering on red now and said with exasperation, "Captain, Herr Mainz is a highly respected member of the Geneva business community and—"

"Monsieur Delmar,"—this time it was Broussard who responded—"Captain Bloom is correct. To be in compliance with American and Swiss law, he should execute the release with Herr Mainz personally."

Delmar's face was working its way toward crimson as he was double-teamed by the two flics in front of him. He inhaled and exhaled rapidly a few times, then his manicured hands gathered up the papers and he said, "I will speak with Herr Mainz."

CHAPTER SIX

Cyril Worsham opened the door of his basement apartment and wearily made his way to the fridge for a beer. It had been a long day in that he'd covered for a co-worker who'd been out sick. There was a major spill in the Level-4 lab where he'd had to drop everything and scrub it all down himself in the bloody plastic suit. Then the high and mighty grand exalted Director Wingate reamed his ass for being slow to mop up and getting in his way. How he hated that bastard. He'd like to shove it all the way up the bugger's ass and break it off.

The anger flared. As he opened the fridge and popped the top on a beer, a wave of depression washed over him. Here he was, closing on thirty and nothing but a glorified mopper, with no prospects of better. He'd tried schooling, but schooling just wasn't for him. And he could endure all the downside of his station in life if only she hadn't gone. Disappeared. It had been three weeks with no sign of her. He had come to the devastating conclusion she would never return.

And then, there she was.

Framed in the doorway, arms extended up against the frame as if holding herself in place. She was wearing nothing but a black, sheer see-through nightie vented in the front and back that accented her long red hair as if each strand were a burnished copper penny.

A rather sardonic smile creased her lips as she pranced the few steps toward Cyril and jumped on him, tipping him off balance. She locked her ankles at the small of his back and her arms around his neck as her lips came down roughly on his—as if the entire movement had been choreographed. Cyril recovered enough from the shock to clumsily embrace her and meet her passion measure for measure. Then after some groping she came up for air to lick his ear and say breathlessly, "Miss me?"

Cyril was beyond speech as he stammered, "M-m-m-miss you? I was d-d-dying for you! Where have you been?"

She pulled back and smiled, not answering his question but saying with that teasing strain in her voice, "Does Ducky want some fekky now?"

Cyril was lost as his hand clutched her buttocks and he buried his face into the fragrance of her hair. "Oh, yes, Fayla. Y-y-yes!"

The Horse Guards had retired from their posts as eventide draped over Whitehall like a mourning blanket. The home secretary gazed out the window as the pair of well-coifed steeds and their cavalrymen in breastplate and polished boots clip-clopped their way down the lane to their mews for the night. However, the minister's mind was far away from horses and empire, trying more to come to grips with the newspapers that littered his desk with banner headlines: VIOLENCE RETURNS TO ULSTER, IRA & PROTESTANT MILITIA EXCHANGE BLAME, and the one he found particularly irksome, HOME OFFICE BEFUDDLED BY BOMBING.

The home secretary was that rarest of species, in that he was a politician with mettle. A rapier-like mind had gotten him through King's College Cambridge to an early post as a classics professor at the University of Bath. But he had tired of the ploddy pace of academic life and given it up to plunge into the hurly-burly of Labour politics. The son of a coal miner, he had that unique ability to quote Chaucer in the House of Commons and tell the Conservative shadow minister to piss off in the cloakroom. He wasn't afraid to turn his ire on his fellow ministers, the opposition, or even his constituents.

Semi-bald with blonde hair, he kept himself trim from a daily four-mile run in Hyde Park. He picked up the paper and read the headline again, then smacked it down on the desk and said, "Well, Chief Superintendent, are we 'befuddled' as the *Evening Standard* suggests?"

The chief superintendent of the London Metropolitan Police had a penchant for uniforms, and his was adorned with such an assortment of ribbons and stripes that he might have been mistaken for a Bulgarian field marshal instead of a cop. He was a stuffy fellow, with slicked-back, dyed hair, and being caught in the laser light of the home secretary's ire was such an assault on his bureaucratic sensibilities that a sprinkle of sweat began to appear on his tinted hairline. He wasted no time in passing off this very hot potato. "If you please, Home Secretary, I would like for Assistant Superintendent Salisbury to outline the situation."

The home secretary turned to the giant of a man sitting on the divan and his demeanor softened a bit. Salisbury had saved his bacon more than once, and the home secretary knew that if anyone could bring the department out of its "befuddlement" it was this man with the oversized feet and hands. "Very well, Assistant Superintendent, was it the IRA?"

Salisbury seemed almost lost in thought as he said, "No."

The home secretary waited for more, but none came, so he asked, "Was it Protestant militia, then?"

Salisbury shook his head and repeated, "No."

"Al-Qaeda?"

"No."

Frustrated, the home secretary blurted, "Who the bloody hell was it then? A cell of radical gardeners?"

Salisbury was unmoved as he replied, "I speak for MI5 as well as the Yard in this matter, and all I can say is we don't know who it was. We only know it is not the IRA or militias, nor al-Qaeda, nor anyone of that ilk."

"And how do you know it wasn't from Ulster or someone from east of Suez?" inquired the home secretary.

Salisbury spoke evenly, as if he were reciting a train schedule. "GCHQ has sifted through all Echo intercepts on Ulster, al-Qaeda, and all possible groups who are on our watch list and absolutely nothing has come to the surface. As you know, our one saving grace is that the Ulster and al-Qaeda types are addicted to their cell phones; and try as they might, they simply can't resist turning up the chatter when something big is afoot. There was not so much as a blip. Additionally, we have squeezed every informant from Derry to Kent and conferred with MI6, and no one knows anything. The fact that Paisley, Adams and Trimble were all topped at the same time in the most heinous way would indicate whoever did it had a burning agenda against both sides."

"And who would that be?"

"That is what troubles me, Home Secretary. On virtually every bombing the bomber, or at least his sponsor, comes to the surface rather quickly and the agenda is self-evident, such as the train bombings in Spain and London. But this . . . it's like a ghost laid this bomb. A ghost with no fingerprints and no agenda."

"What about the surveillance cameras at Wellington Square?"

"All we know is that it was a woman. Thirty, thirty-five years old. Wearing sunglasses and a hat. Unrecognizable. Nice legs, I have to say. But beyond that, a ghost."

The home secretary was about to carp again, but then his intellect kicked in and the enormity of Salisbury's conclusions weighed down on him and his knees went slack, causing him to sit down on the desk overhang. There was a long pause before he said, "So what you are saying is, there is a new force out there—motivations unknown, sponsor unknown—that has surfaced in a most diabolical way, and we have no way of finding them or predicting when they will strike again."

Salisbury nodded. "Quite correct, Home Secretary. Except that you left out something."

"And what would that be?"

"Their intelligence is superb. This was not a zealot with a petrol-filled pipe. This Paisley-Adams-Trimble meeting was as secret as secret things get—even I didn't know about it—yet whoever it was knew well in advance the place and time of the meeting. And if their intelligence is that good . . ."

The home secretary finished the sentence, ". . . then our ability to combat them is compromised."

"Severely compromised," agreed Salisbury.

There was a long silence, then the home secretary said to Salisbury, "I want you to clear your desk. Give this bombing top priority. Report directly to me, and any resources you require let me know. Find me the leader of this new force, Assistant Superintendent, and I will see that he receives a swift and harsh justice."

"At your service, Home Secretary." Salisbury rose to leave, convinced he might be in the presence of a future prime minister.

The chief superintendent with the tinted hair and decorated uniform might not have been in the room.

Cyril Worsham dozed in that blissful state between ecstasy and half-sleep, his body having passed through a sex machine twice in four hours unlike anything he had ever experienced. His naked body was now covered with an epidermis of caked sweat as he lay in the darkness when some sounds came from the kitchen. He raised his head just enough to see her silhouette backlit by the fluorescent illumination holding a beer in each hand and smiling.

"Fancy some refueling, Ducky?"

Cyril dropped his head on the pillow and laughed the exhausted laugh of a sexually spent man. "Refueling? Y-yeah. I'll take some refueling."

Without a stitch on she guzzled one of the beers, then tossed the can in the bin and knelt on the bed beside him. She lifted his head and poured some of the brew into his flower-like mouth, which he gulped greedily. Then she put the can on the night stand, lay down beside him and whispered, "Feel like another turn around the park, Ducky?"

He giggled. "I-I have to go to work t-tomorrow. Besides, I got nothin' l-l-left."

She smiled and purred, "But of course you do, Ducky. You've always got something extra for Fayla. What say we 'ave a go with 'Tell the Truth?' "

His eyes flared at the mere words.

"Tell the Truth? You m-mean it?" he babbled.

"Anything for you, Ducky, you know that. So should we give it a go? You just lay back and relax. I'll take care of everything."

Cyril closed his eyes, not believing his good fortune, and his response was like air hissing out of a balloon as he said, "*Yeasssss.*"

With a giggle she jumped up from the bed and went to her cavernous purse from which she pulled out four leather thongs. Methodically she wrapped a strap around each of Cyril's hands and feet, then tied them off on the stanchions of the old four poster bed.

"Uhhh," he winced. "That's tighter than you done before."

She clucked, "The better to make you tell the truth, Ducky."

And he smiled in anticipation as she knelt down and began to wring the truth out of Cyril Worsham—and being distracted he didn't notice the rolled up sock she'd slipped under the pillow.

Gideon Bloom paused at the apex of the Cresthoff Bridge and took in the exquisite view of the city lights reflecting off the black mirror of Lake Geneva. In a short time he had discerned that the city had a genteel quality to it, imparting the feeling of a safe harbor—that whatever turmoil ransacked the outside world, Geneva was that civilized eye of the storm. Indeed, the city had been founded by persecuted Protestants during the Reformation, and it had hosted expatriates from Hanoi to Kosovo. Yes, the pace of life here seemed slower, the natives kinder, and even the air a bit gentler on the lungs that in other metropolitan centers, yet despite the shock-absorbing effect of the city and its environs, Bloom couldn't shake a feeling that he was on the periphery of something deeply sinister; and as palpable as the feeling was, it was also frustratingly elusive, like a camera lens that refused to focus.

His detective's mind was running eighteen different probability algorithms but all were registering zero, and Bloom knew it would stay that way until he came up with more information. He heard the clock tower chime and figured it was time to move along to his dinner appointment. Perhaps Inspector Broussard could shed some light on the enigma.

Cyril's last line of defense cratered as he gasped, "The shipment's on the seventeenth! *The seventeenth!* That's the truth!"

It was then she smiled again and slipped her hand beneath the pillow to grasp the rolled-up sock. She leaned over him, with a face of a different countenance, and said, "You know what, Ducky, I really believe you . . . *you fekking English pig!*" And before Cyril could react, the heel of her hand shoved the rolled sock into his mouth.

Cyril tried to protest, pushing his tongue against the sock, but before he could eject it, she slapped a strip of duct tape tight over his mouth. He stared wide-eyed into the face of the woman whose eyes glared at him with a rabid intensity. She didn't move for what seemed a long time, then with a swipe she raked a bloody path across his face with her sharp nails as she spat, "*You filthy Tommy pig!*"

Cyril screamed in his throat and thrashed against his bonds, but the sock and tape stifled the sound and the leather jesses held fast.

She rolled off the bed and went to the bathroom, where she vigorously washed her hands, then gargled with mouthwash straight from the bottle. But once her mouth was cleansed, she took a few deep breaths and looked at her naked self in the mirror and whispered with a smile, "Now then, 'tis time for Fayla to have a spot of fun."

She went to the kitchen and opened the small cabinet beneath the sink and extracted a large zip lock plastic bag, then grabbed a rubber band from a catch-all jar that all kitchens seem to have, and reentered the bedroom. Cyril was still struggling and uttering muffled screams. She noticed his wrists were getting bloody, but it really didn't matter as long as the ties held. She reached over and grabbed a fistful of hair to yank his head back. Cyril's eyes were dilated with fear, hanging on to a shred of hope that this was one of her sex games. But she brought her face close to his and said, softly, "Now then, pig, 'tis time to true up the pleasure scales." And in a smooth motion she had the bag over his head and secured it at his throat with the rubber band.

Cyril now thrashed with the vigor of a freshly caught trout in a creel, but Fayla casually went to her purse to fetch her cigarettes and lighter from beside the silenced Beretta at the bottom. Buck-naked she sat down in the cushy easy chair and lit up a smoke, then leaned back in the chair to inhale deeply, crossing her legs to enjoy the show. Cyril was still thrashing but starting to tire as the plastic bag inflated and deflated like a bellows, recycling the ever more toxic carbon dioxide into his lungs.

By the time the cigarette had burned out, the thrashing had subsided, as had the muffled screams, and the ebb and flow of the plastic bag wound down to a halt.

She crushed out the cigarette and went into the bathroom for a long, piping hot shower. That done, she dried off, dressed herself, then cut the jesses free from Cyril's dead limbs, along with the plastic bag. She ripped off the duct tape and plucked the sock from his mouth, then dropped the remnants in her purse before covering Cyril with a blanket. From her purse she extracted something that looked like a black plastic garden hose about three feet in length. She tore off one end of the plastic and began squeezing an orange gelatinous material around the perimeter of Cyril's corpse. Then from a container in her purse she poured a metallic powder all over the bed.

That done, she went to the kitchen and opened the oven door. She set the automatic oven timer to trigger in about thirty minutes, blew out the pilot light and turned on the gas valve full blast. Then Fayla flicked out the light and was away into the night, like a ghost.

Chapter Seven

Emil Broussard wheeled his BMW into the visitors parking space, avoiding the slush on the passenger's side so his guest would set foot on dry land. Gideon Bloom exited the car and gazed upon the edifice of Bernese Laboratories.

Located on the outskirts of Geneva, a pink granite entrance facade led into a campus of low-rise buildings. Bloom followed Broussard past a heated fountain that kept an impressive gurgle of water flowing year round, then they went through a discreet security choke point where Broussard flashed his credentials and was directed to the nearest structure.

As they walked toward the headquarters building Bloom surveyed the scene and commented, "Looks like Bernese Labs is selling a lot of drugs."

Broussard smiled. "Legitimate drugs, I'm sure." He held the door open. Bloom went from a brisk Swiss morning to a tropical, almost greenhouse setting, for the reception area was done in a rain forest motif.

A smartly dressed receptionist smiled at them from behind a marble-faced bunker as Broussard stepped forward to flash his credentials again, saying, "Inspector Broussard and Captain Bloom to see Leopold Mainz. We are expected."

The receptionist gestured to the sign-in sheet and the two men scribbled their names as she murmured into the phone. Then she handed them two visitor tags and said, "Frau Bögner will escort you to Herr Mainz's office."

They turned to see an equally sharp but buxom Teutonic female in a pink business suit approach them. She extended her hand to Broussard and smiled. It seemed to Bloom everyone was smiling today. "*Bonjour*. I am Hanelore Bögner, Herr Mainz's Executive Assistant. He is expecting you. Please follow me."

The two detectives followed the executive assistant in train, with Bloom wondering whatever had happened to secretaries.

They went up to the fourth floor, which was really the fifth floor, Bloom reminded himself, because in Europe the first floor is actually the second floor, and it goes from there. On the ride up Bloom noticed that Hanelore's pink business suit and underlying blouse had a few strategic buttons free, revealing a whiff of cleavage that seemed at odds with Swiss decorum. He made a mental note to ask Broussard why there seemed to be so many Germanic names—Stolz, Mainz, Bögner—at this company in the Francophone part of Switzerland. Perhaps because the company was founded in Bern, located in the German section of the country?

The door parted to a penthouse reception area that was darkly paneled and festooned with Romanesque art. A second buxom secretary, this one a redhead in a burgundy suit, sat typing at a word processor and smiled at them as they marched past. Hanelore knocked once on the double mahogany doors, then opened them and stepped inside, announcing, "Inspector Broussard and Captain Bloom to see you, Herr Mainz."

Bloom entered a room which, unlike the stuffy reception area, was open and airy with big windows looking out on the forest, and appointed with contemporary furniture and modern art. A trim, distinguised executive rose from his leather chair and walked around a rosewood desk that had a surface area only slightly smaller than the flight deck of the USS *Nimitz*. He extended his hand and said, "Inspector, Captain, so good to meet you. Please, sit down."

Seats were taken, and Bloom inspected his host more closely. He had rigid facial features that were somewhat softened by a gray beard and gracefully thinned hair, making him look every inch the senior corporate executive in complete charge of his domain.

"May I offer you something? Tea? Coffee?"

"Coffee would be fine," replied Bloom. "Black if you please."

"Tea for me, thank you," said Broussard. Mainz nodded to Hanelore, who withdrew to fetch the order.

Without hesitation Mainz began. "First of all, I wish to extend my apologies for not personally executing the exchange of poor Erich's remains. This week has been particularly difficult in that we are closing a large licensing agreement for one of our new drugs, and my presence has been required. It was poor judgment to have sent my aide."

"What kind of drug?" inquired Bloom.

"A new treatment for type 2 diabetes. It will be marketed in the U.S. under the name Insulmar."

"Hmm. My aunt suffers from diabetes. I'll tell her to notify her doctor."

"Excellent. Our first sale in America. Your aunt will not be disappointed. The test results on Insulmar are very exciting."

Hanelore entered carrying a tray and began to serve as Bloom regarded his host once more. He had that edge of intellect and streak of smugness Bloom sometimes found in the higher echelons of society; but there was also a trace of the effeminate in Leopold Mainz's mannerisms and voice, and despite the department's sensitivity training it rubbed Bloom the wrong way. He sipped his coffee and decided to get on with it.

"Herr Mainz, from the moment your Assistant Managing Director Erich Stolz met his untimely death in the city of Chicago until this point in time, his remains have been the responsibility of the Cook County Coroner's office. I have seen the Swiss court order appointing you personally as the executor of Herr Stolz's estate, and in view of that I am prepared to transfer his remains to your custody upon completion of some minor formalities."

Mainz nodded and replied, "Of course. And again, my apologies for not being available earlier."

"Not at all." Bloom reached into his briefcase and removed a manila folder. "Forgive me, Herr Mainz. This will be rather distasteful, but necessary." He opened the folder and withdrew an 8 x 10 black-and-white glossy photograph. Holding it by the edge he passed it to Herr Mainz instead of sliding it across the desk. This forced Mainz to take the photograph between his thumb and fingers, and because it was upside down he used both hands to right it as he withdrew his reading glasses from his breast pocket.

"What you are seeing is Herr Stolz's pre-autopsy photograph," Bloom said. "Do you, Leopold Mainz, positively identify the deceased in this photograph as one Erich Stolz employed by Bernese Laboratories?"

Mainz studied the photograph for a few moments, then sighed and said, "Alas, yes, this is poor Erich." He took off his glasses and handed the photograph back. "What a senseless death. He will be sorely missed."

Bloom handled the photograph by the edge and carefully placed it back in the manila folder. Then he slid a form across the desk with the words COOK COUNTY CORONER printed on the crest. "If you will sign the receipt form by the X, the remains will be in your custody."

Mainz scribbled his initials and shoved the form back to Bloom, who picked it up and placed it and the manila folder in his briefcase.

"That should conclude our business, Herr Mainz. By the way, I was curious, what was Herr Stolz doing in Chicago anyway?"

Matter of factly Mainz replied, "He was going to meet with Argon Pharmaceuticals about licensing the European rights for their new anti-depressant. It was his first time in Chicago, so he was taking an extra day as a holiday to see the sights. Not that Erich ever took a holiday; he was totally absorbed by his work. No family, no hobbies. I relied upon him heavily."

Bloom nodded. "His travel itinerary showed that he was in London for three days prior to flying to Chicago." He let the statement hang in the air.

Again, Mainz didn't hesitate in his response. "Yes, he was talking to Thames Pharmacal about their licensing Insulmar for the Commonwealth market."

"I see. Well, we won't take any more of your time. *Danke*, Herr Mainz."

"*Bitte schön.*" He pushed a button. "Hanelore will see you out. Have a safe journey back to Chicago."

They followed the silk-wrapped cleavage back to the visitor entrance where they turned in their tags and made their way back to the parking lot. Once in the car, Broussard looked on quizzically as Bloom opened his briefcase and carefully extracted the manila folder. He opened it and picked up the black-and-white glossy by the edges, then canted it at such an angle that the sun coming through the windshield clearly illuminated the Leopold Mainz's fingerprints pressed into the photograph's emulsion. Bloom extracted a large zip lock bag from his briefcase and deftly placed the photograph inside. He then handed it to a puzzled Broussard, saying, "Get this to

Interpol headquarters in Lyon and tell them to put a rocket under it."

Once the pair of detectives had withdrawn, Leopold Mainz's assistant, Alain Delmar, entered his master's lair to find him at the window, arms folded in contemplation as he stared down at the forest. Delmar was somewhat tentative, concerned he had somehow bungled his earlier encounter with the American detective. He cleared his throat and ventured, "Herr Mainz . . . is everything finished with the police now?"

The managing director did not answer immediately, for he was deep in thought, unable to shake the feeling that the Chicago detective was more than he seemed. He found most policemen barely able to manage their mother tongue, yet this one had brought them up short by taking them to task with a French-language court order. He remained silent for the longest time, and when he finally spoke it was directed more to himself than Delmar when he said, "Always beware the Jew."

CHAPTER EIGHT

The arson investigator was always amazed at how long heat remained with the ashes of a house after it had burned to the ground. Even so, something had cremated this house beyond a gas explosion. The core of the structure had burned with a staggering intensity, turning the house into a pillar of flame before the local fire crew could arrive. The body count was two known dead: an old couple who had since been placed in body bags and removed from the scene.

He probed the pile of ashes with a metal rod while his crew began the painstaking process of sifting the ashes through a strainer.

"'Ey, guv," called one of his crew.

"What is it?"

"Got some bone fragments 'ere, right in the middle of what's left of a bedframe. Looks like the bloke was smokin' in bed."

The investigator pursed his lips. "More like he was smoked in bed. The combustion temperature must have been off the chart to turn bone to ash. Keep sifting."

"Aye, guv."

Experience told the investigator this looked like thermite, which was classified as a controlled armament and not exactly available at your local chemist, but why the hell was a small retired couple's house torched with thermite? He probed some more of the ash and his rod struck something metallic. With his rubber boot he carved out the ash to reveal a cube-shaped object where the basement closet had been. It took him a moment to figure it out, but then he realized it was a small safe—of the fireproof variety.

"Well then," he muttered to himself. "We'll see if it works as advertised."

Gideon Bloom stepped out of the lift and into the lobby of the InterContinental Hotel, lost in a forest of traveling businessmen and tourists. It was a fine hostelry but Bloom was getting impatient, wanting to get down the road to the bedrock of the bizarre enterprise into which he'd been thrust. Every instinct was screaming at him that something nasty was afoot, but it remained ever more elusive; and then there was the feeling he was on the business end of a pair of binoculars, or under a microscope. He tried to shrug it off, but couldn't. Maybe Broussard's summons would yield something. Strange that the young inspector did not want to meet at the police station, but at the restaurant in the hotel.

Bloom entered the main breakfast salon to the aroma of coffee and crumpets, with an undertone of a half-dozen languages on various tongues. He spied Broussard across the way and made his way to the corner table.

"Morning, Inspector."

Broussard nodded and said, somewhat curtly, "Captain."

A waiter came up and took orders for coffee and muffins, then Broussard looked around and said, "It's time for you to tell me what the hell is going on here, Captain. I have extended you every civility since you arrived, but there comes a time when professional courtesy ends and police business begins. It is time for you to tell me why you are here."

Bloom knew this moment had to come. It was an unavoidable reality that in police work you had to give if you were going to get. He was a stranger in a strange land and he needed an ally, and his internal affairs instincts told him Broussard was as straight as they came. He took a deep breath and said, "Emil, I have an incredible story to tell you."

The breakfast crowd had trickled out, leaving them almost alone in the large dining room. As Bloom had recounted his story he had seen Broussard go from surprise, to shock, to disbelief, to a little frightened. Bloom's take on Broussard was that he was a by-the-book sort, and this case was definitely not written in any manual.

"So that is why I am here," said Bloom in completion.

Emil didn't answer at first, and when he did his voice was soft. "It seems to fit."

Bloom cocked an eyebrow. "Fit? Fit how?"

Broussard looked around again, then said, barely audible, "The fingerprint search on the photograph came back from Interpol."

Bloom's pulse quickened. "And . . . ?"

The Swiss detective inhaled deeply, then replied, "It seems that the fingerprints of Leopold Mainz, managing director of Bernese Laboratories, belong to . . . to someone else."

"Someone else who?" demanded Bloom.

Broussard's eyes swept the room, then they locked onto the American's as he said, "The fingerprints belong to one *SS* Brigadefürhrer Walther Schellenberg, chief of the Reichssicherheitshaupamt—the counter-intelligence service of the Third Reich—who died in Turin, Italy, of kidney failure on May

31st, 1952, following his conviction for war crimes."

For the second time in a week Bloom felt the earth shift beneath him—something akin to that sickening crack that ripples across a mountain range before an avalanche cuts loose. From that moment in Sammy Bracewell's office there was a brake on Bloom's intellect that made him think that somehow there had been a bizarre mistake, linking the fingerprints of a long-dead Nazi war criminal to a Swiss pharmaceutical executive. But now, what seemed like a fissure had, in an eyeblink, ripped open a deep, dark abyss. It occurred to him that a lifetime of chasing dirty cops was a footnote compared to what he was facing now. Unconsciously he found himself gripping the edge of the table, as if trying to maintain his balance.

"Captain?" inquired Broussard. "Are you all right?"

Dazed, Bloom refocused on his colleague. "I . . . I'm not sure. Who—who did you say Leopold Mainz really was—is?"

"Walther Schellenberg."

Bloom's mind reached into the recesses. "Schellenberg . . . I've read something about that name before. Who was he? Like you said, head of the *Sicher*-something or other?"

Emil Broussard reached into his attaché case, withdrew a file and began. "Walther Friedrich Schellenberg was born in Saarbrucken, Germany, on January 16, 1910. He studied law at the University of Marburg and University of Bonn. After graduating he joined the Nazi party and the *SS* in 1933, where he worked in counter-intelligence. Then, in 1939, two things happened that catapulted his career into a meteoric rise: he met Reinhard Heydrich and played a major role in the 'Venlo Incident,' which led to the capture of two British agents in Holland.

"Schellenberg had a reputation for being extremely bright and for ingratiating himself to his superiors. A 'brown nose' I believe you Americans refer to it. As a result, he became the youngest general in the *SS* and worked for a time under Heydrich in department Amt IVE of the Gestapo."

"So what was A-M-T IVE?"

"It was the division of the Gestapo that planned and executed the Final Solution against Jews, Gypsies, Russians and partisans, and ran the concentration camps after the plan was green-lighted at the Wannsee Conference."

"So he was an architect of the Holocaust?"

"Precisely."

Dumbfounded, Bloom muttered, "So what happened after 1939 for General Schellenberg?"

"He became something of a pet to Himmler, taking the position of his aide-de-camp."

"Himmler's aide, huh?"

"Yes," explained Broussard, "but his powers far exceeded that of a simple aide-de-camp. Himmler's position was that of Reichsführer, and as such he was Generalbevollmachtigter für die Verwaltung, or plenipotentiary of the whole Reich administration. In other words, Himmler's powers were exceeded only by the Führer himself. Therefore, Himmler appointed Schellenberg Sonderbevollmachtigter, or special plenipotentiary. Arguably, Schellenberg wielded power as the number three person of the entire Third Reich—at times exceeding the reach of Reichsmarshal Göring. This was pretty heady stuff for a thirty-one-year-old man."

"Clearly," mumbled Bloom as he absorbed the information. Then he prompted Broussard, "What happened then?"

"Schellenberg was that rare combination of capability, ambition and confidence. He undertook a series of intelligence missions that were quite extraordinary. He planned Operation Osprey as a precursor to a planned takeover of Ireland. Through his spy Cicero he acquired the plans to the D-Day invasion, but fortunately Hitler discounted them. In 1940 he even tried to intercept the Duke and Duchess of Windsor when they were in Portugal to try and persuade them to work for Germany."

Bloom nodded. "But what kind of a man was he? Was he a firebrand Nazi?"

"You hit upon an intriguing question. On one hand he reveled in the perks of power. An epicurean, he cut a swath through occupied Paris, was always in the company of beautiful women, and became close—but probably not intimate—with Coco Chanel."

"Chanel? The perfume lady? A collaborator?"

"Something of that ilk, but not exactly. As things went south for the Nazis she and Schellenberg hatched a plan to put out peace feelers to the Allies through Chanel's relationship with Churchill, but nothing came of it."

"So, he was a playboy general who was ready to jump the Nazi ship when things got ugly."

Broussard paused and looked out at the whitecaps on the lake, as though his mind was in a different place. He turned back to the American policeman. "At first blush, the historical record would seem to indicate that, but there is a parallel chain of events with Schellenberg that doesn't quite square with that scenario. To my mind at least."

"Explain."

Again, Broussard collected his thoughts before speaking. "According to archive material of his interrogation, in April 1945, Schellenberg convinced Himmler to allow him to travel to Sweden to try and negotiate with the Allies through a count named Folke Bernadotte. While he was there Berlin fell and Schellenberg began negotiating with a U.S. Army officer to essentially turn state's evidence for the Allies. On June 17th, 1945, he was flown to Frankfurt before being transferred to a London prison camp for interrogation. He received a six-year sentence from a military tribunal, but after his imprisonment at the British interrogation center he was transferred to a hospital for gall bladder and liver ailments. This is where things get more than a little strange."

"How so?"

Broussard hesitated, as if he were a doctor about to impart some unpleasant news to a patient. He looked up at Bloom and said, "Although he was arguably the third most powerful man in the Third Reich, his complicity in the Final Solution was without question, and he was found guilty by a military tribunal Walther Schellenberg was never imprisoned for war crimes."

"Never imprisoned! How could that happen?"

Broussard, for lack of a better word, was squirming. "This is where it gets a little . . . complicated."

"So educate me."

Broussard sighed. "You Americans tend to see things in black and white. Cowboys and Indians. Your country is protected by two vast oceans. But in Central Europe the, ah, mindset is somewhat more malleable. Indeed, over centuries about every country, duchy, or principality on this continent has been at war or allied with every other country."

Bloom nodded. "I can appreciate that."

"Well, during World War Two, Switzerland was surrounded on all sides by the Axis forces. Had they wanted to, the Nazis could have made Switzerland capitulate without firing a shot. All Germany needed to do was cut off our importation of food supplies and we would have starved."

"So what is your point in all this, and how does it relate to Schellenberg?"

"My point is that while much of the Swiss populace supported the Allied powers during the war, much of the Swiss government was pro-Nazi and willing to look the other way to accommodate Hitler's demands in return for non-invasion during the war."

"Such as . . . ?"

"Production of war matériel, passage of armaments and supplies from Germany to Italy on Swiss rail lines through Swiss tunnels—and cooperation on intelligence matters."

Bloom made the connection. "And Schellenberg, being in charge of all foreign intelligence for Germany . . ."

". . . developed a close relationship with the chief of Swiss intelligence, a colonel named Roger Masson. As the story goes, Schellenberg convinced Masson he had dissuaded Hitler from invading Switzerland. How much truth there was to that no one will ever know, but apparently Masson bought it; and after Schellenberg received his sentence, Masson made a special appeal to the Allies that Schellenberg be allowed to serve out his time in Switzerland. What back channel, under-the-table dealing went on is open to speculation but, remarkably, the Allies acceded to Masson's request and remanded Schellenberg to Masson's custody."

Bloom shook his head.

With a resigned face, Broussard nodded. "In the netherworld of wartime spycraft, it may not be as outlandish as you might think. It could be Schellenberg had something on Masson and threatened to expose him if he wasn't given sanctuary. Masson, in turn, might have had a marker due from Allen Dulles, who ran OSS operations out of Bern during the war under Masson's protection. In any case, Schellenberg walked right into Switzerland, where he wrote his memoirs and reputedly lived quietly with the financial support of Coco Chanel."

Bloom leaned back and allowed himself to absorb the incredible litany of facts from more than a half century before. A high-ranking Nazi. A deep Swiss connection. The underworld of intelligence. What kind of soup was boiling in this bizarre cauldron? Where did it come from? How deep was it and, more importantly, where was it going? What was its purpose?

Whatever it was, Bloom had the inescapable feeling that some malevolent beast was about to be unleashed, but he had no clue as to its nature or scope. Part of his mind wrestled with the issue of jurisdiction. But another part of him screamed that legalistic niceties were a luxury he couldn't afford now. He had to get to the bottom of this . . . this mystery before the unknown monster was loosed upon its intended victims—whoever they might be. All he had was some outlandish evidence that while incredible, he now believed to be true.

And time? Was the clock ticking? Again, instinct told him the sands were slipping through the hourglass. He weighed the idea of slogging through a series of intercontinental bureaucracies to get action, but who knew how long that would take? And who the hell would he go to? The Department of Dead and Resurrected Reverse-aging War Criminals? Bloom doubted that was in the phone book. . . . No. With an unknown quantity of time, the only course was direct action, of the swift and brass-knuckled kind. He and Broussard would have to bust this puppy wide open, then let the bureaucrats sort out the carnage.

"All right," said Bloom evenly. "I don't know what this is all about, or how it could even be possible, but the evidence speaks for itself. It's my view that something—what, I don't know—is underway, and these resurrected and youthened Nazis intend God only knows what. And time may be of the essence."

"My thoughts exactly," replied Broussard. "And the only thing we may have going for us is that they don't know we know."

"We hope."

"We hope," echoed Broussard. "So, where do we go from here?"

Bloom's mind raced. "We only have two threads, really: Leopold Mainz, managing director of Bernese Pharmaceuticals, and Erich Stolz, or rather Otto von Spinnemann. Can you put a team on Mainz? Maybe get wire taps, phone records, and such?"

Broussard didn't answer at once, and for a moment his face contorted into something like a wince before he replied, "Not a good idea, Captain."

Again, Bloom was perplexed, and more than a little irritated. "So enlighten me."

Broussard sighed. "You must understand, for the Swiss there are skeletons in a closet you just do not open. To the outside world, Switzerland put on a face that it was defiant to the Nazis and struggled to preserve its neutrality, when in fact many businesses and banks profited handsomely from the war. Wealthy Jews deposited their fortunes in Swiss banks thinking they would enjoy refuge if things became untenable in Germany. But when the border was closed, instead of sitting in a safe haven in Zürich with their bank account, they received a one-way ticket to Auschwitz. And not only they, but every relative, friend, colleague or acquaintance—an entire nation, really—disappeared up the chimneys of the crematoriums while Swiss bankers raked in a windfall beyond their dreams. Huge deposits and dead clients, all shielded by draconian bank secrecy laws. It didn't get better than that. Everyone in Switzerland knows that the post-war prosperity that the country enjoyed was propelled in large measure by dead depositors."

"But that was a long time ago."

"To be sure, but a collective guilt permeates my country even today. The deaths of six million are not easily erased. I should think that one with your bloodlines would agree."

"Indeed I do. But why would that stop an investigation with the evidence we have?"

"Because Switzerland is a small place. A very small place.

There are roughly a hundred men who really run the country. And it would only take a few of them to shut this investigation down and put up a brick wall. If I went to a magistrate asking for a wire-tap warrant on someone like Leopold Mainz, by the time I returned to headquarters I would be on the Canton Chief's carpet explaining myself before I was reassigned to traffic duties."

Bloom absorbed what the inspector was saying. He'd been on the receiving end of that kind of heat more times than he could count. "So what you're saying is we're on our own until we can break this . . . 'case' open. Or would I be making a heroic assumption that there is a 'we' in all this?"

The inspector nodded resolutely. "You may rely on me, Captain. This evidence is incredulous and I must tell you it has brought with it a sense of foreboding."

"And a sense of urgency."

"Yes."

"It's my feeling that if we don't break this sooner rather than later, the toothpaste that comes out of this tube may make 9/11 look like a walk in the park. And since you pointed out we have to do this off the grid, does anyone in your department know about this?"

The inspector shook his head. "No. I handled the interface with Interpol personally. I had a sergeant run some traps on Mainz, but I told him to keep it to himself, and he's trustworthy."

"Well, we have to follow our only threads: Spinnemann/Stolz and Schellenberg/Mainz. Spinnemann made a three-day layover in London before he flew on to Chicago. My people ran the traps on his credit cards; he stayed at the Dorchester."

"Rather pricey," the inspector threw in.

"So was the Drake in Chicago. This kind of vermin travels

first cabin. Anyway, I'll head to London and see what I can find. You cover Mainz. Tail him as best you can. Maybe he'll make a move."

"Then I shall be on my way."

"Will you make a copy of that file to take with me?"

Broussard reached into his attaché case and produced a copy for Bloom. The captain took it and said, "I could have used you in Internal Affairs, Emil." He thumbed through the pages and mused, "Where the hell did you get all this stuff anyway?"

Broussard shrugged. "You can get anything on the Internet."

Although he had a global cell phone with him, Bloom went to the lobby and placed a landline call to Deputy Commissioner Bracewell's private home line in Chicago. Sitting in the booth he figured it was 6:30 a.m. Chicago time, and Sammy was not a morning person. A hung-over voice came on the line and mumbled, "Bracewell."

"Sammy, it's Gid."

The voice woke up. "So, my European bureau decides to report in. I was about to put a call in to Missing Persons."

"Skip the repartee and listen." Bloom downloaded a condensed version of Broussard's report, then added, "I don't know where all this is going, but London is about the only thread we've got. I need you to tee me up with an industrial-strength liaison with Scotland Yard and have them set up a meeting with the manager at the Dorchester. Might as well book me in there."

"The Dorchester? They want two Gs a night for a closet! We went to London last summer and my wife—*my* wife—wouldn't stay there it was so expensive."

"*Mmmph . . . wha . . . ?*"

"Go back to sleep, honey."

"Then get the cash out of the drug evidence locker or use your slush fund," Gideon said. "I don't care, just do it. I'll get a flight out this afternoon. Have the Scotland Yard liaison meet me at the plane. I'll text you the particulars."

"But what about—"

"No speculation now, Sammy. There isn't time. Just set it up with London."

"I still can't believe the Swiss won't come down on this guy Mainz."

"Strictly speaking, there is no Swiss law against being a living, breathing dead Nazi, and if we go through channels, Mainz will know something's up. And it takes too long to mobilize a bureaucratic quagmire."

And with that, Bloom hung up.

CHAPTER NINE

The tide was rolling in along the Normandy coast and the wind came with it, roiling up white caps over the Channel and causing Marc Chartain to pull his windbreaker tight against him.

"I can't seem to take this kind of cold," he mused to his sister.

Elise, his younger sibling by two years, gave a chuckle and replied, "The desert can be cold, too."

"Oui. But Algiers was never like this wet cold from the sea."

She shrugged. "You get used to it. The price you pay for a green landscape, I suppose."

Chartain was walking along the beach near Arrowmanches where his sister and her husband lived. Elise was the only living relative from his immediate family, and she alone was the person with whom he could let down his guard.

"Alain!" she yelled at her ten-year-old son playing tag with the waves. "Don't go too far!"

"*Oui, Maman!*" he cried, just before turning around and running farther down the beach.

"He minds well," observed Chartain.

"Just like his uncle."

They both chuckled.

Elise had never seen her leonine brother this vulnerable before. She hadn't pressed, had let the story come out of him at his own pace, and when it did she was surprised at how simple it all was. He had fallen in love and suffered a broken heart. "This Séverine must have been quite the *femme*," Elise said finally.

Chartain looked out to sea. "That she was . . . is."

She took his arm. "You've both been through an ordeal. Perhaps with time . . ."

He shrugged. "Time. . . . Well, I've spent enough of that on your shoulder, moping around here. Time for me to move on. To Paris to visit Caisson, then back to Corsica."

"No rush. Alain can't get enough of you. He counts the days until he can be a *para*."

"See to it he becomes a banker instead. . . . Alain! Time to go!"

With that they returned to the house. Chartain packed his grip and Elise and Alain drove him to the train station. They escorted him to the platform where other travelers were climbing aboard. Chartain gave her a lingering hug, then reached into his grip and handed Alain a small, plainly wrapped package, saying, "This is something to remember your uncle by. But you're not to open it until the train is out of sight. *Comprends*?"

Alain nodded, but was unable to mask his disappointment at his uncle's departure as he gave him a hug.

With that, Chartain climbed aboard just as the car began moving. A final wave and he disappeared inside.

Alain watched as the train pulled out of Arrowmanches Station, then moved on around a curve and out of sight. Alain looked up at his mother, inquiring with his eyes if it was permissible to open the package, and she nodded.

In an eyeblink he had the wrapping off, expecting something like an iPod or at least an action figure; but it was a small, white velvet case with the words *République Française* embossed in gold on the cover. Sensing this was light years removed from a toy box, Alain gingerly raised the hinged cover and looked inside, not prepared for the gasp that came from his mother. Looking at the enameled ivory and the finery of the white ribbon he asked, "What is it Maman?"

Somewhat breathless, she replied softly, "That, my son, is the Croix de Guerre."

Wearing jeans, a leather jacket, stocking cap and designer sunglasses, Fayla Bannon walked past the tenement houses of Falls Road taking in the sights, sounds and smells one last time. It was a kind of requiem to the little girl who had never had the luxury of being a little girl in this kill zone of Belfast, where the tectonic plates of Protestant and Catholic forces had clashed for centuries. Just as when she was a child, scruffy working-class kids still kicked a football around the pavement when they weren't puffin' a fag. She'd never been a sentimental sort, yet with all the demands upon her she had taken leave for this one indulgence to recalibrate her personal compass. Since the bombing in Wellington Square security had been tightened, with British soldiers resurfacing like days of old. At the sight of a Tommy on the corner she graced him with a smile as she strutted past, taking note of his admiring eyes. Yes, she was content, knowing that the deep, searing hate of everything British was still in full flower in what was left of her soul.

She made her way to the Sperrin Peak pub on the Protestant side of Falls Road, confident no one there would have so much as a sliver of a chance at remembering the poor little lass of so long ago. She stopped at the bar for a pint to take to her room upstairs—one of a half-dozen the pub had for rent. She opened the door sipping on the pint and was about to place it on the bedside table when a voice behind her said, "Well, if 'tain't Fayla Bannon back from the grave."

A normal person might have jumped or spun round at the strange voice, but Fayla Bannon had lived on the edge so long she brutally controlled the adrenaline that surged into her veins. With studied nonchalance she set her pint on the bedside table and turned casually, placing her hand inside her shoulder bag.

She faced an overweight, late middle-aged man with gray unkempt hair and bloodshot eyes. He wore a windbreaker, with a hand in the pocket, and she knew what was in it. He might have been a cab driver or a longshoreman—and, indeed, he had been those things—but Fayla Bannon had a hard time accepting this washed-out shell of a shit had once been deputy commander of Regan Fael, an extremist splinter group of the Provisional Irish Republican Army. He had once sworn to expel the British rot from the Emerald Isle or die trying. He had done neither.

"Paddy McDill, as I live and breathe. How did a pig like ye find yer way into my boudoir."

He didn't answer at once but looked her over with an appraising eye. "I sent you off to Gibraltar with a pack of Semtex four years ago, and sadly it went off prematurely. Leveled your hotel to the ground. Nary a splinter left, I'm told. Thirty-three people killed, they think, and Fayla must be one of them, for she never returned."

"And why would I want to return to a bunch of old women who rolled over and spread their legs for the Tommies?"

McDill shook his head and replied, "Still the true blood, I see. You were always the toughest nut of all Fayla, I grant you that, but the war is over. We've made our peace and we were on our way to sealin' it when you leveled Wellington Square and the Lord Mayor's house."

"Ohhh, but ye be wrong, Paddy boy. Ye don't know how wrong. The war hasn't even started yet. But when it does the Orange bastards will be running into the sea to get out of Ulster."

Another shake of the head. "Our friendly RUC men brought me in to view a surveillance video of the Wellington Square bombing. They were squeezing everybody for leads. Asked if I knew the woman who parked the Vauxhall and walked away. I recognized ye, of course. No mistakin'. That was me Fayla."

"Not yer Fayla, Paddy. Not in a million years. So how did you find me? Are the RUC men about?"

"We still have our eyes. Yer not as clever as ye think. But the RUC men are in the dark . . . for the time being. It would be best for all concerned if ye just disappeared, Fayla. I could see the writing on the wall four years ago when I sent ye off to Gibraltar."

"So it was ye who made me pack of plastique go off 'prematurely.' And there I was, sent by ye to finish the job Mairead Farrell had started. Or was it ye who outed Mairead as well?"

"That's history, Fayla. The times have changed."

"Ye have no fekking idea how right ye are, Paddy." And with that the .32-caliber Berretta in her handbag discharged, sending its missile through the leather and into Paddy McDill's forehead above the right eye, just as he was working the Glock out of his windbreaker pocket.

Instinctively, Fayla turned and lunged into the bathroom, kicking out the window in an eruption of splinters and glass. Knowing she only had a moment before a fusillade of bullets ripped through the walls, she pulled a pear-shaped object out of her handbag, plucked out the pin and tossed it into the bedroom before she dove out onto the rooftop, landing with a grunt. The staccato of gunfire broke out, followed by shouts as McDill's backup team stormed into the room. Fayla rolled on the flat top roof, curled into the fetal position and covered her ears as the window she'd just sailed through belched smoke and flame, along with the screams of maimed and dying men. She bolted to her feet and all of a sudden she was thirteen years old again, running over the tiled and angled tenement rooftops with the Orangemen on her heels. Only now, even her own kind had turned against her.

Two blocks from the scene she turned, chest heaving, and scanned the rooftops—satisfied no one was following. The sirens of the Royal Ulster Constabulary pealed in the air as the sense of betrayal welled up inside her and she screamed from the rooftop, "*You'll all run into the sea, ye fekking pigs!*"

And with that she was away and over the next rooftop, like a springbok on the veld.

Gideon Bloom received the stamp on his passport from the Heathrow official and went to collect his bag from the conveyor when a thin and anonymous man in a blue suit stepped up and enquired, "Captain Bloom?"

"Yes?"

The gentleman extended a hand. "Chief Inspector Neville Chatham of Scotland Yard at your service."

Bloom shook it and said, "Good of you to meet me."

"Not at all. We received a most urgent request from your Commissioner to assist you in your investigation. Here, we'll see to your bag." He nodded and a uniformed Bobby took Bloom's grip.

They made their way to an unmarked sedan where Bloom and Chatham settled in the rear. After some light small talk, Chatham asked, "So, what is this about, Captain?"

Bloom was weary and dreading this question, so he deflected it for the moment. "I'll give you the brief tomorrow, Inspector, but the very short answer is we have reason to believe a Swiss pharmaceutical executive is not who he says he is—or was. He was killed in a traffic accident in Chicago, but prior to reaching Chicago he was in London for three days and stayed at the Dorchester. I wanted to see if I could fill out the picture a little."

"Of course. How can we help?"

"Well, first of all, I'd like to reconstruct as best we can his movements while he was here. I thought a good place to start would be the manager and staff of the Dorchester."

"Certainly. I'll set up an interview with the manager first thing in the morning. I understand you're staying at the Dorchester."

"A few notches above my pay grade, but yes. Police business, you understand."

"Quite. One does what one must."

"It is against regulations," murmured Sergeant André Fasson in a low voice.

Emil Broussard leaned over him and rearranged some papers on the Sergeant's desk as if they were discussing a case in the department's day room headquarters. Only two other investigators were in the room, and they were out of earshot—one filling out a form no one would ever read, the other watching a football match on the Internet.

"You would be one to know about breaking regulations, André. I'm giving you the opportunity to clean the slate."

André was whispering through his teeth now. "My mother was dying. She needed treatment the health service and insurance would not pay for. I served this department loyally for twenty-four years. My savings were gone. What else was I to do?"

"It was on the strength of that loyalty that I looked the other way, André. But now it is time to pay the piper."

It had happened seven years ago—Broussard, the rising star in the investigation division—Fasson, the elder sergeant, assigned as his partner. They made a superb team. Fasson's only weakness was that of being the dutiful son. While his mother was on her deathbed, Broussard and Fasson had rolled up a drug ring in Geneva; and late at night Fasson had been in the evidence room taking an inventory of the bust, which included upward of almost a million Swiss francs in cash. While the evidence clerk left to take a leak, Fasson helped himself to about a third of the take. Broussard, however, had seen the whole thing through the wire mesh of the evidence room, staying in the shadows, observing and waiting until Fasson had left the building. Once off the premises, Broussard made the collar.

For the only time in his life, Fasson's Swiss reserve cracked, and he broke down in tears. Broussard simply couldn't bear the man's anguish, so he looked the other way on the condition that he made Fasson sign an undated confession and tucked it away in that file all policemen keep. If it ever hit the fan, Broussard would extract the confession, time stamp the day's date, and say his old partner had just done the right thing. Then slap on the cuffs.

Fasson now squirmed. "What exactly do you want of me, Lieutenant?" he asked with stiff formality.

"That friend of yours at Bern Telecom?"

"What friend?"

"You know very well who. The one you nailed for wire fraud but let him go if he wired the money back. I'm sure you have the evidence hidden away in a safe place. Well, I want him to wire a scanner so I can pick up this cell phone,"—he plunked down a number on a slip of paper—"so when the subscriber dials or answers, I'll pick it up."

Fasson was silent for a moment before he said, "Wait here." He went in the hallway to use his own cell phone, then came back and announced, "It cannot be done. The SIM card in the phone has an encryption algorithm unique to that particular phone. It can only be accessed by Bern Telecom's central registry."

"I know this, André. That's how we monitor calls when we have a warrant. So let me spell this out for you. By eight o'clock tomorrow morning one of two things is going to happen: either I will have the encryption pass key for the scanner, or your signed confession will be on the captain's desk."

"But—"

"Don't make this more complicated than it is. Your friend at Bern Telecom has a choice: he delivers to you or he goes to jail. You deliver to me, or you go to jail. It is that simple."

"But—"

"Tomorrow. Eight o'clock."

Flying the Liberian flag, the tramp steamer *Augsburg* eased through the Adriatic Sea toward Trieste harbor at three knots. Captain Hörst Mannheim peered through his binoculars and saw the pilot launch approach. Soon the pilot-navigator would be on-board to guide his 7,000-ton vessel into its mooring at the pier, where the crew would unload a legitimate cargo of lumber from Borneo. Customs officials would come aboard to execute the paperwork, and were they to take the time to inspect the vessel, they would find everything one would expect to find on a rusting freighter that appeared to be at the end of its service life. The multi-national crew would all have their paperwork in order, but nowhere in their seaman cards would it reflect that nine of the crewmen had their PhDs in various scientific disciplines. Nor would they be able to find the pristine, state-of-the-art Level-5 laboratory cleverly concealed behind the rusty and stained bulkheads of the passageways.

A sister ship named the *Hanover* was just over the horizon and would dock later in the day.

Hörst Mannheim looked the part of the veteran merchant seaman with his gray hair, steely blue eyes, and ruddy skin that had been peppered by salt spray for many years. As the harbor approached he felt his pulse quicken as the culmination of so much preparation was soon to come to fruition, and once again he would be in command of a warship. A different kind of warship to be sure, for to the outside world the *Augsburg* appeared benign; but it would be transformed into the deadliest ship afloat. And the thought of it made Hörst Mannheim's heart race like it had not done since he'd served in the Kriegsmarine aboard the U-288 in the North Atlantic, attacking the Allied convoys with impunity.

CHAPTER TEN

Trevor Burkwood felt flushed as a red hue crept into his face. As general manager of the Dorchester Hotel he was accustomed to dealing with presidents, potentates, kings and rock stars; yet the presence of two policemen in his tastefully appointed office made him uncomfortable. "So, what exactly can I do for you, Captain Bloom?" he asked, with great correctness in his voice, while stroking the lapel of his Savile Row suit.

Bloom was equally uncomfortable because he knew he was in a situation where he had to lie and tell the truth in the same breath. "We are retracing the steps of a Swiss pharmaceutical executive named Erich Stolz who died in a traffic accident in Chicago, and our investigation revealed that he may, in fact, be someone else."

"Someone else?"

"Yes."

"A man named Otto von Spinnemann, we think. He is an ultra-right-wing extremist who, we believe, may be preparing a terrorist attack of some kind."

Burkwood turned cherry red. "A terrorist? Here at the Dorchester?"

"About three weeks ago, yes. He was here for three nights,"

recounted Bloom.

"Well, how may I help you?"

"I'd like you to check your records to begin with. Dinner reservations, theater tickets, limousine bookings, room service. Anything would be helpful, no matter how trivial it might seem."

Burkwood cleared his throat. "Yes, of course. I'll get those for you straight away. Anything else?"

"I presume you have security cameras and archive the footage."

"For up to thirty days, yes. Our security people handle that."

"Well, it will be painstaking, but I would like to see all the archival footage during his stay."

"Very well. Do you have a photograph of this . . . ah . . . individual?

Bloom took out the morgue photograph of Stolz and laid it in front of Burkwood, who recoiled as if a dead rat had been placed on the desk. He really must get these policemen out of his hotel.

"Ahem, ah, very well. Richard Martindale is our head of security and he will assist you."

"Thank you," replied the inspector. "Your cooperation will be remembered at the Yard."

The security video office was confining, little more than a hi-tech broom closet, but Bloom found Richard Martindale capable and efficient, for he had cued up the videos he had retrieved from the hotel's computer in sequence. "All right, Captain, your Mr. Stolz checked in at 2:38 p.m. on the eighth. Here is the video from the front desk for that time frame. . . . Ah, there he is. That your man?"

Bloom leaned forward and squinted at the grainy color

image. "Yes, that appears to be him."

Stolz went through the check-in routine, then asked the desk clerk something and she pointed to the concierge desk. Martindale looked at his clipboard as Stolz went over to the concierge and talked for almost ten minutes.

"Apparently he was booking tickets on the Eurostar."

"Eurostar?" asked Bloom.

"The bullet train that runs from London to Brussels and Paris through the 'Chunnel' under the English Channel. The charge and reservation went through our concierge and was keyed into his room bill about an hour after he checked in."

"Which was on Tuesday."

"That's right."

"When was the Eurostar trip?"

"The following day, Wednesday. Departure St. Pancras Station 3:37 p.m. Arrive Calais 5:14 p.m. Then return at 6:02 p.m. from Calais."

Bloom's brow furrowed. "That only puts him at Calais for forty-five minutes."

"Not him," replied Martindale. "Them. There was a second person on the itinerary."

"Who?"

"A woman. Name on the reservation was Melinda Bishop."

Bloom looked at Chatham who, in the unspoken commo link of detectives, nodded and left to run the traps on all the Melinda Bishops in the U.K.

Bloom thought it through. "He makes a round trip to Calais and likely doesn't even leave the station?"

"A trip to see the countryside?" suggested Martindale.

"On a bullet train? That doesn't make a lot of sense. But what about the woman? Was she a guest?"

Martindale tapped into a computer console and said, "No Melindas or Bishops registered in the last year."

Bloom couldn't connect the data. "Anything else on Tuesday?"

Martindale scanned the sheet. "A room service charge for dinner in his room at 8:14 p.m. By the size of the bill it looks like he dined alone. We don't have surveillance in the rooms."

"A pity."

"Quite."

The American pondered the situation, wondering where to go next. Then he sighed and said, "I know this will be exciting, but I need to view all the footage from his arrival forward."

Clarence Waida probed through the ash in the jar, taking a small sample for the tiny glass bottle that would be shipped to the chemical laboratory for spectral analysis. As head of the pyro-forensics lab of Scotland Yard, Waida was a stickler for procedures, but he already knew from training and experience the cause of this apartment fire in the village of Brentmews Down. Due to the immolation of the bedding fibers it was clear that they had burned at more than 2,500 degrees Centigrade. Waida surmised it was weapons-grade thermite that had reduced the human remains on the bed to a powder, with the exception of a thimbleful of bone fragments. Arson was bad enough. But arson as a means for murder, and thermite . . . well, that was something else altogether.

He labeled the bottle and put it next to the others, then turned his attention to the small charred safe that had been recovered from the ashes. He inspected it closely and nodded in approval, because a fireproof Merton safe was actually, well, fireproof. So many were not.

He hefted the high-speed drill off the workbench and selected a diamond drill bit from the toolkit. He donned the safety goggles and went to work, boring into the blackened metal with a screechy whine. A half hour later he administered the *coup de grace* on the hinges with a hammer and titanium chisel. The door of the safe fell on the workbench with a definitive *clunk*, allowing a small exhalation of warm air to escape from the tiny inner chamber that Waida felt on his face as he looked closer.

Arranged in a row like tiny sentries stood half a dozen video micro-cassettes.

It was late in the day and Bloom was almost cross-eyed from viewing the grainy screen. He'd been able to make some progress by fast-forwarding here and there. He found it to be sort of like a stakeout, but without the excitement.

Martindale had been an attentive host, coming and going, seeing he had lunch sent in with fresh coffee, and giving him free rein with the equipment. He walked in and asked, "How's it going?"

"Tell me again how many cameras you have in this place?"

"Sixty-seven. Three on each floor and the rest scattered about."

Just then the door opened and the chief inspector entered wearing a frown on his face.

"You look like a man bearing bad news," observed Bloom.

Without prelude Chatham said, "There are exactly three Melinda Bishops in the United Kingdom with British passports. One is a seventy-three-year-old retired teacher in Surrey, one is a forty-six-year-old mother of three in Berkshire, and the third, had she lived, would have been a thirty-three-year-old woman from Cheltenham in the Cotswold."

"Had she lived?" asked Bloom.

"I'm afraid so," explained Chatham. "Unfortunately, obtaining a British passport is easier than it should be. Apparently someone used an old ruse to obtain a false ID, presenting herself at the shire records office as Melinda Bishop and asked for a copy of her birth certificate. She used it to file for a U.K. passport."

"But wouldn't the real Melinda Bishop have gotten wind of it?"

The chief inspector shook his head. "The real Melinda Bishop died at age seven. You see, we still have no way of correlating birth and death certificates with passport applications. Not such a good thing in a post-nine-eleven world, but there it is."

"So you've put out the word on Melinda Bishop?"

Chatham nodded. "Yes, but the one and only time she came up on the network was to board the Eurostar on the trip to Calais."

"Used only once?"

"Yes, which would suggest we are dealing with someone very slippery indeed."

Bloom took a deep breath and exhaled slowly. "So we may have struck a dead end. If we can't ID this Melinda Bishop, then we've hit the wall . . . whoa! Hello, Herr Stolz."

On the video monitor the lobby camera showed Eric Stolz stepping out of the elevator wearing slacks, an open collar shirt and an expensive double-breasted blazer. Bloom noticed that the stoic Teutonic demeanor had broken out in a lusty smile, his eyes gleaming as he advanced with extended hand. The object of his attentions was about five-feet-five, wearing a crème silk Armani dress with a black scarf on the shoulder. Striking red hair flowed from under a white fedora. Oversized Chanel sunglasses provided a stylish mask. The view from the camera was off to the side as Stolz took her hand and bestowed a Continental kiss. He was clearly besotted by her, and she was rather giddy herself. She took his arm as they walked into the restaurant.

"I have a feeling this is our Melinda Bishop. Can you bring up the camera in the dining room?"

"Afraid not," said Martindale. "We don't have camera coverage there."

"Damn." One possible lead and it walks out of sight.

"But they have to come out this way." Martindale fast-forwarded the video until seventy-two minutes later, when they both exited the dining room. She was no longer wearing her sunglasses, but the camera angle and the brim of the fedora concealed her face. They stopped in the lobby, Stolz looked at his watch and gestured toward the entrance. She turned and reached into her purse for the sunglasses as they strode toward the exit. She paused, put them on, then walked out the door.

Bloom grumbled. "We just can't seem to get a break."

Martindale said, "Wait a moment." He looked at the date/time notation and rummaged through the CDs. He plucked one out and loaded it into the player. "There is one camera at ground level just inside the entrance. Doesn't provide much coverage and I've given some thought to pulling it out, but maybe . . ." His voice trailed off as the image came up and he rushed it forward to the specific time. "Here we are. . . ."

Stolz and the woman walked into the frame, and in that moment the woman paused and looked square into the camera for just a moment as she put on her Chanels, then walked out of the frame.

Bloom heard a gasp behind him as Chief Inspector Chatham drew breath.

Curious, Bloom asked, "Can you make her?"

"Bring that back up," ordered Chatham.

Martindale complied and froze the image on the screen with the red-haired woman looking directly at them.

"Good God," whispered Chatham, "it can't be."

"Can't be who?" asked Bloom.

"She's dead. Blown to pieces in Gibraltar."

"Looks in one piece to me," observed Bloom. "Who is she?"

Chatham did not answer, but pulled out his cell phone and punched the speed dial. Transfixed, he stared at the image and put the phone to his ear. "Put me through to Grayson Salisbury . . . quickly."

Grayson Salisbury threw another report in the out basket and looked at his watch. It was past 5 p.m. so he unbuttoned the collar of his shirt and loosened his tie. He thought about another cup of coffee, but decided it was time for something a bit stronger. He opened the drawer of his desk, extracted a bottle of Jim Beam and splashed some into a paper cup. He loved the American bourbon more than he'd ever admit, and needed a crutch now more than ever. He'd never been so frustrated in his life. The Wellington Square bombing had not yielded a single clue. The Semtex was generic, the car stolen, the detonator of Czech manufacture but nothing to trace to a perpetrator. Just the surveillance camera of a red-haired woman in sunglasses and a wide-brimmed hat who had disappeared into the crowd.

And there were whispers and rumors from the communities from which these things spring, whether they be Arab, Irish or Asian. But here there was absolutely nothing concrete. Nothing.

The home secretary pinged him daily, wondering what sort of progress was being made. Progress, indeed. Salisbury could hear the tension in the minister's voice, the unspoken truth being that if the Wellington Square bombing wasn't solved— and soon—his position as home secretary would be in jeopardy. Which was a shame, because the reality was, he was a most capable man.

The phone rang and Salisbury winced. It was sure to be the

home secretary. And if he didn't pick up, his BlackBerry would vibrate a few seconds later. He tossed down the Jim Beam, then wearily lifted the receiver and said, "Salisbury."

"Grayson? Neville Chatham here."

That was a bit of a relief. "I say, Neville. Long time. To what do I owe?"

Chatham cut to the chase. "Do you remember Fayla Bannon?"

Salisbury grunted. "That's like asking me if I would remember a cobra in my knickers. Turned into strawberry jam in Gibraltar, the saints be praised. You know that as well as anyone."

"Knew. I'm looking at her face on a surveillance video at this moment at the Dorchester Hotel."

Salisbury was too stunned to respond. Fayla Bannon had been vaporized four years ago in an explosion as big as . . . well, the one in Wellington Square.

"Grayson, are you there?"

"What? Oh, yes, yes. Fayla Bannon? At the Dorchester? How the—"

"I'm here with a Chicago police captain who is pursuing an unusual case. I think it best we come see you at the Yard. This may be, ah, time sensitive."

"Yes . . . yes, of course, Neville. Come straight away."

Chatham rang off and Salisbury sat there dumfounded. Fayla Bannon. Alive? Impossible. Chatham must have it wrong.

Just then the phone rang again.

"Salisbury."

"MacBaine at Forensics, sir."

"Yes, what is it?"

"Well, sir, we have a rather unusual situation. I'm down at the lab with Woolridge and we've been viewing some, ah, explicit video from an arson investigation in Brentmews Down."

"Brentmews Down?"

"A village in Herefordshire."

"Oh, yes, go on."

"Well, sir," MacBaine continued, "seems a small flat was torched with some weapons-grade thermite, killing the occupant. But apparently this fellow was into the video thing and he taped and secured some of his liaisons in a fireproof safe."

"Get to the point, Arthur."

"Yes, sir. Well, the arson people punted the tapes down here to the lab, where we ran the woman's facials through the IdentiScan, and you'll never guess who the computer spit out. . . ."

"Go on."

"You remember that PIRA maiden who you called a devil in a skirt? The one who got blown up in Gibraltar shortly after I joined your department?"

Salisbury felt his pulse shift into high. "Fayla Bannon," he whispered.

"None other. And to confirm, Woolridge and I pulled some of the old surveillance photos and damned if it isn't her. Swear on me mum's grave it is."

There was a moment of silence, then Salisbury said, "If it is Fayla Bannon, she topped her bed mate for a reason. Who was he?"

"Some nobody named Cyril Worsham. A janitor, actually."

"A janitor?"

"Yes, sir," replied MacBaine. "He worked at Heathstone Arsenal."

CHAPTER ELEVEN

Gideon Bloom watched the grainy screen as Fayla Bannon worked over Cyril Worsham's chubby body in the low light. In a prurient technical sense he had to admire the way she became the living, breathing essence of the poor schmuck's ultimate sexual fantasy, extracting bit after bit of information on Cyril's job at Heathstone Arsenal. Unfortunately, the audio, like the video, was grainy and very difficult to hear—except for Fayla's ear-splitting fake orgasm.

"You say he's certain?" said Salisbury into the phone. "Right, then. Get his statement. Every detail. And fax it to me immediately." The assistant superintendent rang off and turned to Bloom and Neville Chatham. Woolridge, the lab tech, and Arthur MacBaine were there, too.

"That was my man in Belfast. He verified that the photos of Fayla Bannon at the Dorchester were the same woman who blew up Paddy McDill in her room at the inn."

Bloom looked at the clock. It was 1:30 a.m. Everyone was exhausted; but as can happen with a case, once something breaks the events followed in rapid-fire sequence.

Chatham had rushed Bloom to Scotland Yard, where he'd been thrust into the office of a huge man named Salisbury with a hawkish face. Bloom didn't catch the title, but it really didn't matter, because it was immediately apparent this dude was in charge. What followed was a gusher of data that all in the room were trying to get their weary brains around. Then Bloom had given this captive audience a lesson in shock and awe as he recounted the story of Stolz/Spinnemann and Mainz/Schellenberg. Everyone was dumbstruck, trying to absorb it all.

When Bloom had learned the background of Fayla Bannon, her story had given a hard ass like him the woolies. But it didn't seem to hold together. "I don't understand why Fayla Bannon would have been in Gibraltar with a load of explosives."

It was Chatham who sighed and took a deep breath. "As younger men, Graham and I were on the Ulster Task Force. You have to understand what it was like during The Troubles. Belfast spawned a number of extremist folk heroes during that era, among them a young woman named Mairead Farrell."

"And who is she?"

"Was," replied Salisbury.

"She led an IRA team to Gibraltar in 1988 that was going to set off a bomb at the changing of the guard ceremony while a gaggle of tourists were looking on."

"What happened? I don't remember anything about a Gibraltar bombing."

"We had totally penetrated their cell. An SAS team intercepted them prior to planting the bomb and shot them all dead."

Salisbury picked up the narrative. "But after Gibraltar, the figure of Mairead Farrell grew to mythic proportions. Fayla Bannon had been a child protégé of hers—an acolyte, you might say. When Farrell was killed the twelve-year-old Fayla vowed to finish the job one day. In the lead-up to the ultimate attempt when she supposedly was killed, she cut a swath through the

British Army unlike anything anyone had ever seen. Like this poor sod on the screen she would seduce them and pretend like she was playing a bondage game. Then she would tie them to a bedpost or a chair, shove a sock in their mouth and tape it over, cover their head with a plastic bag and watch them suffocate. It became something of a trademark of hers."

"And she was never arrested?"

Chatham and Salisbury looked at each other, then both shook their heads. Chatham explained, "While Fayla was topping British soldiers like so many tin cans and placing bombs around Belfast, she was also the mistress of the deputy superintendent for intelligence of the Royal Ulster Constabulary."

Bloom whistled.

"Needless to say," observed Salisbury, "she seemed remarkably well informed. Always one step ahead of us. And it wasn't until after Gibraltar that the deputy superintendent knew who he was actually screwing."

"So what did happen in Gibraltar?" asked Bloom.

Chatham elaborated. "By the time Fayla was ready to make good on her vow to finish Mairead Farrell's last mission, the worm had turned in Ulster. The populace had finally sickened of the violence, the economy was in a shambles, Sinn Fein got the upper hand and the popular support the extremists had enjoyed withered away. They had few safe havens left. Paddy McDill's tribe was one of the last holdouts; but even he called it a day. Rumors were, Fayla was under his umbrella when she went to Gibraltar."

"But how did she, uh, die, so to speak?"

Salisbury ran his hand through his hair and said, "Gibraltar was, and remains, a big tourist attraction—the Rock and all that. As such, much of the island is under surveillance by security cameras. The camera that covered the street of the small hotel where Bannon stayed caught her going in and out over several days, carrying what looked like shopping parcels, when in fact it was probably Semtex. The video showed her entering the hotel, then about two minutes later the whole thing goes up like a volcano. Dozens of remains were pulled out of the rubble, in various states of disrepair. There was never any DNA confirmation because Fayla had never been in custody, so we had no DNA with which to confirm her demise."

"The false assassination was brilliant," said Bloom. "Thinking she was dead, the security services and her enemies would no longer look for her. She'd have free rein to maneuver." He was about to hit the wall of exhaustion, but kept going. "So let's lay out what we know: Fayla Bannon places a bomb at Wellington Square. Shortly thereafter she meets Stolz at the Dorchester for a trendy lunch. They take the Eurostar bullet train to Calais and back again. Stolz goes on to Chicago where he gets pancaked by a delivery truck. Fayla goes to Brentmews Down where she presumably murders and torches a janitor and his flat. What's the connection among these events? What did the janitor have that Mainz wanted?"

"And what would be the significance of Calais?" asked Chatham rhetorically.

Salisbury rubbed his eyes. "Fayla would not be doing our departed janitor without a reason. As best we can hear, she's pumping him for information. What that's about we don't know."

Bloom thought it through and replied, "Well, clearly she isn't pumping him for the brand of toilet bowl cleaner he uses. It's got to be something to do with this Heathstone Arsenal. What is that, exactly?"

Chatham shrugged. "M-O-D. Ministry of Defence. Very hush-hush as they say."

Woolridge chimed in. "It's where, rumor has it, some of the darker arts in the defense of the realm are practiced."

"Such as?" asked Bloom.

"Nobody here knows for sure," said Salisbury, "but probably things like WMD—chemical, bacteriological weaponry. That sort of thing."

Bloom contemplated what Salisbury said when a chill came over him and he shuddered. On one level he was gratified they were making progress. On another level there was a sense of dread about what they would ultimately find. "We better get up there, to this Heathstone Arsenal. Find out all we can about our deceased janitor and what Mainz had—has—his designs on." He turned to Salisbury. "Superintendent, I know this is your turf, but it's my feeling that what we're up against here transcends any jurisdictional issue."

"Agreed," said Salisbury.

"It's also my experience that when an investigation intersects with a government bureaucracy, roadblocks pop up like mushrooms. Are there some levers you can pull to get us access to—and more importantly, cooperation from—the commanding officer of Heathstone?"

Grayson Salisbury regarded Bloom carefully. So unassuming. But underneath the vanilla veneer was an extraordinary mind and an understated mettle. A captain of Internal Affairs? In Chicago no less? What kind of barbarians did he have to slay everyday? No doubt this was a singular man. And a brother-in-arms. "Captain Bloom, I can assure you I can slice the red tape to ribbons in this case. And my colleagues and I would be grateful if you would assist us in our investigation."

"My pleasure."

Salisbury pinched his nose. "Look, we're all in. Captain Bloom, Neville will drive you back to the Dorchester. Get some sleep. A car will call for you at 8 a.m. and we'll head out straightaway for Heathstone. By the way, are you carrying a firearm?"

Bloom shook his head. "Nine-eleven and trans-border paperwork. Decided to leave it behind. Feel naked without it, I don't mind telling you."

"What flavor do you carry?"

"Colt .38 Special. Snub nose in a belt holster."

Salisbury nodded to MacBaine. "See to it, Arthur."

"Aye, sir."

"Neville, you'll come along with Captain Bloom and myself tomorrow."

"Of course," he replied.

"Now if you gentlemen will excuse me, I would like to speak with Captain Bloom alone for a moment."

The other three policemen filed out, leaving the American and Englishman alone. Salisbury stared at Bloom for a few moments, then said, "Captain Bloom, this is the damndest story I have ever heard in my life. Nazis returned from the dead! How incredible is that? How could it be possible?"

"It's Gideon."

Salisbury nodded. "Grayson."

"I'm not a scientist. We can speculate until the cows come home. What I want is to head off whatever disaster is in the making, then bring in this Mainz or Schellenberg or whoever the hell he is and sweat every last drop of information out of him. Get him to Guantanamo if we have to."

"To get the Swiss to give up one of their own is well-nigh impossible."

"I'm sure," Bloom nodded. "But this is beyond a couple of cops. At some point the politicians take over, but not here and not now."

"Agreed." Salisbury looked at his watch. "Might as well let him sleep. I'll ring him first thing and he'll shake things loose for us up at Heathstone."

"Him? Him who?"

"The home secretary."

Chapter Twelve

Emil Broussard pulled up behind the old Opel and got out, wondering if his dependable sergeant had fallen asleep. Fortunately, André Fasson saw his approach and rolled down the window, looking up with bloodshot eyes. There was no greeting between the two men. Broussard simply asked, "Anything?" releasing a puff of breath that condensed in the dawn chill.

Sergeant Fasson shook his head. "Nothing since he arrived home at 8:11 p.m. last night. Anything on the scanner?"

"Just a call from the president of Waldren Pharmaceuticals in New Jersey confirming their golf game. All right, I'll take it from here. Go get some sleep."

The sergeant nodded, then started his car and drove off. Broussard went back to his small BMW and clambered into the driver's seat. He was parked on a residential street on a slight rise that enabled him to view the lakeside estate of Leopold Mainz. Or rather, to view the wall that enclosed the estate of Leopold Mainz. On closer inspection the residence looked like a fortress: solid eight-foot stone fence, steel gates, closed-circuit TV cameras and, undoubtedly, Rottweilers prowling the perimeter. Broussard couldn't begin to guess the cost of such a place. The pharmaceutical business must be doing well.

He looked at the silent scanner on the seat beside him. He was somewhat gratified that his domino extortion play had worked and the sergeant's liaison had coughed up the tech specs to intercept Mainz's cell phone—even though the only harvest thus far had been confirmation of a tee time. It made him wonder how sinister things could be with a golf game looming in the future.

A detective by training and experience, he was always a little in awe of how the evidence spoke to you. How sometimes the dead could yield secrets about where, when, and how they had died, and sometimes even who had facilitated their demise. He'd learned that evidence invariably told the truth. Sometimes it could be misinterpreted, but evidence was evidence, and here it spoke with a resonance he still had a hard time accepting.

How on earth could two dead Nazis—that they knew of— resurface over a half century later, not much worse for wear? Broussard couldn't connect the dots, so he reached in the back seat and retrieved the rapidly expanding file he was compiling. He opened the folder of Erich Stolz/Otto von Spinnemann and went through it again, looking for clues he might have missed.

Standartenführer Otto von Spinnemann had been Commandant of the Schafhausen concentration camp. Located in eastern Poland, it was built after Auschwitz and on quite a smaller scale. Schafhausen was not an extermination camp, per se, replete with a crematorium; rather, it provided slave labor to some of the nearby armaments plants of the Third Reich and served as a reservoir of human subjects for a range of hideous experimentation. Broussard thumbed through printouts of his Internet searches on Schafhausen, involuntarily shivering at what he read. The SS "doctors" had used the camp inmates as targets, among other things, for exploding bullets, mines and shrapnel, then would methodically dissect the remains to determine the efficacy of the munitions employed.

Then there were experiments using poisons, chemical weapons, and newer, more effective extermination gases than I.G. Farben's Zyklon-B that was used at Auschwitz. There were also experiments on how inmates reacted to injections of mercury, copper, and a range of other elements, including gold. Remarkably, one positive thing to come out of such macabre experimentation was the treatment of gold injections for arthritis.

Another inhuman experiment was to observe how the body reacted to cold. Broussard recoiled at the photographs of emaciated inmates as they were forced naked into tubs of freezing water to see how long they would survive.

Broussard felt the guilt very personally. That Switzerland, ostensibly the cradle of democracy in Europe, would harbor the likes of Schellenberg after the war made his stomach turn. And he took a silent oath that if there was any way, he was going to bring Leopold Mainz/Walther Schellenberg to justice. Just then he heard the scanner chirp.

Mainz was in his dressing room. He had showered and trimmed his beard, and was looking through his closet for the right selection. He chose a pair of black flannel slacks, a black turtleneck and a pair of après-ski boots. He would don his black ski parka when he left.

He couldn't help but admire his reflection in the mirror. The women just could not resist his charms. In a way he was saddened that he'd never found his equal. But then, that was what being an elitist was all about, wasn't it?

His cell phone vibrated. Ah, such little marvels they were. He looked at the caller ID and answered, "*Ja?*"

"Herr Doktor Mainz?"

"Ja."

"Hörst here."

"Und . . ."

A brief silence, then Hörst continued, "The packages have arrived."

"Intact?"

"Ja. Intact. She and her sister are ugly on the outside. Beautiful on the inside."

"Sehr gut. Take good care of them."

"Jawohl, Herr . . . Doktor."

Mainz walked into the master bedroom of his castle and surveyed the beautifully appointed chamber one last time. The Louis XIV bed and writing desk, the silk tapestries, the llama rug—to say nothing of the breathtaking view of Lake Geneva. He could have stayed just as he was, in wealth and comfort; but he knew he was cut from a different cloth. To be at the height of his powers and remain a pill salesman? No, he was born to rise—rise so far above the others. Born to make the world dance at his feet. Indeed, what else could a man like himself aspire to?

He held up his hand. Steady as a rock. Yet on this, the dawn of an incredible day, when a plan decades in the making was to unfold, he was sublimely calm. Much like Field Marshal Montgomery at H-hour when the battle of El Alamein had kicked off. The man had been asleep. Asleep in his pajamas! And why not? He'd had an elegant plan that unfolded beautifully. He'd arisen fresh, ready to take command of the battle when flexibility and quick decisions were needed.

Yes, there was excitement in the air. So much preparation now coming to fruition. It was time to leave this luxurious but stifling cocoon and reap the harvest that belonged to him. One last look around, then he grabbed the keys off the dresser and strode through the castle to his waiting Mercedes.

Emil Broussard thought that one through. The "packages" had arrived. What packages? Could be anything. And who was Hörst? Broussard replayed the conversation recorded by the scanner. This Hörst clearly had excitement in his voice. And he had said, "*Jawhol, Herr . . . Doktor.*" It was as if he was about to say something else and had caught himself before uttering the forbidden word. But what was it? *Herr . . . General*? Broussard replayed it again. Another thing. The packages weren't objects, they were both a "she." What kind of packages were feminine in nature? And "ugly on the outside. Beautiful on the inside."

Broussard's mind raced. Perhaps the packages weren't packages at all, but something else. What inanimate object was a "she"? Men projected their affections on things that elicited the machismo factor and they often referred to them in the feminine—fast cars, aircraft, racing yachts. "She's a beauty" would be the refrain of a proud owner. But this was only beautiful on the inside. Beautiful in what way?

Broussard's thoughts were interrupted as the electronic gates to the castle swung open. Mainz's long, black Mercedes rolled out. Broussard started his BMW and dropped it in gear, whipping a u-turn that caused the rear tires to utter a little squeal. He cruised down the slope and slid in behind the Mercedes, keeping far enough back not to be noticed. But the inspector failed to notice the long-lensed camera poking out of the foliage on top of the castle's stone fence as it snapped a photograph of his license plate.

The chamber was a cube, with aerosol nozzles sticking out of the bulkheads.

Six men, looking as if they'd just deplaned from a Martian spacecraft, stood with their arms outstretched as multi-geysers of a pink foamy liquid sprayed over them, then dripped into little rivulets that coursed their way into the floor drain.

"Mind the feet, lads," came a flat voice over the loud speaker, and each knee was bent in sequence to expose the soles of their feet. "Now give the locker a go," ordered the voice, and two of the men lifted the metallic case by the handles, allowing every surface to be sprayed. The case only weighed just over a stone and was but a meter in length.

"Now for the rinse." And the nozzles erupted again, this time with water that cleansed the pink fluid and carried it down the drain.

After five minutes the shower stopped and the louvered ceiling opened, allowing the artificial wind from a giant fan to flow into the chamber. Another five minutes and the sealed door swung open.

"Right, then. Off you go. I know the insides of the container are sealed and this is a redundant wash, but we have to keep to procedures." The two men carried the locker out the door and into a corridor that led to another chamber where they entered, waited for the sealed airlock to close behind them, then the final door to the outside world opened and the Martians stepped into the pre-dawn twilight with their footlocker.

A convoy of three armored vans awaited their arrival. A contingent of security men, all wearing dark suits with white shirts and dark ties—and most with crew cuts—formed a cordon around the locker. Two men wearing gloves stepped forward and took the locker from the Martians. Gingerly they placed it inside the middle van which had been fashioned with a steel cradle to hold the locker securely on its journey.

An older, sanguine-looking man with whitish hair stood to the side. His face betrayed the look of someone who had done distasteful things for Her Majesty's Government one too many times. He had Ministry of Defence written all over him, and as the sliding door of the van slammed shut, a ruddy-looking block of granite in a tie walked up to him and said, "All secure, sir."

The MOD man took stock of the granite block and mused he could have been a professional rugger—which he had been. Nodding, he replied, "Very well, Major, let's proceed as rehearsed. You take the point. I'll be in the rear. Close together. Anonymous. We blend in with the traffic. You have contact with the lookouts posted?"

"Aye, suh. Everyone's in place."

"Let's get on then. We've a long day ahead of us." The MOD man turned the collar of his trench coat up against a light drizzle that had begun to fall, then entered the shotgun seat on the tailing van. The convoy started and weaved its way through the streets between low-lying buildings and past a guard shack where a military policeman waved them through. As the convoy cruised by the sign that read Heathstone Arsenal, the MOD man caught sight of a tall, slender bloke with a beard and glasses watching them as they headed toward the M5 motorway for London. The MOD man was surprised, and not surprised, to see the lone figure watching the convoy go past; because for him it was a kind of requiem for a dear departed one—albeit dark beyond measure.

Séverine duVaal closed her grip and fastened the buckle before slinging the duffel strap over her shoulder.

"Do you have to go so soon?" asked her aunt, somewhat plaintively. "You are welcome to stay as long as you like. I enjoy the company."

Séverine smiled and gave her mother's sister a hug. "You know I'd love to, but I promised André I'd get back to help him with spring planting. The visit here has been quite the tonic.

Since Maman died, you are my connection with her."

Sophie encircled her niece with her arms. "As you are for me, my child. You are the essence of her. And now you must go."

Together they exited the terraced house in Surrey and Aunt Sophie drove them in her aging Morris to the train station. A final goodbye and Séverine entered the station, checking her watch to ensure she'd arrive at St. Pancras Station in time for her connection on the Eurostar bullet train to Paris.

Emil Broussard had his foot flat against the floor, trying to keep up with the black Mercedes 600SL screaming down the motorway along the Rhône River like the proverbial bat out of hell. Broussard had labored under the illusion that his turbo-charged BMW 320i was a peppy little runabout. But trying to keep up with Leopold Mainz had shattered that illusion. What the hell did he have under that thing? The Mercedes had maintained 200 kph with ease as Mainz cruised along the north shore of Lake Geneva to Lausanne, then at Montreux had turned south through Villeneuve.

The road was getting steeper, more winding, and patches of spring snow were starting to appear; but Broussard didn't notice. The Mercedes was so far ahead now he was afraid he might lose it. They were thick into the majesty of the Alps now, with Mt. St. Bernard approaching as they streaked toward the Italian border. The exit for Zermatt approached and the Mercedes suddenly decelerated. Broussard had to downshift. He tried to keep as much distance as possible while keeping Mainz in sight.

As the Mercedes came up to the intersection he expected it to turn left toward Zermatt, but instead it turned right toward the Hérens Valley.

They continued on through the small ski village of Evolène.

Not a major ski resort like Gstaad or Davos, it was just a sleepy town with few ski lifts—which were less employed these days due to global warming.

Broussard had been here before, although some years back. He was more of a climber than skier, and had scaled a few peaks in the area, which were somewhat small-bore compared to other fare along the Swiss-Italian frontier. He remembered Evolène, however. The local populace was peculiar in that they spoke a very thick patois, and the pigment of their skin and eyes was surprisingly dark, raising speculation that they were descended from the Saracens who had conquered the Hérens Valley in the eighth century.

Broussard figured this was the last week the ski lifts would be open, as the chairlifts and slopes were sparsely populated. He expected the Mercedes to halt somewhere in Evolène as they were rapidly running out of road, but still it pressed on. Broussard had never been this far, but when he saw the sign for Arolla, he remembered. Arolla was an even smaller and sleepier ski village than Evolène. The raw beauty of his beloved Alps weighed heavily on him, making it impossible to shake the feeling that somewhere in this pristine snowscape a cancer of the vilest kind had metastasized.

The Mercedes finally slowed as it approached Arolla, then, as it pulled into the town square, Mainz wheeled it into an empty parking slot. Broussard pulled over and watched as Mainz jumped out of the car and marched resolutely toward the ski area. Broussard thought this strange, as Mainz had no skis, so he goosed the engine and pulled into the town square where he found a parking place a discreet distance from the Mercedes.

He hopped out of the heated BMW and was struck by the chill. He was wearing street clothes and a sport jacket. He hustled up toward the ski area, which only had two chair-lifts, one of which wasn't even engaged. His loafers crunched through the slush as his puzzlement grew, then he crested a rise to see a mountain dominating the scene—a white and craggy inverted tooth with the top squared off. He then glimpsed a large cable car rising on steel lanyards toward the summit of the tooth. Inside was the figure of Leopold Mainz, escorted by a muscular attendant on-board.

Broussard searched his memory, and he remembered. The rocky tooth was Mont Collon. He'd thought about climbing it years ago, but it never made his short list.

He inspected the cable car carefully. It terminated inside a hole near the summit. It clearly wasn't for skiing because the sheer face of the alp precluded that. He stood in the cold watching the car grow smaller until it disappeared into the small rocky orifice.

What on earth was this all about? Broussard looked around and saw a gnarled old ski lift attendant who appeared only slightly younger than the mountain itself. He wore a stocking cap that framed a wrinkled and weather-beaten face. He approached and said, "Pardon. I would like to have a ride on that cable car."

The old man shrugged. "So would I, and I was born in this valley."

"I would be willing to pay."

The old man shrugged. "It is *privée*."

"*Privée*? But what is up there?"

Another shrug. "Some say it was to be a restaurant. Others say a hotel. Do not know for certain."

"Who goes up there?"

"Maintenance people live up there. Never come down except to load supplies. Something to do with the Army, perhaps."

That would make it plausible. The Swiss Army was known for having secret installations peppered throughout the Alps.

Broussard pressed. "Who would I see to get a ride to the top?"

The old man was growing tired of the exchange. He shrugged and raised his gaze to indicate the answer was way above his pay grade. "Maybe the canton burger."

Of course, Broussard thought to himself, I'll just ring up the canton burger and ask him about a ride on the cable car. Better I should send Herr Dr. Mainz a note by FedEx. That way it wouldn't be garbled in transmission.

The inspector had never felt more impotent. He couldn't use the bludgeon of his official capacity. He was physically cut off from his quarry by a stupefying physical barrier. He was at the end of the trail. All he could do was wait it out for Leopold Mainz to come down from his eagle's nest and pick up the scent again. But his instincts were in a white-hot revolt—telling him that this was not the time to lie low and wait it out. He had no idea what was unfolding up in that mountain redoubt, but he was damned well going to find out. He spun on his heel and tramped back to the BMW.

He popped the boot, which revealed a bundle of rope, an ice axe, crampons, pitons and carabiners. One way or another, he was heading upstairs to Mont Collon.

Gideon Bloom allowed the doorman to hold the Dorchester's door for him. Somewhat refreshed by a few hours of sleep, a shower, and something called bangers and mash, he was ready for his pick up, which rolled around the corner as if choreographed. It was a cloudy but not drizzly day, yet Bloom still wore his trench coat in case the weather had a mind to change.

The white-haired Sequoia emerged from the passenger seat of the Vauxhall and said, "Get some sleep, Gideon?"

"A bit. Let's roll."

"Right."

Bloom looked at the identical Vauxhall behind them. "We have a convoy today?"

"They've some extra backup should they be needed. Better to have more than less in this kind of situation," replied Salisbury.

"I see." Bloom climbed in the back behind the driver on the right side, which he really couldn't get used to. Arthur MacBaine was driving; Neville Chatham was in the back.

"About two hour's drive," said Salisbury. "Should be well on the ground before lunch."

"Good."

Salisbury reached over the seat and handed Bloom something. "Compliments of Scotland Yard."

Bloom took the .38 Detective Special in the belt holster.

"Did I secure the right size, Captain?" inquired MacBaine.

"Perfect. Feels like it's loaded."

"Of course," replied MacBaine.

Salisbury then handed a file over to Bloom.

"What's this?"

"Fayla Bannon's file from the Yard and MI5. Thought you'd like to read it on the way."

"Definitely," replied Bloom as he thumbed through the pages marked MOST SECRET.

"Any word from your Swiss compatriot?" asked Chatham.

"Last report was that the subject was moving east in a long black Mercedes at a high rate of speed."

CHAPTER THIRTEEN

Fayla Bannon rose that morning with a feeling of expectancy and purpose unlike anything she'd felt since Gibraltar. She had escaped so many times. Dodged so many bullets. And while others faltered, she had remained resolute to her cause. Peering at herself in the mirror of her trendy Mayfair flat, she wondered what Mairead Farrell would say if she could see Fayla Bannon on this glorious day. That Northern Ireland would be purged of every bloody last Orangeman and all the stinking collaborators who caved into their conquest. Their revenge would be complete—beyond even Mairead's imagination. That Fayla had been chosen by such an extraordinary man, with whom she shared a singular vision—well, it was quite overwhelming. But she was confident she was up to the task.

The Wellington Square bombing had been a "final exam" that she had passed with flying colors, and after that she had been anointed into the fold—made a true partner—privy to the plan that was staggering in its audacity, in its simplicity and elegance. She had been exposed to things that were difficult to believe, even though she had seen them with her own eyes. But her inclusion as a member of the inner circle unveiled what awesome resources had been brought into play.

Her mind went backward in time four years to her recruitment. It had been orchestrated like a symphony. She'd been hiding out in a tenement in Dublin in an ever-shrinking network of safe houses. She'd returned one evening to find an envelope on her pillow. There was a Canadian passport—perfect with her photograph—ten thousand pounds Sterling in cash, and a note inviting her to attend a meeting with a "principal" sympathetic to her cause. If interested, she was to be at a designated private airfield at midnight. If not, she could keep the passport and cash with the principal's compliments.

The initial instinct of this being a trap had quickly faded. This wasn't the Tommy's style. And the fekking IRA laggards didn't have the scratch to dangle ten thousand quid as bait. And the passport—that was a clue she was dealing with something beyond her experience. It wasn't just an excellent forgery, it was a genuine Canadian passport in the name of Lucinda Beale. And how did they get her photograph?

By then, the tide had turned in Ireland. Safe havens had dwindled. Betrayal was everywhere. She had resolved to be the last woman standing and never to be taken alive; and the way things were going, that was probably going to be the case. So she weighed the odds, then made her decision.

She primped, loaded her Beretta, grabbed a pint at the pub, and drove out to the deserted airfield in County Westmeath. It was a still, chilly evening and as midnight approached her doubts began to grow. If this was a setup it would be her last shoot out. She was ready for it if it came to that.

At seven minutes to midnight she heard the whine of a jet aircraft as it circled the field. Then something happened that made her jump three feet in the air: a string of intense landing lights flicked on, turning the runway bright as daylight. She fell to the ground and pulled the Beretta, but then . . . nothing. No one. Only the sound of the approaching plane.

The whine faded, followed by the squeal of landing gear tires as they made contact with the runway. She rose to her feet, still holding the Beretta, as the thrust reversers engaged, rapidly slowing the Learjet 35A. The aircraft came to a halt on the tarmac and the door lowered. Something came over her, and she put the Beretta back in her handbag. A white-jacketed steward stepped out and, with great deference, inquired in a heavy German accent, "Fräulein Bannon? Please come aboard. Your appointment awaits."

She found herself drawn to the interior of the plane. Tentatively she peered inside, at once attracted and intimidated by the finery and appointments of the cabin. The glove leather seats, the mahogany trim, and the plasma screen were quite impressive.

"Please have a seat and secure your seatbelt. We would like to get underway without delay," said the steward. "You see, we are here illegally. Once we are airborne I shall be able to offer you some refreshment."

Fayla complied, the door was secured, and within seconds they were wheels up.

As the steward laid out a place setting, Fayla inquired, "Where are we going?"

While pouring a crystal flute of chilled Bollinger, the steward said, "We will be exiting Ireland the way we came in—flying extremely low and slow to avoid civilian air traffic radar until we are sufficiently offshore to climb and blend in with the stream of normal commercial aircraft to our destination." He then placed a tray with Beluga caviar in front of her. "By the way, the captain respectfully requests that you expel the nine-millimeter cartridge from the chamber of your Beretta. Should it accidentally discharge, it would pass through the fuselage of the aircraft and cause catastrophic depressurization."

"Really?"

"Well, better safe than sorry, don't you think?"

An increasingly incredulous Fayla complied, not knowing what to think. She tentatively sipped at the champagne and found it dreamy. Then she eyeballed the caviar, not quite knowing what to make of it. At one level she didn't want to betray her ignorance, but then her curiosity got the better of her and she asked the steward, "What, ah, *is* that?"

The steward replied without a hint of condescension, "Beluga caviar, taken from sturgeon in the Caspian Sea three days ago. You will find the principal has a weakness for it and we always keep the galley well stocked. May I suggest a small spoonful on a wafer. You may find it a little strange to the palette at first, as it is something of an acquired taste."

She shrugged and gave it a whirl. She found it a little granular and salty at first, but it also awakened some taste buds she had no idea she possessed. And in short order she polished off three tins, not knowing she'd just tossed down $1,800 worth of fish eggs.

They had been airborne for about three hours, and the window offered nothing but a dark void in return. Instinct and experience launched her mind on a torturous journey through all the permutations of what the end game to all this could be; but thus far the experience was not only beyond her imagination, it was beyond anything she *could* imagine. So all that was left to her was to play it out.

She felt her ears start to pop as the whine of the jet power ratcheted down a bit. The steward said, "We are beginning our descent."

"Descent to where?"

The steward smiled. "In the fullness of time, as the English say."

Descent into hell, no doubt, she thought. Well, at least she'd be going in style.

The tires screeched, the thrust reversers engaged, and the Learjet taxied to a tarmac in front of a private hangar. The steward offered her a cashmere wrap, which she accepted, and he lowered the door. The inrushing chilled air stole her breath, and she was grateful for the wrap. The steward stepped down to the tarmac and he offered her his hand. Tentatively, Fayla poked her head outside the door. The sky was turning the faint shade of indigo as the promise of dawn lapped at the sky. She took the offered hand and descended the stairs to the hardstand.

Then bowing, the steward said, "It has been a pleasure serving you, Fräulein, and I hope to do so again."

Alongside the Learjet was a Mercedes limousine only slightly smaller than Abu Dhabi, with a uniformed chauffer holding open the passenger door. But what overwhelmed her was the fact this runway and hangar seemed to be out in the middle of nowhere, and in the not so distance she could see the faint silhouette of craggy mountains against the brightening sky. At the base of the mountain, bathed in a golden light, was a villa— a palace, really—that looked like some fortress out of Beau Geste. Parapets and all.

"Fräulein Bannon, if you please," said the smiling chauffer as he gestured to the open door.

Again she hesitated, asking, "Where are you taking me?"

From behind, the steward leaned forward and whispered into her ear, "To meet your destiny."

With that, her hesitancy vanished, and Fayla Bannon decided her destiny had never looked so good. She strode to the chauffer and demanded, "What is your name?"

"Helmut," he said with a curt nod.

"Then let's roll, Helmut." And she clambered into the back seat.

Helmut drove along the private road to the palace, a diamond on black velvet. As the palace grew closer, Fayla realized its dimensions were grander than she had first perceived. The walls were of ocher stucco and at least ten feet high, bathed in a yellow light and set at the foot of a black mountain taken from a moonscape, entirely devoid of vegetation.

The Mercedes approached two wrought-iron gates forged in a kind of Moorish design, but at this point she did not know this was the case. The limousine slowed and, as if on cue, the gates opened wide, allowing it to pull into a circular drive around an elegant fountain. In front of two massive ebony French doors stood a middle-aged woman with gray hair pulled into a tight chignon and wearing a black silk Balenciaga business suit—although by this time it was no later than five in the morning. The limo halted, the chauffer opened the door and Fayla climbed out to her appointment with fate.

The woman advanced with a smile and extended hand. "Fräulein Bannon, how good of you to come. My name is Magrid von Mauerfeld, your hostess. Please come in out of the cold."

Fayla shook the dry hand perfunctorily and followed her hostess into the entry foyer of the palace. Again it was grand in scale, with another fountain and a range of art work adorning the walls. She would find out later they were by artists named Goya, Gaudi, and Caravaggio.

"I'm sure you are quite tired and have many questions. If I may suggest, why don't you retire to your guest chamber for a bath and a sleep, and once you are refreshed we'll have some tea and speak about your future."

Future? Fayla's concept of future these days was to avoid being topped before nightfall. It was an alien concept to her, but she was tired and simply nodded and replied, "'Kay."

"Excellent. Lotte will look after you."

Lotte magically appeared, an older Germanic woman in a

chambermaid uniform.

"Lotte has taken the liberty of drawing you a bath. We've also done a little shopping for you; you will find a few things in the wardrobe for you to wear during your stay. I believe I estimated your size correctly. I have an eye for that sort of thing. Until later, then?"

Fayla nodded, then followed Lotte down the hallway, passing one painting after another.

She'd never been inside Buckingham Palace, but as she entered her guest-chamber she figured it must be something rather like this. The massive four poster bed, tapestries, antique wardrobe and vanity—and again, more paintings.

Lotte opened the wardrobe, which was crammed with designer fare, then she motioned to the bathroom and enquired, "You like the whirlpool, ja?"

Fayla shrugged and said, "Shuh."

Lotte entered the bathroom and soon a gurgling sound emitted from within, and she came out and pointed at a button on the Louis XIV writing desk. "You punch you need someting." And the chambermaid vanished.

After the bubbly of the whirlpool she slept until the middle of the afternoon, and upon awakening there was that moment of disorientation—not knowing where she was or how she had gotten there. Then it sank in and she realized the journey hadn't been a dream. She was genuinely here, wherever "here" was. She stroked the seductive silkiness of her nightgown, then rose, wrapped the dressing gown around her, and went into the bathroom. A range of toiletries were laid out before her, so she brushed her teeth, then began sniffing the bottles assembled on the vanity that made it look like the cosmetics counter at Harrods. The fragrances exerted their seductive force, and she succumbed to one called Heavenly Way, dabbing a drop on her throat as a knock on the door snapped her back to the here and now. "Yes?" she said guardedly.

The door opened with Lotte bearing a large tray. "*Guten Morgen*, Fräulein Fayla. You like the *Frühstück*? Breakfast?"

She shrugged and said, "Shuh." Lotte set a place for her, and she sat down to the most delectable bowl of strawberries she'd ever tasted, and cream and coffee that was smooth as a baby's backside. All addictive. When she finished, Lotte was holding a terry cloth robe and said, "First the spa, then dress for dinner with Frau von Mauerfeld."

Fayla slipped out of her sleepwear and into the robe, and was led through the palace to the center of the grounds, which framed a swimming pool about the size of the Irish Sea, except that it was crystal clear. The adjoining spa and cabana contained every manner of delights, and it was here that she experienced her first massage—delivered by a six-foot Nubian masseuse with fingers made of rawhide. After that a steam, a whirlpool, and a cold plunge bath after which she could have been poured into a bottle. But then it was time for a facial, ironically applied by a veiled Middle Eastern woman, followed by a manicure and a pedicure between caviar snacks. Then an Arab hairdresser coiffed her copper locks into a beautiful chignon.

The veiled facial technician then reappeared and sat her down at a vanity with a battery of cosmetics. After an hour of ministrations, Lotte magically returned and whisked her back to her bed chamber. Night was falling as Lotte began the process of dressing her new mistress. First the *unter* garments. Fayla's instincts railed against someone invading her space like this, but her intellect overrode it, telling her she was on a different planet and she had to play by their rules. And so far this planet looked like it had a lot to offer. Lotte gave her a French strapless bra to support her small but firm breasts, followed by a black full slip that felt like it was made for her—and it was. Then Lotte withdrew to the wardrobe and came out with a stunning forest-green silk Dior evening gown.

Lotte helped her slip in, which was awkward for her. Then a pair of Jimmy Choo slippers, and for the pièce de résistance, Lotte opened a black velvet box, and any vestige of defenses melted. On the black velvet lay a diamond necklace studded with emeralds that took her breath away. Lotte smiled as she placed it around her neck and did the clasp, saying, "It is *sehr gut*. This beautiful thing has not seen the light of day for such a long time. Now then, let us have a look at you." Lotte stepped back and clasped her hands, cooing, "*Wunderbar!* But two small things. Posture. Spine straight as arrow. Shoulders back. Chin up. *Perfekt*." She then opened the wardrobe door with the full-length mirror, allowing Fayla to see the entire package for the first time. The initial impact was one of surrealism, as if she were looking at someone else. Then the shock sank in—how deep the transformation had been—and her knees almost buckled. Numbly her fingers rose to touch the diamonds as she whispered, "Is that me?"

Lotte clucked, "*Ja, mein Liebling*. You are the ugly duckling, yes?"

Fayla couldn't muster a response, the effect was such a rapture. Forty-eight hours before she had been dirty and destitute in a foul Dublin tenement, and now . . . now she looked as if she were ready for a state dinner at Windsor Castle. The butterfly that had emerged from this cocoon was beyond anything she could have imagined.

Deftly, Lotte said, "Frau Mauerfeld awaits. You are ready?"

Fayla fingered the diamonds again as she grinned at herself in the mirror. "You have no idea."

Lotte led her through the hallway, past the gallery of paintings, and into the grand entry where Frau Magrid awaited her wearing a black Dior evening gown, and next to her stood a middle-aged man in a tuxedo. Lotte whispered in her ear, "Posture," then withdrew as a beaming Frau Magrid came forward.

"My, my, my! What a transformation! I hardly recognized you."

"Quite a change, I must say," Fayla agreed. "Never knew it was in here."

"I must confess, you exceeded my most optimistic expectations. Well, turn around. Turn around! Let us have a look at you."

Fayla gave it a whirl, as though she were at the end of a fashion runway.

"*Magnifique!*" cried Frau Magrid in delight. "But now then, where are my manners? Let me introduce to you Herr Otto von Spinnemann."

The tuxedoed figure, who four years hence would wind up on a slab in a Chicago morgue, stepped forward, clearly enraptured with the vision before him. He took her hand and applied a cordial kiss, then said, "An honor, Mademoiselle. The fragrance is Heavenly Way, if I am not mistaken."

"Why, you are correct. How did you know?"

A shrug. "From one of the companies we own. I try to keep a finger on things."

Frau Magrid said, "Otto is much too modest. He knows everything about every company the, ah, consortium owns."

"Consortium?" Fayla had never heard the word before.

"Yes, yes, my dear. All will be explained to you in good time. But now it is time to toast your arrival and the grand enterprise we are to embark upon together. And in celebration of that, it is time you met someone very special—the principal in all this." At this point Fayla heard footfalls on the marble grand staircase behind her as von Spinnemann's heels clicked together and his back went ramrod straight—as if he'd just received a posture lesson from Lotte.

With great drama, Frau Magrid said, "May I present Herr General Walther Schellenberg, director of the Reichssicherheitshauptamt and special-plenipotentiary of the Third Reich!"

CHAPTER FOURTEEN

Fayla would never forget the first time she laid eyes on the General. Wearing a tuxedo, he descended the grand staircase with a casual air, as if he were on his way to a tennis match. There was a wry smile on his face as he crossed the foyer with an outstretched hand. "My dear Fayla," he said, as though they'd known each other for years. "It is a pure delight to meet you." Another kiss. "We are greatly honored by your presence. And Magrid is correct, it is time for a toast. Champagne!"

And champagne appeared on a steward's tray.

Carefully, Fayla took the fluted glass as Schellenberg said, "To a glorious future." On cue the four of them raised the crystals and clinked them together before downing the sparkling beverage.

"Ahhh," said Schellenberg, "nothing quite like Bollinger. And to think that champagne was invented by a bunch of French monks. One of life's little ironies."

In short order Fayla knew she was in the presence of someone from a different world, totally confident and in control of his domain. She felt herself melting under the radiance of his charms.

"But now our guest must have a thousand questions, and it is high time she received answers. But certainly not on an empty stomach . . . Wilhelm?"

"Ja, Herr General."

"We will have dinner now."

"*Natürlich*, Herr General."

"Shall we go in?" Schellenberg offered his arm to Fayla. "I'm absolutely famished. Wilhelm will see to it we are treated to an exceptional culinary experience. He served as the Reichsführer's personal chef for many years."

Reichsführer?

Fayla took his arm and together they walked into the grand dining hall—just like in the movies.

The dining chamber was ornate, with a giant silk tapestry on the wall of Wagner's *Die Walküre*. Inset in the wall was a blazing fireplace, and a massive ebony dining table was set with a brilliant collage of candles. Two stewards held chairs for the ladies as the party of four sat down to dinner.

Schellenberg unfolded his napkin and enquired, "So have you enjoyed your visit thus far?"

Fayla sensed this was an audition of some sort, and monosyllabic answers would not produce a passing grade. With her posture in line, Fayla let loose her own charms on the General and replied, "It has been a rather arousing experience."

The whole table barked in laughter, and the ice was broken.

"I'll take that as a 'yes,'" replied Schellenberg.

"It has been quite fantastic, I must say. . . . But, where am I, exactly? What is this place? And why am I here?"

"Ah," said the General with enthusiasm, "a woman who goes to the heart of the matter. Excellent! Fair questions all. Let me respond to the first two," he began as the steward served the lobster bisque soup. "You are in the Atlas Mountain Range in the Kingdom of Morocco which, I'm sure, will be somewhat surprising given the cool climate. But due to the elevation you may also be amazed to learn ski resorts can be found in the Atlas range, even though the Sahara Desert is located just to the south. We are quite remote, as you have seen, something the previous owner desired."

"Previous owner?" inquired Fayla.

Schellenberg nodded. "He was a Saudi prince. And there are a number of similar castles sprinkled throughout the Atlas Mountains. They are essentially sex palaces for a few depraved individuals whose appetites are financed by American and European motorists. You may have noticed a long hallway of bed chambers—yours among them. It was there he housed his harem. Some were willing prostitutes, but some were unwilling participants procured by white slave traders. This kind of excess is rather commonplace within the upper echelons of the Saudi royal family, but when this particular prince took to drowning women for sport in the large swimming pool, that was too unpalatable, even for the Saudis. So the prince fell from grace, his petro-stipend was cut off and he had to sell, which worked out happily for us. This property suits our needs beautifully. Remote. Comfortable. And in a country whose government looks the other way as long as their stipend arrives uninterrupted. . . . Oh, please, don't let your soup get cold."

From the General's comments, Fayla's earlier idea of taking a swim in the pool vanished, and she tasted the lobster bisque. Again, the effect on the taste buds was extraordinary. "Ummm. This is incredible. Never tasted anything quite like it."

Frau Mauerfeld beamed. "I'm so glad you like it, my dear. Wilhelm will be pleased."

At this point Fayla decided to probe a bit further. "Uh, when Frau Mauerfeld introduced you, I didn't quite follow what she called you. Could you give me that again?"

This time it was the host who smiled. "To repeat, the

name and title are General Walther Schellenberg, special-plenipotentiary of the Third Reich."

"Third Reich . . . you mean like Germans . . . in World War Two? Nazis? Hitler?"

Schellenberg continued smiling. "Precisely! My, my, you are the quick study."

"But . . . I, I don't understand what you're saying. Or how that could be. And why am *I* here?"

Schellenberg reached out and patted her arm. "Not to worry, my dear. All will be explained in the fullness of time. For the moment, let's just say you are here because your interests and our interests are strategically aligned. . . . Magrid."

As the soup was removed and replaced with a hearts of palm salad, Magrid gently inquired, "Fayla, tell me please, what is your attitude toward the English?"

She cocked her head. "The English?"

"Yes. The nation of England. What are your feelings toward the British Crown and its loyal subjects?"

The creamy skin of Fayla's face flushed red as her whole demeanor changed and her nostrils flared. Schellenberg was somewhat taken aback with the transformation as she almost hissed, "They are the vilest scum of this earth who've been a plague on everything and everyone they've touched."

Magrid nodded. "I see. We anticipated this response. And my next question is this: if we provided you with the means to cleanse the island of Britain of every last breathing soul, would you, in turn, be willing to embrace our endeavors?"

She blinked, the gears not quite meshing. "I don't understand. What do you mean by 'cleanse'?"

The General interjected. "We appreciate that what we are saying is difficult to grasp, but on a conceptual level"—Schellenberg took a cracker from the caviar tray and placed it on the tablecloth between them—"let us put it to you this way: let us say this wafer is a button, and if I told you that if you pushed this button every last Englishman on the island of Britain would die a rather horrible death, what would you do?"

The reaction startled even the General, for in an instant Fayla's clenched fist flew up and came down with such a fury that the whole table shook, toppling Otto's wine glass. Fayla's eyes burned with an acetylene intensity as she glared at Schellenberg.

Finally, it was von Spinnemann who spoke, saying, "I think we've found our partner, Herr General."

Again, there was laughter and the ice was broken for the second time. "I quite agree, Otto. . . . Wilhelm, another glass for the colonel!"

"Of course, Herr General."

Schellenberg turned back to Fayla and said, "My dear Miss Bannon, we have arrived at this decision point in our evening earlier than I had anticipated, but so much the better. I have a proposal to put to you. If you accept, you will be brought into our enterprise as a true partner—not a hired gun. Hired guns are expendable. But you will not be because you will be central to our mission. If you elect to join us, the world will be a much better place; and in return we will give you the means to disintegrate England like that wafer under your fist. If you choose not to join us, then you will be returned to the airfield from which you were collected, with our best wishes. However, I have to advise you that if you return to Ireland, your life will be measured in months, if not weeks or days, as we have learned you are targeted for assassination by the remnants of the IRA."

With that, Fayla's gladiator exterior withered.

"So the choice is yours. Join us and get what you want, or

return to Ireland—and certain death."

Fayla felt the three sets of eyes upon her. There was no choice, really. And a chance to exterminate England! Mairead Farrell be blessed, she felt no blarney from these people; if they said it, they meant it. And besides, she'd acquired a taste for caviar. She nodded to the General and said quite formally, "In the memory of Mairead Farrell, I am honored to accept your proposal on one condition."

Guardedly, Schellenberg asked, "What's that?"

"We have caviar served at every meal."

Schellenberg convulsed with laughter again, as did the others. "Every meal, indeed! We have a deal. . . . Wilhelm, more champagne! And caviar!"

After the toasting and the East African quail served with a cranberry glaze, Schellenberg and von Spinnemann took brandy and Cuban cigars as the General leaned back and puffed contemplatively, then turned to Fayla and said, "Now then, my dear. Or may I say, my dear partner, it is time to reveal our mission to you. To begin, tell me how you see the world today?"

Fayla cocked her head. "The world? I don't think much about the world. I think a lot about not being topped before the sun sets."

The General nodded. "Fair enough. So let me outline the situation for you. The world is in a dire situation: population skyrocketing towards seven billion, most of them black, brown or yellow; pollution rampant, petroleum resources largely controlled by a bunch of sand niggers who should be riding camels. . . . But more untenable than anything are nuclear weapons in the hands of rogue states AND stateless rogues. All the while feckless governments are powerless to do anything about it. Simply put, if our planet is to survive, we must take extraordinary measures to cleanse it of the colored peoples of the world."

"Colored people? How does England fit into that?"

Schellenberg looked at the ceiling, and when he spoke it was like an exasperated parent talking about a dim-witted teenager. "That's the tragic irony in all this. If securing your participation means we have to cleanse England of its Englishmen, then so be it. And in a manner of speaking, they have it coming. Quite frankly, I never understood why they felt it necessary to get involved after we invaded Poland. I mean, there we were alone, facing down the Bolshevik horde. The ultimate menace. In order to gain access to the Soviet border to launch the Barbarossa invasion, we had to go through Poland. Had to. The Führer really had no quarrel with England. If England had left us alone, then France would have followed suit, we would have prevailed against Moscow and the world would be clean and safe now. But *no*, that imbecile Chamberlain, and Churchill after him, had to paint us as the forces of evil, allowing the real evil—Stalin—to rise up. We were forced to fight a two-front war, and after the Americans came in following Pearl Harbor, I knew all was lost . . . for the time being.

"But I digress. In answer to your question, England is a special case and on your behalf it shall be purified."

Fayla betrayed her puzzlement. "But . . . how?"

Schellenberg smiled. "That is where you come in."

"Me?"

"Yes. You see, we require your special talents—indeed, the reason you are here—is we need you to screw your way into some highly sensitive information within the British government."

It was a long evening. Indeed, the first rays of dawn were creeping over the mountaintop when the dinner party finally retired for the night. Fayla's head was swirling with all that she'd learned. But after Lotte undressed her, she fell into bed with the General's words dancing like sugarplums in her head. *"England will be cleansed. . . . England will be cleansed. . . . England will be cleansed. . . ."*

Her training began the next day. Although it was rather unorthodox, it began with weapons under Helmut's instruction in the morning, then a massage, spa treatment, and a nap. The afternoons were spent with Magrid in lessons to transform the Belfast urchin into a European aristocrat. Magrid explained, "I will prepare you to enter a new realm, one of culture and refinement, because the men you will have to seduce will be from such a world."

Together they listened to music, read Shakespeare aloud, and immersed themselves in the world of *haute couture*. With her new Canadian passport—one of dozens to follow—the two women boarded the jet and made for the rue Saint-Honoré in Paris. For two weeks they cut a swath through the shops of Armani, Dior, and Gucci, then down to Monaco for a tour through the Côte d'Azur and the casino at Monte Carlo. Otto showed up to squire her at the roulette table, where she drew the lustful glances of men like moths to a flame. At lunch the next day she showed up in a pair of designer jeans, and a stern Magrid sent her back up to the suite to change into a silk suit.

"Haute couture is a way of life. There is no place for denim," she said with inflexibility.

The next evening they returned to the casino, Fayla wearing a white silk Versace evening gown, her red hair splashing down forward over a shoulder. At the baccarat table was a fifties-something British couple. The wife was bejeweled and on her second facelift. Hubby was bored and somewhat pissed off as he kibbutzed to watch a string of his hard-earned Sterling migrate into the croupier's bin.

"See him?" Magrid asked Fayla.

Fayla nodded.

"This is what they call a 'live-fire' exercise." She pressed a small vial into her hand and said, "He is an Engländer, that's all we know. Before the sun rises you are to bed him and put that into his drink. It will make it appear he had a heart attack."

Fayla nodded and put the vial in her Judith Lieber clutch as though she'd just been given a grocery list. It was a few minutes before the ornamented facelift had to obey her bladder and rise to visit the powder room. Her husband was watching over the plaques as Fayla slipped up to him, gave his arm a squeeze, and whispered, "Stay close to me, Ducky, I need some luck," as she glided into the neighboring chair and tossed a wad of bills at the croupier.

Hubby looked as if he'd just stuck his toe into a wall socket as the electricity of her touch ricocheted through his system. He was enraptured by the flame-haired vision.

Facelift returned and assumed her position while Hubby migrated around the table for a better view.

Facelift's luck changed and she became engrossed in the cards, oblivious to Fayla's "come-hither" looks toward her husband. Pouring a little gas on the flame, Fayla ordered a martini with an olive. Holding the olive at the end of a spiked swizzle stick, she worked it over with her tongue as she locked onto his eyes with a seductive gaze. After a couple of minutes of this she slightly cocked her head toward the door that led to the garden, then got up and left. Hubby followed two minutes later.

The next morning, as they were served crumpets and caviar in the Learjet en route back to Morocco, Fayla fingered the gold Gucci necklace around her throat as she peered out the window with a slight smile on her face. "You know, it really is amazing."

"What is amazing, my dear?" asked Magrid.

"A man could be ninety-eight years old and in a wheelchair, and still be convinced he's irresistible to women."

And together they cackled like a couple of hens.

The next day the General flew in—on a large Gulfstream jet, which he piloted himself—to see how the training was going.

He went out on the firing range with Helmut and Fayla, and with an array of weapons she impressed him with her marksmanship. Then at the end of the table she picked up a rocket-propelled grenade launcher like a kid with a new toy. "My favorite," she said with exuberance.

"Then let it fly!" said the beaming General. She did, and the large cardboard target fifty meters away disintegrated in an eruption that reverberated through the Atlas Mountains.

Helmut and the General applauded.

Next came a timed 1500-meter run, then unarmed combat with Helmut, in which she threw him over her shoulder to the General's delight.

This was followed by a break for a spa treatment and nap, then dinner, where Fayla regaled Schellenberg with her views on Yo-Yo Ma's performance of a Bach sonata at Covent Garden and the new Impressionist exhibit at the Musée d'Orsay. Then Fayla treated him and Magrid to a fashion show from the *tsunami* of shopping the two women had inflicted on Paris. Fayla had taken to haute couture like a duck to water, and with each change-up, Schellenberg became more and more enthused. It was finally topped off with the white Versace gown she'd worn in Monte Carlo.

When she told him this, the General said, "Ah, yes, Magrid informed me. Which reminds me. I have something to show you." He reached into his attaché case and extracted a copy of the *Times* of London. He opened the business section and pointed to a two-paragraph obituary about Arthur Medrold, scion of the Medrold grocery store chain, who was found dead in his hotel room in Monte Carlo from an apparent coronary. The story did not mention that the hotel room was not the room in which he had registered with his facelifted wife, as the staff of the Hotel du Paris were known for their discretion.

"So," said the General with authority, "you have performed superbly. You are now ready for deployment." He reached into his attaché case again and pulled out a manila file folder. He extracted a photograph of a middle-aged man and placed it on the coffee table. He appeared a bit overweight and was staring into the camera with an insincere smile. "This will be your first target."

Fayla picked up the photograph and studied it for a moment, then asked, "Who is he?"

Schellenberg held up the folder, "His dossier is in here, but he is a junior minister in the Ministry of Defence. He's a member of Parliament from Dorset and something of a social climber. Married into money and, by all accounts, his wife of twenty-two years is an absolute shrew. So he should be stuffed and ready for plucking."

"What do you want me to do?" asked Fayla.

"You are to seduce him and extract as much information as you can on an endeavor the MOD calls 'Project Gloworm.'"

"And what is Project Gloworm?"

Schellenberg scratched behind his ear and replied, "We have precious little information on the specifics at this point, which is another reason why you are here, but broadly speaking it is the means by which England will be cleansed and the Fourth

Reich will rise to power." And for the next hour Schellenberg outlined for Fayla the scanty but specific details on Project Gloworm. What they knew, what they did not know, and the targets Fayla would go after to fill out the mosaic. When he was finished, Fayla was full of amazement, and any doubt she'd had about the capabilities of these people swiftly vanished.

Schellenberg went on to explain that they had set up three safe flats in Mayfair: one where she would really live and two others where she would take her targets to seduce. If more were needed, they would be arranged.

"And now," he said with a trace of excitement, "a little something to celebrate the commencement of our venture." He withdrew a slender gift-wrapped package and handed it to her with great ceremony.

She giggled like a schoolgirl as she tore off the wrapping to reveal a slim black leather case with gold lettering that read: *Boucheron*. She'd murdered an innocent man in Monte Carlo without batting an eye, but now her heart was all atwitter as she slowly opened the case and gasped with genuine awe. It was a diamond-encrusted bracelet with a series of thumb-sized emeralds implanted like sentries at attention. One that matched her necklace perfectly.

Her gasps continued as the General chortled and Magrid leaned forward and said, "Here, my dear, allow me." She took it from the box and snapped the clasp around Fayla's wrist. The transformed Irish street brat held it up and watched the light beams dance through the faceted surfaces. "Oh, my . . . this is so far from Falls Road, I kinna tell you. If only Mairead could see me now."

"I'm sure she would be proud, my dear," comforted Magrid.

Then a change came over her and she eyed Schellenberg for a moment. She quizzically asked, "Where does it all come from?"

"Where does what come from?"

"The money, of course. For the jets, this palace, the haute couture, this bracelet . . . where does it come from? I mean, Germany lost the war . . . didn't they?"

Schellenberg laughed. "A prescient question. But I'll take the first one first. In simple terms, the money came from Jewish cleverness."

Fayla cocked her head. "Eh?"

The General assumed a professorial posture. "Well, you must understand that the fact of the matter is that Jews believe themselves to be cleverer than everyone else. And quite often that is true. Jews excel at the professions—law, medicine, art, and of course finance. Jews and wealth often seem inseparable.

"Well, after Kristalnacht in late 1938, I conceived of a plan and took it to my new superior at the time, Reinhard Heydrich. A great man, if a little severe. Probably would have ultimately inherited the title as Führer if things had turned out differently, and Czech partisans hadn't assassinated him.

"In any case, I took my plans to Heydrich and he gave them his enthusiastic approval, then dispatched me to Zürich where I found a number of like-minded Swiss bankers—whose distaste for Jews, I must confess, exceeded our own. I also enlisted the covert support of Colonel Masson, chief of the Swiss intelligence service, who shared in the, ah, harvest."

"Harvest?" asked Fayla.

"Exactly. Shortly after Kristalnacht, the roundup of Jews surged dramatically. The wealthy ones were desperately looking for safe havens for their riches. I selected a prominent Jewish banker—a man by the name of Heldmann. His wife and children were arrested by the Gestapo, which was under my command, to secure his assistance. His rich depositors laid siege to him for advice. He gave them the names on our approved list of Swiss bankers. He would also make clandestine arrangements for them to travel to Switzerland, only they were totally unaware it was my department transporting them in the hollowed-out bottom of a truck bed—all very cloak and daggerish and designed to impart the feeling they were pulling the wool over Nazi eyes. It played beautifully to the Jewish sense of intellectual superiority.

"So, as it unfolded, we kept up a steady stream of wealthy Jews into Zürich and back. We kept meticulous records on their identities; their families once, twice, and thrice removed; their business relationships and so forth. Within a year we had rolled up hundreds of millions of Reichsmarks, and when we felt that the cow was done giving milk, we rolled up the entire group in a matter of days and shipped them and their business relations off to liquidation centers.

"So by the time it was over, there was absolutely no one alive who could lay claim to the money. The Swiss bankers then transferred half into accounts I controlled, and the other half went to the bankers' own accounts, minus a stipend to Colonel Masson. Then, following the war, Colonel Masson—who was owed a number of favors from the Americans because he had allowed them to run their intelligence operations on Swiss soil—secured my release from American custody. Then as our rebirth plan took root the Reichsmarks, which had been converted to Swiss Francs long ago, were invested, and over fifty years . . . well, it grew into the billions, and I stopped counting. We couldn't possibly spend it all if we tried.

"So that which is on your wrist—it all comes from Jews trying to be too clever."

A silence fell between them as Fayla surveyed him with an appraiser's eye. Then she caressed the emeralds with her fingertips and smiled at him demurely, saying, "It is an exquisite bracelet. I shall treasure it always."

Schellenberg found himself a bit unsettled, somewhat anxious and excited in the same moment as an alien thought entered his mind. Had he finally met his equal? What an extraordinary idea! This woman was truly partner material. He graced her with a nod of the head and said, "We are honored you have elected to join us. Now we must make some essential arrangements for our plan to go forward."

"Such as?"

Magrid patted her arm. "We must arrange for your assassination, my dear."

CHAPTER FIFTEEN

The anonymous gray van in the center of the security convoy entered the Brixton switch yard as the first rays of a brilliant April morning painted the dull industrial landscape with yellow sunbeams.

It was here in Brixton that the cars of the British Rail system—Eurostar included—would be sifted and sorted like so many cards in a deck. Cars would roll into the lazy Susan, where they would spin and then be hooked up to an engine to head off in a new direction.

The caravan rolled up to a lone Eurostar car. Standing beside it were three armed British Rail police and a middle-aged man in a suit and trench coat. The rear window of the lead sedan rolled down and the man in the trench coat leaned forward, enquiring, "Mr. Davies?"

"Right," replied the MOD man, and he exited. "All ready for us?"

"Quite," said Trenchcoat. "But may I first see your credentials?"

"Of course. And yours?"

The mutual display completed, the MOD man said, "So this is it? Looks like any other Eurostar carriage."

"That's by design," replied Trenchcoat. "Only two of these high-security cars were ever manufactured. Unless you knew what they were, you'd think they were nothing more than passenger cars."

"Right. Give me a walkabout, will you?"

"Already did that with your advance team during the planning stage."

"Humor me," said the MOD man.

"Very well," replied Trenchcoat. "Follow me, please."

Davies exited the sedan and followed him up the steps at the passenger ingress point. He was greeted by a narrow passageway down the length of the car—windows on one side and a smooth floor-to-ceiling metal wall on the other. Trenchcoat knocked on the wall. "Ten-gauge steel and no interior access point, security cameras at each end that are wired into the Eurostar command center in Kent."

"Hmm," replied Davies, as Trenchcoat led him outside to the other side of the car. He nodded to two of the rail police, who unhooked one of the faux windows that swung out on hinges.

Trenchcoat continued his lecture. "As you can see, behind the simulated smoked-glass window is the security panel." He entered a series of numbers on a keypad and two halves of the car bulkhead seemed to burp open slightly like a clamshell. The rail police swung the panels out on hinges to reveal the rather unremarkable innards. Two captain chairs, a table, a small communications panel, and a tiny fridge at one end, and a water closet at the other. Florescent lights above, but the rest was bare walls and floor, except for a metal ladder leading up one wall to the ceiling.

"The car is self-contained. Ventilation can be closed off if necessary and a battery pack can maintain air conditioning and appliances for six hours if need be. Communications to the engineer, train manager, and Eurostar Central are also independent and self-contained."

"Can the guard inside get out in an emergency?"

Trenchcoat replied, "Once the car is buttoned up there is no way for the guards to open the security panels from the inside. However, there is a small panel in the ceiling just above where the ladder terminates. It can only be opened by the detonation of explosive bolts by the guards from that panel over there."

"I see," said MOD man. "And where in the train does this ride?"

Exasperated, Trenchcoat said, "This was all covered in the planning meetings. The security car will be the last element before the rear engine, and sealed off from any passenger access, of course."

"Of course. Well then, it all seems in order. Let's load it up then." He nodded to the Major who put things in motion. The panel door in the van slid back, and two men stepped out carrying a gray gunmetal footlocker.

Trenchcoat was perplexed. "Ah, is that it? I mean, is that all?"

"Believe me, it is quite enough, Major."

The security detail carried the footlocker up the steps to the interior of the car and secured it to anchor points in the floor with straps.

The two SAS men in civilian clothes climbed up with Heckler & Koch submachine guns and took their seats in the captain chairs.

"All right," ordered the Major, "button it up."

The rail police swung the bulkheads shut and then engaged the security panel, ramming the bolts home with a *chung!* Then the faux window was secured and the car was good for go.

Trenchoat motioned to the engineer of a nearby Eurostar engine to approach, and it slowly moved in reverse until it married itself to the security car. Then the two of them were pushed down the rail to link up with a Eurostar passenger car.

"Now then," said Trenchcoat, "I have been advised that no special British Rail Security detail is to be assigned to this mission. I have also been instructed to provide British Rail Security credentials to four men of your ministry. I find this quite irregular, if not distasteful, but I have complied with my instructions."

"That's very good of you," replied MOD man.

Trenchcoat handed over the four leather-bound creds. "Your security people may board the passenger car here. Then they will be connected to the end of the Eurostar train and can remain with the security car without interruption."

"Excellent," he replied, then turned and passed the creds to the Major. "Get on-board with your detail. Have a pleasant journey. I'll be flying ahead to meet you at Lyon."

"Don't understand why we couldn't just fly the bloody things."

"Treaty calls for ground transport, Major, and this is the safest and fastest ground transport in the whole of Europe. So have a quiet day of sightseeing. Low profile and all. Then buy you and your crew a nice dinner at the end of the day."

"Aye, sir. Let's get on with it. Brunton!"

One of the SAS men in casual clothes came forward, his 9mm Glock concealed under his windbreaker and the Heckler & Koch tucked away in a backpack. He grabbed the creds and climbed into the car.

From the ninth floor of a rundown office building three blocks away, a Nikon digital camera with an 800mm lens snapped off a half-dozen shots as the SAS man took his creds from the Major and climbed into the car. Shots of the rest of the team quickly followed. The photographer then transferred the images to his Vaio laptop, rapidly selected the best ones and sent them via Wi-Fi to an encrypted email address. Two minutes later, Helmut was printing them out from a color laser printer in his Mayfair safe house. He hit the speed dial on his cell phone and Fayla immediately answered.

"We have the security team identified," he said.

CHAPTER SIXTEEN

Bloom closed Fayla Bannon's file and shook his head ruefully. "Unbelievable. Her family murdered in front of her when she was eleven?"

Salisbury nodded. "By some Orangemen militia. They were worse than the IRA."

"Was there anyone in the Ulster security service she didn't sleep with?"

"Played them like a violin, she did. And we never had her in custody."

Bloom sighed. "This is one formidable opponent. Coupled with Schellenberg, this is getting scarier by the minute."

"Hopefully we'll get some answers here."

The Vauxhall caravan wheeled up to the curb of the headquarters building at Heathstone Arsenal. A severe man, standing bareheaded on the sidewalk, wore the uniform (Bloom found out later) of a major general in the British Army. A junior aide-de-camp stood a discreet distance behind him.

Salisbury piled out of the car and the general inquired, "Superintendent Salisbury, I presume? Welcome to Heathstone. I am Martin Finch, post commander."

To Bloom, Finch had the look of a fastidious man who was

going to enjoy this visit with the police about as much as a trip to the dentist.

They shook hands perfunctorily, and Salisbury led with, "I presume you were briefed regarding our visit."

A nod. "I have been instructed to offer you our full cooperation. Perhaps we should retire inside."

"Certainly," replied Salisbury. "By the way, allow me to present Captain Gideon Bloom of the Chicago Police Department. He is assisting us in this investigation."

"Chicago? American? I, uh, am not sure he would have clearance to enter any discussion of substance."

"Trust me, he is cleared. Shall we?"

Five minutes later they were in a dismal conference room being served coffee that Bloom thought equally dismal.

"Now then, what can I do for you, Superintendent?"

"To come to the point, General, we have obtained evidence that an employee of the arsenal—thought to have been killed in a house fire—was actually murdered."

"Murdered?"

"Yes, do you know anything about it?"

"Oh, well . . . vaguely. Seems I recall one of the personnel got himself topped in a house fire. I received a report from the provo marshal but it did not go further. We have upwards of eight thousand people here at the Arsenal, and with that big a number death visits rather routinely. Heart attacks, motorcar accidents, that sort of thing. A house fire is unusual, but not unprecedented. Even had a bloke wind up hanging himself while working on his roof a couple of years ago. Who was the person in question?"

Salisbury opened a file and slid a photo across. "A n'er-do-well named Cyril Worsham. Cleaning staff. Ring any bells?"

Finch picked up the photo and studied it as if he were trying to choose between the mahi-mahi or the grilled salmon. "'Fraid not . . . oh, wait, yes. I remember now. He was the janitor in the Q-Lab."

"Q-Lab?" asked Bloom. "What exactly is the Q-Lab?"

Finch peered over his reading glasses, and in his best New England schoolmarm posture, said, "I'm afraid I can't go into any detail on that. Official Secrets, you understand. Suffice to say it is a sensitive area. All I can say is that this poor fellow worked there and that in itself brings a higher degree of scrutiny. But as he was below the bottom rung, it's safe to say nothing was compromised."

Salisbury took a deep breath, then said evenly, "We need to see Cyril Worsham's personnel file. We also need to know everything there is to know about Q-Lab, and I need the director, chief, or whatever you call the top dog in here immediately."

Finch turned to stone. "Quite impossible, I'm afraid."

Salisbury looked around the room and saw a telephone on the far credenza. He pulled out his own cell phone and punched a speed-dial button. A pause, then, "Yes, sir . . . As I suspected. Rather obstinate. . . . Yes. We're in the main conference room on the second floor of the headquarters building . . . a general named Finch. Very well, sir."

Salisbury rang off and said nothing, and for two minutes the silence grew more deafening until the phone on the credenza pierced the air with a shrill ring. The aide jumped up and grabbed it. After a few murmurs he looked up and said, "Uh, General, suh, it's Number Ten Downing Street."

A crack appeared in Finch's veneer as he rose to take the phone. "This is General Finch."

There was a bit of a gasp as he went on to mumble, "Y—Yes, Prime Minister. . . . Yessir. . . . Certainly sir. Full access. . . . I understand. I was only . . . Yessir."

He hung up and, with an ashen face, turned to his aide and

said, "Go find Dr. Wingate and tell him to get in here—immediately."

Jeremy Frost checked his image in the restroom mirror and was satisfied that the battleship-gray Eurostar uniform was perfect. Shirt starched, tie in place, shoes shined, and the gray coat of the steward's blazer had nary a wrinkle. All topped off by the ID tag on the necklace lanyard.

Frost was the sort who would blend in without notice. Short and wiry, he'd been working as a junior steward on the Eurostar bullet train for eight months after a long and exhausting interview process and background check. Well, apparently not exhaustive enough, because Jeremy Frost really didn't exist at all. Or rather, anymore. He'd died at three months old thirty-two years ago and his remains rested peacefully in the cemetery of a Yorkshire churchyard. Frost's real name was Mickey McDrew, and he'd grown up a half block away from Fayla Bannon.

Five years her junior, Fayla had enraptured him before he'd turned ten. He would, and did, do anything to win her favor, including killing seven British soldiers before his sixteenth birthday by placing bombs at Fayla's behest all over Ulster. For her, Mickey was the replacement kid brother for the one the Orangemen had murdered, and she was the goddess he always venerated. Her death in Gibraltar had devastated him beyond comprehension. Then when she'd reappeared two years ago, sitting there in his dingy Belfast hovel as if she'd just gone out for coffee, he'd been transported by the miracle. Tears of joy flowed like a river as she held him tight and told him they were going to roll up the sodding Tommies and send them into the sea.

And now, today was the day. He never knew how she did it,

but an entire false identity—a "legend"—had been created for him in Jeremy Frost: school transcripts, real estate transactions, car registration, passport, Inland Revenue receipts—all authentic with historical dates. He'd applied for and been accepted as a steward, making Eurostar trips to Avignon, Paris and Brussels on a daily basis. Perhaps it was because Jeremy Frost was so benign in his appearance—a bland face and open eyes, hair cut short—that he seemed the perfect sort to refill your teacup. And such a model employee! He was so curious about everything on the job—the train, how it worked, how the engineer drove it, the schedules, the train manager's communications. Always willing to go the extra mile.

But today—today was special. Jeremy Frost would be left behind, and it would be Mickey McDrew and Fayla, just the two of them, for awhile at least. He would make her proud and make those sodding Tommies kiss her feet. He straightened his tie, then left the loo and joined the flow of passengers toward the security queue at St. Pancras Station. He peeled off and entered a door marked STAFF ONLY, totally unaware of a dark-haired French woman nearby as she stepped up to the courteous Eurostar security man, who inspected her passport and ticket.

"DuVaal, is it? Séverine duVaal?"

"*Oui.* Yes."

"Going all the way to Lyon?"

"Yes. Going home."

He handed the documents back. "It will be convenient for you. The new Eurostar leg goes from Paris to Lyon so you will not have to change at Gare du Nord. Have a pleasant journey."

Emil Broussard dropped his gear at the base of Mont Collon and peered up the sheer face before him. He had hiked all the way to the back side of the mountain so his ascent could not be seen by a wandering eye from the village. The sun had come out and patches of ice and snow were dripping onto the slate-gray rock face. Broussard intended to climb to the mesa-like summit, then lower himself into the cable car access hole just below the lip of the mesa. The climb appeared straight-forward and straight up. Plenty of small crevices for hand holds, but the sheer nature of it would be time consuming, so he'd better get on with it. And despite the fact so much hung in the balance, he was not going to climb without a tether. That would take more time, but a slip at this point would be catastrophic on several levels. He sank his ice axe into a frosty fissure and began.

Finding Dr. Wingate turned out to be more of an exercise than anticipated. He was not in the lab or his office, and did not answer his home phone. Finally, two military policemen were dispatched to his residence, where he was awakened from an alcoholic haze.

During the wait Bloom leaned over and whispered to Salis-bury, "Did I hear right, or was General Prig here actually talking to the prime minister?"

Salisbury nodded. "Since time was of the essence, the home secretary—a capable man by the way—anticipated the general would throw up the Official Secrets wall and hide behind the minister of defence. The only person who can trump the MOD is the prime minister, so he made arrangements to cut through the red tape as you requested."

Bloom was silent for moment, then he leaned over and whispered, "It's official, Grayson. I'm impressed."

At high noon an unkempt Dr. Thaddeus Wingate presented himself at the headquarters conference room of Heathstone

Arsenal, with an attitude falling somewhere between indignity and blind rage. Bloom figured on his best day this guy was a consummate prick; and this, clearly, was not his best day.

"Sorry to have to disturb you, Thaddeus," offered General Finch. "But these gentlemen are from Scotland Yard, and we have been instructed by Number Ten to answer any and all questions they have."

"Number Ten?"

"By the prime minister himself, Thaddeus. No Official Secrets here."

Wingate looked them over with a pair of imperious eyes that Bloom thought reflected brilliance, impatience, and intolerance. After another half minute of stone silence, he uttered, "What do you want?"

Salisbury spoke. "Well, for a start, please give us an overview of what goes on in your Q-Lab."

From Wingate's reaction, Salisbury might have asked him to drop his knickers. The scientist jerked his head in Finch's direction as if to say, "Surely you don't mean—"

"Tell them, Thaddeus." The general was firm.

Wingate made a sound Bloom thought akin to a lion growling under water. Then his shoulders sagged and his head bowed as he whispered, "What a hellacious day."

"Pardon?" asked Salisbury.

Wingate raised his gaze with the look of a defeated man. "So you want to know about Q-Lab, Inspector? Are you sure? Better, perhaps, for you to turn away and chase your workaday robberies and murders instead of raising the veil on Q-Lab."

"I'm afraid we must, Doctor Wingate," said Salisbury.

The scientist nodded. "Very well. Tell me, Inspector, what would be the worst that could happen in your line of work—the 'nightmare scenario' as the saying goes?"

Salisbury didn't see the question coming, so he fumbled a

reply. "Well, a terrorist setting off a weapon of mass destruction in London, I suppose."

A wicked smile crossed Wingate's face as he said, "Oh, no,
Inspector there is something much, much worse."

"Worse?" asked Bloom.

Wingate nodded. "Call it a weapon of selective mass destruction."

"Selective?" asked Salisbury. "How do you mean?"

Wingate sighed. "No doubt you've heard of bacteriological
and chemical warfare?"

Nods in reply.

"Well, there is another kind of warfare . . . a warfare that
comes from a cauldron stirred by the devil himself in the inner
sanctum of what is known as Q-Lab."

A pall of silence fell over the room, with Bloom having a
sense of expectation and dread that they had finally hit pay dirt,
but a pay dirt that was an evil soup. "Go on, Doctor Wingate,"
he prompted, "we're listening."

The pompous ass took a fatigued breath, and when he spoke
it was barely a whisper. "The history of mankind is replete with
warfare and weaponry of every kind. From clubs and spears, to
bows and arrows, to flying computers and missiles. And, as
Churchill said, those implements of war were 'made more sinister by perverted science.' To that end we have seen the
mushroom clouds of nuclear destruction, mustard gas in the
trenches of Verdun, and smallpox used to wipe out entire races
of primitive people in the Amazon. But I tell you, gentlemen,
that within the walls of this arsenal, a new type of warfare has
surfaced that is more horrific and ominous than anything
Churchill could have imagined."

No one spoke, until Salisbury said, "And what would that
be?"

Wingate sighed again and replied, "That would be the realm

of genetic warfare."

Bloom's brow furrowed. "How, exactly, does that differ from bacteriological warfare?"

Wearily, Wingate began, "A singular question, Captain Bloom. To reply, I will assume your party knows little, if anything, about genetics or virology."

"Other than lessons in school on Gregor Mendel's experiments with bean plants, I think that would be an accurate assumption," answered Bloom

Nods all around. "Very well, then," said Wingate, "let me give you the thirty-thousand-foot view. When you contract the common cold, a complete virus particle known as a viron is wrapped in a membrane called a capsid. In order for a virus to be infectious, this capsid has to attach—or bind—to the specific receptors of the cellular surface of the host cell. This specificity of receptors determines the host range of a virus. For example, the HIV virus infects only human cells because its surface protein, gp120, can interact with receptors on the T cells surface. Once the virus-host cell receptors come in contact with each other, they induce the viral-envelope capsid to undergo changes that result in the fusion of the viral and cellular membranes. The capsid protein disassociates, or unwraps, the viral RNA, which is transported to the nucleus of the host cell. In the nucleus, something called the viral polymerase complexes transcribe and replicate the RNA. Viral mRNAs migrate to cytoplasm where they are translated into protein. Then the newly synthesized virons bud and multiply from the infected cell and the infection is underway."

"So . . . how is this genetic warfare?" asked Bloom.

Wingate just stared at him for a moment, then went on. "The key issue, Captain Bloom, is the chemical receptors between the capsid envelope and the host cellular wall. If they are not calibrated, attachment does not occur, and the viron passes by the host cell harmlessly, and replication—which is to say, infection—never occurs. What we achieved in Q-Lab is an entire generation of concentrated scientific work. Indeed, we achieved the ability to calibrate the receptors of the capsid to the DNA of the host cell nucleus. Put another way, with the data provided by the Human Genome project, the receptors of the capsid can be calibrated to the genetic code of a human's particular traits."

There was a pause, then Woolridge said, "Let me make sure I understand you, Doctor. You are saying that the receptors can be calibrated to *only* bind to cells with a certain DNA sequence?"

"Precisely."

"I'm afraid you've lost me," said Chatham.

Woodridge tentatively put forward the premise. "If I understand what Doctor Wingate is saying, the envelope of the virus can be activated to bind with the membrane of the cell, based on the genetic coding of certain DNA strands."

"Exactly," replied Wingate.

Bloom leaned forward. "So, you can cause a virus to infect the cells of people only with, say, red hair? Or blue eyes?"

"Correct," said Wingate.

Bloom's mind raced, and when the enormity of what he'd just heard sank in, he fell back in his chair. "And it could be targeted by the color of a person's skin—black, brown or yellow?"

"Yes," said Wingate simply.

"What . . . what kind of virus are we talking about here?" asked Salisbury.

"We have been successful in engineering a range of viruses to bind with the receptor capsid. Our earlier successes were with benign viruses like the common cold. Then with greater potency like roto-viruses. Finally, we achieved a fully weaponized aerosol filovirus."

"What does that mean?" asked Bloom.

Wingate might have been giving an instruction on how to tie a fishing line, as he explained, "The filovirus is similar to the Ebola virus, which has flared up on various occasions in Africa. Our virus, however, has a longer incubation period—days to weeks, not hours—and it can be transmitted by airborne disbursement via aerosol—and if it does not bind with a host cell in five to seven days, it will die."

"So, the virus is transmitted through airborne inhalation?" asked Wooldridge.

"And by casual contact."

There was a pause, until Chatham said, "I find this all very difficult to believe."

Wingate raised an eyebrow. "Really?"

"Yes, really. This all sounds like some kind of pulp science fiction. And even if it were true, I have a hard time believing Her Majesty's Government would underwrite, or even condone, this witch's brew you speak of."

Wingate did not reply. He simply turned to Finch and said, "General, would you retrieve the Gloworm video tape from Q-Lab, if you please."

It pulled into the shiny new St. Pancras Station like an elongated Moray eel approaching its prey. The two yellowish headlights just below the Vader-like smoked-glass windshield gave it the patina of a predator creeping along the track. The steel chain of eighteen cars sandwiched between front and rear locomotives stretched for 394 meters, or nearly a quarter mile. It was elegant, symmetrical, and conveyed a sense of raw power under the vaulted ceiling of the station.

The genesis of this extraordinary conveyance called the Eurostar line arguably began with Napoleon, who, as master of Europe, had contemplated ways to deal with that pesky English Channel so he could invade Britain. He gave serious thought to digging a tunnel under the water; but as technology had not advanced sufficiently at the time, the idea of a "chunnel" was shelved, Admiral Nelson went on to send the Emperor's fleet to the bottom at Trafalgar, and England once more was saved.

Then in the mid-1980s the idea of the Chunnel revived; and with it the idea of high-speed rail from London to Paris and Brussels.

A joint venture was formed between Eurostar U.K. and SNCF of France, with French technology taking the lead as SNCF had been operating the high-speed TGV rail service since 1981.

The French are extremely adroit at conveying the impression that, as a people, they are lazy droids interested in nothing more than wine, cheese, long lunches, sex, and bilking the American tourist. While they do covet those things, the *grande* secret is they are without peer in bringing huge national projects to fruition faster, cheaper, and with better quality than even the Japanese—whether it be a national stadium, an electrical grid powered by nuclear energy, a universal health-care system, or a high-speed rail line.

With the advent of the St. Pancras Station in London in November 2007, the new high-speed line ushered in a new era of Eurostar service, enabling the trains to reach speeds of 186 mph, and bringing the non-stop run time from London to Paris down to 2 hours 15 minutes. And for those who wished to continue to the Eurostar terminus in Avignon, it was a mere 5 hours 40 minutes from London.

Séverine duVaal placed her small carry-on bag in the overhead bin, then sat down in the first class seat and contemplated her future. At twenty-nine, her chosen career now left behind and her convalescence over, she had nowhere to go but home. A life back on the farm? When she'd been in her teens, the tomboy couldn't get away fast enough. Off to Paris.

A brief stint of modeling had ended when a photographer put his hand on her ass and she broke his nose. That had a chilling effect on her fashion career. Dated a flic. He thought he'd impress her by taking her to the range. When she grouped ten rounds in a two-inch pattern within six seconds, it turned out he was the one impressed. As was the range supervisor, who called the talent spotter, and six years later she wound up as the first of three women in the EPIGN (Escadron Parachutiste d'Intervention de la Gendarmerie Nationale). Jumping out of airplanes, scuba diving, shooting off two hundred rounds on the range before lunch, and unarmed combat in the afternoon. Life had been good. She'd been part of several "hot" operations—a hostage rescue in the Cameroons, a rendition out of Algeria, and seducing a drug trafficker in Marseilles while his cell phone was being rewired by the electronic wizards of the gendarmerie. They had been nothing but a warmup for the Libyan operation. She'd been selected because she had the full package—razor sharp military skills, looks that would stop traffic, and the ability to speak Russian like a native.

When the plan had been revealed to her, she'd readily accepted, knowing that she was up to the task. What she didn't see coming was a lieutenant colonel in the Légion étrangère. In the worst possible situation, where absolute focus was required, they were two consummate professionals who had fallen hopelessly in love.

She'd never met the measure of a man like Marc Chartain. A desert rock in so many ways. But she had found that oasis of vulnerability in him no one had ever touched. Just as he had found hers—which was at once frightening and enthralling. Perhaps they were too much alike—so independent and self-reliant. Like Napoleon once said, in order for a relationship to survive, one party must yield. Neither would. On their last night together before she left for Moscow they'd quarreled. He'd asked her to abandon the mission. She'd refused. Then he watched his heart walk off with a snake in an Armani suit. His stomach turned so bad he became physically ill.

When the mission was over, and all the debriefings were done, they'd found themselves alone in a conference room of the Defence Ministry. They just stared at each other, neither saying anything, both of them emotionally exhausted by the experience. After expending so much courage in the desert, neither one had any left to try and recapture the spark. She left for the farm and he for Normandy.

And that was the end of it. Except for the fact she couldn't stop thinking of him. Even now as she absently flipped through the Eurostar travel magazine filled with pictures of smiling families on vacation. There were no pictures of a smart-ass seven-year-old getting whacked on the backside or a toddler throwing up on the steward.

She looked at her watch and figured it was time for the train to get moving, then glanced across the table to meet the eyes of a late-middle-aged woman sitting catty-corner from her in the four-place facing seats. She was gray-haired, matronly and seemed to be cut from the same cloth as her Aunt Sophie. Séverine returned her gaze, which prompted the response, "Forgive me. I apologize for staring. It's just you have that black-black hair and incredibly blue eyes. It's quite a combination, I must say. Never saw anything quite like it."

Séverine smiled. "It is very kind of you. My grandmother was a Cossack. The black hair, blue-eyed gene apparently was passed on to me. It's not uncommon in Cossack tribes."

The lady cocked her head. "Cossack? But you sound French."

"Oui. But I grew up speaking Russian and French."

"Indeed? How did the, ah, Franco-Cossack union occur?"

Séverine smiled again. "My grandfather was part of the post-war occupation forces in Germany on the French side. My grandmother was with the Russian contingent. Love conquered the Iron Curtain you might say."

"And here you are. Going home?"

"Oui. A farm in the Vercors region, along the Rhône. Have to go home for spring planting."

There was movement.

"Oh! Well, it appears we're on our way. Paris in a little over two hours."

Two cars ahead of Séverine, Fayla released a long, slow breath as she smiled and took a flute of champagne from the steward. Their eyes locked for a moment, then with great flair she tossed it down.

"Will there be anything else, madam?" asked Mickey.

"Perhaps . . . when we reach Calais."

CHAPTER SEVENTEEN

The general's aide slipped the videotape into the player as the conference room screen dropped down. The video came up with the stenciled words PROJECT GLOWORM keyed over a black background. Bloom squinted at the grainy black-and-white images as Dr. Wingate broke the awkward silence.

"This is a prison cell in the Republic of Gabon in Central Africa. This surveillance video was taken under a secret agreement with the Gabonese government. The chamber has been sealed to Level-five bacteriologic standards. As you can see, one prisoner is white—a Gabonese citizen of French extraction—and the other is black—also a Gabonese national. Both prisoners are under a sentence of death for crimes that were, I can assure you, quite heinous."

And both of them look scared as hell, thought Bloom. It was a small cell with two wood bunks and a bucket for human waste. Both men were barefoot and wore gray cotton pajama-like prison garb. The man of French extraction was skinny, with chiseled features and thinning, dark hair in a prison brush cut. The other man was younger but more heavyset, and rivulets of sweat could be seen on his fleshy cheeks. Both men were pacing the cell incessantly as Wingate droned on.

"I would direct your attention to the date-time notation at the bottom of the screen."

Bloom squinted at the other script that read DAY: 01 TIME LAPSE: 00:00:45. Just then a small circle near the ceiling opened and an object that looked like the rear end of a flashlight protruded into the cell, causing the prisoners to stop and gape upwards.

"It is at this point the viron capsid is injected into the atmosphere of the prison cell."

Bloom watched carefully as the two prisoners jabbered excitedly to each other. And then . . . nothing. The prisoners settled down and resumed their pacing. Then the scene remained the same, but a cut in the tape had advanced the notation to DAY: 02 TIME LAPSE: 37:04:02. The two men were lying on their bunks, making bored conversation, with the remnants of a meal on trays on the floor.

Another cut to DAY: 03 TIME LAPSE: 66:42:28. Still nothing. Then two more cuts to DAY: 07 TIME LAPSE: 161:31:22. At this point the white prisoner was bent over the bucket vomiting as the black prisoner looked on rather curiously.

Another cut. DAY: 08 TIME LAPSE: 186:52:38. The white prisoner was shivering uncontrollably, drawn up in a ball on his bunk as the black prisoner leaned over him.

"At this point the filovirus has invaded vital organs, impairing blood flow to extremities and creating a chill. The body reacts by shaking violently to try and keep itself warm. But at this point hemorrhaging begins."

Bloom looked on as the white man started a racking cough, projecting blood from his mouth. The black man then stepped back.

"Lungs are rapidly filling with fluid and blood," explained Wingate.

Final cut. The white prisoner gave a final spasm, then lay

still. The black prisoner then lost it and started pounding on the door, releasing a silent scream.

The screen went dark, and no one spoke for what seemed to be a very long time. The aide flicked the lights on and Wingate continued his lecture. "One of the key aspects of this engineered viron is that it is infectious for approximately a hundred hours before the onset of symptoms. That is to say, unlike other filoviruses like Ebola that manifest themselves and 'burn out' rather quickly, enabling them to be identified and quarantined, this viron has a longer incubation period of almost seven days.

"This enables it to be passed among a much larger target population before the opposing leadership is aware of its presence."

It was Bloom who spoke first. "I take it this virus of yours was engineered to attack the white prisoner."

"Yes."

"How did you do that?"

Wingate sighed, "In lay terms, it was straightforward. The capsid was calibrated to activate off the DNA sequence providing white pigmentation to the skin."

"But what if both opposing forces were of the same race. White on white? Black on black?" asked Salisbury.

In an antiseptic response, Wingate replied, "No one can predict exactly what kind of scenario our national leadership would encounter, but we have developed the engineering of the viron to the point it can be calibrated to a particular, ah, ethnicity."

Another pregnant silence.

"You mean, you can target, say, French as opposed to Greeks?" asked Bloom.

"Not with surgical precision," said Wingate. "But with greater precision than you might imagine."

"This is madness!" barked Chatham. "How could you

possibly differentiate between two Mediterranean populations that have intermingled for centuries—indeed, millennia."

Wingate sighed again. "You have no doubt heard of the lost tribes of Israel?"

"Yes," replied Chatham, "but what—"

"Well, we can't say if this was one such tribe, but in 1999 a DNA study of the Lemba tribe in Mozambique, Africa, conducted by the University of London's anthropology department, discovered a genetic marker called the Cohen Modal Haplotype in the Lemba tribe."

"So, what is the Cohen Modal . . . Hap-something . . . ?"

"Haplotype. It is a specific genetic marker that is common among Jewish men of families named Cohen. Cohen, or Cohane, comes from the Biblical Hebrew word for 'priest,' and men in this Jewish family are understood to be the descendants of the Israelite priesthood. Therefore, this is direct evidence that—genetically speaking—this Lemba clan was directly descended from a priestly family of ancient Israel some millennia past. . . . So, strictly speaking, if we were tasked to target individuals within an African tribe of Jewish extraction, we could do it."

Salisbury shuddered. "This sounds like ethnic cleansing brought to a high art form. I have to say—"

"Dear God! The map!"

Everyone turned to look at Bloom, who had turned deathly pale.

"What is it Gideon?" asked Salisbury. "What map?"

"The map. Spinnemann had it on him when he was run down in Chicago. It was a map of the greater Chicago area, the town of Skokie circled in red."

"I don't understand," said General Finch. "What is the significance of a town in the Chicago area?"

"It's a town known for its heavily Jewish population. I know,

I was born there."

"So, what is the significance of that?" asked the general.

"We can't say for certain, but maybe Skokie was to be a test run for this . . . this 'Final Solution' weapon of yours."

Wingate started to bristle as Salisbury injected, "That may be the case, Gideon, but luckily we have tracked this down in time. General, I'm going to order in extra security. Lay on whatever on-call security you have here. I'll have a full special weapons team up here from London, and we'll turn this Q-Lab into a fortress within the hour."

"I think that's rather a moot point at this juncture," said Wingate wearily.

"Why is that?"

Wingate looked at Finch as if trying to decide who should respond. Finally, Wingate shrugged and said, "Let me explain, Superintendent, why I seem a little taciturn today. At the behest of Her Majesty's Government I have spent my entire career—thirty years if you'd care to count—developing this weaponized genetic warfare capability. For three decades I received unlimited funding and delivered breakthrough after breakthrough. All in a cocoon of oppressive secrecy. Unable to publish. No recognition, even from my family, who couldn't know what their husband and father actually did for the government.

"Well, after a thirty-year career that in any outside endeavor would have garnered me one or two Nobel prizes, I was informed my work 'was no longer required' by Her Majesty's Government."

At this point General Finch cut in with a defensive tone. "You have to understand, Superintendent. We were not the only ones working on this kind of weaponization. Russia, France, China, and the United States were all moving in the same direction—although through Dr. Wingate's efforts we were far, far advanced over the other countries. But as the political leadership of these countries began to realize that the ramifications of such a weapon were, shall we say, distasteful, the idea of it being turned on themselves was even more frightening. Therefore, the treaty was born."

"Treaty?" asked Salisbury. "What treaty?"

Wingate and Finch looked at each other again, then Finch responded. "A secret protocol among Britain, France, Russia, the United States, and China. Under the terms of the protocol, all research into genetic weapons was to cease. All data, memoranda, research papers, and key lab specimens were to be reduced to microfilm and transported to the Interpol head-quarters in Lyon, where they would be destroyed under the witness and certification of the director general of Interpol."

"Interpol?" questioned Salisbury.

"Yes, the countries involved wanted some third-party cer-tification on the destruction that could remain very hush-hush. The UN is a sieve. I dealt directly with the director general myself. No intermediaries. No aides."

"So, when were the materials destroyed?"

"Well, that won't be until next week when all the countries have transported their materials to Lyon."

"And the British materials? When are they being trans-ported?"

"Ah, well, they left this morning. It was decided to use the safest means of travel from here to Lyon." Finch looked at his watch. "They are en route as we speak."

"En route?" asked Bloom. "En route how?"

"On a special security car attached to the Eurostar bullet train that left Saint Pancras Station not quite an hour ago."

CHAPTER EIGHTEEN

The manicured patchwork green of the Kent countryside whizzed past the cabin windows at 170 mph as the Eurostar hurtled toward the entry of the Chunnel.

Mickey McDrew moved about the cabin, ever the solicitous steward in first class. Everyone comfy, eh? Care for a pillow? Today's paper? He couldn't imagine what tomorrow's headlines would look like as he leaned over the gorgeous redhead in the white velour Versace jumpsuit. There was no one else in her quad seating arrangement as Mickey placed a champagne cocktail at her elbow. She sipped demurely and whispered, "Have you made them?"

Mickey slowly cleared the small plate of cakes, taking extra care to wipe up all the crumbs. "I have them pegged. Just say the word."

Fayla checked her watch, then tossed down the champagne and said, "Today is our day, Mick. And now is our time." She squeezed his hand. "Time to kick the bloody Tommies out of Ireland. And it all starts here and now. Go!"

The electricity of her touch was all the urging that Mickey needed. Resolutely he made his way to the bar, dumped the trash, then said to the barman, "A half-dozen lemon squashes, if you please."

Peter Hereford was as tough and as mean as they came, and more than a little smart. Just the sort of cloth for the SAS. Born in Liverpool to a working-class family, the six-foot-two staff sergeant had a lanyard-like body, sandy hair, and a ruddy complexion, punctuated by a broken nose from a brief boxing career prior to his entry into Her Majesty's service.

Hereford had been battle tested in Afghanistan and Iraq, had disrupted drug production facilities in Colombia and been on special embassy security details. He took nothing for granted and had a suspicious nature. So when the automatic sliding door of the car made its pneumatic *hiss*, his right hand instinctively went under his windbreaker to his nine millimeter Glock. Then the twerpy steward came through bearing a tray of drinks with a towel over his arm. Hereford would have preferred his team have the car all to themselves, but orders were to blend in. Even so, there were only four other passengers in the car.

Perhaps it came from the experience of being in uniform that caused his guard to slip. The "us-vs.-the-enemy" mentality. Seeing the steward in uniform imparted the feeling he was with a comrade of sorts. And the guy was so benign, smiling as he bowed in the cramped aisle and served drinks. He made his way toward the four SAS men sprinkled through the latter half of the car and bowed to Hereford. "A new flavor of lemon squash. Compliments of Eurostar. We're seeing how our passengers like it." And he set it down at the table before moving on to the Major wearing a business suit and sitting alone in the quad seats across the aisle.

Such a kind smile. "As we enter the Chunnel, I will be taking lunch orders should you gentlemen care for anything."

Emil Broussard sank his ice axe into a small fissure, and perhaps because his adrenal glands were already working overtime, he overreacted when the startled pigeon fluttered and shot out of the crevasse like a rocket. He fell back, losing his grip on the rock outcropping. The safety rope went from slack to taut, breaking his fall in a yo-yo motion until he heard the sickening *pop* of the anchoring piton spring free from the rock fissure. Down he went again, performing another yo-yo until the next anchor engaged. This time it held firm, but Broussard didn't waste a moment. He scrambled to get a foothold and, between curses at mountain pigeons, he offered up prayers of thanksgiving that he'd retained the presence of mind to hang onto his ice axe.

He sank it into a fissure and took a long slow breath to get his pulse back under a hundred and fifty beats a minute. He had contemplated hanging it up as a climber; maybe this was the appropriate juncture. He gazed upward and saw the summit maybe forty meters away. He grunted and pulled himself up to the next toehold.

The central nervous system of the Eurostar is located outside London in a command post building. As you would expect, the central command looks something like the bridge of a starship, with flat screen monitors, digital readouts, and a controller who manages the on-duty staff.

The Eurostar system isn't just the train, but an intricate hairnet of different elements to keep unwitting passengers humming along in safety and comfort at incredible speeds—and part of that is underneath the seabed of the English Channel.

A pathway of rails, sensors, electrical grid, security fences, and cameras made the Eurostar a hermetically sealed system— off limits to the outside world. Delivering the correct electrical load to the locomotives, communicating with the trains, ensuring nothing untoward was on the tracks, and monitoring the timetables of trains zipping north and south to Paris, and east and west to Brussels. All of this computing power came to a locus point in the central command post on the U.K. side, and in a similar facility near Chantilly on the Gallic side.

After years of operation without a single fatality, the Eurostar and the French TGV systems were largely routine. The central control station was so hugely automated that the operations had become virtually robotic. Shift workers monitored readouts, talked with engineers and, as required, reported upstream . . . then they went home for dinner.

After 9/11 in New York—and the train bombings in London—security had increased; but as time wore on, complacency set back in and vigilance waned, even though Eurostar was a very inviting target. In the absence of a major security incident, active measures had also waned. Except for today. At the controller's elbow stood two men from the Ministry of Defence, along with the assistant managing director for Eurostar security, a former Scotland Yard bloke with a grousy demeanor.

"So where are we now?" asked the man from MOD.

The controller brought up the real-time camera feed from the engineer's cockpit in the nose of the locomotive and put it center screen. "There you are. Five minutes away from entry into the Chunnel."

The Ministry man said, "Right," and punched in a speed dial on his cell. It was answered immediately and he said, "You're five minutes away from the entrance to the Chunnel. Handing you off to the Frogs. Have a pleasant trip."

The Major said, "Right. I'll check in with Chantilly when we exit the other side." He hit the CALL END button, gazed out the window at the fast-moving countryside, then took a pull on the lemon squash. Hmmm. Not bad.

France's Gendarmarie Nationale contains a number of specialized and elite sub units, and the most famous of these units is the GIGN counter terrorist unit. Another of these units, although less well known, is the gendarmerie's EPIGN (Escadron Parachutiste d'Intervention de la Gendarmerie Nationale). Little known outside France, this highly skilled special operations and counterterrorist unit routinely operates alongside its better known counterpart.

Originally raised in 1971 as EPGM (Escadron Parachutiste de Gendarmerie Mobile), the initial members were drawn from mobile gendarmerie units throughout France. The Squadron underwent several name changes over the years before settling on its current designation.

EPIGN gendarmes have participated in a range of French military interventions over the years and across the globe, as one would expect of a former colonial power. Teams have also been deployed to many of France's former African colonies to help quell disturbances, including supporting French military units operating against Libyan-backed opposition forces in Chad. Afghanistan has been a magnet for their particular skill set of dropping in at night via HAHO (high-altitude, high-opening) parasail, striking quickly and silently, then disappearing into the hills. Domestically they are given the stickier security and VIP protection tasks, opting to ask for forgiveness rather than permission to strike at the heart of a potential threat, like against heavily armed ETA terrorists in Basque provinces where, in the wake of the Madrid bombings, EPIGN platoons operated on a rotational basis throughout the Spanish countryside. They also get pulled into exotic law-enforcement tasks that are largely enabled by the French penchant for interpreting their laws on defendant rights and civil liberties with great suppleness.

Of particular note was their action against the terrorist battle on French soil with Algerian extremists. On the 26th of August 1995, during a bombing campaign conducted by such terrorists, a gas bottle equipped with a detonation system was found near the Paris-Lyon TGV railway, near Cailloux-sur-Fontaines in the Rhône region. The device had not exploded and was found to be similar to the one that had been set off on the 25th of July in the Saint-Michel RER station.

Fingerprints of an Algerian extremist named Khaled Kelkal were found on the bomb, and a frantic search immediately followed, with Kelkal designated as Public Enemy Number One in France. 170,000 photographs of him papered every public venue in the country.

Kelkal was then located in the Lyon region, and after several days of pursuit in the forest of Malval, he was cornered in La Maison Blanche. He attempted to resist arrest and was shot dead by members of the EPIGN. Kelkal's death was shown on television, and a polemic arose about the exact reasons for the shooting. On the television footage, as the gendarmes got close to the body of Kelkal, one of them could be heard yelling, "*Finis-le, finis-le!*" Finish him, Finish him! However, it seems that even though he was shot in the leg, Kelkal had aimed a pistol at the gendarmes, who opened fire in self-defense.

The EPIGN is composed of 135 men and three women commanded by a captain. It draws its recruits from the police and military forces, and is organized into four 30-man platoons and a small HALO detachment. One of the platoons specializes in VIP protection and operates alongside of the Groupe de Sécurité du Président de la République (the French Secret Service). Another small detachment has the anti-terrorist responsibility for the TGV high-speed rail system throughout the country.

Marc Chartain was a graduate of the St. Cyr military academy, so it was with familiarity he walked into the barracks building at Camp de Satory—a military enclave outside Paris that houses a smattering of various units, including GIGN and EPIGN. The "barracks" was a rather all-encompassing term for a hodge-podge of structures that housed admin offices, training facilities, living quarters and communications. He trudged up to the second floor and down the hall to a doorway with the EPIGN guidon perched by the frame, and a plaque on the door that read COMMANDANT EPIGN. He entered and a uniformed clerk behind a desk looked up with surprise. "Colonel Chartain! What a surprise! I thought you were back in Corsica."

"Hello, Matthieu. That's where I'm headed after I have lunch with your boss."

The clerk looked at the day book and then huffed like the mother hen that he was. "Lunch? It's just like him not to tell me."

"Is that the crazy Legionnaire out there?" came a voice from the inner office.

"Guilty!" replied Chartain.

A sinewy captain with black cropped hair and black eyes came out smiling and took Chartain into his embrace. "I thought you were a dead man walking when I saw you last. And now? The Croix de Guerre I heard. Awarded at the Élysée Palace no less."

"I cannot confirm or deny, Philippe. However, I will say your intelligence—as always—is first class."

Captain Philippe Caisson was the commandant of the EPIGN and relished the role. One of France's top commandos, he was on the short list to be on the Libyan operation; but the powers that be had decided they wanted someone with more desert experience, and Chartain got the nod. A lesser man would have smoldered, but as Séverine was under his command, he placed his unit and resources at Chartain's disposal for preparation of the mission. Chartain was indebted to the younger man, but especially so because his acute antennae picked up what was happening between himself and Séverine

Rather than raise a stink, he'd provided air cover to the pair of lovers, making sure they received discreet interludes together when and where it was possible. They knew he knew but no one said anything, and for that Chartain was eternally grateful—to the point he was buying lunch.

He eyed Caisson curiously, for the captain was wearing the special black one-piece operational jumpsuit, while Chartain was in civilian clothes and a sports jacket. "I thought we were going off post for lunch?"

Caisson shrugged. "We're on a short leash today. Word came down this morning: We're on alert status. No drill. Knew it was coming but not exactly when. Probably means a boring afternoon. But no matter, we can have lunch here. Matthieu, rustle up something from the canteen, will you?"

"Oui, mon Commandant."

And with that, Caisson threw his arm around Chartain's shoulder and led him into his office.

CHAPTER NINETEEN

When General Finch uttered the word "Eurostar," an apoplectic silence gripped the conference room. The Heathstone men, unaware of the food chain of evidence the lawmen brought to the table, thought it quizzical that everyone's jaw dropped in unison—and remained silent.

Salisbury's and Bloom's minds were racing like tandem computers, running in parallel as they sorted through the permutations and combinations of different avenues of attack to bring the Eurostar train to a screeching halt. They both knew they had only minutes—if not seconds—to intervene before this devil's brew headed out of the country at lightning speed.

"Security," Bloom croaked, barely more than a whisper. "There has to be a security team on-board."

"And someone in charge," echoed Salisbury as he hyperventilated, turning to Finch. "Who is in charge of security for the transport to Lyon?"

"Uh, why a man from the Ministry. Chap named Davies."

"Get him on the phone," ordered Salisbury.

The general, unused to taking orders and particularly not from civilians, reluctantly turned to his aide and said, "Go to my office and retrieve Davies' number from the transport document. It's in my safe. Call me here for the key—"

"*NOW!*" roared Salisbury. "Get your bloody arse down there yourself, or I'll have you broken down to a subaltern before I throw you in jail for the rest of your life. And don't think that uniform will save you. Now move!"

Finch looked like he'd just taken a rather generous one up the ass as he stood and executed a hurried strategic withdrawal with his aide.

Salisbury was already gripping his cell phone, as if trying to strangle it. "Central Dispatch, this is Assistant Superintendent Salisbury. Patch me through to the Eurostar security office, immediately! There is an active threat in progress."

The Eurostar controller watched the illuminated flat panel display of the string of lights showing the progress of the Eurostar under the Chunnel. At the hash mark in the middle he breathed a sigh of relief and turned to the MOD contingent and said, "Looks like you chaps can call it a day. Handoff completed to Chantilly Central."

One of the MOD blokes punched a number into a special encrypted cell phone and put it to his ear. "You've got it? . . . Right, then . . . very well. We will stand down." He killed the connection and turned to the controller. "Well, looks like you won't have us underfoot any longer. Our work is done here. Anyplace you can recommend for a spot of lunch?"

The chain of command for a Eurostar train is a bit different than you'd think. The person who is responsible for all aspects on-board is known as the Train Manager, or "T.M." Technically, the engineer reports to the T.M., but the engineer's station is so computer driven and in-sync with the command center that his interaction with the T.M. is less than with central control. That leaves the T.M. to run the steward staff, the on-board maintenance engineer, the kitchen staff, and the on-board security officer.

In the compartmentalization of information that the Ministry of Defence loved to embrace, the T.M. had been told next to nothing about the security car on the train he was responsible for, except that the usual security man had been dispensed with and replaced with a special team with whom he had virtually no contact.

The Train Manager—one Leonard Gaines—had eight years experience with British Rail before transferring to Eurostar. He was more than a little miffed his train had been commandeered by a bunch of nameless gorillas over whom he had no control. But, one followed orders. He was standing at the bar going over a clipboard with the liquor inventories when a feminine hand enveloped his upper arm and gave it a little squeeze. He turned to see a ravishing redhead in a white velour jumpsuit. Her smile was disarming as she said, "Excuse me, but I wondered if you could help me."

"Uh, why, of course, madam. What is it?"

She crooked her finger and leaned forward in a conspiratorial way, and being a tall bloke, Leonard had to bow slightly to enable her to whisper into his ear. "There seems to be a bit of a problem with the loo in my car. I wondered if you might come and have a look." She was close enough that her hair brushed against his face and he inhaled the scent of her high-octane perfume. Then she pulled away much more slowly than she had to, as if with reluctance.

To the T.M., a loo problem never looked so good. Ordinarily he'd just buzz the maintenance engineer, but for this damsel in distress he'd handle it personally. "Why, of course, madam.

Rest assured we'll put it right."

"Would you? How sweet. Come, let me show you." And she gave Leonard another squeeze on the upper arm that sent an electric surge down his spine.

Séverine flipped through her third magazine, then looked out the window into the blackness of the Chunnel going past. The woman across from her was starting to get a little tiresome as she waxed on about her third grandchild who was such a brainiac, and so well-behaved.

Then she noticed a redheaded woman leading a uniformed Eurostar man down the aisle and into the next car and, thinking nothing of it, she returned to her magazine.

Peter Hereford looked over at the Major. His head was leaned back against the cushion and his eyes were closed. That didn't seem right. He went to stand up, but found his arms and legs didn't want to respond. He felt the crushing onset of sleep. Then the steward appeared. Standing over him with a smile. With an incredible effort, Hereford managed to move his hand under his windbreaker to touch his 9mm. But the Steward's hand closed over his and gently moved it away, saying, "There, there, now. You go on and have yourself a nice sleep. I'm going to need to borrow this." And he withdrew the Glock and placed it with the others in the Eurostar zipper bag he was carrying. Standing in the aisle, he admired his handiwork. The entire car sleeping like babies. The fact that he had neutralized Britain's finest SAS men with a round of lemon squash was most gratifying.

But no time to tarry, he had to make it up to the engineer's cockpit straightaway.

"Here 'tis," said Fayla as she pushed open the accordion door. "Doesn't seem to be flushing right." She stepped back and let the Train Manager enter the cramped lavatory, which was much like you would find in an airliner.

"Let's have a look," he said helpfully. He leaned over and raised the toilet seat. And that's when he simultaneously heard a small pop, like a bubble of chewing gum exploding, together with a bee sting on his neck. He slapped the patch of skin on his neck and spun round, seeing the woman return something into the pocket of her jumpsuit. He started to protest, but then felt woozy and grabbed onto the doorframe for support.

She leaned into him, grabbing his belt and gently pushing him backward as his knees gave way and he wound up sitting on the toilet. "There, there, Ducky. Off to dreamland you go." And she folded his arms and leaned him against the bulkhead. Then she eased out of the lavatory and took a small gummed label from her pocket. She peeled off the backing and stuck it on the door. The label read: TEMPORARILY OUT OF SER-VICE. WE APOLOGIZE FOR THE INCONVENIENCE.

Just then Mickey McDrew entered the car. Their eyes locked, she nodded, and he resolutely headed toward the cockpit as he handed her one of the Glocks wrapped in a hand towel.

Wearily, Emil Broussard looked up and estimated that he was twenty meters from the summit. Once more he swung the ice axe into a crevasse and hit something unexpected. "What the . . . ?" He withdrew the ice axe with a plastic cube attached. It was about a meter for each dimension and was extremely light, fashioned on one side to be identical to the rock face of the cliff. He shook it off the blade of his axe and watched it on the long fall to the floor below. He reached up with the axe and dislodged another cube, then another, which provided an opening one meter tall by three meters wide. Not having seen this coming he hesitated, then scrambled through the opening.

The U.K. Eurostar controller was watching the train in question move toward the Chunnel exit when the phone to the security office buzzed. "Chilton," he answered.

"This is the security office. I have some high-level Scotland Yard official on the line. I'm putting him through."

"Hello. This is Eurostar Central Control. To whom am I speaking?"

"This is Assistant Superintendent Salisbury of Scotland Yard. We have an active terrorist threat on the Eurostar train bound for Lyon."

"Oh, the one the security team was here for?"

"Yes. Let me speak with the head of the team, quickly!"

"Well, I'm afraid that's not possible."

"What!"

"Well, the train, you see, has been handed off to French control. The security team that was here stood down and left a few minutes ago."

"Then patch me through to the French control station."

"Well, I can call them, of course, but I can't transfer an outside call to them. You'll have to call them directly."

Grayson Salisbury wanted to scream in frustration as he bellowed, "Get me that number!"

Just then General Finch reappeared and placed a piece of paper on the table in front of Salisbury. "Andrew Davies' cell number." Frantically he punched in the number and endured an excruciating pause before receiving a voicemail introduction.

The Eurostar bullet train roared out of the Chunnel and onto French soil. David Hazeltine had long experience in the engineer's cockpit of the Eurostar. He knew all the computer readouts, but he also had that intuitive feel for the machine with a gazillion moving parts. Carefully he pushed up the speed from 90 mph in the Chunnel toward its top cruising speed, merging onto the rails that would bypass the Calais-Fréthun station, as it was an express to Paris. After one stop at Gare du Nord it was on to Lyon. He was curious about what the cargo was in the security car at the rear, but was told it was none of his affair. Only that he was here today because he was the best driver in the organization. So drive.

He brought the throttle up to 133 mph and navigated a few gentle curves on the flat coastal plain before the tracks straightened out for the high-speed run towards Paris. He pushed it up to 180 mph, then gave the instruments a once-over and engaged the autopilot.

The British Ministry of Defence representative watched the illuminated lights on the flat panel display in the Chantilly Eurostar control room depicting the progress of the security train. He punched in the number on the special phone set up for him. He was trying to reach the team leader on-board, but there was no answer. He tried the other members of the team, also without success. "I cannot reach my team," he said to the controller. "Ring up the men inside the security car."

"Oui," replied the controller. He fiddled with the phone, than handed it to the MOD man, who said, "This is Jeffers at the Chantilly station. I can't reach the security team. Is everything all right in the security car?"

"Roger that. But as you know we're cut off from everyone but you. Better assume something's up. Keep us informed."

"Right-o. Stay on the line." He turned to the controller. "Get the bloody Train Manager on the horn."

The controller punched in more numbers on a train comm line, then said, "No one is picking up. But that's not unusual. He may be away from his station at the moment. I can ring the driver and ask him to raise the Train Manager on the internal train radio."

"Do it," ordered Jeffers.

The controller grabbed another handset and waited for a pickup, then said, "Chantilly control here. Are you having any problems on-board? . . . No? You are certain? . . . Very well. Will you page the Train Manager or send a steward to fetch him and have him report in to me immediately? And notify us at once of any suspicious activity. Do you understand?"

"Yes. Certainly. I understand," said the driver, and he hung up the handset as a bead of sweat trickled down his cheek and onto the barrel of the Glock automatic held under his chin by Mickey McDrew.

"Nicely done," said Mickey. "You see, we've already taken out their security team and that prick of a Train Manager, and we knew of course that the next call would be to you. Now then, you must understand that we're going to be spending the day together. Follow my instructions precisely and you'll walk away intact. One little fudge and your kneecap is gone. Two fudges and you are gone. Got it?"

The driver nodded vigorously.

"That's a good pig-o. Now then, to business. You're to bring the train to a halt precisely six miles south of the Lille-Europe station. And since this bugger takes five miles to stop at this speed, you best get the math right. If you get it wrong, I'll have no further use for you."

And to make sure he got the point, Mickey raked the barrel of the Glock across the driver's teeth.

Helmut Kruger came down on one knee and leaned over the sniper who was lying prone on the camouflaged sniper pad peering through the scope. He'd arrived by private helicopter not ten minutes before.

"Do you have it zeroed in?"

"Jawohl, Herr Oberst."

"*Gut.* I buy you a lager you take each one with a single shot."

"Done," said the sniper. Kruger rose, dusted off his Eurostar maintenance jumpsuit, and looked at his watch. Timing was critical now. And they would have to move with speed and precision. Which was fine with Helmut. He liked speed and precision. It was in his DNA. Just then his cell phone jingled and he answered, "Ja?"

"This is your star pupil," came Fayla's voice. "The train is ours. Be ready to come on-board."

"*Ausgezeichnet!*"

Jeffers was getting frantic. "Why hasn't the bugger called? My security team is still off-line. Better call him again."

Just then a phone line winked and the controller grabbed it. "Oui?" He listened for a few moments, then handed it to Jeffers, saying, "Someone from Scotland Yard, for you."

He grabbed it and said, "Jeffers."

"This is Assistant Superintendent Salisbury with Scotland Yard. We have information of an imminent threat to the Eurostar train from Heathstone Arsenal. Alert your security team immediately."

"Uh, well, there's a problem there. I've been trying to raise them, but they are not responding."

"Not responding?"

"No, sir. Can't raise them."

"Then take whatever measures you have to, but stop that train in its tracks! Alert the French authorities to secure the train. My team and I will arrive shortly."

"Right," replied Jeffers as he turned to his French counterpart. "Stop the train and secure it. Something's afoot."

Alain Dassault from the French Defense Ministry nodded and gave the order, but the quizzical controller squinted at the screen and said, "It, uh, seems to be stopping on its own."

"What?"

"It has come off autopilot and is decelerating rapidly."

"Jetzt!" **ordered Helmut**. "Take it down!"

The sniper squeezed the trigger on his Weatherby .223 and the small video camera perched on the fence post disintegrated. He quickly shifted position and the second quickly followed suit.

"The fence," ordered Helmut.

The explosives expert hit the hand plunger and a staccato of little pops echoed through the forest, allowing a section of fence to fall away.

"What the . . . ?"

"What is it?" asked Dassault.

The controller pointed. "The video feed from the section of track that the Eurostar is approaching—it just went black. And so did the cockpit video feed!"

A light buzzed and the controller tapped on his keyboard. "There is an intrusion on that section of fence!"

Séverine felt the train decelerating and looked up from her magazine. That was odd. She'd taken this express before and knew it didn't stop until Paris. And just then a voice came over the loud speaker.

"Ladies and gentlemen, this is the Train Manager speaking. We apologize for the inconvenience, but I have been advised by the driver that one of the locomotive's magnetos is indicating a malfunction. In the interest of your safety we are bringing the train to a halt to allow an engineering team to come aboard and repair the equipment. Hopefully the delay will be brief and we'll be on our way shortly." The statement was repeated in appalling French.

Séverine thought nothing of it until she heard the steward at her elbow murmur, "Huh, that wasn't the T.M."

She tugged at his sleeve. "What do you mean?"

"Nothing, I'm sure. It's just that the announcer sounded like Jeremy, one of the other stewards. Not the Train Manager."

A faint alarm bell went off in her subconscious.

"So, where is the Train Manager?"

"Can't say, really. Been looking for him myself. Oh, maybe he'll know."

"He? He who?"

"Rupert. Our maintenance engineer. Say, Rupe, what's with the magneto or whatever?"

The dumpy looking man coming up the aisle shrugged. "It's news to me. Can't raise the T.M. or the driver on my radio. Trying to track him down."

The subconscious alert was working itself to the surface now.

The train came to a complete stop, and waiting alongside the track were eight men wearing identical Eurostar maintenance jumpsuits—and behind them was a gaping hole in the protective fence.

Peptides emptied into Séverine's bloodstream. Her mind

raced like a rabbit caught in a snare. All eight men were cut from the same cloth: lean, hard, athletic—in other words, military. Her mind went into hyperdrive. Eight men. Eighteen cars. They would face a gap initially. Maybe she had time to sound an alarm. She shoved her hand into her purse and retrieved her cell phone and scrolled to the speed dial for the one person she knew had a security role for the Eurostar.

Chapter Twenty

Emil Broussard stayed in a low crouch and allowed his eyes to adjust to the darker environ of the—what? A cave? A tunnel? He felt the various plastic cubes that plugged the opening, which from the other side must now look like the cliff face was smiling with a couple of missing teeth. He decided not to disturb any more of the cubes and started to make his way up the tunnel carved from the rock—at least as far as the limited light would allow. He took two steps and promptly bashed his shins on something and fell to the stone floor.

He moaned while grabbing his leg and looked down to see the obstacle that had felled him. It was a pair of small, narrow gauge rails. They extended about fifteen meters into the tunnel, which was quite wide but not very high. He followed the rails deeper into the cavity and could just barely make out some long object against one wall, covered in a tarpaulin. He passed it by and continued on until the light was almost too faint . . . until he reached out and touched something man-made and metallic—a door, or rather something akin to a hatch. It had no knob, but a lever-like gizmo with a handle you raised from its receptacle.

He listened, but heard nothing. So he gulped, said a silent

Hail Mary from his Catholic upbringing, and gently eased the lever up. No sound was made, but the hinges could be a different story. He softly pulled it inward two inches and peered through the crack. More tunnel, but this was a lighted passageway with a concrete floor. He eased it open wider and cringed when the hinges gave a mild protest. But now he had an opening and stepped through.

Grayson Salisbury let the cell phone drop from his grasp with a clatter and covered his face with his hands. Never had he felt so impotent. For all the Herculean effort, the painstaking detective work, the lack of sleep, the stress and the politics, they had come up ten minutes short. "We are too late," he said finally. "They've neutralized the security team and have halted the train. The French have mobilized their SAS types, but I would venture they've got a way around that." There was a silent pause, then the ham hock fist came down on the table like a hammer. "*Ten bloody minutes*! If we'd had ten bloody minutes we could have stopped them on this side of the Channel!"

In the face of such ferocity, no one wanted to venture; but Bloom knew they couldn't raise the white flag just yet.

"Grayson, we all share your frustration. I'm not sure what we can do, but we're pretty useless here. Can you call the prime minister and get us some rapid transport to the scene? Maybe there's a way to head this off."

A sigh. "You're right, Gideon. Neville, you, Anthony, and Arthur stay here in case we need information from the arsenal. Arthur, hand me the phone and let's get the hell out of this devil's workshop."

Philippe Caisson and Marc Chartain shared a belly laugh over some bread, cheese, wine, and one of Caisson's more ribald tales. It was quite the tonic the older man needed. Nothing like a testosterone-laced barracks with good company, canteen food, and cheap wine.

Chartain shook his head. "How did you build such a library? I've never heard you tell the same story twice."

Both men had their feet up on Caisson's desk as he clasped his hands behind his neck and stretched. "Rigorous research, Colonel. You can do wonders with the Internet. Like the one about the two flics in Marseilles who—"

The cell phone on his desk chirped. He picked it up. "*Allo?*"

He listened for a moment, then eyed Chartain and said, rather awkwardly, "Well, this is quite a surprise—particularly at this moment—"

Chartain saw Caisson's face turn white as he whispered, "Mon Dieu!"

Just then Matthieu, the clerk, burst in. "Captain! You have an alert-five call coming in on your console!"

"Stand by, Séverine," he said and he put his cell phone down before reaching behind him to grab a buzzing handset on the credenza.

Without hesitation, Chartain grabbed the cell phone and gasped, "Séverine?"

"Marc?"

"Oui. I am here with Philippe. What is happening?"

"I am on the Eurostar train headed for Paris. The train is stopped, and I think we're being commandeered by hijackers disguised as Eurostar engineers."

"Where is the train at this moment?"

"Southbound, somewhere north of Paris," she said, then added, "The train is starting to move again."

Caisson dropped the headset. "Matthieu! Scramble the choppers and the Eurostar detachment. This is not a drill. Squad leaders to the Com Center!" He motioned for Chartain to follow and took his cell phone back.

As they headed out of Caisson's office, Chartain grabbed Matthieu by the arm and pulled him along.

"Matthieu, is my room still in the barracks?"

"Oui, mon Colonel."

"Grab my assault gear and meet me at the helicopter pad."

Séverine slipped the cell phone inside her boot as a Eurostar "engineer" entered the car carrying a Schmeisser and a grim smile. "Good afternoon, ladies and gentleman," he said with a Westphalian accent. "I confess I am not a member of the Eurostar staff, but my colleagues and I now control the train. As long as you comply with our instructions, no one will be harmed. Understood?"

Heads bobbed up and down.

"Excellent. Now then, I need all of you to get up and move two cars down. It will be a bit more cozy, but leave all purses, baggage, and cell phones behind. So move along. . . . *Now!*"

Four of the "engineers" entered the next-to-last car carrying a footlocker. As rehearsed, two of them took it to the security car while the other two took out a bunch of handcuffs and began securing the lemon-squashed security team to their chairs.

The two carrying the footlocker entered the narrow passageway of the security car. It was well choreographed as they halted halfway and opened the box. One of the men took out a small collapsible platform and deployed it next to the wall. The other pulled out two small tanks connected to hoses that terminated at a welder's torch.

One of the men stood on the platform, donned welder's goggles and gloves, opened the oxygen and acetylene valves, and flicked the flint starter in front of the nozzle. A foot-long flame roared out of the torch and the welder adjusted the valves until an inch-long blue flame came out the tip at 3,000 degrees Celsius. He chose a spot about nine feet above the floor. This had been calibrated previously to insure the men inside could not easily reach the opening to employ their firearms against them.

In moments a saucer-shaped outline had been burned into the heavy gauge steel and rivulets of molten metal were running down the wall.

"This is the officer-in-charge of the Defence Ministry Threat Center," came the voice through the speaker. A second voice conferenced in with, "This is Alain Dassault of the Defense Ministry at the Eurostar control center in Chantilly."

Caisson hit the transmit button on his microphone. "This is the commandant of EPIGN with the TGV hostage rescue detachment."

The faceless voice of the Defence Ministry Threat Center was clearly the senior man in charge. "Very well, Monsieur Dassault, what is the situation?"

"It appears the security team protecting the 'special cargo,' has been neutralized, as have the Eurostar staff. The train was brought to a standstill and the video feeds cut. An intrusion alarm indicated the protective fence had been breached. Then the train started moving again. Just as all this was happening, we received a call from Scotland Yard that a threat against the Eurostar train was imminent."

A groan came through the speaker.

Dassault continued, "The British have requested the train be halted and not be allowed to continue."

Caisson spoke up. "Sir, if I may interrupt, by happenstance one of the Squadron's people is on the train in question."

"Indeed?" said the O.I.C.

"Yes, sir. She called me just as the alarm was being sounded. She stated eight men disguised as Eurostar engineers boarded the train after it halted on the line."

"She?"

"Yes, sir. An extremely capable 'she,' if I may say so."

"Can you communicate with her?" asked Dassault.

"The cell connection went dead. If she can, I'm sure she will reestablish contact."

Dassault interrupted, "Wait a moment, we are receiving a communication from the train. I will put it on speaker."

Chartain listened intently as a female voice with an Irish accent came through the speaker. "Hello, Duckies! This is your new captain speaking."

CHAPTER TWENTY-ONE

Séverine sat down in the standard class car that was rapidly filling up as passengers of the sparsely loaded train were being shoe-horned into three cars—with an empty car between each occupied car. Each occupied carriage had an "engineer" posted at the upstream door, toting a submachine gun. Their eyes were dark, beady and bloodless; and Séverine knew the look. These were professional killers, not the hot-headed zealots likely to make a mistake. And they spoke German to each other. With this kind of meticulous planning it begged the question of who was behind this seizure. Then it dawned on her: there was something or someone on-board that they wanted. But who? Or what?

More passengers were forced into the car: retired tourists, a middle-aged business man, a mother with three small children, a pair of American college students. The initial shock was giving way to fear and apprehension. The mother looked beside herself. Séverine reached across the aisle and stroked the hair of one of the children.

"What is your name?"

"Pierre," he answered, somewhat bewildered.

"Well then, Pierre, these are bad men. We may be here

awhile, but we should get through this. How old are you?"

"Ten."

"No talking!" yelled the nearest hijacker.

Séverine glared at him, then gently patted Pierre's shoulder and guided him back to his mother's embrace.

"Now do you understand me, Duckies? One little fekking deviation and we will start tossing hostages off the train like a flower girl."

"*Oui.* Yes," replied Dassault. "We will comply."

"That's a luv. Don't be too stupid to fek with us. Ta-ta for now."

There was silence until the O.I.C. said, "I am open to suggestions."

Ted Brighton and Marvin Stanley were two crack troops of the SAS. But now they were totally helpless. They had the open line to Eurostar Central and knew what was coming. They heard something like a water spigot, then up near the ceiling a tiny spit of molten metal popped out of wall, followed by small blue flame and a tiny stream of the detritus running down the wall.

Stanley keyed the mike, and said, "They're cutting through the wall with a torch."

Caisson and Chartain ran at the double time towards the four Panther Eurocopters spinning their rotor blades at idle. Matthieu was on the tarmac by the lead chopper, where he handed off a small duffel to Chartain as if he were a halfback.

The two men scrambled on-board and Caisson spun his

finger in the air, which the pilot acknowledged. He increased power and pulled up on the collective, causing the rotor blades to bite the air and take the Panther airborne.

Caisson put on the headphones as the pilot asked, "Where to, mon Commandant?"

"Crécy protocol on the Lyon line."

"Oui, mon Commandant."

Chartain put on a pair of headphones, then started pulling his assault gear out of the duffel as the other members of the team looked on curiously.

"I am allowing you to accompany us strictly as an observer, Colonel. Do I make myself clear?"

"Perfectly, Captain. So give me the brief."

While Chartain had trained with the Squadron and knew the troops in the chopper, the specifics of hostage rescue on the Eurostar line was not in his training portfolio.

Caisson explained the procedure as the Panther rose to cruising altitude and began racing to the intercept point. "There are certain points along the rail line where we have preplanned protocols. The hijackers have demanded the train continue from Paris to Avignon without stopping at Lyon. We will comply with this. Our assault team has enough lead time to get into position at a pre-selected point where we have rehearsed many times. Eurostar Central will cut power to bring the train to a stop where the assault team is in place. When the train halts, we will assess the situation as quickly as possible, then strike before they can react."

Just then Caisson's cell phone chirped, signaling receipt of a text message. He flipped it open and said, "It's from Séverine!" The message read:

8 MEN PROS

HEAVY ARMD

The turbofans of the Sidley-Hawker jet whined as they spooled up to full power and raced down the runway at Heathstone Arsenal. After the takeoff rotation, the steward said, "I am under instruction from the prime minister to offer whatever assistance I can."

"Communications," said Salisbury.

The steward slid open a panel next to Salisbury's elbow. "Satellite phone. You can dial normally. Push this button and you are connected to Number 10 comm center."

Salisbury ripped the receiver out and punched in the number to the Chantilly control station.

"Jeffers here."

"Situation?"

"Hijackers have demanded the train bypass Lyon to the Avignon line. The French are complying and have deployed their TGV hostage rescue team in advance of the train. Power will be cut and they are under orders to assault the train and secure the hostages."

"The cargo?" demanded Salisbury. "What about the package?"

"The hijackers are cutting through the wall with a torch."

A hammer clanged on the circle of steel that had been burned by the acetylene torch, and the hot metal disc fell into the security chamber. Ted Brighton knew what was coming next, but being SAS they were not going down without protest. He took careful aim with his Heckler & Koch and squeezed off several rounds. They sailed through the saucer-like hole and rattled around on the other side.

He was rewarded with a scream as the ricocheting bullet found a spot of flesh. But his success was short-lived as a cone-shaped object with a burning top was tossed through the hole.

He and Stanley knew exactly what it was because they used it in their line of work. "Oh, shit," he said. They dropped to the floor and curled into fetal positions, their forearms over their ears. However, the defensive posture really didn't matter as the flash-bang stun grenade detonated and the compression wave rendered the SAS troopers unconscious.

On the other side of the wall, Manfred Leinz held his bleeding side where the ricochet had taken a nip out of a rib. Angry now, he tossed in a gas canister, along with curses against the *Engländer*.

Emil Broussard peeked ever so carefully around the corner, but only saw an extension of what he'd traversed so far. A wide tunnel with craggy rock-hewn walls and a smooth concrete floor. Electric lights were hung in the fixtures that made them look like torches, and there was clearly a ventilation system. He'd come a short way from his entry point, and around the corner he saw the tunnel come to a T. Heart pounding, he softly stepped down to the junction and peeked to the left and right. To the left was a longer stretch of passageway that led to another corner, but also to open chambers off the corridor. In the distance he could faintly hear voices. To the right, the corridor terminated at an opening that led down to a stairway.

Broussard gulped, then turned left, treading softly. He came to the first opening and carefully looked around the corner. He was greeted by something that appeared to be a military-style barracks, with bunk beds and footlockers. There were, in fact, two men asleep while maybe twenty bunks remained empty in the dimly lit chamber. Gingerly he snuck by and approached the next opening. This was another passageway, but of smaller dimension, and it appeared to be a common hallway to a suite of offices.

The next one opened to what appeared to be a communication center. One man, his back to the doorway, was wearing a black jumpsuit and had a pair of headphones covering his ears as he thumbed through a German sports magazine.

Broussard eased past, knowing he was getting deeper into the snare, and approached another corner and looked to the left. Here was a large viewing window grafted into the rock wall. He tiptoed forward and looked in—or down, rather—where he saw a laboratory the size of a gymnasium with several space-suited figures moving about. There was a range of lab equipment—centrifuges, microscopes, Petri dishes, and the like—and several large aluminum canisters where the lab androids were packing items . . . for transport?

There was a large hatchway at the end of the passageway, and Broussard heard and saw the wheel spin, which told him it was time for a strategic retreat. He hastened back the way he'd come—past the comm center, the office suite, and the barracks—and sought refuge around the corner, his heart pounding in his chest.

Catching his breath, he couldn't help but wonder, Where did all this come from? Who had chiseled or blasted a warren of tunnels into an inaccessible fortress? And why? Carving up a mountain was no small feat of engineering. Indeed, it was a massive undertaking. And how long had it been here? What the devil was going on in that laboratory? No good, of that Broussard was certain. But what was the purpose of this . . . this . . . whatever *this* was? Again, it occurred to him that it might be one of the Swiss Army's various redoubts sprinkled through the Alps, and if he didn't know better, he would've guessed that was what it was. But he hadn't seen so much as a Swiss Army knife, so ownership was up in the air.

So, next step? Hightail it out of here while his head was still attached to his shoulders and reconnect with Bloom and see what forces they could muster? Or dig for more evidence? The stairwell at the other end of the corridor seemed to beckon him. He took a deep breath, then crossed over and started a descent down the poorly lit circular metal steps. He came to another hatchway that was slightly ajar. He listened.

Silence.

He pushed gently and the hinges gave without a sound.

The scene that greeted Broussard was shocking in its contrast. The lighting was better, but not by much. He was at the apex of a wide, spiral marble staircase chiseled into the wall that led down to a kind of narthex. The walls were not exposed rock, but had been covered with a veneer of smooth Italian marble, with scenes of knights with lances on horseback, knights in sword play, and various Teutonic coats of arms carved in relief. Carefully, he made his way down to the bottom, where a massive oaken double door waited. On each door was a giant S etched in the form of a lightning bolt which, when put together, formed the dreaded insignia of the *SS*.

Broussard approached, at once horrified and fascinated by what he might find on the other side. Deftly, he pulled one of the doors open and stepped inside. At first, he didn't quite know what to make of it. It was a chamber, maybe ten meters square, lined with marble. The bulk of the chamber contained a circular platform raised a couple of steps from the floor, and around the platform rose a series of ornate columns that stretched to the high ceiling. Tentatively, he took the two steps up to the platform and inspected the floor. Inlaid in the marble was a mosaic that formed swastika-like patterns. And then it dawned on him: this was some kind of twisted temple where who knew what kind of ceremonies were performed.

On the far side was another double door, this one of black ebony with the Latin *SANCTUS* carved in Germanic script.

By now Broussard's fight-or-flight instincts were screaming, *"flight!"* with great resonance as sweat soaked his shirt. But he was, at his core, a detective, and the door called to him like a siren's song. He moved closer to the ebony door, then carefully tried the handle. It responded and he pulled it open a crack. He listened carefully and his tympanic membrane picked up a low electric hum—but no voices. He peered through the slit and could only make out a rock wall that was reflecting a weak, flickering light. He eased the door open further and ventured a look inside that made it stupefyingly clear he'd reached the black heart of a hellish beast.

The proportions were of a small cathedral where the exposed rock face towered up each side into a Gothic arch, with gas flames burning at the end of simulated torches implanted in the walls. Suspended above the transept hung a golden eagle of mammoth proportions, with a swastika clutched in its talons. A center aisle led along the floor up to an altar—on either side of which stood rows of pedestals, each supporting a coffin-like object that glowed with a ghostly light. They were arranged in herring-bone fashion, guiding the eye up the aisle to where a single coffin rested under the unforgiving gaze of the eagle.

Numb with fear and curiosity, Broussard stepped closer to one of the coffins and saw that the glass was lined with frost. He'd visited Moscow once and seen Lenin's tomb. It was similar in many respects, but he realized each coffin's pedestal housed some kind of refrigeration unit. And the face that was entombed looked as if it were frozen.

Overwhelmed, he made his way up the aisle, feeling the cold more acutely the deeper he went. A few of the coffins were dark and empty, and as he approached the altar, he saw that the final three on each side were not of gray metal, but of what appeared to be silver, with raised Germanic lettering on the side that was like a silent roll call from hell—Bormann,

Goebbels, Hess, Schellenberg, Göring, Himmler. He took note that the Schellenberg coffin was among the dark and empty.

With trepidation he paused at the steps of the altar, looking up at the lozenge-shaped gold coffin with the raised letters: *FÜHRER.*

With a feeling that went beyond the surreal, he mounted the steps and peered through the frost-framed glass at the frozen image that had harvested so much blood and death in this world. Albeit frozen, even here the trademark smudge of a moustache was distinct.

Broussard shook his head, unable to absorb what was right before his eyes. He knew his history: the Führer had shot himself in the bunker and his body burned along with Eva Braun's; Himmler had been captured by the Allies at war's end disguised as a workman and had taken a cyanide pill—as had Göring on the morning of his scheduled execution; and Hess died an old man at Spandau.

Was he in some kind of macabre dream? With a shaking hand, he reached out to touch the gold lettering—and at that moment a bank of blinding klieg lights came on and a surprisingly cheerful voice from behind resonated in the cathedral, saying, "Good afternoon, Inspector! And welcome to Wewelsburg Fortress!"

CHAPTER TWENTY-TWO

Grayson Salisbury stared out the window of the jet as the French coast approached. "How bloody stupid," he said to himself.

"What's stupid?" asked Bloom.

Salisbury sighed. "I can't believe those MOD idiots put that kind of weapon on a civilian form of transport. Should have been a military convoy. Armed to the teeth."

Bloom replied, "Quite frankly, Grayson, I don't think it would've made any difference."

"No difference?"

"We are dealing with an organization with resources and intelligence capabilities beyond anything I've ever experienced. If it had been a convoy, they would have found a way to strike just the same. They penetrated the most secret facility in Britain. Maybe they have a source inside Interpol. Maybe even in the Yard. In a normal world, traveling stealthily on the Eurostar may have made sense. At any rate, they'd have found a way to strike no matter how it was transported."

Salisbury didn't respond, his shoulders sagging.

"Oh, dear, luvie, that's a nasty scratch," observed Fayla.

Manfred Leinz pulled the torch away and said, "Nothing serious, Fräulein. It is bandaged and we will continue."

"How long?"

"The wall is quite thick, and we have to have a large enough window to extract the package. At this pace I would say ninety minutes. Maybe more. That will keep us on the timetable," added Helmut.

"See that it does," ordered Fayla, and she turned to leave.

Helmut instinctively brought his heels together. "Jawohl, Fräulein." The General had given him precise instructions to follow Fayla's lead, but the General had also given him explicit confidential orders to do nothing to jeopardize the mission. Beyond that, they were to take whatever measures were necessary to ensure the physical safety of the woman, as she was no longer considered expendable.

Put another way, the General was telling him this red-haired lass was to be the new Empress of the Fourth Reich.

The four Panther Eurocopters skimmed over the treetops of the Gallic countryside on a beeline for the intercept point outside the small village of Crécy. Chartain listened through his headphones as Caisson sifted through information with Alain Dassault at the Eurostar control room.

"Current position of the Eurostar?" asked Caisson.

"Entering the northern outskirts of Paris. Speed, over two hundred kilometers per hour. Switch has been made to bypass the Gare du Nord station."

Caisson did the math in his head. "That's about forty-five minutes to the Crécy intercept point."

Dassault said, "I have been advised by the Ministry that the train is not to be allowed to continue. Safeguard the passengers as best you can, but the train is to be seized and the hijackers captured, or killed, if necessary."

He made it sound so easy. Caisson said, "We have received a message from our person inside that there are eight heavily armed professionals on-board. This is not an untrained zealot with a pipe bomb."

"You have your orders, Captain."

Caisson met Chartain's gaze, both thinking, *Bureaucrats. You gotta love 'em.*

Emil Broussard turned slowly to see the personage of Leopold Mainz standing inside the doorway, flanked on each side by two hard-looking men with Schmeisser machine pistols trained on him.

"I must say, you are quite persistent. We had you under surveillance ever since you left my residence this morning. A most impressive climb, I might add."

The naked fear aside, Broussard found himself somewhat disarmed by Mainz's casual manner.

"In a backhanded way this is something of an honor, Inspector. You are the first guest—albeit uninvited—we have ever had at Wewelsburg Fortress. I'm sure you have many questions and, although time is pressing, I will do my best to satisfy your curiosity. Come, let me enlighten you." He approached and joined Broussard on the Führer altar. Looking down, Schellenberg's tone was reminiscent of an exasperated offspring dealing with an aging, cantankerous parent.

"Ah, Adolph. He missed such an incredible opportunity." Schellenberg swept with his arm in a grand gesture. "You see all of this, Inspector? The genesis of it began on the outskirts of Moscow. You are too young to remember, but the Wehrmacht was advancing toward Moscow. It was ours for the taking. In one move we could have taken the head off that snake Joseph Stalin, and Europe would have been completely ours. But as the advance of Operation Barbarossa was unfolding beautifully, even with the early onset of winter, the Führer here—whose military judgment had proven to be so prescient in the conquest of France—ordered the advancing thrust to split, one north to Leningrad and the other south to Stalingrad. Why? For some inexplicable reason, he said his true mission was for more *Lebensraum*—living space—for the German people.

"So for two weeks the Wehrmacht was going north and south, then he changed his mind *again* and ordered them to backtrack, regroup, and head for Moscow. By that time a fearsome winter had set in, and the Russian reinforcements from the Pacific Coast had arrived because the Japanese refused to land an invasion force to hold down the Soviets in Eastern Siberia. That freed up the Russians to travel west in the defense of Moscow.

"On December 6, the Wehrmacht was in sight of Moscow when the battle was joined and German forces were encircled by the Russian horde. And then on December 7, instead of holding down the Russians in Siberia, the Japanese attacked Pearl Harbor and brought America into the war with a vengeance. So, by year's end 1941, I knew it was over, and so did Heinrich." He gestured to the frozen coffin next to the altar. "So we began to take measures to preserve the Reich and its ideals when Germany ultimately fell. And that is what this is all about."

Broussard's only response was to gawk at the whole scene as he mumbled, "But how did you accomplish all this?"

Schellenberg couldn't help but be a little flush with himself, now that he had an appreciative audience. "I'm glad to see you are impressed. Let me tell you about it. . . ."

On August 26, 1346, the pivotal battle of the Hundred Years War was fought on the plain of the French countryside, where Edward III faced off with King Philip VI of France.

The French were arrayed with armor and lances on horse-back, while the English formed a wedge of longbowmen who proceeded to mow down wave after wave of the charging Frenchmen at long range. After eleven mounted charges, what was left of the French army retired from the field, which was near a small village name Crécy.

However, there was a second Crécy, unrelated to the bat-tlefield, and this was a small town south of Paris where the Eurostar line snaked through the farmland and forest of north central France on its way to Dijon (of mustard fame).

The Panthers put down in a field next to the treeline of a forest. Each helicopter disgorged its complement of Squadron troopers, plus Chartain, and they headed out at the double time into the woods without a word from Caisson. The protocol had been rehearsed multiple times and every man knew his task.

They soon came to the rise just outside the massive Eurostar fence. Sergeant Major Pascal Rocard motioned to the two ord-nance men, who quickly found the hidden wires leading to the fence. They attached the leads to the hand plungers, then played out the wire and took position behind the trees.

The rise in the landscape sloped sharply down to the fence that cordoned off the dual rail lines of the Eurostar. There was a ten-meter swath on either side of the rail lines that was cleared of all trees, foliage and cover. The site was selected for an assault because of the positions it offered to snipers to fire above the fence, and the cover it provided the rest of the assault team. Most hijackings are by radicals who have little or no experience in such matters. So usually the methods employed by the assault teams tend to be applied very early—before the hijackers are aware an assault is underway—or after a long, drawn-out and fruitless negotiation that would leave the hijackers tired, with slow reaction times, or even asleep.

Caisson knew the protracted version was off the boards, and that for the Crécy protocol to work the Eurostar had to be halted precisely at this assault point. It had been practiced multiple times, but . . . He switched on his tactical radio and ran through the roll call. "Snipers?"

"One in place and laid in," replied a voice.

"Roger that on Two."

"And Three."

"Assault team One?" radioed Caisson.

"In place," came the response.

Four more responded similarly.

While Caisson was working the team, Chartain punched in a text message to Séverine:

CRECY PROTOCOL
TEAM IN PLACE

The assault protocol called for the power to be cut at precisely the correct moment to bring the train to a halt in front of them. Observers would quickly diagnose the situation, zeroing in on the hijackers, then on the commander's order, the snipers would lay down cover fire. They would blow the fence, and the assault teams would race across the open space and yank the emergency lever to open the sliding access door. The number one man would duck inside and do the same thing to the internal sliding door to the cabin, while number two tossed in the flash-bang stun grenade. After detonation the commandos would enter with their HKs and sweep the car, killing any remaining hijackers.

It was all choreographed with the precision of a ballet, but it required the Eurostar to halt at just the right spot.

Caisson punched in the speed dial on his cell to the Eurostar central control room, and it was immediately answered by Alain Dassault.

"Oui?"

"The assault team is in place," said Caisson. "Stop the train."

"The train is moving at 283 kilometers per hour. Our engineer is doing the math now. Stand by said Dassault. "Cutting power . . ."

Chartain heard the electric hum in the line spool down as he received a reply, then grabbed Caisson's elbow and shoved the screen in his face.

DO NOT ASSAULT
DANGER

Chapter Twenty-Three

"You see, Inspector, I am sure you are familiar with the experiments we had conducted on concentration camp inmates on the human body's reaction to cold. We would immerse them in frigid water and study the reaction. Taken to cold enough temperatures they would, of course, freeze to death, but our scientists found something amazing at the cellular level. There was a very narrow range—two-tenths of a degree Celsius, to be precise—at which cellular and organ function slowed down to almost zero before freezing set in. If the body could be maintained at this exact temperature, it could remain in a state of hibernation, or suspended animation, for an indefinite period of time, because the oxygenation requirements at the cellular level drop to virtual zero. Then at the proper time the temperature could be brought back to normal, very slowly, and the subject resuscitated." Schellenberg gestured over the rows of coffin-like chambers. "Of course, it wasn't always perfect. Sometimes the equipment failed, sometimes the subject had other medical issues to which they succumbed. But this enabled us to preserve the cadre of key people to establish the Fourth Reich when the time and the means revealed themselves."

Dumbly, Broussard gestured to the silver coffin marked

Schellenberg. He asked, "How long have you been . . . ?"

"Resurrected? I was revived seven years ago under a set of criteria long established. Also, being 'on ice' for a half century, I did not wish to push my luck. Ha ha! But beyond that we've made some remarkable discoveries. Come, let me show you."

Broussard docilely followed Schellenberg back into the marble temple chamber. Dumbfounded, he mumbled, "How did you build all this?"

Schellenberg shrugged as if the answer was obvious. "Well, Switzerland was largely an annex of the Reich. Wait . . . did I say 'was'? Ha ha. With Colonel Masson's sponsorship, this was constructed under the auspices of the Swiss Army, and construction was completed before the war's end, actually. Perfect cover story, wouldn't you say? Our people were—and remain— liberally sprinkled throughout the Swiss intelligence service, the Army, the banks and, of course, the police force."

"But . . . Hitler . . . Himmler . . . your death . . . ?"

"Not terribly difficult when you come down to it, as long as you have sufficient foresight and planning time. The Arabs were not the first to come up with the idea of suicide bombers. Ever hear of the *kamikaze*? Plenty of zealots were willing to make the final sacrifice for a cause they believed in. In terms of candidates, there was selection, training, surgery, and so forth. Finalists received a personal interview with the Führer himself, and after that their commitment was total. Ever wonder why 'Adolf' went to the bunker in Berlin in the final phase of the war when he could have withdrawn his forces into the Bavarian Alps and fought on for another year or more? To let the Russians find the burned remains of a corpse, of course. And since the Russians were such a secretive bunch, it served our purposes perfectly."

As they passed the marble pedestal surrounded by columns, Schellenberg pointed. "I suppose I should explain that this fortress was designed to replicate, in many respects, Wewels-burg Castle in the Westphalian region of Germany. After we came to power, Heinrich took over the castle and had it revamped as a kind of Vatican to the knightly order of his *SS*. Heinrich, you see, was obsessed with the occult, which, quite frankly, I always thought was rather silly. But, he was the boss, so what could you do? In any case, he would hold *SS* investiture ceremonies in this kind of temple at Wewelsburg. Lots of chanting. Incense. That sort of thing. And we've even done some of that here with the younger recruits. But this is old news. I have something truly exciting to show you. Come along."

Broussard felt the muzzle of the Schmeisser in the small of his back pushing him forward.

David Hazeltine's upper lip and bridge were swollen like a melon, and hurt like hell; but the Glock in the small of his back was the focus of his attention. The cockpit access door slid open and Fayla entered.

"Is our pilot being a good boy?" she enquired,

"A regular Boy Scout," said Mickey.

"That's a luv. Just keep doing what you're doing, and you may get out of this with your head intact."

Just then the instruments blinked, and the feeling of deceleration was felt by them all.

"What was that?" demanded Mickey.

The driver ran his fingers over the instruments, then said, "Power's been cut. Battery current has kicked in to keep the instruments on."

Fayla sighed. "How predictable is that? Keep our Boy Scout in the saddle, Mickey, my luv. Power will be restored shortly." She put the small radio to her lips. "Helmut?"

"Ja?"

"Bring my favorite weapon to the middle hostage car. And have our dear passengers assume the position. It appears the Crécy protocol is in play."

"At once, Fräulein."

Marc Chartain heard its approach before it came into view. The kinetic energy of all those tons of steel decelerating filled the air with vibrations. He was reminded of stories about Native Americans tracking the great buffalo herds by literally putting their ear to the ground and feeling the rhythm of hoofbeats traveling through the earth.

His pulse throbbed. He'd watched his love face danger through binoculars once before, and now he was to do it again.

Fayla entered the first hostage car and scanned the apprehensive faces. She found one in an aisle seat. Maybe sixty-something. White patrician hair. British military moustache. Expensive blue wool pinstripe suit. She fixed on the tie and leveled the Glock at the bridge of his nose, saying, "Where did you go to school, Ducky?"

"Uh, what?"

She shoved the muzzle into his nose. "I *said*, where the fek did you go to school?"

"Uh, why, Eton."

"I thought so." She reached down and yanked the lapel of the suit open and looked at the label. "Ohhh my goodness. Huntsman tailors. I am impressed, Duck. You must be a managing director mucky muck of some kind. Born with a silver spoon up your arse. Don't tell me you're an Earl or something."

"Well, baronet, actually."

"*Woooo!*" Fayla howled. "This is my lucky day! You'll be purrrfect. Come along, Ducky. You're getting a free ticket off the train." And she yanked him out of the seat by his Eton tie.

"*Raus! Raus! Raus!*" shouted the German with the machine pistol. "All passengers stand up and extend your arms. Place them against the window. *Jetzt!* Now!"

Slowly, Séverine rose and leaned over to whisper to the boy next to her, "Stay behind me, Pierre."

The frightened boy nodded.

The cramped space made the entire exercise awkward in the extreme as Séverine leaned over her matronly travelling companion to place her palms on the window, hoping Marc had received her text.

Salisbury grunted into the air phone and slammed it down on the cradle. "Power has been cut so a French commando team can assault the train."

"Let's hope they can avoid 'collateral damage,'" replied Bloom.

"And that they recover the bloody package!"

Luc Gaston was sniper number two and was taking deep breaths to lower his pulse rate. He was a competitive biathlete— an athletic contest made in hell that combined cross-country skiing and target shooting. Those who competed in biathlons were perhaps the most adroit people in the world at lowering their heart rate, but at this moment even Gaston's pulse couldn't turn down. This was the real thing. Game day. Lying on his sniper pad he peered through his scope as the Eurostar engine slowly went past, followed by a series of empty cars. Then he panned his view, paused, and keyed his mike to whisper, "Commandant, we have a problem."

Caisson swore under his breath as he looked through his binoculars at the passengers, arms raised, pressed against the glass in a giant human shield. Frustrated, he said to Chartain, "No way the snipers can get a bead."

Chartain only half heard him, for he was looking squarely at Séverine. She knew the drill and was slowly shaking her head from side to side. "Hold off, Philippe! I see Séverine and . . . what now?"

The sliding door on the Eurostar car opened, and a middle-aged man in a blue pinstriped suit was shoved out. He pancaked on the rocky railbed with a thud. Behind him in the doorway appeared a red-haired woman wearing a white jumpsuit and a malevolent smile.

Fayla grinned down at him and yelled, "Run, Ducky, run! Pick your baronet ass up and run to the fence before I lose my patience!"

Stunned, winded, and wheezing from cracked ribs, the portly baronet heaved himself up and began a slow plodding trot toward the fence.

Fayla stepped back and held out her hand. Helmut placed the pistol grip of the rocket propelled grenade launcher into it, saying, "The safety is off." Helmut then opened the opposite door to vent the backwash of the thrust.

Fayla hefted the launch tube onto her shoulder and sighted in the baronet as he limped toward the fence. She put the crosshairs between his shoulder blades and slowly squeezed the trigger.

With an exhilarating *WHOOOOOSHH!!!* the RPG roared out of the tube and left a smoke trail that terminated at the baronet's back in a cataclysmic explosion. The riptide of the concussion wave disintegrated the baronet in a bloody fireball that sent his remains into the fence like so much strawberry jam.

Screams reverberated through the train, and Caisson yelled through the mike, "Hold your fire!" to quell the itchy trigger fingers on his team.

Fayla held out her hand and said, "Bullhorn." Helmut complied.

She keyed the mike and yelled, "Now listen to me you fekking froggies! You restore power in five minutes or we start tossing out one dead hostage every thirty seconds. We've got plenty of firepower and surprises in this train, and as of this moment the clock is ticking. So get on with it!

"Aging is a fascinating process," Schellenberg exuded as Broussard looked on. They were in a laboratory, but not one that required a spacesuit. "Most people think your skin and organs wear out over time, and they call it the aging process. Actually, for example, your epidermal skin is replaced every four weeks. This makes it clear that aging is triggered by something else. Through ground-breaking research at Stanford University by Doctors Stuart Kim and Marc Tatar, we have found that aging can be slowed and managed by manipulating signaling circuits within cells. We built on that research and have achieved an extraordinary breakthrough." He waved his hand and one of the lab assistants started a small inclined conveyor belt on the lab bench. There were two lab rats confined to individual chutes. One of them plodded along, continually bumping his rump on the bottom barrier, hardly able to keep up. The other one easily kept pace on the conveyor.

"Do you see?" asked Schellenberg.

Broussard nodded.

"One of them is old and decrepit; the other is youthful and full of vitality. And the surprising thing about it is they are from the same litter."

Broussard didn't quite get it at first—he'd been through a lot over the course of the day—but then it dawned on him, and he looked at Schellenberg incredulously, eliciting a grin from the smug Nazi.

"Exactly, Inspector. We have begun human trials, and if they prove successful, I am to be the first to receive this method of genetic manipulation to fool father time and retard to a severe degree—if not cease it all together—the aging process. I would say my resuscitation was timely, wouldn't you? You are perhaps seeing the beginning of the Reich without end."

Numbed by it all, the only thing Broussard could say was, "You are mad."

Schellenberg laughed. "Quite the contrary, Inspector, it is the world that has gone mad. Think of it. Everywhere you look there is chaos. And I am just the person to put it right. And I can take the longer view of things, you might say. Ha ha." He looked at his watch and sighed. "But I'm afraid we're out of time. A great pity, Inspector. I could have used a man of your talents. But, you chose your side and I chose mine. So I bid you farewell. I really must be going." He nodded to the gun-toting gorillas and two of them grabbed his arms.

He tried to struggle but he might as well have been caught in a vice. They dragged him as if he weighed no more than a child—back through the tunnel and to the chamber where he had first crawled into the mountain fortress. The two guards grabbed his ankles, and with him fighting for his life they gave him the heave-ho through the opening from whence he had come—then brushed the dust from their uniforms to the sound of a descending scream.

CHAPTER TWENTY-FOUR

The voice through the speaker said in monotone, "The president is in the air, along with the defense minister, returning from a conference in Singapore. The interior minister is recovering from a heart bypass operation, and the chief of the gendarmerie has informed us he considers this a Defense Ministry issue and will take his instructions from the prem—"

"We have two minutes!" yelled Alain Dassault.

The voice coming through the speaker would not be rushed. "The premier is, well, the premier, and for anything that does not involve a flattering press conference he has no interest . . . or spine, I might add. So the decision has been passed down to us, or more specifically, to you, Monsieur Dassault."

"*Me!*" shrieked Dassault.

"Exactly. As the Defense Ministry's man on the scene, you are to decide to assault the train or restore power."

Alain Dassault was a mid-level bureaucrat who was accustomed to deflecting responsibility of any kind. As sweat wilted his starched collar, he saw the clock gave him thirty seconds. Having the blood of hundreds of people on his hands was not in his job description. And in a voice that was little more than a croak, he said to the controller, "Restore power."

Séverine's arms were feeling the fatigue as her eyes searched the woods on the rise above the fence for the face of Marc Chartain. The phantom that he was would not allow himself to be seen, of course; but she knew he was there. She could sense his presence—once again, her protector. If there was any way, she knew he'd find a way to save her. Save them all.

What a bizarre way to come to grips with her own folly, she thought. Caught between two menacing batteries of weapons, it was here she realized that to possess the love of a man like that . . . she'd been the fool of fools.

So when she felt the car surge and begin to move, she let out an unbridled exhalation of relief, as did the rest of the passengers, but hers was also with the realization she'd finally found the true compass of her heart.

"*Setzen Sie sich!*" barked the hijacker. "Sit! No talking!"

Séverine complied and looked across at the little, ashenfaced Pierre.

Mickey McDrew tapped the back of the driver's neck with the Glock. "There you go, me bucko. Keep us on track to Avignon." Then he keyed his handheld radio and said, "Nicely done, Miss Fayla. Very nice, indeed."

"So glad you approve, Mickey me luv. Our driver behaving?"

"Like a gem."

"Wonderful," replied Fayla. Then she looked at Helmut and murmured, "You know, the General was right."

"In what way, Fräulein?"

"He said France was corrupt from top to bottom, and that he bought the secrets of the Crécy Protocol from a bureaucrat as though he was ordering a pair of trousers through a Harrods catalog."

Chartain watched the train disappear with a now familiar anguish. But his reverie was cut short as Caisson barked, "Back to the choppers!"

The detachment responded and double-timed back to the helicopters. Keeping apace, Chartain asked, "What now?"

Caisson replied, "Daisychain, or the sled."

Chartain was not familiar with either. "I don't know what you mean."

"No time now. Metz! Bouvain! Dormont! You're with me on the Daisychain."

The three hardened soldiers stopped in their tracks and turned white with an ethereal look that seemed to say, "You can't be serious."

The one named Bouvain ventured, "You mean, for real, mon Commandant?"

"It is either that or the sled."

Hearing "the sled," Bouvain and the others came unstuck and clambered into the fourth helicopter with the wedge on the underbelly. Chartain started to climb in, but Caisson put a hand on his chest. "No, Colonel. The aircraft cannot handle the added weight. You go with Sergeant Major Rocard in chopper one."

Chartain climbed on-board the other Panther, and all four choppers spooled up to full power. Chartain clapped on Caisson's headset and flicked to the central net so he could listen into the exchange with Eurostar Control.

"The train has left the scene," said Caisson. "The assault team is back in the air shadowing the train. We need authorization to 'go' or 'no go' on the Daisychain."

Chartain looked at the Sergeant Major. "What is a Daisychain?"

Rocard looked at him balefully with sad-sack eyes. "The Daisychain is a very bad idea."

"And what's the sled?"

"Even worse," replied the Sergeant Major.

The voice of Alain Dassault came through Chartain's headphones. "I have been ordered by the Defense Ministry to tell you that you are authorized to employ the Daisychain. I understand you will have a window on the track after Dijon."

"Roger, Central," came Caisson's voice. "We will comply. . . . Colonel, are you there?"

Chartain keyed his mike. "Roger."

"I will need the other choppers to fan out and shadow the train. Close enough to be a distraction, but not close enough to provoke a response. We need you to be a diversion."

"I will pass the word."

Heinz Müller put on his gas mask, then applied the acetylene flame to the last bridge that was holding the cutout in place. He had burned out a large rectangle in the heavy-gauge steel of the wall, and all that was holding it in place was a small divot of metal on the top border. The torch burned through, then there was a tearing, screeching sound, and Heinz jumped back as the panel fell down with a crash, allowing the knockout gas to billow into the passageway.

Heinz killed the torch, then he and his cohort gingerly stepped through the opening. Beyond the haze he could see the two SAS troopers, and beside them was the prize. He was struck at how benign it appeared. Just a simple footlocker. He keyed his radio and said, "We are in, Helmut. Notify the Fräulein."

Séverine saw the front door slide open and the red-haired woman streak through the car at a trot. She was perplexed at how the hard-looking Germans deferred to her. Who the hell was she? And what were they after? Except when they had been cornered, they were treating the passengers as if they were an afterthought. Having studied the terrorist mind, she concluded there was not a political agenda here. More like customers caught in bank robbery while the bandits drilled the safe—they were after the money. But what could possibly be aboard this train? She racked her brain and came up empty. Then when the cell phone in her boot vibrated she nearly jumped out of her skin. Discreetly, she fished it out and opened the clamshell screen to view the message:

DAISYCHAIN

Oh, Lord, no, she thought. Then she realized that if this was a political hijacking, the authorities would let things play out and make rescuing the hostages a priority. Employing the Daisychain was a desperation move, and that told her the authorities wanted whatever was on-board as badly as the hijackers—which meant that at the end of the day, the passengers were expendable.

With a sense of dread she looked up and saw four helicopters fanning out behind the train as they passed the outskirts of Dijon.

The Eurostar locomotive is an intricate maelstrom of mechanics and electronics. The engine is manufactured by SNCF, which draws electric power converts it into a massive stream of horsepower to pull (or push) 18 cars at ultra-high speeds.

The source of all this juice that makes high-speed rail possible is an exposed electrical power line that is suspended above the train like an old-time electric trolley. The suspension points for this power line are a continuous series of arches made up of a steel exoskeleton. Simply put, the Eurostar is continually passing through these arches like a croquet ball through an endless string of wickets—which is to say, the train is constantly covered with a kind of electric and steel hairnet as it races along.

The access to this power line is achieved through a device called the "pantograph," which is a praying mantis-like arm that has a conductive bar of carbon that connects to the raw power in the line while it slides along. A slight pressure against the line to keep the contact continuous is provided by a springy hinge in the arm of the retractable pantograph.

Using an exposed power source has its upside and downside. Repair crews have easy access, but the line is exposed to the elements. Therefore, in the constant upgrades that go along with ultra-sophisticated rail lines, the new T1 rail line laid on the Dijon-Lyon-Avignon leg had a new generation of pantograph that accessed the power line laid alongside the rail via an undercarriage stem of the locomotive. This eliminated the need for the hairnet of steel arches for the suspension power line. Eventually, all the Eurostar lines would be replaced with the undercarriage power system, but for the moment the only section of the Eurostar line that did not have an electric and steel exoskeleton covering its path was part of the segment between Dijon and Lyon. It could be covered in about twenty minutes, and this was the window through which the assault team had to deploy the Daisychain.

Heinz applied a portable sonogram device to the latch on the footlocker, then ran it around the periphery and issued his judgment. "I see no booby traps, Fräulein. It is a simple locking mechanism."

"Break it open, then," ordered Fayla.

Heinz applied some ministrations with a crowbar, causing the lock to spring free. She lifted the lid and it was almost anti-climactic. Sitting in a steel housing was a sealed package of space-age plastic about eighteen inches by eighteen inches and about eight inches deep, but with sloping edges. Inside the sealed package were vials that contained the seeds of selective mass destruction, along with microfilm of the project's documents over the last two decades—the only remaining record.

Greedily, Fayla picked up the package and clutched it with an exultation she'd never known before. She smiled at Helmut and Heinz. "Well done, gentlemen. Very well done, indeed!" She looked at her watch. "And none too soon. It's almost time for you to make your exit."

"Jawohl, Fräulein."

She placed the package in a bulky satchel-like purse and turned to leave. "Get the others in place. I'll radio you from the cockpit when to pull the plug."

Then she looked out the window and said, "What are those bleeding helicopters doing?"

"Keeping an eye on us, I suspect, Fräulein," replied Helmut.

The wicked smile returned. "So much the better."

No one knew exactly what the genesis was for the Daisychain system, but broadly speaking it was probably a combination of the surge in government spending following 9/11 and some Aerospatiale engineers getting blind drunk in a bar in Toulon.

The question raised at the bar was, how do you get commandos on-board a soft target like a moving high-speed train? Through an alcoholic haze, the idea emerged, and on the next day of sobriety some concept drawings were made.

And in an environment where money was thrown with abandon at anything labeled "anti-terrorist," the Daisychain program was born.

Caisson strapped on the helmet, wind-goggles, and gloves, slid his boots into the stirrups, and grabbed the hand controllers.

"Are you sure about this, Commandant?" shouted Bouvain.

"If I wanted to be sure I would work in a bank," he said into the voice-activated microphone. "Is it clear?"

"Oui, mon Commandant," replied the pilot.

"I will aim for the car next to the rear locomotive. Lower away."

"Roger, Commandant."

Chartain looked out the window at Caisson's chopper, and could only say, "What the hell . . . ?"

From the belly of the Daisychain chopper an object emerged that looked like an anchor or an upside-down T. The bottom of the crossbar had an airfoil shape where Caisson inserted his feet into stirrups along the trailing edge, while the shaft was a windshield that protected him as he held onto two hand grips. At the apex of the shaft was a coupling that hooked onto a cable, which fed into a winch in the helicopter. The design of the contraption was for the airfoil to keep stabilized downward pressure on the cable, so as not to flail wildly in the 100+ mph airstream. The air-control surfaces were manipulated by the hand controllers, and it was a deft exercise, because too much downward pressure would pull the helicopter down and too little would create slack, compromising control.

The idea was to descend over one of the cars in the hijackers' blind spot. Once the bottom of the air frame came in contact with the roof of the car, an adhesive bladder was broken and a kind of superglue fixed the airfoil in place. Then, one by one the assault troops would slide down the cable. Once on the train roof, they would employ handheld suction grippers to make their way to the windshield of the rearward facing locomotive, blast it open, and gain entry for the assault.

The advantage of the Daisychain was that it allowed the commandos a chance of getting on-board undetected, but only a chance.

Chartain was mesmerized by the scene. "Who is riding that thing?"

"The commandant," replied the Sergeant Major. "He is the only one crazy enough to try."

The howl of the wind was deafening, even behind the transparent armor of the windshield with his helmet on. As the Daisychain came clear of the helicopter, Caisson maneuvered the hand controllers through the fly-by-wire systems so the control surfaces of the airframe bit into the air to keep the craft aligned with downward pressure on the cable.

The drum spooled out and the airspeed indicator read 202 kph. As the length of the cable increased, it formed something of a reverse bow despite its weight.

Caisson looked down at the racing serpentine figure of the Eurostar. He was about forty feet above the train, three cars up from the rear.

He pressed the DOWN button on the hand controller, and he continued a slow descent. He was grateful for the microchip controller that kept the vibrating airframe in trim, for the view of the treetops zipping by at eye level was enough to rattle even a battle-hardened commando. He halted the descent and saw he was two cars ahead of where he needed to be, so he spoke into the stem mike to the chopper pilot.

"Throttle back," he shouted. "I need to fall back farther."

The pilot eased back and Caisson saw the train cars move slowly ahead beneath him, as if in slow motion. "There. Hold it there! Resuming descent now." And he eased the hand controller to the right as the train negotiated a curve.

Inside the cockpit, Mickey McDrew was intently watching the kilometer markers as they went by, then he keyed the radio to Fayla. "Number three-seven-seven just went by, so we have about fifty kilometers to go."

"Got it," replied Fayla, and she turned to Helmut. "Fifty clicks out. You know what to do?"

Helmut nodded as he stood in the empty car behind the last hostage car with Heinz and two other hijackers. "Jawohl, Fräulein. Just radio us at the proper moment and we will . . . what in the world?"

Fayla followed his gaze, but all she could see was the ceiling. "What is it?"

"I saw . . . some object above one of the rear cars. I just saw it for a moment through the angle on the curve. It must be one of the helicopters. Heinz! *Komm mit mir, schnell!*" And they ran toward the rear of the train.

Marc Chartain watched in fascination as the bizarre wing-walker contraption slowly descended toward the rear of the train. It had a surreal quality about it, as if it were a UFO of some kind. It had fallen back to hover above the rear locomotive, where Caisson halted its descent just above touchdown. The roof of the locomotive had a slight curve to it and not enough flat real estate for the Daisychain to anchor itself.

"Forward. Carefully!" ordered Caisson.

The Panther responded, and as if levitating, the Daisychain moved forward inch by inch until it was perhaps two feet above the security car.

"Ready to deploy," shouted Caisson

"Ready," replied the pilot.

"Now!" and he mashed the red button.

The spool released three feet of slack, and the under carriage of the Daisychain slammed down on the roof, breaking the bladder holding the super adhesive. The adhesive only took ten seconds to set, but ten seconds in this environment was a very long time, indeed. The pilot had to keep the line precisely taut enough to hold the Daisychain upright against the wind. And it almost worked.

The pilot let out too much slack, and the Daisychain rocked backward. Caisson's feet slipped out of the stirrups and the wind lifted him up, but he held fast to the hand controllers as his torso and legs airplaned behind him.

The good news was the adhesive held, securing the Daisychain fast to the roof, albeit at a cockeyed angle.

Caisson curled his body and legs into a ball to get into the windbreak of the Daisychain where he grabbed the hand loop on the trailing edge of the airfoil. Then he pulled one of the suction grippers out of the housing at the base of the upside down T. The gripper had the circumference of a dinner plate with a handle on one side, and on the other was a three-inch hard-rubber rim with a rubber membrane stretched around it. Embedded in the handle was a lever that worked a piston that, when you placed the rubber rim on a flat surface and pushed the piston down, created a hard and fast suction. Window washers use them to reach hard-to-get places on skyscrapers.

Caisson pushed the piston down and then pulled the handle to ensure it was secure. Then he plunked down the second one. He was now holding onto two grips and they held fast, but the airstream was lifting his legs above his head.

"Twenty-three kilometers left, Commandant," radioed the pilot.

"Send the team down. We are secure."

"Roger." And the pilot gave the hand signal.

Immediately Bouvain snapped the carabiner onto the cable and hooked it into his safety belt. The Heckler & Koch sub-machine gun was strapped tightly to his back and his two grippers to the belt. His gloved hands held tightly to the cable as he wrapped his legs around it, then began the slide down. The whipsaw of the wind was brutal—like fighting against invisible white-water rapids. On his way down he felt the cable slacken a bit as the train increased its speed, then it grew taut again as the helicopter pilot increased the pitch of his blades to keep pace.

Helmut was a resourceful man. He'd had to be. As Chief of U-171 he had performed heroically on many occasions in the North Atlantic. He'd been one of the Kriegsmarine's finest, to the point of receiving his Knight's Cross from Admiral Dönitz himself. He was intimately familiar with all things mechanical, and was not intimidated by the technical intricacies of the Eurostar.

The carriages had two sets of double doors between them. There was a sliding glass door that separated the cabin proper from the side entry point that allowed ingress and egress of passengers when the train was halted at the station. Then there was another heavy metal door with a glass oval that opened into a small vestibule between cars, where the plastic accordion-like membrane allowed some flexibility between cars. In the ingress and egress space was a panel marked UTILITY, where Helmut took a crowbar and jimmied the lock. He shouted, "Hold on!" to Heinz, then hooked his arm into the handrail and reached into the open panel and pulled the lever, causing the side exit door to slide open.

The airburst nearly ripped him out of the entrance alcove, but he put his foot against the opposing wall to brace himself against the wind. Holding the rail he leaned out as far as he could and looked up. Because they were in a slight curve he could see the Panther dead above him, and a black-suited figure sliding down a cable.

With his eyes he followed the cable down to the top of the security car. Then they came out of the curve, the train straightened, and he lost sight of it. But no matter, he'd seen enough. He reached back into the utility panel and pulled the lever to close the door.

He released the rail and yelled, "*Schnell!*" as he hustled into the next car.

Sergeant Bouvain reached the Daisychain anchor and fought against the airstream as he unhooked the carabiner from the cable and grabbed the hand loop embedded in the airfoil. He slipped, and his legs airplaned upwards, but he held fast to the hand loop. Then he reached ahead and grabbed the gripper handle the commandant had placed down. As rehearsed, he passed his gripper to Caisson, who set it down in a chain toward the locomotive like lily pads across a pond. Bouvain advanced to the next gripper as the third commando slid down the cable.

Helmut Kruger entered the connecting cubicle between the heavy metal doors one car removed from the trailing security car. Grabbing the radio he pressed the mike button. "McDrew! How far?"

"Close," came Mickey's voice. "Forty kilometers to go!"

At 220 kph, that would pass in eleven minutes.

Helmut took the crowbar and forced a floor panel up. Inside was a labyrinth of cables, wires and switches. One lever was painted in red and white striping with red lettering that displayed: EMERGENCY USE ONLY. He reached down and pulled with his ham hock forearm.

The lever gave way to the German's muscle, followed by a hissing, popping, screeching sound. Helmut and Heinz fell back to grab the handrail by the upstream door as a violent tearing noise reverberated through the vessel. Then suddenly the trailing car pulled away, ripping away the plastic membrane between the cars and opening up a ring of daylight. A punishing backdraft rushed into the void and pummeled their bodies against the interior walls of the vestibule.

The fourth commando was sliding down the cable when suddenly the line sprang taught as a bowstring, whipsawing him like a rag doll.

Caisson felt the vibrations ripple through the car, drawing his attention upward; and with a sickening sense of dread he watched the helicopter as it pitched forward and headed down.

Chapter Twenty-Five

From his perch in the chopper, Chartain looked down and sensed something was amiss, but couldn't diagnose the problem until he noticed the gap grow between the security car and the rest of the train.

He watched as the tethered Daisychain Panther, suddenly anchored by tons of drifting steel, reacted like a calf roped at full gallop by an American cowboy, with the horse rearing up and locking down.

The pilot cut power, but it was too little too late, and almost in slow motion the chopper made a groaning sound as it edged over in a nosedive into the gap between the jettisoned car and the Eurostar proper. The moment before the chopper's impact the cable snapped, the black serpentine line sailing backward with the kinetic energy of a steel bullwhip, and the last image Caisson saw was of the orange fulmination erupting in front of him before the cable sliced him and his comrades off the roof like a scythe.

Chartain watched in horror and felt the shudder of the concussion wave as the Daisychain chopper impacted with a *KA-WHUMP!!!* and formed an orange inferno that billowed out to consume the security car rushing into it.

In all his years, the hardened Legionnaire had never witnessed anything so horrific; and it was with a sense of shock, dread and impotence that he watched the expanding conflagration fall behind.

When the cable broke, the helicopter lunged toward Helmut and Heinz, and crashed on the railbed almost close enough to touch. The fireball bloomed out, reaching for Helmut, the fringe of it singeing his arm, but the escape velocity of the Eurostar got him out of the kill zone just in the nick.

With fascination he watched the trailing cars plow into the debris and send it off in a starshell pattern. The security car almost derailed, but held fast to the track.

Helmut then looked over at Heinz, who had an otherworldly look on his face. A meter-long shard of a rotor blade was sticking out of his chest. Slowly, Heinz's grip relaxed from the handrail, his eyes rolled back, and the roaring slipstream of air lifted him gently off the platform. He floated onto the tracks, then tumbled, and at over 125 mph it was with a mixture of revulsion and amazement that Helmut watched his comrade's body cartwheel along, breaking into parts in so many directions.

But no time for remorse, the Kriegsmarine had taught him that the middle of a battle was not the time to grieve. He opened the door and headed upstream. It was almost time for him to get off.

Chartain was in shock as well, but he knew if he was going to pull Séverine out of the firestorm, he had to get on top of the situation, or the situation was going to get on top of him.

"Sergeant Major!"

He didn't answer at first. He was staring glassy-eyed out the window, mumbling, "Commandant . . ."

Chartain cuffed him on the shoulder. "Sergeant Major Rocard!"

"Uh, oui, Colonel."

"What are our options?"

"I . . . I fear we are out of options."

"What about this sled you spoke of?"

"Well, it was experimental. And the experiment did not go well."

"How does it work?"

The Sergeant Major explained. Chartain then understood the Sergeant Major's reluctance. "Where is this sled now?"

"In a railyard in Lyon."

Chartain's mind raced. What should he do? Hang back and see how things played out? Or seize the initiative? By nature his proclivity was for the latter, not the former. He put on the headset and keyed in to the Eurostar control center.

Séverine had heard the explosion and felt the train shudder, but it had kept moving. She immediately felt a sense of foreboding and knew in her heart some of her comrades were gone, all in the attempt to save her and the innocents on-board. A rush of grief washed over her, but that was soon supplanted by a deep, searing anger. All she wanted now was some small window of opportunity to be let off the leash, then the spitfire within would wreak havoc in every way she could.

Just then the rear door opened and one of the older hijackers rushed down the aisle. Séverine noticed the arm of his uniform was blackened with burn marks.

Then she felt the phone vibrate in her boot. Carefully she retrieved it and flipped up the screen that read:

WILL ATTEMPT SLED
SOUTH OF LYON

"Dijon?" repeated Salisbury into the phone. Then he listened further and said, "Right," before hanging up.

"What's happening?" asked Bloom.

"We're putting down in Dijon. Apparently some French commandos require a lift to Lyon."

Helmut was standing just outside the cockpit door conferring with Fayla and McDrew as Mickey kept the door open—the gun on the driver, lest he get any ideas.

"So if we separate as planned, but you miss the bridge, chances are we'll lose the package."

"Jawohl, Fräulein. The inertia of separated cars without the weight of the engine and cars we left behind cannot be accurately calibrated. But if we stay on the train we have no means for extraction for my part of the team. And we lose the diversion."

Fayla thought fast. She always did in a pinch—a trait of survival. "I'll take the package with me. You and your mates separate as planned. You make the extraction point, fine. Just don't be taken alive."

"I made that decision in 1942."

She placed her hand on his shoulder and gave it a squeeze. "You've been a superb teacher." Then she turned to McDrew. "Mickey, you were always good with numbers. Figure as best you can the separation point. Helmut, get your crew into position."

"Jawohl."

Chartain keyed his mike to the squad leaders in the two helicopters flying abreast. "This is Colonel Chartain. I am assuming command of the assault team. My aircraft and team will return to Dijon to transfer to a fixed-wing in order to leapfrog the Eurostar and employ the rocket sled. Continue to shadow the Eurostar until you receive further orders."

"Oui, Colonel," came the simultaneous response, followed by, "Uh, Colonel . . . what is happening?"

Chartain looked down to see two more cars on the trailing end of the Eurostar separate from the rest of the train and start to fall behind.

"Now what?" he grumbled.

Helmut leapt onto the trailing platform and grabbed onto the handrail as the screeching metallic sound reverberated in the small passageway, followed by daylight spewing in with tornadic winds. Since he was on the leading face of the separated car, the wind pancaked him against the door, but he did not panic; he had anticipated this. All he had to do was wait for the cars to decelerate.

"Assault team Leader, your rendezvous aircraft is nearing Dijon. What is your location?"

"Wait one, Central," replied Chartain. "Something is happening."

Chartain watched the disengaged cars fall behind. He had to make a decision. He prayed it was the right one and keyed the mike.

"Team One leader?"

"Here, Colonel."

"You follow the main train. Report into Central continually. Team Two leader?"

"Oui, Colonel."

"Stay with the section of the train left behind. When it stops, stay airborne and keep it under surveillance. Continue reports going to Central."

"Roger, Colonel."

Chartain then flipped the switch to the internal intercom and told the pilot, "Make like hell for Dijon airport!"

Then the formation of Panthers split to take three different vectors.

Jochen List read the text message on his cell phone, then peered through the windshield to the bridge above him. A complication. *Nicht gut.* But the plan allowed for flexibility. If they were able to reach his van, all should be well. If not, his orders were to not let the operation be compromised.

The trailing cars had slowed to 100 kph, enabling Helmut to raise his hand and push the button to open the sliding doors. He fell into the aisle where his two comrades helped him to his feet.

"Where are we?" he demanded.

"Maybe three kilometers away. We may overshoot!"

"Follow me!" And they raced toward the end car.

The Sidley-Hawker jet touched down at Dijon airport, then did a rapid taxi away from the main terminal to the end of an adjoining runway.

Bloom looked out the window and saw a black helicopter without markings land in the grass nearby. Immediately the door slid back and four men wearing black jumpsuits and helmets jumped out, all of them carrying submachine guns. The resoluteness of their approach made Bloom hope they were on the same side.

The steward lowered the door ladder and they piled in. The first one was older, hard looking. Clearly the man in charge. He stuck his head into the cockpit and barked, "Lyon. Quickly!"

Bloom, who had never served in the military, had an unusual urge to stand at attention and salute.

The commando turned and saw Salisbury, then stuck out his hand. "Colonel Marc Chartain of the Second Regiment of the Légion étrangère. Temporarily assigned to the commando force of the gendarmerie."

Légion étrangère? wondered Bloom. The Foreign Legion?

Salisbury took the hand. "Grayson Salisbury, Scotland Yard. This is Captain Gideon Bloom of the Chicago Police Department."

"Chicago?" queried Chartain.

"It's a long story, Colonel. I think you best get your men strapped in."

"Thank you, Captain." And in short order the door was sealed, the engines revved, and the aircraft was wheels up.

Chartain pulled off his sweaty helmet and set it down. Then

he removed the magazine from his MP5 and yanked the bolt back to eject the cartridge from the chamber as a safety precaution.

The he looked up to see the white-jacketed steward as he said, "May I offer you and your men some refreshment, Colonel?"

Helmut Kruger stuck his head into the wind and saw the small bridge that would take the train over the two-lane road. The cars were coasting at what Helmut estimated to be around 40 kph. The railbed was on an embankment, and to Helmut it looked like they were going to overshoot. He looked up at the helicopter shadowing them over the French countryside and made his decision. "We are going to jump!" he yelled to his two comrades.

The underpass approached. The moment it slid beneath the car, Helmut jumped. His heels hit the incline and he pitched over on his shoulder, rolling down the grassy embankment.

The copilot pointed at the train and yelled, "Look!" The pilot needed no urging. He saw the three figures jump from the slowing car. What were they? Hostages? Hijackers? He held his position and noticed they did nothing to signal him. Two were running and one was hobbling toward a small underpass. Seconds after disappearing from view, a van pulled out from underneath, and as the lead jumper approached the restraining fence, small puffs of smoke rose from the chain-link mesh.

Helmut held back until the last charge fired, then he reached forward and ripped the fence section out. He stepped through and scrambled to the back of the van and yanked open the door. Waving frantically he yelled, "*Schnell!*"

First one, then the second with a broken ankle piled into the back. Helmut looked up at the helicopter, hovering like an angry wasp, and he couldn't help but smile. Then he jumped in and yelled to the driver, "*Fahr! Fahr!*"

And the van peeled rubber.

"Eurostar Central, this is Panther Two. Three subjects jumped from the train, blew the fence, and climbed into a waiting van. We are maintaining surveillance."

"Roger, Panther Two. Stay with them. We are alerting the local gendarmerie."

"Roger, Central. We will stay with them until . . . wait . . . what are they . . . ? They have stopped, Central."

One of the jumpers stepped out of the back with a tube-like object.

Martin Raux was the sixth generation of his family to farm the fertile soil outside of Lyon. He was on his tractor, plowing the rows for the planting of spring wheat when he saw a helicopter maintaining its position in the distance. That was strange? Why would it be doing such a thing?

As if in answer to his question, the helicopter suddenly banked away and headed for the ground, just as a smoky trail rose up from the farm road and overshot the diving aircraft. But then the smoke trail executed an aerial pirouette and corkscrewed down into the chopper, turning it into an orange fireball.

The Gauloise cigarette fell from Martin's mouth as the fiery remains plummeted to the ground with a *WHAM!!*

It was the second helicopter catastrophe Helmut had experienced inside of an hour, but unlike the first, although this one was close enough to feel the heat of the impact, it wasn't close enough to concern him.

He patted the spent tube of the American-made Stinger missile and said, "*Ach*, if only I'd had something like you in forty-four." Then he tossed it in the van and climbed in.

In terms of private aircraft, the Pilatus PC-6/B was a real draft horse. With a large shoebox cabin and a high-wing configuration, the utility plane could seat six passengers comfortably. It had a single quad-bladed propeller off the nose, powered by a 550-horsepower Pratt & Whitney engine, and was manufactured in Switzerland. So of course it was engineered to the nines. One of the features of the Pilatus and its high-wing configuration was the ease of passenger ingress and egress from the tarmac. This particular one had some special modifications, which General Walther Schellenberg intended to make use of.

He eased the throttles forward to wind up to full power and the aircraft responded. At nearly 200 kph, he pulled back on the control column and the nose slowly rose into the air. The takeoff roll took longer because of the thin Alpine air, but finally it became airborne and Schellenberg navigated through treacherous peaks before locking in a vector for the south of France.

It had always pissed him off that Göring wouldn't arrange for him to take flying lessons from the Luftwaffe. *"We shan't squander the resources of the Reich on pleasure flying,"* he would say. *Harrumph.* Using the "resources of the Reich," that fat pig had looted half the art works of Europe and stashed them in his private collection at Karinhall. But then, he'd broken his pick on Spitfires in the Battle of Britain.

Well, at least there was a little justice in this world after all.

"**You want me** to do what?" asked Luc Besson as he stared quixotically at the contraption in the railyard as workmen removed the covering tarp.

The yardmaster was waving his radio as he explained, "The Eurostar has been hijacked! You are to drive an engine and push this sled to approach the train from the rear. Commandos are on their way to man the sled, and they will assault the train."

Besson blinked. "I would need to talk to the union about this."

"This is a national emergency! One hostage has already been murdered! There are children on board! You will drive this engine or I will strangle you myself!"

Besson swallowed. He was admittedly not a brave man. But children? He squared his round shoulders and said, "Very well. Show me how it works."

Using the hand radio antenna as a pointer, the yardmaster gestured to the trailing edge of the sled, which had a curved rubber bumper. "You will bring the nose of the engine against this bumper." Then he pointed at the flatbed car with four plastic outcroppings. "The commandos will lie flat behind these windshields. Then, when you get within three hundred meters of the train, you will cut power."

"Cut power?"

"Yes, and apply a little brake. This will allow you to fall back as the sled shoots forward."

"But, how does the sled reach the train?"

The yardmaster pointed at two tube-link objects welded to each edge of the sled. "The commandos will trigger the rocket engines. They will propel the sled the final distance. It will impact with enough force so this boarding ladder will smash through the windshield of the trailing engine, allowing the commandos to board."

Besson gawked at the titanium ladder sticking out of the leading edge of the sled like a unicorn's horn. Then he blinked.

"I am to fall back?"

"Oui."

"Very well, I will do it. But who are the kamikazes who are riding this 'sled' as you call it?"

"They are arriving momentarily. The Eurostar will be by-passing Lyon in minutes. So get in the cockpit."

Besson shrugged and complied.

Marc Chartain extended his hand and said, "My thanks for the lift, Superintendent. Hope to see you on the backside of our assault."

Salisbury shook the cast iron grip. "Good luck, Colonel. We will leapfrog you to Valence. The French gendarmerie has a helicopter waiting for us there."

Chartain nodded to Bloom. "Captain, a pleasure. Perhaps I will make it to Chicago some day."

"Take care, Colonel. This sled business sounds extremely hazardous to me."

"And you are quite right, Captain. *Adieu.*"

"*Bonne chance,*" replied Bloom.

The stairway door deployed and the commandos hustled out to a waiting van with a spinning red light on top.

The Eurostar was in a wide sweeping turn, enabling Séverine to look back and see that fully a third of the train was no longer there. What had happened?

And the sled? Mon Dieu! Surely they would not try that. It had been tested before Séverine had joined the Squadron, but she'd heard about it. Two men dead in the live-fire exercise. The rockets had been fired too close to the target and the sled impacted with too much force and derailed, killing the two Squadron members and severely damaging the engine. And what of Marc? He was just bull-headed enough to ride that rocket to rescue her . . . and she prayed he would.

The cell phone vibrated. Carefully she extracted it and spied the message:

SLED LEAVING YARD
ON SIGNAL CREATE DIVERSION
JE TAIME MARC

A lump formed in her throat. *Je t'aime*? What a time to face the truth!

But a diversion? How could she provide a diversion? She peered at the hijacker and he was still alert. Finger on the trigger, eyes flicking to the window, then canvassing the cabin that was crammed with passengers. And what about a weapon? She didn't have so much as a nail file. In her frustration, she gripped the armrest and noticed it wobbled a little. She felt under the arm and fingered a concave groove running the length of the underside of the arm rest, beneath where a passenger would lay their forearm. At either end of the groove was a bolt protruding through a frame that was fastened by a screwed-on nut. One was already loose and she easily unscrewed it, prompting the matronly Auntie in the neighboring seat to whisper, "What are you doing?"

Séverine put her finger to her lips indicating silence, then she tried to work the second nut loose, which was proving to be tough indeed. Try as she might, her bare fingers couldn't get traction on the slippery metal. She looked at the white pocket square in the breast pocket of Auntie's suit jacket. "I need your handkerchief," she whispered, and warily Auntie handed it over. Using the fabric as a buffer, she applied so much torque to the nut that she feared her knuckle might break. But finally it gave way and she unscrewed it the rest of the way. Then she deftly lifted the 18-inch object out of its housing and turned it over to see the anchoring bolt sticking out like a spike. She hefted it, then replaced it back in the frame.

Now she had a weapon. But how to deploy it? She was in the middle of the car, the hijacker at the front. No way to rush him. He had to come to her. But how? She looked across the aisle to the frightened ten-year-old boy who clung tightly to his mother's arm. Carefully she whispered, "Pierre, can you pretend to be sick?"

"Access rail has been switched. You are cleared to go," barked the disembodied voice through the cockpit speaker.

Luc Besson keyed the mike switch. "Understood, Central. Will comply." He eased the throttle forward, allowing the current to surge into the coils of the massive electric motor that caused the heavy axle to rotate. The engine eased forward and the nose engaged the rubber bumper of the sled.

Marc Chartain felt the bump against the flatbed car, then saw the railyard slip away. He and the three troops were literally strapped onto the sled, each with a broad canvas belt. He turned to Sergeant Major Rocard, lying alongside him, and yelled, "Tell me again how this works."

The Sergeant Major pointed to a small LCD screen between them. "This is the readout from the laser range-finder. This button engages it. When the readout shows three hundred meters, I will hit this button and it will fire the booster rockets."

"But on the test the sled impacted too hard?"

"Oui. But assuming we impact correctly, release your belt and use these handholds to get to the ladder. The air current will lift your body up, so you will have to walk with your hands grabbing the loops."

Chartain saw the feeder junction of the track go past, then they were on the main line and the croquet wickets of the electric arches started to whip past. The roar of the wind started to grow as he watched the speed indicator go past 200 kph. Then up ahead in the distance he saw the black Panther helicopter shadowing their quarry. In his left hand he tightly held the cell phone.

CHAPTER TWENTY-SIX

Fayla listened intently, then said, "Excellent! See you on the backside." She closed the cell phone and said to McDrew, "Helmut made the safe house transfer. They're home free. How far to the rendezvous?"

McDrew looked out the windshield at the marker as it whipped past. "Eight-six kilometers."

"Our driver has just been Ducky. Be sure and give him a nice reward when we're done."

"My pleasure."

The mood in the Eurostar central control room was of resigned fatalism. They had been bested at every turn by their adversaries, and their final recourse was the wildest of wild cards.

Alain Dassault looked at the large electronic Eurostar map on the LCD screen. The moving light of the train was progressing south, while the light of the engine pushing the sled was closing the gap.

He heard a phone ring. Some junior staffer answered. A muffled exchange, then the staffer approached deferentially.

"Monsieur Dassault?"

"Oui?"

"It is the press office. They are getting calls about gendarmerie stations being alerted from Lyon to Avignon. And a helicopter being shot down. What do I tell them?"

Dassault closed his eyes and cursed softly. Then he sighed and said, "Tell them it is an unannounced exercise of a simulated hijacking."

That might buy them a little time, at least.

The readout on the display read 227 kph, and Chartain could see they were closing the distance. Without the push of the trailing engine, the Eurostar couldn't get past 205 kph even though a third of the train had been jettisoned.

The rails were relatively straight as they coursed through the flat patchwork-quilt farmland of central France. And as the wind roared over him, it began to sink in on Chartain how many things could go wrong with this plan. This was their last chance to save the hostages and retrieve the footlocker. In the distance he could see the trailing car. The ledge that was normally a walkway between cars was now a small cliff that led to nowhere. Through his windshield he could see that the sliding metal door to the passenger cabin was closed, but he couldn't see through the glass oval whether anyone was beyond the door. They moved into a long stretch of straight track. Chartain hit the laser range finder and the display read 323.5 meters. It was now or never. He hit the SEND button on the cell phone.

The vibration in her boot nearly sent Séverine through the window, but she recovered and flipped the phone open. One word was on the screen:

NOW!

She looked up at Pierre. Behind him his mother returned her stare with a face that imparted her escalating feeling of terror that this could not be happening, that putting her little boy in danger was the key to keeping the passengers safe. Reluctantly she nodded, squeezed her son, and whispered, "If you must, *mon cher*. Go now."

Nervously, Pierre grabbed his stomach and let loose a wail. Everyone's head in the car turned as he rolled over the armrest and fell into the narrow aisle on his hands and knees. The guard was instantly tracking the disturbance as the little boy writhed on the floor. Séverine saw the guard mutter something into his radio, then with machine pistol at the ready, he advanced down the aisle.

Pierre's mother had moved into the aisle seat and was leaning over the armrest speaking a stream of nervous French.

The guard approached and motioned at the mother with the muzzle of the gun, shouting, *"Aus dem Weg! Zurück!"*

The mother looked at him and said, "My boy has a peptic ulcer!"

The guard halted directly beside Séverine, blocking her, but as if on cue, Pierre tried to get up and then collapsed two steps towards the rear of the car. This kid was good. The guard hesitated as Séverine chanted to herself, "Take the bait. Take the bait. . . ." Then he took another step and leaned over the boy to shake him by the shoulder.

In one fluid motion Séverine lifted the armrest out of its cradle, stood, and rotated into the aisle. Had the hijacker and Séverine's position been reversed it would have had a sexual connotation, and indeed, as she raised the arm rest like an axe handle, her crotch bumped against his buttocks, causing him to rear up. But it was too late. The farm girl's sinewy arms brought the spike of the bolt down and drove it into the base of his skull as if she were chopping wood for the kitchen.

A geyser of blood spurted out at the junction of spine and skull as the hijacker's body pitched forward, then went into a spasm as he collapsed with his gun on top of Pierre.

"*Light the candle!!!*" shouted Chartain, and the Sergeant Major slammed the button.

Chartain had been near explosives up close and personal before, but nothing like this. The speed and wind were frenetic, but in an eyeblink they became stupefying with the earsplitting roar of the rocket thrust. It felt like the sled had been kicked in the ass by an angry mule, and with a feeling of sheer terror, he watched the Eurostar car hurtle toward him in a rush.

After the final spasm, Séverine saw the hijacker's eyes freeze open, telling her he was quite dead. She turned around and saw another hijacker in the empty upstream car running toward the sliding glass doors. She yanked the dead man's shoulder and ignored Pierre's cries underneath as she tugged the canvas gun strap over his head. She grabbed the pistol grip and brought the weapon over her head in an arc as she intentionally fell backward. The hiss of the airlock door reached her ears as her back hit the floor. Then she arched her spine like a gymnast as the intruder fired a round from his weapon that zinged past her torso to bury itself into his dead comrade. But by then she'd framed him in the upside-down sights and squeezed off a short burst.

The projectiles sailed out of the barrel and crashed through the hijacker's upper bridgework before splashing the detritus of a red mash exit wound on the bulkhead.

Screams rippled through the car as the second dead hijacker fell over. Séverine was pulling herself up when something jarred the train and knocked her back to the deck with an "*Ooof!*"

The titanium ladder crashed through the glass oval of the metal door with the grace of a medieval battering ram, triggering spring-loaded spikes that deployed like barbs on a fish hook.

Chartain felt the sled buck with the impact—the front wheels even came off the rails a little—but then settled back down in alignment.

The rocket engine expended, the Eurostar began pulling away, causing the spikes to grab the doorframe like the barb setting the hook on a fish's lip. The metal groaned but held, and the sled was violently taken in tow by the larger train.

Chartain looked behind him at the two commandos and got thumbs up in reply. Then he nodded to the Sergeant Major before grabbing the handgrip and hitting the release on the canvas belt. Sure enough, his legs were uplifted by the wind as he started the trek up the ladder like a circus acrobat walking on his hands.

The Sergeant Major followed.

"What the hell was that?" demanded Fayla.

Hazeltine, the driver, scanned the instruments. "Nothing that I can see."

She put the radio to her lips. "Dieter, what's happening back there?"

"Something hit us."

"No shit. Find out what the hell it was. Where are you?"

"Guarding my passengers. . . . Heading into the trailing car now. . . . *Was ist*— We are being boarded!"

Fayla's confidence cracked and in a shrill voice she screamed into the radio, "Shoot them off. Wolfgang, get back there and help Dieter. . . . Wolfgang . . . Wolfgang! . . . Hans! . . . *Answer me!*"

Then came Dieter's voice, "*Grenade!*"

Dieter had entered the empty trailing car, and for a moment he was mesmerized by the spider web of twisted metal protruding through the broken glass and two black figures climbing through the opening.

The German raised his machine pistol, causing the two figures to duck as he sprayed the rear of the compartment. Chartain and the Sergeant Major found protection behind the metal door, but the bullet stream caught the two figures still doing hand stands on the ladder. And in a heartbeat they were gone with the wind.

Dieter started to advance when a small black object arced through the window and tumbled near his feet, emitting a hissing stream of smoke. He turned and ran toward the door, screaming into the radio when the flash-bang stun munition went off.

Séverine was watching forward and backward. Not sure which move to make. Then she heard the muffled report of the flash-bang and knew immediately what it was. That meant the Squadron had landed. If she went downstream she could take any remaining hijackers from the rear. She pulled the dead German off Pierre, yanked him up, and reunited him with his mother, saying, "You'll get a medal for this."

She turned and started toward the rear, yelling, "Stay in your seats! Commandos are on-board."

Fayla turned to her acolyte. "Mickey, go back there and hold them off. We're almost home."

At this point McDrew's true nature came to the surface. Quietly leaving a pipe bomb to explode amongst unarmed civilians was one thing; going into a pitched battle against heavily armed soldiers was quite another.

"I . . . I don't know, Fayla. I didn't sign on for this kind of—"

The palm of her hand came across his face with the ferocity of a bull whip. "You'll bloody do *exactly* as I tell you, you little cretin! Is that *clear?*"

A chastened Mickey had no defenses as he quivered and said, "Y-yes, Fayla," before reluctantly turning to head toward the rear.

Not satisfied with his progress, she kicked him in the ass.

Dieter tried to pull himself up off the floor, but it was like he was moving in slow motion as he recovered from the haymaker blow of the flash-bang. Every fiber ached as he tried to turn and raise his weapon. He was halfway there when two short bursts from Chartain and the Sergeant Major grouped on his left ear, severing his cranium from the apex of his neck.

Fayla eyeballed the kilometer markers and felt her confidence start to return. From her thigh pocket she extracted an object that looked like a transistor radio. She extended the antenna of the single sideband transceiver and pressed a button. A few seconds later she was rewarded with the illumination of a little yellow light, which brought a smile to her lips. Timing was everything.

She looked through the windshield and saw the kilometer marker she'd been waiting for. She smiled at the driver and cooed, "You've been an absolute luv, my dear Ducky." And with that she put the muzzle of her Glock to his chin and pulled the trigger.

Séverine was midstream in the empty car when she heard the twin bursts of automatic-weapons fire . . . then silence. At this point discretion was the better part of valor, and she ducked behind a seat. The door slid open and she knew what was coming. "*Marc!*" she screamed.

Chartain had pulled the pin on the stun grenade and was about to toss it when he heard the familiar voice call his name. He held the safety spoon fast and shoved the pin back into place. Tentatively, he peered around the bulkhead and saw those Mediterranean blue eyes peeking over a headrest.

It was an unlikely reunion—the grimy commando of the Legion and the fashionable farm girl. Both of them smelling of cordite and keeping their weapons out of the way as they fell into each other's arms—while the Sergeant Major looked away rather awkwardly.

Just as Helmut had shown her, Fayla twisted the hand grip, then raised the floor panel in the passageway until it swayed over and fell back with a *clung!* Below was the red-and-white-striped handle with admonitions of danger painted around it. She took a deep breath, then with all her might she pulled until it gave way with a cacophony of hissing, popping and screeching. She leapt onto the platform of the trailing car and dove through the sliding door as the engine pulled away, peeling away the protective membrane. The wicked smile reappeared as she raced by the empty seats toward the passenger-filled cars with her weapon drawn.

McDrew entered the middle passenger car, and his eyes grew wide at the two dead Germans on the floor. He waved his pistol over the cowering passengers and screamed, "Nobody move!" Then he felt a vibration and noticed the train starting to slow markedly. What was happening? Not knowing what to do, he feared Fayla's wrath more than the unknown, so he continued tentatively toward the rear.

Their embrace was short-lived as they both felt the vibration. Séverine looked out and said, "We're slowing down."

"What is the situation?" asked Chartain.

She jerked her thumb towards the passenger cars. "Two dead hijackers upstream."

Chartain nodded. "And one behind us. How many left?"

"Not sure. Eight came on-board, and I presume some bailed when the trailing cars were separated. But I can't say for certain. Maybe some are even disguised as passengers."

"All right. We'll clear it one car at a time. I'll lead. You and the Sergeant Major bring up the rear."

Séverine did not protest.

"What's the layout?" asked Chartain.

"Two more empty cars. Then a hostage car. Then empty. Then hostages, then empty, then hostages. Beyond that I don't know. They have radios."

McDrew had passed through the last hostage car and just entered the vacant carriage, where the empty seats stared back at him, when he peered ahead and saw through the far glass door to see the commandos coming toward him. A riptide of panic overwhelmed him and he turned to flee. Entering the last hostage car in the string, he started a sprint up the aisle—only to see Fayla emerge with her Glock pointed dead at him. But panic blinded him as he ran towards her screaming, "Fayla! They're coming!"

Like Helmut had taught her, she held the pistol in profile—arm extended—and squeezed off two rounds. Screams ricocheted through the car as McDrew collapsed at her feet, a crimson stain spreading over the back of his white Eurostar shirt.

She shook her head in a tut-tut way and whispered, "Always knew you'd wind up like this, Mick." Then she fired two more rounds into the ceiling and screamed, "There's a bomb on this car that's going to blow all you pigs to hell!"

Then she turned and ran upstream, repeating the shots and bomb threat in the successive hostage cars.

Chapter Twenty-Seven

At five thousand feet above the rails, Walther Schellenberg looked down with his binocular glasses and captured the engineless train as it rapidly decelerated. He peered ahead and saw the flat pastureland they had surveyed earlier. Absolute precision. That woman was a wonder. They were going to pull it off.

He put the Pilatus into a shallow spiral dive toward the pasture, ever mindful of the helicopter escort. He even took note of a second chopper approaching from the south.

Gideon Bloom looked at the slowing train in the distance. "I don't see an engine on that thing."

Salisbury squinted. "Neither do I . . . and it appears to be slowing."

"And what . . . people are jumping off!"

Chartain was halfway up the empty car when the door slid back and a wave of panicked passengers stampeded down the aisle. They seemed oblivious to the gun-toting commando as they screamed, *"Bomb! Bomb! Out of the way!"*

In the water closet of the lead empty car, Fayla secured the lock, then unzipped her white velour jumpsuit. She stripped it off to reveal a frumpy cotton dress underneath, and from a pocket in the small of the back, she extracted a wig and pulled it on before scrubbing off her lipstick and putting on a pair of globby sunglasses.

She looked in the mirror at a different person.

She peered out the small porthole and estimated the train was probably doing 25 mph, and younger passengers were starting to bail onto the railbed. She stared intently at the base of the steel poles holding up the perimeter fence. The chain-link barrier kept livestock, wildlife, hobos, and such off the high-speed pathway. It was peppered with sensors, but it took significant pressure on the chain link to trigger the alert. A little splash of paint wouldn't sound the alarm.

Fayla looked down at the base of the orange-colored poles and saw the first spot of yellow paint. Then another, and another. The train was slowing right into the kill zone. She hefted the large floppy purse onto her shoulder—the one holding the viral container covered with a scarf. Then she extended the antenna on the small transceiver and held her thumb over the red button.

Séverine tried to calm the flow of passengers, with little success. There wasn't much Chartain could do as they streamed past, but his instinct told him he was at the end of a marionette's string.

"Put it down there!" ordered Salisbury, pointing to a flat open pasture next to the train that now was creeping to a halt. Bloom saw the assault team helicopter descending as well; and one was putting down close to the fence when the earth erupted like Vesuvius.

From his perch above the fray, Walther Schellenberg witnessed two parallel waves of explosives race down the fence lines, sending sprays of earth into the air and turning the chain-link fence into so much shrapnel. One section of the mesh fence cartwheeled into the air and wrapped itself around the rotor blades of the low hovering chopper, and in a heartbeat it fell to the earth near the train with an unceremonious *thud*.

Séverine picked herself up off the floor, wondering what else could happen. The car had been rocked by the explosions and windows cracked, but she looked around and saw the passengers were unhurt. But any residue of restraint had now vanished, and the passengers fled for the exits in stark panic.

Gideon Bloom's senses were numb. This was a war zone where a policeman's .38 was little more than a peashooter. Their pilot had climbed higher to get above the swirling dust cloud. Even so, Bloom could see the passengers pouring out of the cars like ants out of a ransacked nest.

Everyone's attention was on the ground, so no one saw the Pilatus circling just above them.

The Eurostar engine, at full throttle and without the weight of a train behind it, was approaching 180 mph as it neared the village of Saulce-sur-Rhône. Normally it would be traveling at 50 mph at this point to negotiate the curve that brought it along the bank of the river on the outskirts of the village.

Madame Valerie was pushing her fourteen-month-old grandson in a stroller on the far bank of the river. Such a lovely day for an afternoon stroll. And little Jean asleep and missing it all. She had moved from Lyon to enjoy a quiet retirement in the country.

She heard it before she saw it. A kind of screeching sound, like the protest of a hinge on a rusty gate. She looked up and saw the distinctive headlights of the Eurostar rounding the curve, heading right for her. Then, as if in slow motion, its right wheels began to lift off the rail, and it lay over on its side. With a sausage grinder sound, the fast-moving leviathan slid along the gravel railbed in a shower of electric sparks as it knocked out the power-line arch before crashing through the perimeter fence and going airborne off the embankment.

The nose slammed into the mud of the shallow river, causing the body of the engine to arc over like the arm of a metronome, before releasing the last of its kinetic energy in a bellyflop splash.

Frozen in a hypnotic trance by the spectacle, Madame Valerie gaped with open mouth as a wall of water rose out of the river like a tidal wave and broke over her and her grandson. But once it surged past she was able to right herself and the stroller with the crying child, wondering how fast she could move back to Lyon.

Chartain surveyed the car, empty except for himself, Séverine and the Sergeant Major. His mind raced, then he said, "They're getting away."

"Using the panicked passengers for cover," chimed Séverine.

"Can you ID the hijackers?"

"Maybe. There was the red-haired woman."

"Then let's get outside. Maybe we'll get lucky."

Bloom and Salisbury put down fifty yards from the train. The dust cloud hung in the air as the two policemen moved in. Almost immediately, terrorized passengers began emerging from the haze, the younger ones doing an adrenaline-laced sprint out into the pasture, followed by the older ones, who were moving slower, but with no less panic.

Bloom tried to aid an elderly man who was hobbling, but he got a stiff arm in the throat and an ornery, "Out of the way!"

An older gray-haired woman in sunglasses shuffled along lugging a bulky purse. Salisbury tried to offer some assistance but she pushed him away, yelling, "Bomb! Bomb!"

With the other chopper a compacted hulk, there were no troops to gain control over a hundred passengers spreading across the landscape like ripples in a pond.

The dust cloud was dissipating and Bloom recognized a familiar silhouette. "Colonel! Over here!"

Chartain and the two others jogged over—one a woman carrying a machine pistol with the nonchalance of a tennis player toting her racquet. Chartain extended his hand, saying, "Captain Bloom. Superintendent. These are my people."

"The situation?" queried Salisbury.

Chartain jerked his thumb. "Three dead hijackers on-board. We don't know who might be escaping at this moment." He moved his arm in an arc. "We'd need fifty men to round every-one up."

"Might anyone be left on-board?" asked Bloom.

"Good point," replied the colonel. "Sergeant Major, cover the train as best you can until reinforcements arrive—although I fear we're locking the barn after the horses are out."

"Oui, Colonel."

As the dialogue was underway among the policemen and soldiers, they did not notice that as the old woman staggered by the helicopter, she tossed something to the ground underneath the tail boom.

The passengers continued to put as much real estate between themselves and the train as fast as they could, and Walther Schellenberg surveyed the refugees populating the pasture with his binoculars. There were perhaps a dozen stragglers making their way across the field. He looked carefully and, yes! There she was! In the blue frock, gray wig, and the floppy purse. She'd done it!

Immediately he pulled a lever on the control panel, and the sound of whirring servos kicked in. A specially modified door on the high-wing aircraft recessed and slid back like the side door on a minivan. A howling wind filled the empty cabin as a titanium arm swung out and locked, and a power winch started playing out a weighted cable.

"Any sign of the red-haired woman?" asked Bloom.

Séverine shook her head. "Not that I've seen. Could be anywhere."

"Do you think she jumped when the trailing cars were separated?" asked Salisbury. "We know some of them escaped that way."

Séverine shook her head again. "She went forward before the separation, so she is either still on-board or scattered with the wind."

Bloom sighed in frustration. "Well, we must be fifty miles from anywhere. It will be an hour before we get reinforcements to get control of things. Grayson, can you call in backup? Alert the local gendarmerie to search for . . . Grayson?"

Salisbury looked white as a sheet as he murmured, "Wait a moment . . . Impossible . . . I touched her." And then he wheeled around, scanning the pasture beyond the helicopter. "That was Bannon. The old woman. She was wearing the same sunglasses we saw on the Dorchester surveillance video!"

"And what's that airplane doing?" shouted Bloom as he pointed.

Fayla was in a dead sprint now, and then she abruptly halted in midfield. She pulled off the wig, dropped the bag, and ripped off the blue frock. Underneath she was wearing a knee-length Lycra stretch workout suit. Over that was a harness made of high-strength webbing with a mountaineer's carabiner dangling from the chest strap. She grabbed the purse and pulled it over her head like a bandolier and yanked the cinch strap tight.

Now, like they'd practiced so many times in rehearsals, she stood still and let the Pilatus turn in a tight circle around her as the cable descended.

Chartain, Séverine, Bloom, and Salisbury ran toward the field, then halted.

Chartain only said, "Séverine?"

In the shorthand that practitioners in the art understood, Chartain was asking his best marksman if she could make the shot.

"Not with this." She raised the German-made machine pistol. "Out of range."

"Then run for it!" ordered the colonel.

Like a greyhound let off the leash, she sprinted across the

pasture with Chartain in tow. Bloom followed as fast as he could, while Salisbury brought up the rear, his lung power diminished from a lifetime of Players cigarettes. He spun his finger in the air, indicating to the pilot to fire up the rotor blades. Maybe they could continue pursuit by air, although he felt they were already too late.

The cable was weighted with something that looked like a lead shot sinker. And just above that were five loops: one for each of the hijackers who could make it to the extraction point. For those who did not make it, or were captured, no matter; they knew the risks. Even if they were captured and water-boarded to sing like canaries it didn't matter now. Schellenberg had planned for compromises. As long as he had the prize, he could shape the world to his liking and dictate his own terms.

The weighted line began dragging on the ground. Fayla fought the compulsion to run after it and, as Helmut had taught her, she remained stationary to let the cable come to her. Methodically, she pulled the canvas gloves from her pockets and put them on.

Running across an open field in high-heeled boots while carrying a firearm was a problematic exercise to say the least, but pastureland was nothing new to the farm girl. Even so, she stumbled, fell, cursed, then pulled herself up.

At a hundred meters she went down again. This time on purpose. She had to decide—the plane or the red-haired woman. She probably didn't have the firepower to bring down the aircraft, so she put the sights on the woman and was just about to squeeze off a short burst when the helicopter exploded behind her.

Bloom was maybe thirty yards away and out of the kill zone, but despite that he was knocked to the ground with a sledge-hammer blast. Dazed, ears ringing, he weakly pulled himself up and saw a bonfire where the helicopter had been a moment before. Lying prostrate nearby was the figure of the assistant superintendent. "Grayson!" cried Bloom as he limped toward the charred body. He knelt down and felt the neck for a pulse, but found none. He'd seen enough corpses to know when a soul had departed the body.

The steel cable did a pirouette around Fayla and she grabbed it, letting it run loosely through her gloved hands until the loops arrived. She grabbed the middle one and clipped on the carabiner, then held her arms straight up, indicating she was ready for the skyhook maneuver.

The Pilatus turned away from the mayhem, drawing out the slack on the cable, and a moment before Mairead's disciple went airborne, a bullet tore out a plug of flesh near her left elbow, eliciting a yelp.

In frustration, Séverine and Chartain emptied the rest of their magazines at the retreating plane and the figure dangling underneath, but they both knew the targets were out of range.

As the gun smoke hung in the air, Chartain asked, "Think you connected?"

She shrugged. "Impossible to know."

The winch pulled in the cargo like a fishing reel. When it was complete, the titanium arm swung in and the servo door slid closed.

"Success?" asked the General from the cockpit.

"Yes!" screamed Fayla. "Yes! . . . But, I-I'm hit."

"Oh, dear," replied the General, genuinely concerned. He put the plane on autopilot, unbuckled his seat belt, and went back into the cabin.

He unhooked Fayla's carabiner, then took off the bag. He was a fastidious man by nature, and a lawyer by training, as opposed to a doctor. He found the blood streaming from her arm rather distasteful. But, in truth, it didn't look all that bad. "Nasty, but not to worry. You'll go into shock, but we'll get the medical team onto you straightaway after we touch down. In the meantime . . ." He went to the rear of the cabin and retrieved a first aid kit. He placed a cushioned bandage over the wound and said, "This is called a 'gouging wound.' Bernese Laboratories developed a vacuum bandage just for this sort of injury. Sold them worldwide. Made a fortune. We'll apply one after we land, but for now we'll fix you up the old-fashioned way, just like Josef taught me."

"Josef?"

"Mengele. Probably the brightest physician in the *SS*. Gave the senior officers a course in first aid for battle dressings. Heinrich insisted. Said we were all soldiers, as we were . . . are. There now, keep pressure on it. . . . And this? Is this our prize?"

"Yes, General. Mission accomplished."

He bestowed a genuine smile upon her, then peered into the purse to see the simple sealed object, not much larger than a couple of loaves of bread. The means to reshape the world. So incredibly benign. So incredibly powerful.

"My dear, words cannot express my feelings at this moment. Your achievement is Promethian in scope. I am a man of my word. England shall be yours. Now let us get you into the cockpit before you go deeper into shock. We'll be on the ground within the hour."

CHAPTER TWENTY-EIGHT

". . . and a person can be infectious for one to three weeks before the onset of symptoms, infection being passed by casual contact and, to a degree, even by airborne transmission."

The minister of health squirmed in his chair as he chimed in, "So what you are saying, Dr. Wingate, is this genetic virus can be in a stealth mode for upwards of three weeks, expanding its footprint through an unsuspecting populace before the first victims even exhibit a symptom?"

"Yes," replied Thaddeus Wingate. "That is how it was engineered. You see, this was the technical issue we spent years—"

"Yes, well, I think we get the picture, Dr. Wingate," interrupted the prime minister. "That will be all."

Chastened, Wingate rose and exited the Cabinet room at Number 10 Downing Street. A butler ushered him out, leaving a dozen men behind. On one side of the table sat the president of France, his defense, interior and health ministers, and a general named Bertrand. They had been flown in covertly that morning, driven into the underground garage of the Treasury, then taken via secret tunnel from Treasury to Number 10.

Across from the president of France was the prime minister, his health, foreign and defense ministers, the home secretary, the head of Scotland Yard, chief of the Joint Intelligence Committee (JIC), and three guests.

It was the prime minister who broke the silence with his aristocratic voice. "We could waste a lot of time dissecting how we fell into this mess. We could spend even more time convincing ourselves that the resurrection of Hitler's long-dead inner circle is impossible. But as surreal as the situation appears, I am convinced we have to deal with the reality that a most diabolical weapon has fallen into the hands of a most diabolical force."

"Agreed," said the president of France.

"Very well," replied the prime minister. "As our two nations are the ones who have been directly victimized, it is my view we must move swiftly and resolutely to identify the whereabouts of these renegades, put them down, and recover or destroy this virus mechanism."

"*Assurément,*" replied the French president.

"As this enterprise seems to have emanated from Switzerland, I spoke with the Swiss president by phone three days ago, followed by a personal briefing presented to him by my home secretary."

"And the result?" asked the French president.

"All we could obtain was his promise to 'look into the matter,'" said the prime minister

"Fortunately," said the chief of the JIC, "based on the assistance of Inspector Broussard, we at least have a departure point upon which to focus our resources."

Emil Broussard nodded with difficulty. His head in a neck brace, his right arm in a cast, and various bandages on his face. Despite an angled impact on a deep snow drift, much like a ski jump landing, the 370-foot fall had inflicted a rash of injuries.

The chief of the JIC continued. "We have had Mont Collon under surveillance for the last forty-eight hours, a team of three

MI6 agents covertly in the village, and a team of three SAS men in the surrounding hills. All have satellite phones and we will be notified immediately of any activity. The mansion of Leopold Mainz has also been under surveillance. Thus far, no activity has been detected in either place. Government Communications Headquarters has focused its eavesdropping resources on the Swiss government, but has picked up nothing of consequence."

Bloom leaned forward, "Prime Minister, Mister President, may I interject something here?"

"By all means, Captain Bloom," replied the prime minister.

"As Inspector Broussard's jaw has been injured and Grayson Salisbury gave his life in the line of duty, if I may I would like to speak for my comrades." A silence fell over the table. "Inspector Broussard's penetration of this Nazi redoubt revealed two things: one, this hijacking was years in the making; and two, Inspector Broussard witnessed the laboratories in the process of being packed up, but not packed up and abandoned."

"So what is your point, Captain?" asked the British home secretary.

"The Eurostar hijacking was meticulously planned and executed. If the packing up of the Nazi redoubt was not completed, it was because Schellenberg felt confident he had sufficient time post-hijacking to complete the task."

"So what are you saying, Captain?" asked the French defense minister.

Bloom took a deep breath and put it on the table. "What I'm saying is if Schellenberg felt that confident, he had to have sufficient collaboration within the Swiss government to cover his ultimate escape."

"I would agree," said Broussard, again, with difficulty.

"Therefore," continued Bloom, "if you are encountering foot

dragging from the Swiss government, that tells me that Schellenberg is still in country, probably at the redoubt itself. And the Swiss won't take any action until after he's gone. As such, we may never catch him."

"But if the Swiss government is stonewalling, what recourse do we have?" asked the French interior minister.

"I would say the course of action is obvious: a direct military assault on the Nazi redoubt. Destroy the guts of the place. Kill or capture everyone inside."

The British foreign minister looked as if he'd had a coronary. "Captain Bloom, have you taken leave of your senses? Invade a sovereign nation in the heart of Europe? Such a suggestion is preposterous!"

Bloom sighed again. "Gentlemen, the time is too short and the threat too grave for the luxury of political correctness. The truth is, if that Nazi fortress was in Botswana or Indonesia or Paraguay, you'd launch an assault in a heartbeat. And who's to say the Swiss haven't cut a secret deal with Schellenberg already: sanctuary in return for immunity from the virus. Hell, the man cut a deal with the Swiss when he worked for Hitler. Maybe he's done it again! His verbatim remarks to Inspector Broussard were that his 'people' were liberally sprinkled throughout the Swiss intelligence services, the military, the banks and the police force."

The room fell silent. The British prime minister looked at the French president, who nodded, and they turned to the men in uniform sitting at the table. "General Bertrand is such an assault feasible?"

The general was matter-of-fact. "A small commando force inserted by air from across the border in Italian airspace, then landing on the flat summit of Mont Collon. In fast with explosives, rappel down and extraction by land vehicle at the base of the mountain. Transport to a nearby airfield where the team is flown out. All communications into and out of the village will be cut just before the assault is launched."

"How large a team?" asked the British defense minister.

"Eight in the air assault."

"Only eight?"

"Our purpose will not be to engage in a pitched battle, but to deliver satchel charges and pyro-munitions to destroy the fortress, and capture or kill Schellenberg and the Bannon woman."

"What is this pyro-munition you speak of?" asked the British home secretary.

"The English do not have an exclusive franchise on the development of sinister munitions," explained General Bertrand. "It is called 'ragepalm,' not to be confused with napalm. While napalm is quite impressive in its own way, it is essentially gasoline in a gelatin form. Ragepalm is a pure liquid that is stable until ignited, then it releases energy along the lines of burning thermite."

"So how do you intend to deploy it?" asked the British defense minister, who'd never heard of the stuff.

"We will land three three-hundred-gallon bladders on the summit of Mont Collon, then run hoses into the redoubt and let gravity do the rest. According to Inspector Broussard, the Nazi redoubt is multi-layered. The ragepalm will be poured in on the upper level so it will trickle down to the lower levels. In terms of energy released, think nitroglycerin in thermal form."

"I see," said the home secretary. "But how do you get these bladders on top of Mont Collon?"

"Leave that to us."

The British foreign secretary was still squeamish. "But is this worth the risk? The key components for this virus that was hijacked from the Eurostar are no bigger than a football."

"That is true," said the French president, "but what this

renegade has done against the nation of France is an act of war, and the Swiss government is complicit as far as I'm concerned. Therefore, Prime Minister, we are going to execute General Bertrand's plan without delay."

"I concur," said the prime minister "Whom do you intend to lead the assault? Or do I have to ask?"

All eyes turned to Marc Chartain as the French president said, "Colonel, it appears the nation of France requires your unique talents once again. However, I have to say that in view of your recent exploits in North Africa and on the Eurostar rescue I cannot, in good conscience, order you into harm's way again. I will only say the mission is yours if you want it."

Chartain met the president's gaze. "Schellenberg murdered my friends and comrades. I accept the mission."

"*Bon*," said the president. "And what about the woman? Mademoiselle duVaal? The one who keeps avoiding me? Will she be on the assault team?"

Chartain cracked a smile. "She is at her family's farm in the Vercors helping with spring planting. But she has authorized me to speak for her: she insists on being part of the team."

"Very well," said the prime minister. "I will have some disappointed gentlemen in the SAS, but the French team will have responsibility for the insertion and the assault. We will provide surveillance and the resources for extraction.

"Now let us adjourn so that General Bertrand and Colonel Chartain can get on with it. However, before we leave, I must say to Inspector Broussard, you have brought this information to us at great personal risk to yourself. Arguably, in so doing, you have made yourself *persona non grata* in your own country. Therefore, should you choose to avail yourself of the option, Her Majesty's Government is prepared to offer you political asylum."

"As is the government of France," said the French president.

"*Merci*," was all he could manage.

"Then we are adjourned," said the prime minister, adding, "Mister President, would you stay behind for a moment?"

The men at the table filed out, leaving the young prime minister and the Frenchman of Eastern European extraction behind. The two men stood at the window, looking out through the bulletproof glass. For some seconds they silently communicated with the empathy that only heads of state understand. Then finally, the younger man said mournfully, "I had great hopes for reforming our financial system."

The Frenchman shrugged. "I was going to focus on reviving the economy."

The prime minister sighed and said, "I wish you luck with the assault. It must be done. But I fear we may be too late."

"As do I."

The prime minister shook his head. "I am absolutely at a loss to understand how this malicious alchemy could go on in this country for years—decades. And once it is out of the bottle the consequences are too horrible to contemplate."

"True. But do not underestimate our own resources or capabilities."

The prime minister nodded. "That fellow Chartain seems quite the tough customer. He really pulled off that Libya business?"

"With the woman duVaal, oui."

"Incredible. And they almost saved the day on the Eurostar. A formidable team."

"As is that Chicago policeman. It might be prudent to have him on the extraction team."

CHAPTER TWENTY-NINE

The twin Rolls-Royce Tyne engines strained against the 30,000-foot service ceiling as the Transall C-160 cargo aircraft made its way through Italian airspace—on a "milk run" to the American air base at Aviano.

The loadmaster made sure his oxygen mask had a snug fit, then clipped on his tether line and threw the switch to lower the cargo door in the arse of the aircraft.

Despite the thermal flight suit, the sub-zero chill was a shock to the system as he motioned to the two airmen. They followed his hand signal and pulled the safety restraints on the slats holding a large cubed object in place. Then the two airmen joined the loadmaster on the interior side of the cube and began pushing it across the floor rollers towards the open sky. It moved slowly at first, then gained momentum as it approached the lip of the door. Automatically, a drogue chute deployed, catching a gulp of the 250-knot slipstream of the aircraft. This yanked the cube into space, where it began to plummet like a stone until the drogue plucked a giant canopy into the air, and the descent slowed.

The loadmaster peered down at the wing-shaped object and hit his intercom button to say, "Cargo away and canopy deployed!" Then he flipped the switch and the cargo door began to close . . . and he was happy about that. Sharing the same space as nine hundred gallons of the most flammable liquid known to man was a little disconcerting. He was looking forward to getting on the ground and having a smoke.

The DragonFly air cargo delivery system was not a parachute per se. More precisely, it was a ram-air pressurized gliding canopy, enabled with a GPS navigation system that could guide a payload to a predetermined landing zone—in this case, the summit of Mont Collon.

General Alois Bertrand hated his desk. So much so he often fantasized about taking the fire emergency axe and hacking it into so much kindling. He'd spent too many years pushing paper and he damn well was not going to miss this one—even if it was as a straphanging observer.

In the cargo bay of the second C-160, Bertrand heard the pilot's voice through the headset, "Canopy away from lead aircraft! Prepare to disembark!"

Bertrand clipped on his oxygen mask and his eyes met Chartain's through the visor of the Legionnaire's HALO helmet. He stuck out his gloved hand and shouted loud enough to be heard, "No Geneva rules here! We're dealing with a menace!"

Chartain nodded and shook the hand. "That goes without saying."

Bertrand turned to Séverine and said, "God go with you, Captain."

"Merci, General," she replied. "Not to worry. This is what you trained us for."

Bertrand nodded, wondering how someone could wear a

one-piece black assault suit and a crash helmet, and still look fabulous. Next fashion season the Paris runways would be full of assault suits and safety helmets. He was sure of it. "Time to strap in," he said finally.

"Roger, General," replied Chartain.

Chartain, Séverine, Sergeant Major Rocard, and five other members of the Squadron took a deep breath, then quickly unplugged their oxygen hoses from the receptacles along the cargo bay's bulkhead and clipped them into the pressurized bottles on their thighs. They had been pre-breathing oxygen for the last hour to "wash" the nitrogen out of their system prior to the HALO descent. Otherwise the rapid freefall from this altitude would give them the bends. Once satisfied the oxygen flow was operative, they went to their assigned contraptions lying on the deck.

Chartain and Séverine lay down on their respective apparatus in the prone position as the airmen secured the restraining strap over the small of their backs. These were the "Switchblades," or in the military vernacular PHASST gliders, meaning "Programmable High Altitude Single Soldier Transport." Literally fulfilling the dreams of Icarus, the single-person vehicle gave the pilot wings. Séverine lay down and inserted her arms into the grooves, then took hold of the hand controllers. Her torso was snug against the flat carbon composite fuselage, while her boots rested in the saddle of the V-shaped tail. She made sure her oxygen hose wasn't crimped as the airman did a final check on the parachute regalia.

The Switchblade was developed by a small American company with the view of inserting commandos into a hostile environment from a "stand-off" position. Described more as something you wear than something you ride, the Switchblade was contoured to fit the pilot's body, with arms and legs fitting into recessed grooves in the fuselage. The wings were swept back for deployment, but could be electronically expanded into a maximum wingspan of eight feet for longer cruise and slower flight.

The summit of Mont Collon was a mere three kilometers from the Italian border, but to ensure a stealthy approach the planners had factored in an additional sixteen kilometers for the DragonFly cargo and Switchblade deployment.

The loadmaster looked at Chartain, who surveyed his team and gave a thumbs-up. The loadmaster hit the switch and the ramp began its descent to a howling wind. Once it was locked down, the crewmen began pushing Chartain's aircraft tail first toward the void.

To the unaccustomed observer, parting company with an aircraft in such a manner would imbue stark terror, but with 484 jumps under his belt and as one of a handful of troops qualified on the Switchblade, Chartain let the training kick in. Once free of the transport he put his tiny glider into a moderate dive and deployed the wings to their full extension. That done, he checked the GPS readout and rolled it into a shallow bank toward the Swiss frontier—knowing his team would follow in his wake.

Gideon Bloom had an overcoat and ski cap on as he stood on the edge of the forest looking up at the summit of Mont Collon. The SAS sergeant with him had not said three words in three hours. Hadn't moved, in fact. Not an inch. Bloom thought he knew something about stakeouts, but this guy was a machine. Where did they find these people? And what did they do to them once they found them?

His cell phone chirped and he answered, "Hello?"

"Mr. Crestway?"

"That's me."

"Yes, sir, this is Riverbend Floral. We wanted you to know the flowers you ordered were just delivered to your wife."

"Thank you. I'm sure she'll enjoy them." He rang off and said over his shoulder, "Curtain's going up."

No response.

He turned and the SAS man who'd been a statue for three hours was nowhere to be seen.

The Switchblade glider really came into its own along the no man's land of the Afghanistan-Pakistan tribal area. Faced with foot-dragging from the Pakistanis to clear out the Taliban/al-Qaeda riff-raff, plus the distances involved and lack of natural cover, it was well-nigh impossible to get a strike force in place when "actionable intelligence" came in. Helicopters could be heard miles away. HAHO jumps took too much time. Predator drones were, well, drones.

Enter the Switchblade.

If intel came in about a bunch of Taliban mucky-mucks sipping tea in some tribal village, three troops could be deployed via the Switchblades fifteen miles away and on the ground before the Taliban could scrabble back to their holes. Then airstrikes could be called in by the observer team.

At a 160-mph cruise, the twelve-mile distance to Mont Collon was covered in 4.5 minutes.

Séverine was about four hundred meters behind Chartain, her ponytail flapping and jumpsuit cracking in the slipstream as they entered the airspace above Mont Collon. Despite the double layer of thermal underwear the icy wind cut deep as the snow-capped peaks of the Alps seemed to reach out for her. They were five thousand feet above the summit as she watched Chartain begin a wide banking turn to the left. She applied a little left rudder to follow him down, and the assault team began their descent in a wagonwheel spiral. To the left she caught sight of the DragonFly cargo chute coming in.

Through his binoculars, Bloom saw the big DragonFly canopy approaching the summit and could barely make out a number of gnats circling above. Then one of the gnats bloomed into a parasail.

Chartain separated from his Switchblade, went into a brief freefall, and deployed his chute.

Séverine reached back and hit the handle to release the restraining strap. The airflow ripped her out of the Switchblade like a rag doll, and into a freefall she went. She angled into the air to carry herself closer to Chartain before yanking on her ripcord and bracing for the whipsaw action of the billowing parasail. She looked up to ensure she had a fully deployed canopy, then grabbed the control risers and watched her spent Switchblade head for the forest below. She hoped its carcass would be found by the Swiss authorities so the American manufacture would throw them off.

Manfred Jost had been given the security post, and like any *SS* man he took his duties seriously. Since the General's extraordinary operation had proved successful, the Fourth Reich would rise up, and Jost would be a part of it. So now more than ever vigilance was required: the Reich's informers were placed throughout the village; sensors and motion detectors were installed on the mountain approaches; and every square meter of the mountain was under video surveillance, which all fed into Jost's station, where he monitored a numbing array of video monitors. However, even with the increased watch-fulness, Jost had to obey his bladder from time to time, so he was absent when the DragonFly cargo canopy landed on the summit. He had just returned when he saw the first commando parasail land. Then another . . . and another! He brought his fist down on the alert button and a klaxon reverberated through the fortress as he grabbed the red phone and shouted, "General, we are under attack!"

General Walther Schellenberg winced and held the red phone receiver away from his ear. He calmly took off his reading glasses and said, "Jost, get a hold of yourself. Now then, what exactly is happening?"

"*Fallschirmjäger*! Paratroops! Landing on the summit! Four! . . . five! . . . six!"

Schellenberg sighed, thinking he really must do a better job of vetting these people. Kriegsmarine veterans like Helmut were the personification of grace under pressure. These young people . . .

"Now, Jost, six Fallschirmjäger are hardly an invasion."

"Seven!"

"All right, seven. Just make sure the fortress is secured and I will be there directly. Have Helmut meet me there."

"Jawohl, Herr General!"

Schellenberg hung up the phone and looked at Fayla. "Well, my dear, it appears the timetable for our departure has been moved up a bit. No matter. Come along."

And with that they rose to exit. On the way out he paused for a moment to gaze at his "Eagle's Lair." The chamber had been burrowed out of solid rock and he always looked upon it as a little fortress of solitude. The golden eagle and swastika that hung behind his chair, the autographed photos of himself with the Führer, and with Coco Chanel. The tea service he had spirited away from Berchtesgaden before the Allied troops arrived, the paintings from the private Jewish art collections, the tiny Rodin sculpture he used for a paperweight. He would've preferred to take them along as keepsakes. But perhaps it was better this way. Closure, you might say. He grabbed the satchel off the 18th-century table that held the prize from the Eurostar, then took Fayla's hand and led her to the security post.

Marc Chartain hit the release on his parasail rigging, then turned to watch Séverine and Sergeant Major Rocard land not a hundred feet away from him. He looked up and confirmed the remainder of his team had successfully separated from their Switchblades and were descending in stairstep fashion.

Not wasting time, he unstrapped his Heckler & Koch submachine gun and began trudging through the meter-high snow toward the terminus of the cable car station.

Séverine followed him, as did the Sergeant Major, while the others headed for the cargo cube. No one said anything. It had all been rehearsed.

"So, what do we have here?" asked Schellenberg.

"We count eight troops on the summit," replied Helmut. "As you can see, some are moving toward the cable car and some are going to some object over there." He pointed and said, "Manfred, zoom in on that . . . ah, *gut*. An air drop."

Schellenberg peered at the screen. "Quite right. Are we buttoned up?"

"Of course, Herr General."

"Any word from our people in the village?"

"Nein, Herr General. It appears communications have been cut."

"Hmm. Well, they cannot be Swiss. Half of the government is on our retainer and the other half shares our view of the world—what's left of it, anyway. If they were Swiss we would know about it and they would approach from the base of the mountain. That means they are probably French, or British. I smell that American Jew policeman behind this somewhere. No matter, let us be on our way. Is the exit prepared for myself and the Fräulein?"

"I triple checked everything myself, Herr General."

Schellenberg graced him with a smile and patted his shoulder. "As I knew you would, *meiner gute Freund*. Leave a couple of surprises behind for our visitors. Better yet, have Jost here and one or two others put up some resistance, then off you go down the chute. I wouldn't want to make it too easy for them."

He and Helmut shared a hearty laugh.

Jost wasn't laughing.

Schellenberg clapped Helmut on the shoulder again and said, "See you in Trieste. Come along, my dear. Time to complete some unfinished business." And he took Fayla's hand in his right and led her away, the satchel in the other.

Chartain, Séverine and the Sergeant Major approached the opening of the cable car station with caution.

"Wait!" barked Séverine, and she pointed. A small object on a pedestal.

"Camera," replied Chartain. "Take it."

From the hip Séverine fired a three-round burst and the camera disintegrated.

Chartain continued his approach and peered over the edge.

In the cement chamber was the cable car, a hairnet of wheels and gears, and a vault-like door, similar to what you would see in a bank. Chartain motioned them back, then pulled the pin on a grenade and tossed it in. There was a *whump!* and smoke belched out of the opening, followed by silence.

"It appears no booby traps in place," Rocard muttered into his radio. "Bring the munitions forward."

CHAPTER THIRTY

Fayla had faced down the business end of a gun more times than she could count, had provided sexual rapture to a series of men who would have topped her had they known her true identity, but nothing imbued pure fear and intimidation in her like this Nazi temple. Meekly she allowed the general to lead her down the grand winding staircase, past the carvings of Teutonic knights on horseback on the marble wall, then into the columned temple and on to the black double doors with the giant *SANCTUS* inscribed on it.

"Now, my dear, you have seen everything but what lies behind these doors. I promised you that you would pass through them at the proper time. Now is that time." He opened the door and led her into the inner sanctum.

Louis DeMar was the explosives expert of the Squadron. Rapidly he unwrapped a snake-like tube of material with the consistency of silly putty, then pressed it against the vault door in a circular pattern. It possessed an adhesive property and stuck. To this he attached a detonator lead, crimped it to the wire and then played out the spool, saying, "Everyone back!"

Fayla trembled at the sight before her. The coffin-like lozenges that filled the vaulted chamber, the gas-fired torches, the giant swastika eagle, and the gold coffin on the altar with the word Führer in raised letters. The General brought her to the altar and through the faceplate she peered down at the unmistakable countenance that had sent an entire world into war.

She looked at Schellenberg, who gazed into the coffin contemplatively. Finally, he said, "Ah, Adolf. We have come to this moment. I needed you,"—he gestured with his hand—"needed all this to rally the troops at war's end. But now? I am afraid the times have passed you by. You really were such a simple man. No education. A corporal. A failed artist. This world would only confound you."

And with that he turned to Fayla and said, "You have delivered to the Fourth Reich the means to rule the world. Therefore, I shall be the Führer and you shall be my queen. Do you accept?"

"I accept," whispered the Belfast street urchin.

"Very well. It is time to bring an end to the Third Reich, and out of its ashes our reign shall begin."

And with that, Schellenberg reached into his satchel and withdrew an object that could only be described as a Medieval mace, with a spiked sphere on the end. Then with a savagery that frightened her, the General brought the iron mallet down with a vengeance to shatter the face plate and crack the skull of Adolph Hitler until his brains were revealed.

Not stopping there, Schellenberg went to the coffin labeled Himmler and said cryptically over his shoulder, "You have no idea how I had to suck up to this insufferable chicken farmer." And with that he shattered glass and brains again. Then on to . . .

Göring. "You drug-addicted pig!"

Goebbels. "You pathetic prick!"

Bormann. "You drunken doorstop!"

And on it went until the brains of the Nazi inner circle had been reduced to pulp.

Then they heard a muffled explosion.

Schellenberg tossed the bloody mace aside with a *clang* and took Fayla's arm, saying, "Our visitors are knocking on the door. Let us be on our way."

Jost gripped the stock of his machine pistol nervously as Helmut sat on the edge of a hole in the floor, his legs dangling out of sight.

Helmut turned his torso and said, "Now just fire off a magazine, keep their heads down, and follow us down. We need a little distraction to make our escape. *Verstehst du?*"

"Uh, *ja*," replied an unenthused Jost.

"Very well." Helmut folded his arms, slid off the edge and disappeared down the hole like a rabbit.

Sergeant Major Rocard tossed a grenade through the portal of twisted metal that had been the vault door. They waited for the *whump!* and without a word Séverine—because of her smaller size—dove through the hole and rolled, bringing her MP5 to her shoulder.

"Clear!" came the shout from within.

Chartain squeezed through the hole, followed by the Sergeant Major. They were on a concrete landing of a flight of stairs.

"Follow me," ordered Chartain, and he started down toward the opening to a passageway.

After suffering the ravages of World War I and the Great Depression, the German economy finally started to revive in the late 1930s, propelled by military spending. In so doing, the aristocracy began building new mansions, or refurbishing old ones, in the trendier districts of Berlin. In a quirk of fashion that for a brief period became all the rage, the idle rich would host dinner parties where cocktails would be served in a drawing room and dinner in a lower-level dining room. Instead of walking down a flight of steps, someone installed a children's slide—like the kind you would find on a playground—and the guests would slide down to dinner. The picture of middle-aged aristocrats descending a playground slide wearing their evening gowns, tuxedos and uniforms made for a ridiculous image; but for some reason it caught on.

Schellenberg, of course, was a fixture on the Berlin dinner party circuit and he "slid" on a number of occasions. And it was out of that experience that he had the idea for the chute.

It was simplicity itself. A tunnel burrowed from the fortress at an angle to the termination point within the treeline at the base of the mountain. It was lined with smooth aluminum and illuminated by a series of LEDs strung along the ceiling.

With unlimited funds, it took three years to dig and construct, but the General was always one to plan ahead.

With arms folded, Helmut leaned back and watched the lights whip by overhead like white stripes on the road. The truth be told, this was actually fun. Made all the better by besting the opposition. The General was going to make a fantastic Führer. He was sure of it. So much stronger and wiser than those weak-kneed party hacks.

As he approached the terminus point the descent angle became more and more shallow until his momentum brought him to a halt at the moment he slid into daylight and his feet touched the bottom of the chute.

German physics and engineering. Best in the world, ja?

Helmut swung his legs over and stood up on the small concrete apron. The camouflage bush that concealed the terminus
had been removed, and twelve of his men were removing
mountain bikes from a subterranean storage area.

"The rest of you mount your bikes and head for the rallying
point. I will wait here for Jost and the others."

After a few *jawohl*s, the group headed down the mountain
trail on their Peugeots.

Chartain peered through a large bay window at the vacant
laboratory below. The stainless steel work tables were there,
along with some discarded lab equipment, but empty cabinets
and storage bins yawned back at him.

"We're too late," he said laconically. "They've cleared out."

"Maybe so, maybe no," replied Séverine. "This is where
Broussard was. Let's go this way."

She led on past the opening to the hallway with offices, past
the radio room and the entry to the empty barracks. She
approached the dogleg of the corridor and ever so carefully
peered around the corner—to see Schellenberg and Fayla
crossing the passageway to enter a doorway.

Séverine raised her weapon to fire as the royal couple of the
new Reich ducked inside. Fayla slammed the heavy metal door
closed as a burst of bullets ricocheted off it. She dropped and
locked the lever, then turned to see the General raise the
Plexiglas canopy of the glider resting on the launch rails. He
tucked the satchel in the small storage area behind the rear
passenger seat, and said, "My dear, would you mind pushing
the camouflage blocks out of the way. Then we'll be off."

"Of course," replied the empress, to the sound of someone
trying to force the door open.

Chartain strained against it to no avail. "We'll have to blow it."

"No!" said Séverine. "This is the way Broussard came in. Come on!" And they turned and ran back the way they'd come.

Manfred Jost was creeping up the stairs from the chute chamber when he heard the weapons fire. He and his two cohorts halted, not sure what to do.

One of the men raised his eyebrow to Jost, and Jost croaked, "We stay here."

Séverine, Chartain, and the Sergeant Major ran pell mell back up the stairs, through the blown vault, and across the snow to the summit's edge. They looked down and saw the last of the camouflage cubes tumbling down the cliff face. Séverine pointed at one of the bundles of rope DeMar had pre-positioned for their escape and said to Chartain, "Belay me!"

Chartain replied, "I'm not sure about this."

"Do it!"

Chartain sighed and said, "Come along Sergeant Major. Always give a woman what she wants."

Fayla pushed off the last of the camouflage cubes and a horizontal opening wide enough to accommodate the wingspan was cleared. Schellenberg helped his consort into the rear seat, then climbed into the front and said, "Strap yourself in." And he dropped and locked the canopy.

When Emil Broussard had found his way into the chamber he'd passed an object covered by a tarpaulin. That was a disassembled glider that was now assembled and sitting on the launch rails.

With the sub-machine gun on her back, Séverine held onto the looped end of the rope with both hands as she walked backwards down the cliff face. Chartain and the Sergeant Major played out the rope until she was just above the opening cut into the rock for the glider's tail section to clear. But she didn't know that's what it was.

She looked up and nodded; it was time to do the "swing-in" maneuver. Designed to crash through windows, the commando would push off hard, drop a few feet on the rope before swing in to crash through the window feet first, guns ablaze. At least, that was how it was supposed to work.

Schellenberg pulled the knob on the control panel, releasing the weighted line to engage the pulley. Fayla's head bobbled back from the abrupt acceleration as the daylight of the opening rushed toward them.

What happened next was a hefty dose of shock and awe to all parties, and it took them a few moments to absorb and process exactly what had happened. Just as the nose of the glider cleared the opening some object dropped out of nowhere and smashed onto the canopy.

The glider cleared the opening and was immediately caught in a strong updraft rising along the cliff face.

Chartain and the Sergeant Major could only stand with open mouths as they watched the glider rise in the air with Séverine duVaal clinging to the canopy.

Schellenberg struggled with the controls to compensate for the unexpected weight on the nose. He brought it roughly under control, but as he flew out of the updraft he realized the added weight drove them in too rapid a descent. He waggled the wings, but couldn't dislodge the uninvited passenger who was hugging the canopy with her arms and legs, so he banked around to reenter the updraft.

The Sergeant Major raised his gun to shoot at the returning glider, but Chartain put up a hand to hold the fire. "I fear she has gone too far this time."

Séverine and Fayla were almost face to face, separated only by a thin layer of clear CycloShield canopy glass. Séverine's gun was strapped behind her but it might as well have been on the moon. Fayla realized this and smiled her most wicked smile.

Schellenberg looked at the altimeter and said, "I think it is time to say *auf Wiedersehen* to our unwanted guest."

"I agree completely." And she waved bye-bye.

Higher and higher they climbed in the updraft; then the General pushed the nose over into a steep dive.

As the nose pointed down Séverine started to slide off, but as can happen with aerodynamics, the physics of a given situation can play out differently than you'd expect. The on-rush of air first pinned her in place, but then drove her along the fuselage, past the canopy and onto the fuselage stem toward the tail—as her arms and legs refused to let go.

Determined to dislodge her, the general yanked back on the stick and the nose reared up, sending Séverine into the cruciform tail. Her crash helmet bashed against it as the glider's momentum took the aircraft straight up. The General cursed and struggled with the stick as he tried to nose the glider over again to regain airspeed. But Séverine's body weight disrupted the aircraft's balance, freezing it in a vertical, nose-up/tail-down position as its kinetic energy bled off. They all hung in the air for a moment before the glider began to sink into a tailslide, falling to earth—tail first.

An accomplished pilot, Schellenberg knew how to handle a Hammerhead aerobatic maneuver—but not with an uninvited adversary literally on his tail. He wrestled violently with the stick as they began falling backwards, and for once terror gripped the terrorist as Fayla screamed, *"General, what's happening?"*

With her legs wrapped around the fuselage and the ground rushing up towards her, Séverine pulled on the elevator control surface of the tail section with all her strength until she felt something give way, then the aircraft flipped nose-down and flung her into space like a slingshot.

Mesmerized, Chartain watched his love separate from the aircraft on an upward trajectory, along with a small piece of the tail. Then she seemed to hang in the air for a moment before starting to fall. A wave of impotence washed over Chartain as he watched the tiny figure of his heart fall down . . . down . . . down . . .

She was only about two hundred feet from the valley floor when she popped her reserve chute.

The glider, now tipped into a nosedive, regained much-needed airspeed, wobbled and pulled up a little, but clearly still out of control as it disappeared behind a ridge.

"Did you see that!"

Bloom turned and saw the SAS man had returned out of nowhere. "Indeed, I did."

The reserve chute was much smaller, and the thin Alpine air

caused her descent to be uncomfortably rapid when she landed near the bottom of a neighboring mountain with a *thump* and a puff of snow.

"Sergeant Major?"

"Oui, Colonel."

"When we get off this mountain you are going to buy me a very large brandy."

"Oui, Colonel."

"Courvoisier."

"Oui, Colonel."

"Now it is time to dispatch this accursed place back to hell. Send the men down to snap a few pictures, then hose it down with the fire water."

"Oui, Colonel."

Shaken by what he'd seen in the warren of tunnels below, Louis DeMar opened the valves, allowing the gravity flow of the ragepalm to surge through the hoses and into the guts of the fortress. The pungent-smelling liquid trickled down the steps, and into fractures and crevices as it found its way to the lower parts of the fortress—down the Wagnerian staircase, across the temple floor and under the door marked *SANCTUS*, and it was there the vapors floated upward to caress the gas-fired torches.

Jost and his two compatriots had retreated behind the door and locked it, the weather stripping on the bottom acting like a little dam to the liquid building up behind it, but not to the vapors.

Jost sniffed, then ventured to open the door. A tiny wave

washed over his boots and swished into the chute entry.

Raw terror seizing him, he dropped his weapon and jumped into the hole.

Later in his debrief, Chartain told the scribes it was a good thing he had no idea of the explosive force of the Rage-palm; otherwise he never would've signed on. Once the vapors reached the torches in the sanctum chamber the entire mountain seemed to convulse, belching smoke and fire out of the cable car entrance and literally knocking Chartain's team off their feet as flames raced up the hoses and immolated the bladders in a kind of funeral pyre.

Chartain pulled himself up and said, "I believe that is our cue. Over the side with us."

The old ski-lift operator was just returning to his post from a schnapps break when he heard a rumbling sound like thunder, drawing his attention up toward Mont Collon. A black cloud was rising above the summit. "A volcano? In the Alps?"

Helmut had watched the aerial dance of the glider with alarm. Then he heard the explosion and saw the smoke curling into the air. Shortly thereafter he heard a scream coming from the chute. In a dance of the macabre, Jost popped out of the exit on fire. Screaming and waving his arms, he took a few steps, then fell and rolled on the forest floor. Helmut sighed and shook his head, then approached the charred and whimpering figure. He withdrew his Luger and put the muzzle to Jost's temple and administered the *coup de grace*.

Then he climbed on his bike and was on his way. There was

much to be done, and not much time to do it.

Bloom watched the seven French commandos rappel down the sheer face of Mont Collon. They made it look so easy, and once on the ground they trotted over to the three SUVs that the SAS men had made appear out of nowhere. Bloom stuck out his hand. "Colonel Chartain, glad your team all made it down. I'm told it's a short drive to the airfield. We'll be wheels up inside of forty minutes."

Chartain shook Bloom's hand and asked, "Captain duVaal?"

Bloom gestured to one of the vehicles. "Sprained ankle and maybe a cracked rib or two. But otherwise no worse for wear. What did you find?"

Chartain shook his head. "Something that should have gone into the flames a long time ago."

EPILOGUE

Ordinarily, investitures are awarded in the Victorian Ballroom of Buckingham Palace, but as this was a private ceremony the more intimate Prince Albert Music Room was selected. There, an elderly woman had some kind words for a middle-aged woman, her two grown sons and three grandchildren. Tea was served to the utter boredom of the four-year-old, who fidgeted in the suit purchased especially for this occasion.

In a sense, it was an awkward audience because the hostess had access to state secrets, but the widow of Grayson Salisbury did not. So it was with a degree of ignorance Mrs. Salisbury accepted the Order of the British Empire posthumously for her husband, taking it on faith from the sovereign that the title was given for "extraordinary service to the Crown."

At the opening reception of a European summit conference on global warming held in Madrid, the British prime minister, the French president, and the Swiss president bumped into each other at the canapé table. A brief discussion ensued about the economy, the lovely Spanish weather, and polite inquiries as to whether the French president's fashion-model wife would put in an appearance at the conference.

No one mentioned anything about Hitler and his inner circle being cremated inside a Swiss Alp by a French and British assault team.

Gideon Bloom trudged up the stairs of Chicago Police Headquarters and entered the office of the newly appointed Police Superintendent Samuel Bracewell. No greetings were exchanged between the two men as Bloom sat down.

Bracewell lifted two letters, one in each hand saying, "This is from Number Ten Downing Street. This is from the Élysée Palace. Both of them say words to the effect that you saved Western civilization.

"I send you to Geneva with a corpse and you come back with these? What the precise hell went on over there? Besides a bill from the Dorchester that wiped out half my budget for the next year?"

Bloom sighed. "I knew this question was coming, Sammy, so to preface my response, let's say things are now in the hands of people above our pay grade. I was asked to keep a lid on this adventure by the prime minister and the French president, and I agreed with the proviso I could inform my boss. They agreed, providing you give me an oath you'll keep your mouth shut."

"If I do, will this come back to bite me in the ass?"

"Possibly. . . . Probably."

Bracewell groaned. "Okay, so give it to me."

"In that case you better get some coffee in here."

Two hours and six cups later, the coffee had been replaced by Jim Beam as an ashen-faced Bracewell sat gaping at Gideon Bloom.

"This cannot be for real!" he said finally.

"You wanted to know. I'd say it's a history lesson you'll remember."

A prolonged silence followed, until a plaintive Bracewell asked, "And this Schellenberg, the woman, they're dead?"

Bloom shrugged. "Their glider was headed down, the French woman ripped off the tail section in midair. Something they don't teach at the police academy by the way. But the aircraft went down behind a ridge and never came up again."

"You didn't answer my question."

"I didn't answer it because I can't. They went down inside the Swiss border so we couldn't hang around, and I can't give you a wiseguy confirmation."

"Meaning?"

Bloom sighed. "I didn't see their brains, Sammy."

On an isolated Corsican beach, the sun was going down as Marc Chartain watched Séverine emerge from the surf like Aphrodite from the sea. She walked toward him with the trace of a limp from the ankle that had not yet completely healed. Chartain took some comfort in that, for it was evidence she wasn't made of iron after all. He wrapped her in a towel and they both lay down on the sand that held the remnants of the sun's warmth.

It should have been a refreshing holiday after their exploits, and initially it was, but slowly the aftershock of the stress started to weigh upon them, as did the loss of their comrades.

Chartain built a fire, and in silence they watched the stars come out, Séverine lying in the crook of his arm—both of them wondering what the future held.

On the tramp steamer *Augsburg* a figure emerged from

below and came out on deck. She was wearing a pea jacket and her red hair was tucked under a bosun's cap. A chill had set in with the night air, but she was glad to be on deck after staying out of sight all day. She moved to the bow railing where another figure, sitting in a wheelchair with an extended leg in a cast, awaited her.

"Ah, my dear, so good of you to join me. I hope Helmut has not been boring you with stories of his adventures in the Kriegsmarine?"

She shook her head carefully, being cautious not to aggravate her arm in the sling from a dislocated shoulder. "Not at all. I had no idea he'd had two submarines shot out from under him in the North Atlantic."

"Helmut. What a capable man. Pried us out of that glider and got us to Trieste. And here we are. By the way, how is the shoulder feeling?"

"Much better, although we must get off this boat before too long; Wilhelm has stuffed me silly. I must have put on five pounds."

The new Führer laughed. "And who could blame him? No one, myself included, can resist your charms. And besides, there is a sense of excitement in the air."

"I must say I picked up on that. All those white-jacketed eggheads below seem giddy as school girls."

"As well they might." He pointed to a distant shoreline where faint pinpoints of light shimmered on the horizon. "You see, the Fourth Reich begins there, my dear, and we will enjoy success beyond the imagination of those weak old men we left in the mountain cave. As soon as you and I have mended, which will not take long, our dreams will be realized."

Fayla peered at the faint lights in the distance and asked, "Walther . . . Ducky . . . ah, where is that, exactly? You've kept me below decks and out of sight for so long I have no idea where we are."

Schellenberg was sincerely apologetic. "Forgive me, my dear, I suppose I am overly zealous when it comes to operational security. I was head of Reich counter-intelligence, after all." Then he nodded toward the distant illumination and said, "Those are the coastal lights of Tel Aviv."

On behalf of our friends, Steve Berry and Random House, please enjoy a sample of the newest Cotton Malone thriller

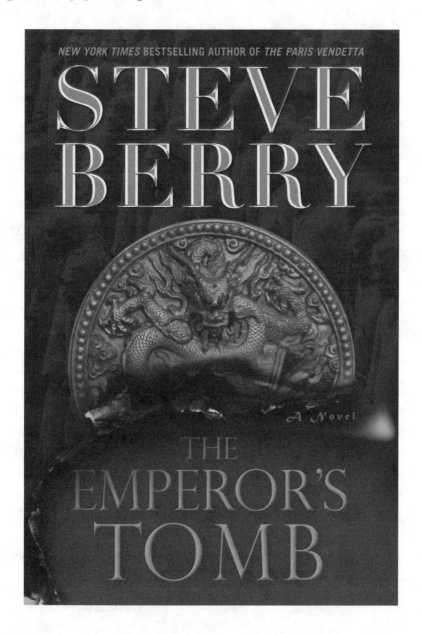

NEW YORK TIMES BESTSELLING AUTHOR OF *THE PARIS VENDETTA*

STEVE BERRY

A Novel

THE EMPEROR'S TOMB

Available Fall 2010

ONE

COTTON MALONE TYPED THE WEB ADDRESS WITH TREMBLING fingers. Like a phone that rings in the middle of the night, nothing about an anonymous message was ever good.

The note had arrived two hours ago, while he'd been out of his bookshop on an errand, but the employee who'd accepted the unmarked envelope forgot to give it to him until a few minutes ago.

"The woman didn't say it was urgent," she said in her defense.

"What woman?"

"Chinese lady, dressed in a gorgeous Burberry skirt. She said to give it only to you."

"She used my name?"

"Twice."

Inside had been a folded sheet of gray vellum upon which was printed a Web address with a dot- org suffix. He'd immediately climbed the four flights of stairs to his apartment above the book- shop and found his laptop.

He finished typing and waited while the screen blackened, then a new image appeared. A video display console indicated that a live feed was about to engage.

The communications link established.

A body appeared, lying on its back, arms above the head, ankles and wrists bound tight to what looked like a sheet of plywood. The person was angled so that the head was slightly beneath the feet. A towel wrapped the face, but it was clear the bound form was a woman.

"Mr. Malone." The voice was electronically altered, disguising every attribute of pitch and tone. "We've been waiting. Not in much of a hurry, are you? I have something for you to see."

A hooded figure appeared on the screen, holding a plastic bucket. He watched as water was poured onto the towel that wrapped the bound woman's face. Her body writhed as she struggled with her restraints.

He knew what was happening.

The liquid penetrated the towel and flowed unrestricted into her mouth and nose. At first a few gulps of air could be stolen—the throat constricted, inhaling little of the water—but that could be maintained only for a few seconds. Then the body's natural gag reflex would kick in and all control would be lost. The head was angled downward so gravity could prolong the agony. It was like drowning without ever being submerged.

The man stopped pouring.

The woman continued to struggle with her restraints.

The technique dated back to the Inquisition. Highly favored since it left no marks, its main drawback was harshness—so intense that the victim would immediately admit to anything. Malone had actually experienced it once, years ago, while training to become a Magellan Billet agent. All recruits had to take their turn as part of survival school. His agony had been amplified by his dislike of confinement. The bondage, combined with the soaked towel, had created an unbearable claustrophobia. He recalled the public debate a few years ago as to whether waterboarding was torture.

Damn right it was.

"Here's the purpose of my contact," the voice said. The camera zoomed tight on the towel wrapping the woman's face. A hand entered the frame and wrenched the soaked cloth away, revealing Cassiopeia Vitt.

"Oh, no," Malone muttered.

Darts of fear pierced his skin. A light-headedness overtook him.

This can't be happening.

No.

She blinked water from her eyes, spit more from her mouth, and gained her breath. "Don't give them a damn thing, Cotton. Nothing."

The soaked towel was slapped back across her face.

"That would not be smart," the computerized voice said. "Certainly not for her."

"Can you hear me?" he said into the laptop's microphone.

"Of course."

"Is this necessary?"

"For you? I believe so. You're a man to be respected. Former Justice Department agent. Highly trained."

"I'm a bookseller."

The voice chuckled. "Don't insult my intelligence, or risk her life any further. I want you to clearly understand what's at stake."

"And you need to understand that I can kill you."

"By then, Ms. Vitt will be dead. So let's stop with the bravado. I want what she gave you."

He saw Cassiopeia renew her struggle against the restraints, her head whipping from side to side beneath the towel.

"Give him nothing, Cotton. I mean it. I gave that to you for safekeeping. Don't give it up."

More water was poured. Her protests stopped as she fought to breathe.

"Bring the item to Tivoli Gardens, at two pm, just outside the Chinese pagoda. You'll be contacted. If you don't show—" The voice paused. "—I think you can imagine the consequences."

The connection was severed.

He sat back in the chair.

He hadn't seen Cassiopeia in more than a month. Hadn't spoken to her for two weeks. She'd said that she was headed out on a trip but, characteristically, offered no details. Their *relationship* was hardly one at all. Just an attraction that they both tacitly acknowledged. Strangely, Henrik Thorvaldsen's death had drawn them closer, and they'd spent a lot of time together in the weeks after their friend's funeral.

She was tough, smart, and gutsy.

But waterboarding?

He doubted if she'd ever experienced anything like that.

Seeing her on the screen tore at his gut. He suddenly realized that if anything happened to this woman his life would never be the same.

He had to find her.

But there was a problem.

She'd obviously been forced to do whatever was necessary in order to survive. This time, however, she may have bitten off more than she could ever chew.

She'd left nothing with him for safekeeping.

He had no clue what she, or her captor, was talking about.

OTHER TITLES AVAILABLE FROM VARIANCE PUBLISHING

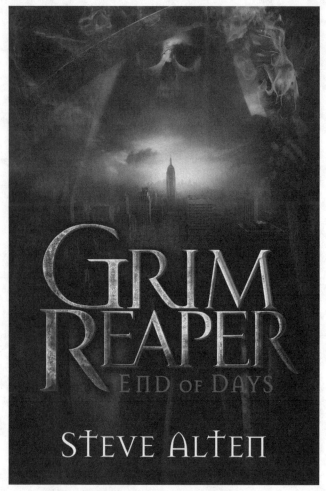

WIRED KINGDOM

WHEN A MURDER AT SEA IS CAUGHT
ON CAMERA, THE HUNT BEGINS

RICK CHESLER

ISBN-13: 978-1-935142-07-2

"A whale of a tale by first-time author Rick Chesler."

-- Steve Alten, NY Times bestselling author of
GRIM REAPER and MEG

**"WIRED KINGDOM is a fast-paced thriller. . . . A
superb debut novel and killer concept."**

-- Jeremy Robinson, author of PULSE and INSTINCT.

AVAILABLE NOW!